I0726953

Pawsitively
A
Purrfect
Trilogy

The Cat's Meow

The Cat's Meow

A PAWSITIVELY PURRFECT TRILOGY

PEPPER MCGRAW

P
M
G
Publishing

Contents

CATNAPPED

THE REAL MCCAT

UNBEARABLY CUTE

Catnapped

Description

**A matchmaking cat may be their only hope
for a happily ever after.**

Maggie isn't a fan of people. Or maybe it would be more accurate to say that people aren't a fan of Maggie. Therefore, when she inherits a house and enough money to retreat from the world, she happily embraces the opportunity, bringing only her cat along for company.

Jackson is the sheriff of his shifter town. He deals with people all day long and for the most part, enjoys his job. Until the crazy human who just moved to town reports a catnapping. He's not exactly leaping at the opportunity to track down a missing pet. Then he discovers the crazy human is his mate.

Genghis Khat has a mission: find his human companion a mate. The only problem? Maggie's mate is the sheriff and she's not exactly a fan. It's going to take a lot of work to make this match a pawsitively purrfect one.

One

B YGUL DESPERATELY NEEDED some time off from Pawsitively Purrfect Matches.

He was the cat companion of a goddess, after all, which made him practically a god himself. He deserved the time off, especially after working so hard on his latest matches.

He planned to make his report, then escape the PPM as soon as possible.

The sun was high overhead and he had grand plans for that bright patch of sunlight he'd seen just a few moments before.

He was almost to Freyja's office door when he realized she wasn't alone.

"I've never known a human in more desperate need of companionship."

Bygul twitched his whiskers and laid his ears back in dismay. That was Bastet's voice. He'd really rather not deal with her today.

"Agreed." And *that* was Ceridwen. Even worse. "Who's available to match her?"

Bygul backed away slowly. He'd come back later, catch Freyja when she was alone.

"Just Bygul," Freyja said.

Bygul froze in mid-step. Well, that was rather rude! He wasn't *just* anyone. He was her cat companion, for goddess' sake!

"Not Bygul." Ceridwen groaned. "He'll make a total mess of things."

Bygul growled low in his throat. He didn't make a mess of anything! His matches were perfect in every way.

"He has the best success record of all our matchmakers and you know it, Ceri," Freyja said.

Exactly! *Thank you, Freyja.* Bygul would have to remember to bring her a special gift next time he visited.

"Yes, but he'll insist on making more than just the companion match."

That's it. Scratch Ceridwen off his Christmas list. No more decapitated birds for her!

"Actually," Freyja said. "The likelihood of him succeeding in this particular case—"

"Practically zero," Bastet said.

What? How insulting! Bygul was the best matchmaker they had on staff!

"Then why are we even having this conversation?" Ceridwen demanded. "We shouldn't waste our resources if she's not a good candidate."

"Oh, she's a perfect candidate for a companion," Freyja said.

"But terrible for a mate," Bastet said. "Which is excellent news for us. If Bygul fails to find her a mate—"

As if!

"He might finally give up his quest to mate-match all of his humans," Freyja said.

"But if he succeeds," Ceridwen wailed, "he'll *never* stop!"

Ceridwen was so melodramatic. And wrong, of course. Nothing would convince him to stop matching his humans, not even failure, a word that had never been associated with *any* of Bygul's matches—and never would be, if he had anything to say about it.

"Trust us," Bastet said. "There's no way he'll succeed with *this* human."

Now, that was just insulting. Bygul was a Norwegian forest cat, for goddess' sake, and they never gave up!

Forget the nap.

Bygul took a moment to mourn that patch of sunlight he'd been looking forward to, then shook it off. In his lifetime, patches of sunlight would come and go, but the matches he made would last forever and this particular match definitely called for the number one matchmaker at PPM.

As far as Maggie Winters was concerned, life was nothing but a series of increasingly annoying events.

Nothing made sense.

Ever.

And people were the worst of all.

She simply didn't get along with any of them, beginning with her parents and continuing with pretty much everyone she'd ever met in her thirty-six years on the planet.

They were just incomprehensible.

Take the woman who'd asked Maggie's opinion at the retail

outlet she used to work for. *Used to* being the key words in that sentence.

The woman had asked, point blank, whether the dress made her ass look bigger.

Maggie was simply telling the truth when she said, "Oh, yes, it's quite prominent in that dress, actually."

She had more to say, of course, but the woman didn't appear to be listening as Maggie went on to explain that the dress did a beautiful job of accentuating *all* of the woman's assets, backside included.

Unfortunately, the woman had thrown a fit in middle of the department store and had demanded Maggie's manager fire her on the spot.

Maggie's protests that she was just answering the woman's question and that it was a compliment in any case went completely unheard.

Maggie really didn't understand why the woman was so upset. Why would she even ask such a question if she didn't want to know the answer?

Even more perplexing was the concept that having a large ass was somehow undesirable. Everyone was built the way they were built and Maggie just didn't understand people's obsession with hiding what made them unique.

It was entirely too confusing.

So that was approximately job number seven hundred fifty-three that Maggie had lost since she began working at age thirteen.

It was the same story over and over again.

Either people didn't appreciate Maggie's honesty or they were assholes.

Or both.

And Maggie frankly didn't put up with assholes.

Like the man who copped a feel when she was serving him a burger and fries.

Or the boss who insisted on calling her sweet cheeks and slapping her ass.

She'd dumped an entire pitcher of iced tea over the head of the first one (job number four hundred ninety-one) and the second, she'd laid out with a single punch (job number one hundred eighty-six).

Overall, Maggie was fine with her rather vagabond, work lifestyle. She usually had no less than three jobs at any one time because she always knew at least one would be ending imminently. Most of her jobs never even lasted a month and that was fine.

Maggie liked variety.

So far, she'd worked almost every job you could possibly imagine. She'd even worked for a city morgue once upon a time. That had been the perfect job as the only people she ever interacted with, given she worked the nightshift, were dead.

Unfortunately, she discovered she really fucking hated the dead.

They were creepy and disturbing and she kept imagining the zombie apocalypse starting right there in the morgue where she was working. She'd be the first zombie victim and she really wasn't okay with that, especially since she was pretty certain the recently dead would be too hungry to leave any bit of her behind.

This, of course, wasn't what she liked to imagine her role to be in the zombie apocalypse.

At best, Maggie hoped to be a survivor fighting the zombie horde.

At worst, she expected to become a zombie herself.

But entirely consumed by zombies?

No way.

Maggie Winters had no intention of ever becoming the first zombie dinner.

Or would that be breakfast?

Well, it didn't really matter.

The point was Maggie wasn't cut out for working with dead people.

So that was job number three hundred forty-eight, one of the very few she'd quit on her own.

Most jobs Maggie simply endured, at least until she was fired, but keeper of the dead wasn't one of them.

Maggie often wondered, though, if she'd perhaps been too hasty in walking away from that particular job.

After all, the dead weren't anywhere near as annoying as all the living people she'd encountered in her many, varied jobs since.

And so far, as far as she knew, the zombie apocalypse hadn't happened yet, which meant she could have stayed and avoided people and not been eaten by zombies, but she hadn't known that at the time, now had she?

Nor had she realized that most jobs she would be qualified for, as someone blessed with only average intelligence, a GED and a work history that resembled a ping pong ball, would require some form of human interaction, even if only with co-workers and a supervisor.

So there she was, working dead-end, stupid jobs or getting *fired* from dead-end, stupid jobs when something extraordinary happened.

She received a phone call from a lawyer who informed her she'd inherited a small house and some money from a great-aunt she'd never even met.

After much back and forth, as she tried to explain he had to have found the wrong Maggie Winters because no, she did not have an aunt named Becky, although, yes, she *was* the daughter of Joseph and Sarah, but as far as she knew, her mother had no living relatives at all.

Nevertheless, it appeared Becky did exist and Maggie was her only living heir.

After a rather long conversation that utterly taxed Maggie's patience and communication skills (she had very few, after all), she ended the phone call with a visceral understanding of what people meant when they referred to life-changing events.

Maggie's heretofore unknown aunt was apparently quite well-off or perhaps she simply hoarded her money. Either way, Maggie's life was changed forever.

She couldn't say whether the house or the money was more important. Truthfully, one without the other, wouldn't have provided the freedom they did together.

The money was great, but not so great that Maggie could have purchased a house and had money left over to live on. And while the house was wonderful, without the money, Maggie would have had to continue to work to pay for groceries and utilities.

With both house *and* money, however, Maggie now had the means to retreat from civilization forever.

She would never have to deal with people again!

She'd never have to see that look on their faces when they realized she was serious when she gave them a truth they didn't want to hear.

She'd never have to deal with an asshole boss or an entitled customer or all the tiny misunderstandings that happened day after day when people got all worked up over things Maggie didn't even realize were problems.

Like voting. Why was everyone so worked up about

someone getting voted off an island? Maggie didn't even know such a thing was possible. Could anyone be voted off? This island didn't seem a very good place to live if that were the case.

And royal marriages. Why in the world would anyone care about someone else's marriage? Her parents' had been a disaster and Maggie didn't even care about *it*, so why would she worry about the state of a stranger's marriage?

None of it made any sense.

And in a world where nothing made sense, the unexpected gift of being able to retreat from it all was like a dream come true.

So Maggie quit her three jobs. She'd possibly already been fired from one of them, but since she wasn't quite sure about that, she went ahead and quit that one as well.

Her boss looked surprised, so perhaps she really had been fired. Why wouldn't he have just said that though? Maggie couldn't understand why some people never said exactly what they meant.

"I don't think this is the right job for you," wasn't the same as "you're fired," now was it?

She never quite knew how to interpret that statement, so would always show up for the next shift to see what happened.

Sometimes they came right out and said, "You're fired. Go away."

Sometimes, however, they didn't say anything at all and she got to keep the job. For a while anyway. Until something else happened.

But this unpredictability was why she never really knew.

If "I don't think this is the right job for you" was a synonym for "you're fired," then she shouldn't have been able to continue working at any of those jobs, right?

Only that's not what happened approximately thirty-six percent of the time.

Usually (sixty-four percent of the time to be exact) it *did* mean you were fired, but all those other times, it meant you could keep working if you just showed up.

So that being the case, Maggie always showed up and sometimes she got to keep working.

It was really quite perplexing and yet another reason to be absolutely thrilled to no longer have to work with people.

Maggie actually took quite a bit of pleasure in quitting her jobs.

She didn't even given them notice.

She figured after all the years she'd spent dealing with being fired from job after job with no notice whatsoever, the world owed her the opportunity to do the same back.

So when she quit her final job, the one she was probably fired from already, but maybe not, she delighted in informing her boss, "I'm sorry, sir, but *you're* fired."

She then walked out, leaving him sputtering in her wake, which was really quite awesome.

A couple hours later, her Honda Civic was packed full of clothes and other essentials and she was ready to hit the road.

Her apartment was on a month-to-month lease so she simply handed her key to the landlord and said, "You can keep the deposit. Use it to get rid of everything I left behind."

"Wait. What?"

She left the landlord sputtering behind her as well, which was also quite delightful. After all, he was just another human being who never said exactly what he meant.

When she first moved in, he'd offered to let her earn her keep in other ways, but everything she suggested, he turned down. She offered to do maintenance, yard work, change lightbulbs, paint the hallways, vacuum the stairs, but he never took her up on any of those offers, and when she demanded to know what he wanted her to do instead, he hemmed and hawed and said to just pay him his rent and get out of his face.

Okay, so maybe he did say what he meant there at the end, but still. She'd wasted so much time trying to think of ways to earn her keep and he never did take her up on any of it. Not even when she offered to run errands for him. Rude.

In any case, that was all behind her now.

No more landlords.

No more bosses.

No more customers.

No more people!

Two

THE FIRST THING Bygul had to do was find the right cat.

According to the PPM's mission statement, this was not a task to be taken lightly. Every cat was unique, after all, and deserved the very best of human companions.

Which was what made this particular matchmaking more challenging than usual. Typically, they started with a cat and then went in search of the perfect human match.

This time, however, a human had come to the attention of PPM and now the task was to find the right cat.

At first, Bygul thought a full-grown cat would be best. One who was big enough for hugging and cuddling. An affectionate cat who wouldn't mind the constant handling.

Then Bygul discovered the human was moving, and more importantly, *where* the human was moving to.

Suddenly, he was on a time crunch.

He had to find the cat and get it bonded with the human *before* she reached her destination. Otherwise, he might not succeed in recruiting a cat to bond with her at all.

Of course, there were *some* cats who would be thrilled at the challenge of living in shifter territory, but they were all a bit crazy, even feral, and possibly not the best match for a woman as lonely as Maggie Winters seemed to be.

In addition, a full-grown cat—especially a feral one—might actually challenge the local shifters, which could result in instant death, a raw deal for both the cat *and* the human.

So perhaps a kitten instead.

After all, shifters were very protective of their young, a protectiveness that might extend to the young of *all* species.

So, Bygul turned his attentions to selecting the perfect kitten companion for Maggie Winters.

Unfortunately, the human was uncooperative in the extreme.

Bygul found three different candidates along the journey toward shifter territory—three!

He placed each of the kittens in the human's path at a different location each time, but did the human do anything Bygul expected in response?

Did she scoop even one of the kittens up into her arms and snuggle him?

Did she carry even one of the kittens home with her?

No, she did not.

Instead, she called the local humane society and informed them of a kitten abandoned in this parking lot or roaming that park.

Bygul supposed he should be grateful she recruited help for the kittens at all and that she waited until someone showed up to trap them, but all he could really think about was how she left immediately upon the rescue worker's arrival without even a "Goodbye, hope you have a nice life," to the kitten left behind.

This human was most unusual and Bygul was getting desperate.

As the hours passed, she got closer and closer to shifter territory without accepting a single one of the companions he'd specifically chosen for her.

Clearly it was time for new tactics.

Especially when he overheard the human saying to the third candidate, right before she called the Humane Society (again), "Don't look at me with those pathetic little eyes. I'm not the right family for you. You'll find one though, so don't worry. You're cute enough, you'll be adopted right away."

Great.

As much of a risk as it would be to bring a full-grown cat into shifter territory, Bygul was back to thinking this would be the best choice.

So off he went on the hunt for yet another companion for this human who was turning out to be a most difficult human to match indeed.

The human was barely eighty miles from her destination when Bygul finally found the perfect cat.

He was a big, lean tom cat, full of attitude and arrogance.

He'd been in a number of fights over the years. One ear was partially gone and he had a scar and a small, bald spot toward his hindquarters, where something bigger than him had taken a bite.

He wasn't cute and he definitely wasn't adoptable.

He was also quite independent and rather cranky.

He liked living on his own and wasn't exactly looking for companionship, which meant convincing him was no easy task.

It was only when Bygul mentioned living in shifter territory that the cat finally showed a bit of interest, in the form of one good ear perking up.

From there, it was a simple matter of enticing the cat with the promise of endless treats and bright patches of sunlight.

When the cat finally deigned to agree, Bygul transported them both, with seconds to spare, from the alley where he'd found the sad-looking feline to the rest stop along I-70 where Maggie was currently using the restroom.

Bygul hoped this match did the trick because if it didn't, he'd be stuck bringing a slew of cat candidates into shifter territory and *that* had disaster written all over it.

Maggie exited the building at the rest stop and froze.

A giant, raggedy looking gray cat lay stretched across the sidewalk directly in her path.

"For goodness sake!" Maggie set her hands on her hips. "Are these rest stops breeding grounds for cats everywhere?" She looked around, but saw no one who might claim responsibility for this cat. The same thing had happened at the last three stops she'd made.

The only difference was this was a full-grown cat.

One who looked rather the worse for wear.

She inched closer and he didn't move.

He just blinked up at her as if to say, "Well, move around me if you want, but I'm quite content to stay right here."

Maggie crouched down beside him and reached out a hand.

He eyed the hand, but made no aggressive moves, so she gently pet him on the side, then scratched his head, noting one mangled ear and some crusts in his eyes.

"Poor love," she murmured to him. "Has no one been properly caring for you?" She could certainly relate to that.

A rumble started in his chest as she pet him and she couldn't help the tiny thrill of delight that raced through her at the sound.

He was purring!

She really needed to be moving along, but then again, she wasn't exactly on a tight schedule.

She was free.

Free to do whatever she wanted.

No jobs.

No bosses to report to.

No customers to try and please.

It was just her and the open road and the eventual house that had belonged to her aunt Becky, whom she'd never met or even knew existed.

Perhaps her aunt Becky's house needed a cat.

And perhaps this cat needed a house.

Maggie had never considered getting a pet before, mostly because she lived in a series of low-rent apartments that didn't allow for pets, but if she'd ever thought to get one, she'd definitely have chosen a cat.

Maybe even this gray one here.

"Well, then, what do you think? Would you like to come with me? It's your choice. I won't make you." She stood and waited.

The cat let out a rumble, then slowly climbed to its feet.

"Right then." Maggie grinned and led the way to her car. She opened the drivers' side door and the cat jumped inside.

It padded its way across to the passenger seat, where it sat on a mound of clothes and stared out the passenger side window.

Maggie climbed into the car and started it.

She reached to put the car in drive, then hesitated. She really needed to figure out her next steps.

As much as she wanted to get to her new home as soon as possible, she also needed a few things for the cat—a litter box and food, at the very least—and the cat definitely needed medical care.

She looked up the closest vet and headed that way.

It turned out the cat was long overdue to be neutered and those surgeries were only ever scheduled for the morning hours, so Maggie ended up checking them into a motel room for the night.

"I wish I knew your name," she said to the cat as they drove to a local pet store.

Gray Cat was what they'd put on the intake form, but Maggie knew she'd have to come up with something better than that.

She spent an hour at the pet store buying and shoving cat things into the tiny bits of space left in her car, all while the cat watched her from the front passenger seat.

Not once did he attempt to leave the car, which struck her as rather odd, but she was terribly grateful all the same.

Eventually, she carried the cat into their motel room, where she set up a litter box and food and water bowls for him.

He snarfed down the food, then settled on her chest as they watched a documentary series about big cats.

She fell asleep with him curled there, his purr a soft rumble that filled her heart with joy.

Three

WITH THE MATCHING of Maggie to a companion cat, and fairly quickly if he did say so himself, Bygul knew he'd be hearing from the trio goddesses, demanding his immediate return.

He'd ignore them, of course, as no match was complete until he deemed it so.

He'd hold them off by claiming he needed to make sure the cat was adjusting to shifter territory and would be healthy and happy there.

Everyone would know it was just an excuse, of course, but that was okay. Excuses worked.

He'd be using the extra time to match Maggie again, this time to her mate.

Unfortunately, she wasn't cooperative when it came to mate-matching either.

Maggie might have a truly excellent wardrobe and impeccable fashion sense, catching eyes everywhere she went, but unfortunately, she also had a way of offending people that was truly epic.

The first evidence of this was when they visited the vet, whom Bygul thought might be a good candidate. If not the vet, then perhaps his assistant.

However, neither one seemed to appreciate Maggie's arched eyebrow and acerbic, "That's rather highway robbery, now isn't it?" when paying the bill.

Then he thought perhaps the trucker when they stopped for gas, but Maggie didn't even notice the man was checking her out and before Bygul could somehow manipulate the situation—cause her to trip and fall into the trucker's arms or maybe have the cat escape right in front of the trucker— Maggie was back in her car and driving away and it was too late to arrange anything.

The rest of the trip was spent with Maggie asking the cat over and over again how it felt about this name or that name.

Of course, the cat never had a response in return, though Maggie didn't seem to hold that against him. She seemed to believe that no response meant he didn't approve, which must be why she kept suggesting new names.

Finally, Bygul could take it no longer. "For goddess' sake, just call him Max!"

"Max," Maggie repeated, startling both the cat and Bygul. "What do you think of that name, Mr. Gray Cat?"

The cat, as far as Bygul could tell, had never had a name before and wasn't quite sure what to make of all this naming nonsense. As far as the cat was concerned, he was a cat and that was that.

"I'm not really quite sure about Max. It seems a little common," Maggie told the cat, who simply yawned in response and didn't seem that interested in the conversation at all.

"It's a perfectly good name and he'd be lucky to have it,"

Bygul snapped. He'd mate-matched a shifter named Max once, quite by accident.

It was a rather convoluted story. He'd been trying to match a cat with a human and a couple bear shifters in the area kept scaring the cat away, so he'd made the shifters go away, sent them on a new quest.

Who knew they'd end up on the other side of the country, opening a Shenanigans right in between cougar and wolf territories, and that one of the bears would mate a wolf named Max?

He hadn't even been *trying* and he'd managed to set into motion a sequence of events that had not only resulted in the matching of a cat companion with a human, but also the mate-matching of not just the one bear and one wolf, but eventually the other bear with *his* mate plus a whole slew of paranormal matings after that.

That was when Bygul decided he was a matchmaking genius who needed to get serious about expanding beyond just matching companion cats to their human counterparts.

Thus he added mate-matching to his services.

His humans were always quite grateful, though the goddesses didn't exactly appreciate his initiative and the other matchmakers thought he'd lost sight of the mission.

He knew the mission, he just knew his cats would be happier if their companions were happy too.

Happily Furever After — wasn't that what they guaranteed? He was pretty sure it was.

"I'm just not feeling Max," Maggie said. "And since you don't seem to love it either, Mr. Gray Cat, I think we need some help."

"For heaven's sake, woman!" Bygul exclaimed. "Just call him Cat then!"

"Cat's not a name. Nor is Gray Cat, nor is even Mr. Gray Cat. We need something better than that."

How the human was even hearing him, Bygul had no idea, especially since he was only visible to the cat population and she didn't seem to realize someone was talking in the first place.

This Maggie woman was the strangest human he'd ever tried to match and he'd had a few really strange matches in his time.

"You look like you've been in a few battles there, my friend," Maggie said to the cat. "So I'm thinking we need a warrior's name. It's really unfortunate the vet confirmed you're a boy. I kind of wanted to call you Bastet."

Bygul choked and almost hacked up a fur ball.

What a wonderful idea!

How he'd missed this opportunity in the past, he had no idea.

Why, he could encourage all his humans to name their companion-cats after the gods and goddesses. Imagine the uproar!

"Catphrodite would be hilarious," Maggie continued. "Or maybe Cleocatra."

Bygul was laughing so hard, he almost fell off the dash where he'd settled early in the trip. He was completely shielded from human sight, but the cat could see him and kept an eye on him the entire time.

"Actually, I don't see why I can't go ahead and give you a girl's name," Maggie said. "We could push those gender barriers, right?"

The cat lurched to his feet and hunched over, beginning to gag.

"Oh, no, don't hack up a furball in here!" Bygul exclaimed. "She might decide you're more trouble than you're worth."

"Okay, okay," Maggie said. "I guess Purrsephone's out of the question. Settle down. I'll come up with a boy's name for you soon enough."

With a satisfied air, the cat walked in a circle, kneaded the chair a moment, then flopped back onto his side, a smug look on his face.

"You're not as dumb as you look," Bygul informed him. "Nice job."

"I've got it," Maggie announced. "And just in time because I think we're here."

Bygul looked out the windshield and saw that they'd pulled up to a large farmhouse in the middle of nowhere with no neighbors in sight.

"Come along, Genghis Khat." Maggie turned off the car and scooped the cat into her arms. "Let's go explore our new home!"

THE HOUSE SEEMED TO BE IN PRETTY GOOD SHAPE.

Maggie walked up onto the porch and found the keys under the doormat, just where the lawyer had said they'd be. It seemed a little trusting to leave keys under the doormat, but Maggie wasn't going to complain, especially since it meant she didn't have to socialize.

The first day in their new home Maggie spent cleaning and unpacking.

The second day she did a lot of online shopping, arranging for Amazon to deliver everything from canned goods to a cat tree. She then went exploring.

The third day, she had an appointment with her aunt's

lawyer, a Mr. Wilson, to get all the paperwork signed and to take final possession of her inheritance.

The worst part of that entire experience was having to actually talk to people. First his assistant, who looked rather surprised to see her, then the lawyer himself, who looked utterly stunned.

She had no idea why. She'd told him she'd never met her aunt, so she couldn't imagine why he seemed so surprised.

Mr. Wilson asked a couple questions about her parents and where she'd grown up and where she'd gone to school and seemed a little disturbed at her answers.

He asked if she was planning to stay or to sell the house and he seemed even more disturbed when she said she'd be staying. He seemed to feel it would be better for her to go, but that wasn't happening. "I'm good here and that's that," she told him and he nodded, though the look on his face said he did not agree with her decision.

Why it mattered, she had no idea.

He then asked if she planned to look for a job in town and she said, "Absolutely not."

He looked relieved at that—weird—then asked if she already had a job.

At this point, Maggie was done with the entire conversation so she just stared at him.

He waited for her to answer and she waited for him to realize she wasn't going to.

The silence stretched on long enough that Maggie wondered if it was an awkward silence. It didn't seem awkward to her, but she'd come to realize over the years that her definition of awkward was not everyone's else's.

Silence didn't bother Maggie, but wasting her time did, so she eventually broke the silence by asking, "Are we done here?"

A look of surprise flashed across Mr. Wilson's face—again —but he just nodded and said, "We are. Good luck with everything."

Maggie, though, was already striding out the door, quite relieved to have this last bit of required socializing behind her.

She was famished after the meeting and desperately needed food. She really wanted to just go home, but wasn't looking forward to yet another dinner made up of canned green beans.

Unfortunately, her only other options were to eat out somewhere, which would involve dealing with people, or to go grocery shopping, which would also mean dealing with people.

However, if she went grocery shopping, she'd have more options than green beans for tomorrow's meals as well.

She'd been severely disappointed when she'd discovered the town of Greensboro only had one grocery store and they did *not* deliver. She'd already found a meal subscription service and had placed her first order, but it wouldn't arrive for another week and she'd never survive that long on green beans.

So, though she dreaded it, grocery shopping it was.

She hurried through the grocery store, avoiding people and trying not to notice as they stopped and stared every time she came near. It had to be because it was such a small town. They probably didn't get many strangers here, that was all.

Still it was unnerving and by the time the cashier had finished ringing up her groceries, Maggie was exhausted, especially since the woman insisted on asking invasive questions.

"Why are you here?"

"How did you find us?"

"Where are you staying?"

Maggie really wasn't in the mood to answer any of the cashier's questions, which meant her responses became increasingly curt as time went on.

"To get groceries."

"You're on a public street."

"None of your business."

It was the last reply that finally stopped the litany of questions.

Maggie paid and helped bag the last of her groceries. She then grabbed the bags and muttered, "Have a nice day," before hurrying out of the store.

She didn't even know why she'd added that bit at the end.

She certainly didn't *care* whether the nosy cashier had a good day or not, which meant that Maggie was guilty of the one thing she hated the most. She'd said what she didn't mean.

Because what she really meant was, "Don't ever talk to me again."

Maggie hurried to her car, slung the groceries inside and raced home.

When she walked inside, Genghis Khat greeted her with a symphony of meows and wound himself around her ankles, making her smile.

"Yes, I know, I'll never leave again, how's that?" She began putting the groceries away, all the while talking to the cat about the snippy assistant, the disapproving attorney *and* the nosy cashier. "We have enough groceries to last until I manage to get my meal subscriptions delivered. So we should be fine, Genghis Khat. Just fine!" With that, Maggie retreated to the very comfortable recliner in the living room.

Genghis Khat settled on her lap and they spent the evening together, Maggie reading a stream of books on her Kindle and Genghis Khat snoozing and purring on her lap.

Four

IT WAS UNFORTUNATE, but Bygul was beginning to think the goddesses might have been correct. The horror of it all!

This particular match was practically impossible.

As it turned out, Bygul was increasingly impressed with the fact he'd managed to match Maggie with a cat at all. She'd truly fallen in love with Genghis Khat, which Bygul now considered to be a minor miracle seeing as the woman was a recluse the likes of which Bygul had never seen before.

In four weeks, she hadn't returned to town, not even once.

The woman did leave the house to work in the yard, to do some gardening and to go on early morning strolls along the deserted stretch of road that led to town. However, she always turned back before reaching any signs of civilization.

Genghis Khat accompanied her on these walks and serenaded her from the screened porch when she worked in the backyard and from the bay window when she worked in the front.

In other words, the only contact the woman had had with

another living being was the cat. She hadn't spoken to a single human since that disastrous trip into town.

Bygul had hoped perhaps to set her up with the attorney, but he'd been entirely too old and had clearly disapproved of Maggie. Probably because she wasn't a shifter, which was definitely a bit of a wrench in the works.

He'd then hoped she'd meet someone at the grocery store, but everyone there had given her a wide berth and she'd been epically grouchy with the cashier, potentially solidifying a reputation that was already on shaky grounds due to being human.

After a week of no progress, the goddesses had demanded Bygul turn his attention to matching a feral cat in desperate need of a home. As a result, he'd had to put his attempts to mate-match Maggie on hold while attending to other business.

Over the following three weeks, he'd popped in every once in a while just to check on her progress. He'd hoped in his absence she'd simply gravitate toward her mate the way the wolf and the bear had gravitated toward each other.

Unfortunately, Maggie was, as usual, completely uncooperative.

According to Genghis Khat, she'd sworn off human interaction entirely.

Bygul wondered whether she would change her mind if she knew the humans in town could all shift into animals.

Probably not.

She seemed a stubborn sort.

Unfortunately, Bygul couldn't stick around to force the issue as he had many humans to find for the cats on his match-making list. This meant he needed to recruit some help and the only candidate for that was Genghis Khat himself.

Genghis Khat, much like his human, wasn't super cooperative at first—more evidence that Bygul was an excellent matchmaker—but then Bygul reminded him that the town was full of shifters.

Of course, a cat with one mangled ear, scars along his backside and a name like Genghis Khat would perk up at the thought of tangling with some shifters who in shifted form were approximately ten times his size.

The trick was to somehow get the woman to meet the many eligible shifters in town, and as far as Bygul was concerned, the cat was the key.

MAGGIE WAS ONE MONTH INTO HER NEW LIFE AND she absolutely adored it.

She loved living so far out, there were no sounds of any neighbors.

She loved her aunt's house and the garden and the cat most of all.

She loved having enough time in the mornings to really think about what she wanted to wear and what items would look amazing together.

Okay, so no one ever saw her fantastic fashion sense, but she didn't really care. She modeled her clothes for Genghis Khat and absolutely loved that as well.

Who knew that one not-so-small and not-so-pretty cat would become so important to her happiness in such a short amount of time?

Genghis Khat followed her throughout the house, moving from room to room and listening to her ramble about whatever she wanted to talk about on any particular day.

He rarely responded, though he *did* have quite a strong

meow, which she was treated to the first time she left him behind to go on a walk without him.

After that, she ordered a harness and leash from Amazon and though Genghis Khat was *not* a fan of either one, he did enjoy their walks outside and thus tolerated them both.

He woke her every morning by patting her on the cheek and on one memorable occasion, biting her on the nose. After that, she made sure to respond by the third pat as she rather liked her nose where it was.

So it was with trepidation that Maggie woke one morning without the usual paw and kitty breath in her face.

She got up and dressed swiftly and went in search of Genghis Khat.

Only he was nowhere to be found.

Literally nowhere.

He'd gone to bed with her the night before and all the windows and doors had been locked. Yet, when she woke the next morning, the window in her study was wide open and Genghis Khat was long gone.

Most disturbing, however, was the one footprint right outside her study window, in the middle of her flower bed.

Someone had broken into her house and catnapped Genghis Khat!

JACKSON HEWITT LOVED HIS JOB, BUT THERE WERE some days it just didn't pay to get out of bed.

Most days, as sheriff of an entirely shifter town, his days were busy.

Between the cougars always riling up the bears and the full

moon making the wolves act like idiots, his job as peacekeeper was never dull.

The night before had been rather eventful, with two bar fights in the span of as many hours, so all the jail cells at the station were full of belligerent, angry, hungover idiots.

Nine times out of ten, those idiots were men, but on this particular occasion, *three* were women.

The Donnelly sisters. They were an utter pain in his ass and he *lived* for the day they found their mates and became someone else's problem.

For now, they were the problem of the very angry wolf facing him.

"I can't believe you locked up my sisters, Hewitt!" Mark Donnelly growled. "You should have called me."

"Now why would I do that?" Jackson demanded. "Your sisters were each told they could make one phone call and not one of them took me up on the offer. I figured they preferred to just sleep it off."

"You shouldn't have arrested them in the first place!"

"Have you talked to Steve this morning? Because I'm telling you right now, I may have saved your sisters' lives by locking them up."

Mark growled. "That bastard. What's *he* got to be pissed about?"

"It's his bar they destroyed!"

Mark gave Jackson a skeptical look.

"Fine," Jackson sighed. "Their actions incited a fight that destroyed the bar."

"So you arrested them because some assholes got into a fight?"

"No, I arrested your sisters because they were belligerent with my officers *and* they caused the damn fight."

"Sheriff, I'm sorry to interrupt." Connie poked her head through the door, demonstrating once again that she had epically perfect timing.

"No problem, Connie. Mark, go talk to Danny. Tell him I said to let your sisters go."

Mark let out a huff, turned on his heel and stormed out.

"What's up, Connie?"

"There's a woman on the phone. She's crying and saying her kid's been catnapped."

"What?" Jackson leapt to his feet and grabbed at the phone. He stabbed the light indicating a call on hold and said, "This is Sheriff Hewitt. How can I help you?"

"Sheriff, my name's Maggie. My cat's been taken."

"Right. I need some details from you. Name, age, description."

"Okay. Um. His name is Genghis Khat. I don't know how old he is. Old enough to have gotten into a lot of cat fights. Let's see. Description. He's gray and he's got a mangled ear and he's missing some fur, probably because of those cat fights, right at the tail area. If you see him, you'll know him right off. You can't miss the mangled ear."

Jackson had a pencil in hand, ready to take notes, but he only got as far as Genghis before his brain caught up and he realized what he was hearing.

"Hold on, lady. Let me get this straight. You're calling about your pet cat?" He could hear the incredulity in his own voice.

"Yes! He's been catnapped and I need you to come out and dust for fingerprints and–and–and catch whoever took him."

"Okay, ma'am, why do you think someone took the cat?"

"Because when I went to bed the doors and windows were all locked, but now the study window's open and there's a footprint in the flowerbed right under the window and my cat is missing!"

"Listen, ma'am, the thing is, we're the police. We help with — um — human problems."

"Well, I'm a human and I have a problem, so please help me!"

"One moment, ma'am." Jackson put the crazy woman on hold and banged his head on the desk.

"I take it the cat's not a shifter," Connie said, a wealth of humor in her voice.

Jackson glared up at her. "Did you know she was talking about a freaking pet?"

"I had no idea," Connie laughed. "I just heard catnapped and came running."

Jackson nodded. "All right. Damn. When Danny's finished with Mark, send him in here please. We'll let him deal with the missing pet report."

Connie snorted. "That's just mean. Are you *ever* going to forgive him for backing into Miss Maura's mailbox?"

"Are you kidding me? I had to listen to her complaining for an hour and then I'm the one who had to replace the damn mailbox because she refused to let Danny back on her property and said she wouldn't trust any of the other deputies either. And then I had to endure her litany of complaints about her body aches and pains and the horror of getting old—old, my ass—the entire time I was out there installing her new mailbox. So no, there is no forgiveness here. Danny gets the shit jobs for the rest of his career. The end."

Connie laughed, "Right. Well, can't say I blame you there." Still laughing, she headed back out to her desk, calling over her shoulder, "Your crazy cat lady's still on hold."

"Damn."

MAGGIE WAS *NOT* A HAPPY CAMPER. THE SHERIFF seemed to take her seriously enough. He told her a deputy would be out right away to help her find Genghis Khat, but then it turned out the deputy was a bit of an idiot.

"Well, ma'am, there really aren't any clues as to where the cat's been taken. I don't rightly know what you expect me to do."

"Dust for fingerprints! Make a cast of the shoe print. Why am I telling you how to do your job? Just find my cat!"

The deputy, who had introduced himself as Danny Morris, gave a big sigh.

"Fine, ma'am. I'll dust for fingerprints, but it's doubtful the catnapper left any behind. Truthfully, if someone was feeling peckish and stole your cat, well, the cat's probably a goner."

Maggie gasped, then screeched, "What?"

Danny winced. "Well, you know, ma'am. I mean, it is the countryside and—and there's a lot of wildlife around and—"

"I'm quite sure the local cougars didn't open my damn window themselves!" Maggie snapped. What was wrong with this man?

At that moment, her cell phone rang in her pocket, making them both jump.

Maggie pulled out the phone and answered, "Hello?"

"Maggie, this is Sheriff Hewitt."

"Yes, Sheriff."

"I may have some good news for you. The owner of the diner just called and said a gray cat sneaked in with one of the customers and has made himself at home."

"Someone took my cat all the way into town, to the diner? But why?"

The sheriff cleared his throat. "Yes, well, I'm not quite sure that's what happened, but you might want to get over to the diner to collect your cat."

"Oh, but couldn't you bring it out to me or–or maybe Danny could collect the cat for me?"

"Ma'am, we are not a taxi service nor are we a pet rescue. If you want your cat back, I'd suggest you go pick him up. I'd also suggest you hurry. You never know in this town. People have all kinds of strange appetites." With that, he hung up on her.

"What the hell does that mean?" Maggie shrieked, staring at the phone.

Danny shuffled his feet. "Um. What's that, ma'am?"

Maggie rolled her eyes. She was starting to hate that word —ma'am. "Apparently my cat's shown up at the diner. Would you be able to go get him for me?"

Danny shook his head and backed up. "Oh no, ma'am. I need to get back to work now." He hurried toward his patrol car.

"Hey, wait! Aren't you going to dust for fingerprints?"

"Nah, that'd be a waste of time, especially now that you've found your cat and all. Have a good day, ma'am." With that, he climbed into his car and drove away.

"Damnit." Maggie couldn't believe she was going to have to go into town. She glanced down at her phone. And right at lunchtime! This was a nightmare. She hurried into the house, grabbed her keys, locked everything up and climbed into her car.

"Just in and out," she muttered to herself as she set off for town. "You don't have to talk to anyone. Just grab Genghis Khat and go."

Five

"THIS CAT IS either the bravest or the stupidest cat I've ever met," announced one of the humans Genghis Khat had followed into the diner.

"You've got that right, George," the waitress said as a murmur of agreement rolled through the diner.

Genghis Khat thought it perfectly obviously that he was *brave* not stupid, but since humans never understood his meows, he didn't bother to correct them. Instead, he continued making his way through the customers, giving each one a solid sniff.

Some smelled better than others, but they *all* smelled wild and Genghis Khat like that. An awful lot.

He was wilder than they were, of course, but for now he was too busy enjoying the tiny bits of meat and other morsels falling to the floor to impress them with his wildness.

Perhaps later.

As he wandered under the tables and accepted the occasional scratch on the head, he listened to the conversations happening above him.

"Where do you think he came from?" someone asked.

"The sheriff said a woman named Maggie's looking for him," the cook called form the kitchen. "She lives out on Cutter Lane."

"Becky's niece, Maggie?"

"I didn't know Becky had a niece."

"Nobody did. I only know because I handled her affairs after she died. Even then, I had no idea her niece was human." This must be the attorney Maggie was going on and on about, the one who disapproved of her staying.

"Becky's niece is human?"

"There's a human living in town?"

"That must be the woman I saw grocery shopping a while back. She wasn't very friendly. Poor Lindsay kept asking questions and the human refused to answer any of them."

"Well, good for her. Lindsay's a busybody." Lindsay must be the cashier Maggie had told him about.

"She was just curious about the human."

"Still."

"I can't believe we have a human in town."

"How long's she been here anyway?"

"It's been at least a month." That was the attorney's voice again.

"I'm surprised we haven't seen her in town more often."

"Do you think she's someone's mate?"

Genghis Khat perked up at the question.

"I hadn't thought of that." The attorney again. "I was so worried about a human moving to town, it didn't occur to me that mate magic could be in play."

"Well, if she's not a mate, something will pull her away. It always does."

"Surprised it hasn't happened yet if she's been here a month."

"Yeah, by now they've usually moved on or found their mate."

"Well, I'm sure the magic will kick in soon enough and she'll be gone."

Interesting.

Genghis Khat had decided he liked this town.

He liked their house and he liked the scent of all these people.

But if there was magic that would send them away from this town if Maggie didn't find a mate here, they were in serious trouble.

The woman hated people, which was why Bygul's mate-matching plan was surely destined for failure.

Genghis Khat had only agreed to help because Bygul kept talking about people shifting into animals and Genghis Khat was curious to meet these peculiar humans.

He knew Bygul wanted him to somehow get Maggie to interact with as many people in town as possible, but he'd really only planned to laze about and wait for her to pick him up and take him home.

Unfortunately, it sounded like he might have to actually be proactive when it came to the mate-matching efforts, if he didn't want to have to move again.

The thought was really quite horrifying.

Genghis Khat, fiercest feral from the streets of Chicago, was now reduced to mate-matching.

"You can do this," Maggie coached herself as she pulled into the parking lot at the town's diner. "No one will be watching. No one is *ever* watching you, not even when you're convinced they are. Just control the crazy, batten down the paranoia and get in and out, preferably without interacting with anyone. In and out. That's it. You can do this."

Dragging in a deep breath, she locked the car and strode toward the door to the diner. "You used to do this every day. You've worked in hundreds of restaurants and stores and dealt with all kinds of people. You can handle five minutes in this diner."

Except, honestly, Maggie wasn't sure she could.

She stopped halfway up the sidewalk, swung around and paced back toward her car.

The past four weeks had ruined her! She'd been working since she was thirteen and had rarely had more than three days off in a row until her unknown aunt Becky changed her life.

Four weeks without having to interact with people had been an incredible blessing, but now she was completely out of practice!

She no longer knew how to talk to people.

No, that wasn't right. Of course, she knew how to talk to people. She'd been doing it her entire life. Just because people didn't like what she said didn't mean she didn't know how to talk to them.

"You can do this, Maggie." She glanced down at the sassy skirt and sleeveless blouse she was wearing and gave thanks that she'd chosen this outfit for today. "You can do this, Maggie," she repeated to herself, "and even better, you'll look fantastic while doing it."

"THERE'S A CRAZY WOMAN ON THE SIDEWALK," PAUL Davis reported from where he was sitting by the window. "I'm betting it's the human."

Annie rolled her eyes as she delivered drinks to the table across from his booth. "Could you be any more of a bigot, Paul?"

"What?"

"You're saying just because she's human, she's also crazy?"

"Noooo. I'm saying she's crazy because she's talking to herself, pacing back and forth and waving her arms in the air."

By this time, a number of people were crowded around the windows staring out at the human, who Annie saw, really did appear to be having an entire conversation with herself.

In public.

"Maybe she's on the phone," Livi suggested.

"I don't see any earbuds," Tom said.

"Maybe they're just really small," Erica said.

"Not seeing any wires," Adam said.

"Maybe they're wireless," Annie said.

"And maybe she's just crazy," Paul said.

Annie threw her arms in the air. "Whatever. Just get away from the windows before you scare the human away." She shooed them all back to their tables. "She probably saw you and that's why she's freaking out. Act normal for goodness' sake!"

"Normal?" Bud called from the kitchen. "What's normal about this town and these people?"

That was a good question. "Fine!" Annie snapped. "Just

don't act like shifters. No sniffing the human and no growling!"

Paul groaned. "Having a human in town is going to be a real pain in the ass."

ALL MAGGIE HAD MANAGED TO ACCOMPLISH WITH that pep talk was to freak herself out even more.

Time to just grab that bull by the horns and get it over with.

She barreled into the diner, then skidded to a stop.

They were *definitely* staring at her.

All of them.

It wasn't her paranoia this time.

She knew it, she knew it, she knew it.

They weren't just staring with their eyes, they were staring with their bodies too!

Some of them had turned clean around in their chair so their bodies were pointed at the door where Maggie was standing.

"Not cool, not cool, not cool," she muttered under her breath. "Just grab the bull by the horns, just grab the bull by the horns, just grab the bull—"

"What bull you talking about there, Maggie?" Mr. Wilson called from across the diner.

"Yeah, there aren't any bulls in here," a man in a booth by the window informed her. "No bulls in town, in fact."

"Paul, knock it off." A woman walked up to Maggie and handed her a menu. "Come along, dear, let's get you a table." She grabbed Maggie's arm and started to pull her through the dining room.

"Oh–oh–oh, no. I don't—I—I'm not—hungry or–or thirsty. I just—I need—"

"Oh, hon. You have to eat a good meal in the middle of the day if you want to keep up your energy. Now what are you in the mood for? Burger and fries, turkey club, fish and chips, meatloaf—"

It appeared the woman was ready to recite the entire menu, so Maggie cut her off. "A turkey club will be fine."

"With the bacon?"

"Sure."

"Fries?"

"Sure."

"What'll you have to drink?"

"Um, I—" Maggie caught sight of a gray blob on the floor under the table next to her and lunged out of the booth. "Genghis Khat!" She landed on her knees beside the table, crawled beneath it and scooped her cat into her arms, thrilled he was safe.

Genghis Khat started to purr the minute she held him close and she slowly backed out from under the table, realizing as she did so, that there were several pairs of legs also under the table with her.

Oh, well.

Most people would apologize, but Maggie didn't believe in apologizing for things you weren't sorry for and she'd have crawled under a hundred tables to rescue her cat again.

She settled back in the booth with Genghis Khat in her arms and set him on the table in front of her. "Oh, Genghis Khat, I was so worried," she whispered to him. "You have to tell me who catnapped you." She sent a narrow-eyed glare around the room, noting that *everyone* in the room was *still* staring at her.

In fact, even though she was now on the opposite side of the room from the door, everyone had swiveled around so that their bodies were now turned her way again.

She looked back at Genghis Khat, who flopped onto his side and let out a huge yawn. "Seriously?" she whispered. "It wasn't anyone in the diner?"

She cast another suspicious look at the diners.

No one looked guilty, though they all seemed somewhat surprised. Or disturbed. Or something, she wasn't quite sure what.

But guilty?

No.

"This doesn't make any sense, Genghis Khat. Why would someone break into our house and catnap you, only to drop you off at the diner in town?"

The sound of a throat clearing interrupted Maggie's train of thought, bringing her attention back to the waitress, whose name according to the tag on her shirt was Annie. "Oh. You're still here?"

"Waiting for your drink order, hon."

"Oh, right, uh, coke for me please and maybe a bit of milk for Genghis Khat?"

Annie smiled. "You got it."

Maggie waited until the waitress was out of earshot, then turned back to Genghis Khat. "Nothing to say, eh? I assume that means your catnapper's long gone."

Genghis Khat wasn't the greatest of communicators, but Maggie was still pretty sure he'd implicate the person responsible if they were still in the diner, so Maggie mentally crossed everyone present off her suspect list.

Unfortunately, since Maggie's list only consisted of the

people currently inside the diner, there was no longer anyone on it.

"You're the best cat ever. If I'd catnapped you, I'd never let you out of my sight. I certainly wouldn't leave you behind at a diner full of strangers. I can't imagine why your catnapper abandoned you. Unless—did you *escape*, Genghis Khat?"

He nudged Maggie's hand.

"Sorry, sorry, didn't mean to stop petting you." Maggie scratched his head and began to stroke him again.

"I bet you did escape. You're so smart, but you know what that means? It means the catnapper's still out there and he may come back for you later. I'd call the sheriff, but I have to tell you, I'm not that impressed with his deputy, and the sheriff seemed a bit unwilling to handle it himself. That's okay, though. We can handle a catnapper between the two of us, right?"

"Here you go. One turkey club and fries, one coke and one saucer of milk." Annie set each item on the table as she announced it.

In addition to not apologizing for things she wasn't sorry for, Maggie didn't believe in saying thank you for things she wasn't actually grateful for. She just didn't understand false gratitude, and as a result, hadn't been planning to thank Annie since she hadn't wanted food in the first place.

However, when Annie settled the plate in front of Maggie and she inhaled the delicious scents of the turkey club and fries, she realized she was quite hungry, and therefore, grateful after all. "Thanks, Annie."

Without waiting for a response, she carefully peeled apart the sandwich, removed two slices of turkey from its center and reassembled it. She then began to methodically tear the turkey into tiny bite-size pieces for Genghis Khat, who was busy lapping up the milk.

"So." Annie plopped into the seat across from Maggie, startling her and Genghis Khat, who let out a soft hiss of surprise.

"It's okay, sweetheart." Maggie stroked her hand down his back and he went back to lapping up the milk.

"What's your name?" Annie asked.

"Oh, um, Maggie."

"Nice to meet you. I'm Annie. My parents own the diner."

Maggie nodded. She had no idea what to say in response. Was she even expected to reply?

Annie hadn't asked a question so Maggie wasn't sure.

Maybe Maggie was supposed to share about her own parents, but she didn't want to, so she didn't.

Once again, as the silence stretched out, Maggie wondered if it was becoming awkward.

Since Maggie loved silence, she wasn't sure how long it had to last before it became awkward for others.

In truth, Maggie thought silence was a beautiful thing.

She could sit in silence all day long, even when surrounded by people, even if none of them spoke a word to her. In fact, she'd prefer that.

However, she knew from countless prior conversations that most people were uncomfortable with silence.

She waited to see if Annie was one of those people.

If she was, she'd either make an excuse and rush away or she'd break the silence by asking a question, thus forcing Maggie to participate in the conversation.

The silence stretched long enough that Maggie managed to finish tearing apart both slices of turkey and to cut her sandwich into fourths.

Without looking up, Maggie ate one-fourth of her sandwich with her left hand, while feeding tiny bits of turkey to Genghis Khat with her right.

Genghis Khat happily ate each piece from the palm of her hand and when he was done licking it clean, would nudge her hand for more.

And so it went.

Maggie ate the next three-fourths of her sandwich, one by one, and hand-fed Genghis Khat the rest of the turkey.

She'd carefully divided the pieces of turkey into four equal sections so that they were both finished with their lunch at approximately the same time.

Genghis Khat never tried to steal a single piece of turkey from her plate. He simply waited for her to feed him one piece at a time.

"You're the best cat ever, Genghis Khat," Maggie whispered to him. "So polite, so smart, so sweet." She scratched him on the head and fed him the final bit of turkey. "Last bite, darling."

Movement from across the table caught Maggie's attention and she realized Annie was still sitting in the booth with her. "Oh. You're still here?"

Annie smiled. "Still here. Your cat is beautiful. And I love the name."

Maggie completely agreed. Genghis Khat *was* beautiful. He was a scarred warrior with a beautiful soul. "I know."

"So who have you met in town so far?"

There it was.

The question.

Maggie considered questions to be a way for extroverts to manipulate and force introverts into participating in conversations they normally wouldn't.

Most of the time, Maggie simply refused to answer people's questions.

Either by giving non-answers or by not responding at all.

Of course, she knew most people considered that to be very rude, but honestly, Maggie just didn't care.

This time, in response to Annie's question, Maggie gave a half-hearted shrug in response, which to her meant she was making a real effort.

She wasn't sure how she'd been roped into eating at the diner, but now she was trapped in this booth with a ton of people between her and the door, and it hadn't escaped her notice that no one seemed inclined to leave anytime soon.

However, Annie *had* brought her this incredibly delicious meal that *almost* made up for Maggie having to interact with people.

"Well, let's take care of that right now," Annie said.

Maggie had no idea what that meant, but she was pretty sure she wasn't going to like it.

That turned out to be the understatement of the century.

Six

GENGHIS KHAT HEARTILY approved of this diner-place where Bygul had transported him earlier that day.

He'd had no idea when he walked in that he'd be treated to so many tasty, meaty morsels in such a short amount of time.

First, he'd wandered the diner, enjoying snack after snack.

Then, when Maggie had come to pick him up, she'd stayed and fed him more tasty, meaty morsels.

This was definitely his second favorite place on earth, the first being the recliner at their house, where he loved to stretch out on Maggie's lap.

He was so busy enjoying the taste-testing that he completely forgot he was supposed to be helping Maggie interact with the people at the diner.

Luckily, Annie, the woman who had brought him the cream in a saucer and the meaty morsels on a plate, took care of that task for him.

When they were done eating, Annie stood, grabbed Maggie

by the arm and started dragging her from table to table, introducing her to everyone in the diner.

Genghis Khat followed, feeling a little put out that Annie wasn't bothering to introduce him as well.

Maggie took care of that, though, because she was the best human companion ever.

She scooped him up from the floor and proceeded to introduce him to everyone she met.

Annie would say, "This is Maggie. Maggie, these are the Donnelly sisters, Kate, Mary Lou and Hannah."

Then Maggie would nod and say, "This is Genghis Khat. He's the best cat in the world." Only Maggie never said the same thing about him twice. She came up with new ways to introduce him every time.

"This is Genghis Khat. He's a warrior with the scars to prove it."

"This is Genghis Khat. He has the most amazing purr. It rumbles like a steam engine."

"This is Genghis Khat. He's a hunter who specializes in decapitating his prey."

By the time they finished with all the introductions, Genghis Khat felt about ten feet tall. He hadn't realized all those wonderful things about himself.

Of course, he knew he was a good hunter, but he didn't know that about his purr or that Maggie loved his scars.

She really was the best human companion ever.

MAGGIE GOT THROUGH THE ORDEAL OF BEING introduced to so many people in such a short amount of time by focusing on Genghis Khat. She spent time in between introductions coming up with new ways to describe the best cat in the world.

Suddenly the terror of speaking with new people was almost fun. It was like a game.

A game of words and a way to let Genghis Khat know how much she appreciated him.

It got her through the endless rounds of conversations until finally she had met every single person in the diner for lunch that day.

Grateful she'd survived the onslaught, Maggie was edging toward the door when Annie exclaimed, "You have to come to the party Saturday night."

Gasps of shock resounded through the room, making it pretty obvious that no one else agreed with Annie's declaration.

"Oh, I'm not much for parties," Maggie said with a shake of her head.

She couldn't help but notice how relieved everyone appeared.

"Oh, but you haven't met everyone yet. Until you meet everyone, we won't know if—" Annie broke off with a look of consternation on her face.

Maggie was probably supposed to ask a question at that point, something like "What won't you know?" But she figured this was just another tactic to get her to engage in the conversation, and would probably result in her being manipulated into attending this party.

As Maggie considered the word party to be synonymous with hell on earth, she had no intention of being manipulated in such an obvious way.

So she simply stood there and waited.

When Annie never finished her sentence, Maggie decided it was time to move on. "I have to go now," she said.

Annie had never given her the check, so Maggie wasn't sure how much her meal had cost, but she set a couple twenties onto the counter on her way out.

THE MINUTE THE DOOR CLOSED BEHIND MAGGIE, Annie whirled around and glared at the shifters in the diner. "You should all be ashamed of yourselves. Just because she's human doesn't mean we can't be nice."

"You invited a human to a shifter party, Annie. What were you thinking?" Paul demanded.

"I was thinking that most of our eligible men and women aren't even here in the diner today. She could be the mate of any one of them. I figured most of them will be at the party Saturday night, which makes it the perfect gathering for her to find her mate."

"There's no way that human is the mate of any shifter," Bob Wilson said.

"How can you say that, Bob?" Annie demanded. "Her mother's a shifter, for heaven's sake!"

"Yeah, a shifter who couldn't wait to get away from her shifter roots. You never met Sarah Madison, but let me tell you, she was something else," Bob said. "The woman did everything she could to kill the cougar inside her and then she left this town and deliberately mated with a human. She did nothing to pull him into our world and instead, immersed herself into his. Worse, she had not a shred of compassion, honor or loyalty, and as far as I can tell, her daughter's nothing but a miniature Sarah."

"You don't even know her," Annie said.

"I know she was pretty damn unfriendly when she came to my office last month," Bob said. "And I know that nothing I saw in her today convinced me she wasn't anything but a clone of her angry, hateful mother."

"Don't be ridiculous. Someone who's full of anger and hate can't hide that from us, you know that. Emotions have a scent, Bob, and the only thing I scented around Maggie today was anxiety and uncertainty. It seems to me the only one lacking compassion around here is you." She sent a glare around the room. "All of you."

Jackson was sitting in his office the next day, just about to bite into the burger he'd picked up from the diner on his lunch break when Connie appeared in the doorway, a giant grin on her face.

Jackson sighed and set down his burger.

This was not going to be good.

Anything that made Connie smile that widely was sure to be a disaster for him and hilarious for everyone else.

"What is it, Connie?"

"The crazy cat lady's on line one again."

"You're joking."

"Nope."

"What's the problem now? Cat climb a tree?"

"Oh no. Apparently the catnappers are back." Connie barely got the words out before she burst into laughter.

"You've got to be kidding me."

"Nope. She's quite serious. She wants you to send Danny back out, only this time he has to actually do his job and dust for fingerprints and take a cast of the shoe print in her flower bed."

Jackson dropped his head into his hands, then without even looking, grabbed his headset, hit the button for line one and answered the call.

Five minutes later, he was convinced that Maggie Winters was nuttier than a Planters factory.

She was absolutely convinced someone kept breaking into her house to steal her cat.

"Lady, why would anyone want your cat?"

"A better question would be why *wouldn't* they want him? I'll have you know that Genghis Khat is both a warrior and a lover. He's utterly perfect in every way and there's no other cat like him. Anyone would be thrilled to have him as a companion cat, and I daresay, many of those people wouldn't hesitate to catnap him if necessary. Now why don't you do your job and catch the crooks who keep traumatizing the two of us?"

"Have you tried the diner yet?"

"Why on earth would he be at the diner? Genghis Khat may have escaped the catnapper yesterday and found refuge in the diner, but there's no guarantee he'll manage to do that again. He needs rescuing!"

Jackson heaved a huge sigh, then said, "I'm going to put you on hold for a moment, ma'am. I'll be right back." He didn't wait for a reply, just stabbed the hold button and yelled, "Connie, call the diner. See if the cat's shown up over there."

A few minutes later, Connie appeared in his office door, once more grinning like a loon. "You're psychic, Sheriff. The cat walked into the diner ten seconds into my conversation with Bud."

"Wonderful. I hope this isn't going to become a daily occurrence."

Connie chuckled. "Well, if it is, you might want to start eating your lunch at the diner rather than bringing it back here. Maybe then you'll catch those catnappers in the act."

"WHAT DO YOU MEAN MY CAT'S AT THE DINER AGAIN? What is up with these catnappers?"

"Well, ma'am, I think you should perhaps consider the possibility that your cat is managing to escape your house on his own."

"Seriously? Sheriff, I don't have a whole lot of confidence in your investigative skills if *that's* the conclusion you've come to. Do you have any idea how far of a walk it is from my house to the diner? It takes me a good fifteen minutes by car. Are you seriously suggesting my cat walked that distance all by himself, all without being attacked by any of the local wildlife?"

The sheriff sighed. "All I'm saying, ma'am, is we don't have the resources to investigate missing cats. Maybe get a better lock for your windows. Have a good day, ma'am."

Then, quite unbelievably, *he hung up on her.*

"Oh, that man. He makes me crazy!" Maggie grabbed her purse and stormed out to her car.

The entire way to the diner, she fumed and mimicked his superior attitude, sneering, "I'm sorry, *ma'am,* your cat just isn't important enough for us to investigate his disappearance. *Bastard.*"

By the time she got to the diner, she was so angry, she completely forgot to be nervous. She stormed inside and immediately started searching under every table.

She didn't even pause to greet any of the people whose

tables she was peeking beneath, regardless of whether she'd met them the day before or not.

"Hey, Maggie!" Annie called from behind the counter. "Genghis Khat's around here somewhere."

Maggie waved a hand in acknowledgment and kept peeking under tables, refusing to make eye contact or greet anyone along the way.

She was peripherally aware of the conversations above her pausing every time she peeked under a table, then starting up again as she moved on.

A few people tried to engage her in conversation, greeting her by name, but she just focused on the job at hand and ignored their overtures.

Finally, at the table in the opposite corner from the diner's door, she found Genghis Khat sprawled on top of a pair of boots.

Maggie didn't acknowledge the owner of those boots in any way.

She simply crawled under the table, scooped up Genghis Khat and backed out with him in her arms.

She ignored the sound of the owner of those boots chuckling and refused to look at him when he reached out to pat Genghis Khat on the head.

She climbed to her feet and turned away from the table, intending to leave immediately, but found Annie blocking her way.

"I've got you and Genghis Khat all set up in the same booth as last time, Maggie," Annie said, nodding to the booth across the way.

A saucer of milk was already sitting on the table.

"So what are you thinking today, Maggie? Turkey club again, or maybe a tuna melt, or the meatloaf or—"

Maggie sighed. "Let's try a tuna melt this time."

Genghis Khat let out a loud, rumbling purr and Maggie grinned, barely registering Annie's, "You got it," as she walked away.

"Yes, I know," Maggie murmured to Genghis Khat as she headed for the booth. "Tuna makes you *very* happy."

She'd barely settled in the booth, Genghis Khat still in her arms, when two women swooped into the seat across from her. Between the two of them, they were carrying three wine glasses and two unopened bottles of wine, both of them red.

"Hi. I'm Kate and this is Olivia, in case you don't remember us."

Maggie did.

"Call me Livi. And we love your cat."

Maggie smiled a bit. "Did you hear that, Genghis Khat? They like you." She settled him on the seat beside her, then watched as he immediately set both front paws on the table in front of him and stared across it at Kate and Livi.

"Sorry, no wine for you, Mr. Khat," Livi said as she opened one of the bottles of wine. "But the good news is that means more for us." She poured them each a glass and lifted hers in the air. "Cheers."

Kate held hers up, so Maggie did the same and watched as they tapped their glasses to hers.

This was an odd ritual she'd never before participated in.

Both the toasting and the drinking.

"Bottoms up," Livi said and she drained her glass.

Kate followed suit.

Maggie wasn't sure this was a good idea, especially since she had to drive herself and Genghis Khat back home later, but she *was* curious to know what red wine tasted like, so she tried a sip, found it to be palatable and took a larger drink.

Surprisingly, she didn't hate it.

She'd had a sip of champagne once and the bubbles had made her shudder.

This was smooth though and rather tasty.

She had another gulp and then drained the glass as she'd seen the other two women do.

"Right on!" Livi exclaimed, then poured them each another round.

This glass, they drank slowly.

Maggie savored the taste and found it surprisingly soothing.

She might have to add a red wine subscription to her monthly orders.

"So, how are you liking Greensboro so far?" Kate asked. "Is it super different from the last place you lived? Did you live in a big city or a small town like ours?"

Questions.

Always questions.

Maggie shrugged and took another large gulp of wine.

"Don't mind Kate," Livi said. "She chatters like that all the time. You don't have to answer her questions, especially since she rarely gives anyone a chance to get a word in edgewise."

"Hey!"

"You know it's true, Kate." Livi topped off Maggie's glass.

"That's beside the point," Kate said.

Maggie took another big gulp.

So good.

Genghis Khat lost interest in staring at the women and dropped his front feet back down into the booth, where he circled and kneaded the seat for a couple minutes before finally curling up and falling asleep.

Maggie found him to be so adorable lying there, she turned

her attention to petting him, and for long moments, lost track of the conversation as Livi and Kate argued good-naturedly.

She drank down her glass of red with her left hand while adoring Genghis Khat with her right.

"So, Maggie." Kate dragged her attention back to the two of them. "Do you have a boyfriend? Girlfriend? Gender neutral friend? Lover? Significant other? Whatever you want to call them?"

"Uh." Maggie snickered, unexpectedly amused by Kate's frenetic questioning style. "No."

"Cool. Would you like one? And if so, which would you choose? Boyfriend? Girlfriend? Gender neutral—"

"Please, do *not* go through that list again," Livi said as she filled Maggie's glass once more.

"Psh." Kate waved a hand. "So?"

For some reason, Maggie was charmed enough that for once, she didn't mind answering a question. "I guess boyfriend if I wanted one, but I don't."

"Well, why not?"

Maggie shrugged and drained her glass. This was not a conversation she'd ever expected to have, but definitely not with two virtual strangers.

Livi filled Maggie's glass again, which was a really welcome development, given the subject matter.

Maggie took a gulp.

"Come on, why not?" Kate asked.

"Why not what?" Maggie couldn't remember the question. What were they talking about again?

"Why don't you want a boyfriend?"

"It's not that I don't want one. It's that people don't like me and it's just better to not even try. A boyfriend would be too much hard work—trying to make him like me, trying to be whoever he wanted me to be instead of who I am. No. I'm better off alone."

At that moment, Genghis Khat stood and put his front paws on Maggie's left shoulder and nuzzled her cheek, thus reminding her that she was not alone at all.

"Aw, you're the best, Genghis Khat." She scooped him up and kissed his forehead, right above his nose. "I love you, baby boy."

Annie arrived at that moment, delivering Maggie's tuna melt, Livi's burger and fries and Kate's fish and chips. "Enjoy, ladies."

The rest of the afternoon passed in a bit of a blur for Maggie.

When they finished eating, Livi, Kate and Annie, who ended her shift early to join them, dragged Maggie to the local salon, where they got manicures and pedicures.

Unbelievably, they insisted that Genghis Khat accompany them and no one at the salon protested his presence. Instead, all the workers in the salon fussed over the cat and treated him like the king he was.

The women talked and laughed while their nails were being painted, and enjoyed a third bottle of wine provided by the salon.

Maggie chose a brilliant red for her nails and spent a bit of time envisioning all the different outfits in her closet that would look amazing against that red.

Once their nails were done, the women dragged Maggie and Genghis Khat to the only movie theater in town where they watched a terrifying film about a serial killer clown.

The women ate too much popcorn and washed it down with a gallon of coke, all the while cringing and squealing and peeking between their fingers at the screen during the intensely scary parts.

Genghis Khat was the only one who seemed undisturbed by the events onscreen. He snoozed quite happily in Maggie's lap the entire movie, not even waking when Maggie shrieked and sent popcorn sailing everywhere.

The movie was freaky and terrifying and Maggie wouldn't give up the experience for anything in the world.

In the end, it was the most beautiful day of Maggie's life.

By the time they made it back to the diner, Maggie was no longer feeling the effects of the wine, but she was giddy with the realization that at thirty-six years of age, she may have finally made her very first, real friends.

Seven

WHEN BYGUL SHOWED up and cast a bit of magic at the kitchen window the next day, Genghis Khat was ready for him.

He sailed through the window and just like that, Bygul transported them both to the alley behind the diner.

Genghis Khat decided he was beginning to like this job. The diner was a wondrous place, full of yummy food (the tuna the day before had been divine) and people willing to scratch any itch he had.

"Come along, G.K." Bygul said and led the way around to the front of the diner, where they stood at the big picture window and peered inside. "Are there any new people inside or have we been wasting our time with the same people over and over again?"

How in the world was Genghis Khat supposed to know the answer to that question? He didn't pay attention to people's faces. He mostly saw their shoes and their boots and sometimes their fingers that came down to offer a tasty morsel or a head scratch.

And he needed to be inside the diner if he wanted to identify them by scent.

"Right. Let's go inside then," Bygul said. "I've got a bit more time this morning, so I'm going to stick around, just to see what's going on in here. We might need to choose a new place tomorrow if the diner's a bust."

A new place! What if there wasn't any food or head-scratching humans at the new place?

Maggie wasn't happy when she discovered for the third day in a row that Genghis Khat had somehow disappeared from her house.

This time, the window over the kitchen sink was open.

Maggie had tried to open the window when she'd first moved in, but it had been stuck and she'd been unable to budge it.

Yet somehow, while she'd been cleaning upstairs, someone had managed to pry the window open and entice Genghis Khat outside.

She had no idea how this kept happening, especially since paranoia had her checking all the doors and windows before going to bed at night and once again when waking each morning.

She'd even closed her bedroom door the last two nights to keep Genghis Khat close, which had seemed a genius plan yesterday morning when she woke to a paw on the cheek and kitty breath.

Her mistake had been thinking the danger was over when he hadn't been stolen in the middle of the night. She'd gone out into the garden as usual yesterday and when she'd returned, the window in the study had been open again and Genghis Khat nowhere to be seen.

Today, she'd been determined there wouldn't be a third catnapping.

More paranoid than ever, she'd kept Genghis Khat with her as she moved about the house, dusting and vacuuming.

Unfortunately, Genghis Khat hated the vacuum cleaner and he'd gotten away from her when she'd opened the guest bedroom door. She'd raced after him, but somehow it was already too late.

The window was open and Genghis Khat and his catnapper were long gone.

She couldn't understand it. She'd been seconds behind him and yet somehow, he'd managed to leave the house and completely disappear.

Not a single car or person was in sight of the house in any direction and yet there was no denying the cat was missing.

This time, Maggie didn't even bother to call the sheriff's office. The man was infuriating and if he wasn't willing to do his job and investigate these catnappings, Maggie would damn well do it for him.

At this point, she was fairly certain the catnapper was just messing with her. He probably had some secret way of getting into her house and back out again without being seen.

So Maggie's first step—after rescuing Genghis Khat again, of course—would be to find the catnapper's secret entrance.

And block it forever.

Grabbing her car keys, Maggie stormed out of the house and for the third time in as many days, drove into town, headed for the diner.

She was annoyed, yes, and worried about Genghis Khat, of course, but there was a tiny part of her that was happy to have an excuse to go into town again because maybe Annie would be working this morning or maybe Livi and Kate would be there having lunch.

Maybe even all three of them would be there and she'd get to hang out with her friends again.

JACKSON HAD TO ADMIT IT WAS PURE CURIOSITY that had him sitting in a booth toward the back of the diner the following day, rather than ordering his lunch to-go.

"Well, Sheriff, it sure is nice to see you here in the middle of the day," Annie said with a grin. "You here to meet our resident cat or the human?"

"Definitely the cat," Jackson said dryly.

At that moment, a huge gray monstrosity leapt onto the bench seat across from Jackson.

"Good lord, is that the cat in question?"

"The very one," Annie said cheerfully as the cat glared balefully at Jackson over the top of the table.

"He doesn't seem too happy to see me," Jackson observed.

"Well, you are sitting in his booth."

Jackson gave Annie an incredulous look. "You gave the cat his own booth?"

"Not exactly, but Maggie sat here the first day she came to collect Genghis Khat and it's kind of been her booth ever since."

"Ever since two days ago," Jackson said dryly.

"Well, no one's really wanted to use it since, so..."

Jackson wasn't even surprised to hear this.

Shifters could be utterly ridiculous sometimes.

He leaned forward a bit and called to the other diners, "What, did you think her humanity's catching or something?"

"Or something," David Humphreys growled.

Jackson shook his head.

Wolves.

So damn superstitious.

Jackson sat back in the booth and stared at the cat across from him.

Genghis Khat—a name so ridiculous, Jackson couldn't help but smile at the audacity of it—was sitting straight and tall and staring right at him.

Over the next several minutes, Jackson indulged in a staring contest with a domesticated cat.

It was ridiculous, but once he'd started, he couldn't figure out how to extricate himself without appearing weak to the other shifters, not to mention the damn cat.

"There you are, Genghis Khat!"

The staring contest was mercifully ended when the cat was suddenly swept up into a woman's arms.

And what a woman!

Jackson was struck dumb at the sight of her.

She was wearing a bright green dress that came to mid-thigh and the sassiest sandals he'd ever seen. They had ribbons that wrapped around and around her calves, accentuating what had to be the sexiest legs he'd seen in a long time.

Her hair fell in long, brown waves almost to her waist and her bangs fell across her eyes like curtains.

She peeked at him, just once, giving him a glimpse of hazel eyes, before she plopped into the seat across from him, cuddling the ridiculous cat in her arms.

Her scent reached him in a delicate, floral wave that had the panther inside stretching and pressing against his skin.

Before Jackson could really do anything other than blink at this vision in front of him, Annie showed up with two plates. She slid the one with a burger in front of Jackson and the other —a tuna melt, it looked like—in front of the human.

"Hi, Maggie," Annie exclaimed. "I hope you don't mind. I went ahead and put in an order for a tuna melt for you. I noticed how much Genghis Khat enjoyed the tuna yesterday and since the sheriff is here for his lunch, I thought it'd be nice if the two of you could keep each other company."

Jackson couldn't help but notice that Maggie never took her attention from the cat in her lap the entire time Annie was speaking. However, the minute Annie said sheriff, Maggie's head came flying up and her eyes jerked from Annie to Jackson.

"You!" she exclaimed.

Jackson opened his mouth, without any real inkling as to what he was going to say, but whatever it was, he didn't have a chance to say it, because Maggie cut him off in a rush of words.

"I don't appreciate you dismissing my concerns. There's quite obviously a catnapper at work in this community causing all kinds of mischief. Maybe it's just some prankster, but I'm not finding it funny. And it's your job to stop criminal activity."

She stood and swept from the booth. She had the cat cradled in her left arm and used her right to grab the plate with the tuna melt on it. "You should be ashamed of yourself. Your deputy refused to take fingerprints the first time Genghis Khat went missing, and here we are, two days later with three unsolved catnappings you haven't even bothered to begin to investigate. Well, I'll tell you what, if you won't solve this spree of catnappings, I will!" With that, she turned on her heel and flounced out of the diner.

Silence fell in her wake until the diner's door opened again and Maggie poked her head back in to call, "I'll bring the plate back tomorrow, Annie, if that's okay."

"Sure, sure!"

"Just charge it to my account, or better yet, charge it to your condescending, inept sheriff's account!" With that, she was gone again.

"Ooooh, doggie," Travis Norton exclaimed. "You done riled up the human, Jackson."

Jackson didn't reply. He was too busy processing what had just happened.

"Jackson, honey, you okay?" Annie was starting to look concerned.

She couldn't possibly be as concerned as Jackson was though.

"What's the matter, Sheriff?" David's wife, Natalie asked. "Haven't you ever seen a human before?"

"Sure I have, Natalie. Just haven't met one that's my mate before." With that, he lunged from the booth and raced toward the door, with only one thing in mind.

Soothing his mate's temper.

"Darn that sheriff, Genghis Khat." Maggie sat in her car in the diner's parking lot, fuming. "He ruined everything. I was looking forward to chatting with Annie again. Although there *were* a lot of people in the diner I hadn't met yet, so maybe it was better to just get out of there. No use pushing my luck."

Genghis Khat, who was sitting on the console between the two front seats, rubbed his head against her shoulder and let out a deep, rumbling purr.

"I know, baby." Maggie lifted a hand and stroked it all the way down his back. "You're the best kitty ever."

A knock on the window startled both of them, making Maggie jump and Genghis Khat hiss fiercely.

A peek at the side window told Maggie it was the idiot sheriff knocking.

Damn.

"It's okay, Genghis Khat. Everything's going to be just fine." Maggie stroked him several times, soothing down his fur and crooning to him.

Interestingly, the sheriff didn't knock again, just stood outside the door waiting patiently.

Or maybe not so patiently, Maggie didn't know.

Still, he didn't knock or hurry her along, so Maggie counted that as a tiny point in his favor.

One tiny point that barely made a dent in all the ones he'd racked up as marks against him.

Finally, she turned and rolled the window down a couple inches. She stared at him, but didn't say anything. After all, she wasn't the one knocking on his car door window. She had nothing to say.

He was silent for a minute before he finally seemed to realize she was waiting on him to speak. "Would you mind stepping out of the car for a minute?"

Maggie scowled. What could he possibly want from her now? She turned to Genghis Khat and said, "Be good, boy. I'll be right back."

She opened the door and the sheriff stepped forward to offer a hand.

She froze and stared at his hand.

What was he doing?

He just waited.

Was she supposed to give him something?

Well, he *was* a cop. Maybe he wanted her license and registration.

Or maybe he paid for her lunch and wanted her to pay him back.

She couldn't imagine what else he'd want her to give him.

She felt Genghis Khat's paws on her shoulders and glanced back to see that he was now standing on his hind legs and peering over her shoulder at the sheriff.

She turned back to the sheriff just in time to see him reach toward her.

She shrank back, but all he did was catch both of her hands in his and gently pull her from the car.

Oh.

He'd been offering his hand to help.

Now Maggie felt foolish.

At least she hadn't tried to give him money or her license or anything like that.

Genghis Khat meowed at her and she turned to see he was now sitting in the drivers' seat, watching her and the sheriff.

"It's okay, Genghis Khat. We won't be long."

The sheriff closed the door and pulled her toward him.

That was when Maggie realized he still had hold of both her hands.

He guided her around so her back was to the car, then stepped in so he was standing right in front of her.

Closer than she was usually comfortable with.

He was in her space and Maggie was usually very territorial about her space.

This was her space, that was his space, and never the twain shall meet.

Except right then, her space and his space were all tangled up together and she was feeling a bit lightheaded.

"Breathe, Maggie."

She dragged in a deep breath. "You know my name."

"You called my office the past two days, gave your name each time."

Maggie scowled at the reminder. "Yes, and you didn't take my concerns seriously."

He raised an eyebrow. "I took your concerns seriously enough to send a deputy out to your house."

Well, she supposed that was true. It wasn't his fault his deputy had refused to dust for fingerprints.

"I also tracked your cat to the diner and you got him back both days, didn't you?"

Maggie sighed. Well, when he put it like that, sure. "Yes, but you haven't done anything to keep this from happening again. Today was the third time someone opened a window at my house and stole my cat."

"Right."

From the look on the sheriff's face, Maggie was pretty sure he didn't agree with her assessment of the situation. Still, he didn't argue with her, which was probably another point in his favor.

"Well, how about I come out right now and help you problem-solve? We can take a look around, see where the intruder might be getting in or possibly how—" he hesitated, then continued, "—Genghis Khat might be getting out."

She wasn't sure what that hesitation meant, but had a feeling it was related to her cat in some way. The sheriff probably thought she hadn't noticed, but he'd been in a pretty intense stare-down with Genghis Khat when she'd arrived at the diner.

She'd planned to admonish him for trying to intimidate her cat, but then she'd found out he was the sheriff and she had a much bigger lecture to deliver.

Oh, well, she'd just save that one for next time.

"Maggie?"

"Fine, Sheriff. You can follow me back to the house."

"First, call me Jackson."

Maggie hesitated, then said softly, "Jackson."

He smiled at her, then stepped back, pulling her with him. He opened the car door and held it as she climbed in. "I'll meet you at your house. Drive safe." He closed the car door and stood there, hands on hips, watching as she pulled out of the parking lot and headed toward home.

Within minutes, he was behind her on the winding roads leading out of town.

By the time they reached the house, Maggie was a bundle of nerves.

Genghis Khat could obviously sense her nerves because he'd paced in the passenger side seat the entire trip home.

Scooping Genghis Khat into her arms, Maggie met Jackson on the front porch, and let him into the house, feeling more nervous than ever.

She'd never had a man over to her place before—any place, not just this one.

"So I thought I should look for a secret entrance," she said. "I figure that's the only way someone could sneak into my house without me knowing it."

"What about the locks? If your Aunt Becky gave keys to anyone—"

"I changed the locks when I moved in. No one has the keys but me."

"Right, then. Let's get to the searching."

As strange as it was, the afternoon and evening went by quickly.

Maggie found Jackson's presence to be both soothing and agitating, all at the same time.

Genghis Khat followed them from room to room as they searched for a false entrance. They tapped all the walls, explored every closet in depth, and found nothing.

Jackson spent some time looking at both the study window and the kitchen window and couldn't find anything wrong with either lock.

"This just isn't possible, Genghis Khat," Maggie said, hands on hips.

Genghis Khat was sitting in the center of the kitchen table, watching carefully as Jackson flipped the lock on the window back and forth.

"I just don't understand how you keep getting out. I know you're not doing it on your own, but I don't know how someone's getting in."

"Well, you could certainly have a security system added, wire the windows so the alarm blares when they're opened, but it seems like overkill."

Maggie sighed. "Yeah. I guess. Well, thanks for trying to help, Sheriff."

He raised an eyebrow.

"Jackson."

He smiled. "It was my pleasure, Maggie. It's getting on to dinner time. I was going to go to the diner, if you'd like to join me."

Maggie shook her head. "Oh, no." She'd spent more than enough time socializing and talking for one day, and while the sheriff wasn't quite the idiot she'd once thought him, she needed him to leave now.

She'd enjoyed listening to him speak and watching him wander through her house. She'd enjoyed watching his capable hands knocking on walls and testing the locks on her doors and windows.

She'd enjoyed the feel of his hand in hers when he'd led her down the stairs and into the kitchen just a few moments before.

But it was too much.

Entirely too much for one day.

"Time to go, Sheriff." Maggie hurried toward the front door and flung it open.

He followed at a more leisurely pace, then stopped right next to her and slid one broad hand around to the back of her neck, where he cradled her head.

He nudged her chin up with his other hand and leaned down and kissed her.

It wasn't her first kiss.

There were a few teenaged fumblings in her past.

And one tentative kiss with a roommate she'd had a girl-crush on in her early twenties.

This, though, was her first kiss from a man.

And oh, what a man.

His kiss was gentle and light and sent shivers down her back.

He came back for more and laid a series of kisses on her lips, one after the other, making her shiver in delight.

Her hands came up of their own accord and latched onto his shirt where they clung as he coaxed her lips open and swept his tongue inside for a hotter, more devastating kiss than she'd ever known.

Long moments later, he pulled back, then leaned down and kissed her again, one short kiss that left her breathless.

"Lock the door behind me, Maggie," he murmured against her lips.

She nodded dazedly and followed him out the door.

He stopped on the porch and gently nudged her back inside the house. "I'll see you tomorrow. Close the door and lock it now."

She nodded again.

He stepped back and in a daze, she closed the door and locked it. She stood there and listened as he said, "Sweet dreams, Maggie mine." She staggered to the picture window and watched as he sauntered down her front walkway, climbed into his car and drove off into the night.

Maggie sagged down onto the couch, touched shaky fingers to her lips and let out a soft whimper.

Genghis Khat leapt up onto her lap, nudged her chin and she caught him up in her arms, hugging him close in an almost compulsive move. "Oh, Genghis Khat," she whispered. "What just happened?"

Eight

GENGHIS KHAT DIDN'T understand humans at all.

He wasn't sure why his Maggie was shaking, but he knew it had something to do with that sheriff, so he spent the night guarding his human and making a plan to avoid the sheriff from now on.

Unfortunately, that plan was pretty much destroyed when Bygul showed up the next morning.

"We've found Maggie's mate," Bygul explained, "so instead of going to the diner today, we're going to the barbershop where her mate has an appointment."

Genghis Khat didn't like this idea at all. He doubted the barbershop would be a food paradise like the diner.

However, to get Maggie the mate she needed so they could stay in this town, Genghis Khat was willing to make the supreme sacrifice.

It was a good thing too because the next thing he knew, he was inside a long, narrow room that had all kinds of hair on the floor, but no tasty morsels.

Genghis Khat growled his displeasure at Bygul.

"Oh, get over it. There's Maggie's mate. Go make friends with him."

Genghis Khat was horrified when he realized Bygul was referring to the sheriff.

The sheriff who'd left his scent in every room of their house the day before and who'd upset Maggie so much that after he'd left, she'd been a mess, constantly asking Genghis Khat to explain what had just happened.

Apparently, the answer was that Maggie had met her mate.

And Genghis Khat *hated* him.

MAXWELL HAD JUST FINISHED SHAVING THE BACK OF Jackson's neck when Maggie's crazy cat appeared out of nowhere and leapt onto Jackson's lap.

Both Maxwell and Jackson let out yelps of surprise.

Laughter sounded around the room as the cat from hell began kneading Jackson's legs, full claws extended.

Jackson winced and tried to lift the cat away, but it just sank its claws in deeper.

"Okay, okay. Ow, ow, ow, you freaky feline." In desperation, Jackson shoved his hands between the cat and his family jewels.

Just in case.

"Damn." With one hand blocking the cat from full access, Jackson extricated his phone with the other and called Connie. "Get ahold of Maggie and let her know her cat's at the barbershop today."

Five minutes later, Maggie burst into the shop. She must have already been in town to have gotten there so quickly.

She froze for one moment when she caught sight of Genghis Khat on Jackson's lap.

"Hey, sweetheart," Jackson said, sending her his best smile.

Maggie's face darkened in response. "Is *this* why you refused to investigate the catnappings?"

"Huh?"

"And then insisted on coming over last night to *help*?" She made quotes in the air around help. "Were you really helping at all or were you just setting things up for the next catnapping?"

"What? Maggie, no!"

"Well, what else am I supposed to think, Jackson? Someone keeps stealing my cat and here you are, cuddling him like he's *your* cat, not mine!"

"Does this *look* like cuddling? Because I assure you there is no cuddling happening over here." Jackson winced as the demon cat flexed its claws.

Maggie made a sound of frustration, stormed toward him and swept Genghis Khat into her arms.

Jackson winced as ten claws peeled from his skin all at once.

Maggie whirled and stalked toward the door.

The cat stared over her shoulder at Jackson with what he would swear was a smug look on its face.

"Maggie, wait!" Jackson jumped up, peeled a couple bills from his wallet, pressed them into Maxwell's hand and hurried after her, a symphony of "Good luck!" and "You're going to need it!" following him out the door.

Maggie stamped toward her car, fuming.

She couldn't believe Jackson was trying to steal her cat!

"Maggie, hold up!" Jackson darted into her path and held out his hands in the universal stop position.

She skidded to a halt and scowled at him.

"Sweetheart, I *promise* I am not the one stealing your cat. No one was more surprised than me when he jumped into my lap at the barbershop."

Maggie eyed him suspiciously. He sounded sincere, but she just wasn't sure whether to believe him or not.

"I assume you didn't touch your windows or doors after I left last night."

"Of course not. That didn't seem to matter today though."

"What do you mean?"

"Genghis Khat was with me all morning long. He was sitting right on the kitchen table and we were having a lovely conversation." She paused at the odd look on Jackson's face, but before she could interpret what it meant, he smiled and the look was gone.

"Go on. You were talking with the cat and then what?"

"I turned away to get something out of a cabinet and when I turned back, he was gone. I searched everywhere, but he was nowhere to be found and all the windows and doors were closed tight. Now how do you explain that, Jackson?"

He looked perplexed. "Frankly, it's starting to sound a bit like god magic."

Maggie took a step back. "I don't believe in god or heaven or hell or any of that." She saw no condemnation on his face, which she had to admit, was a huge relief. "There's just no scientific proof that any of it really exists."

Jackson grinned. "Valid point, but I'm not *really* talking about that kind of god. I'm more talking about *the* gods, as in plural. You know, the ones who occasionally like to meddle in

—" he cleared his throat "—people's affairs. This sounds like the work of a mischievous god."

Maggie thought his theory was as lacking in scientific evidence as every other god theory she'd ever heard, but since at this point, she had zero *logical* explanations, she supposed she might have to accept an illogical one instead. And now that she thought about it, an illogical explanation might be the only one that actually made sense, in some weird, alternate universe kind of way, of course.

She hefted Genghis Khat away from her shoulder and held him up high so she could see his face. "So, what's the story, Genghis Khat? Are the gods responsible for you coming into town every day?"

Genghis Khat let out a sound that seemed to start as a purr and ended as a meow. This was unexpected as he rarely responded to any of her questions.

"Well, I wouldn't say that's a no." She settled him back against her chest, so that he was once again resting his head on her shoulder, and smiled at Jackson. "Of course, I'm not sure it was a yes, either, so I guess that means it's not outside the realm of possibility. A weird and crazy realm, to be sure, but I've been unable to come up with any other explanation."

"Crazy." Jackson grinned. "Right. Well, I have a couple other crazy things you should probably know. Why don't we head over to the diner? We can get some lunch and chat for a bit."

Maggie hesitated. Was she really up for yet another round of social interactions?

"I bet Genghis Khat would enjoy a treat and he must be getting a bit heavy to carry."

She supposed one more round wouldn't be so bad. Especially since most of the people in this town gave her a wide berth and didn't seem to take offense when she chose not to reply to their greetings. She started walking toward the diner, which was just a few doors down, and Jackson fell into step at her side.

When they reached the door of the diner, he opened it for her and rested a hand on her lower back to gently guide her into the restaurant.

She moved forward, intensely aware of the placement of his hand.

Genghis Khat shifted on her shoulder and hissed.

Jackson let out a yelp and jerked his hand away from her waist.

By this time, they were several steps into the restaurant and laughter swept like a wave through the diners.

"Having a bit of trouble there, are ya, Sheriff?" one of the diners called out.

Jackson let out a soft growl of annoyance.

Maggie glanced over the opposite shoulder from where Genghis Khat was.

Jackson had his hand to his mouth and was—licking it?

He saw her watching and jerked his hand back down, quickly covering it with his other one, but it was too late.

She'd already seen the scratch.

"Oh, Genghis Khat." She shook her head and made her way through the tables, ignoring the many greetings called her way, focused on reaching the booth she was starting to think of as belonging to her and Genghis Khat.

When she reached their table, she set him on it and bent down to stare into his eyes. "Be nice to the sheriff and he might buy you a treat."

Jackson made a scoffing sound as he settled into the booth.

Maggie scowled, settled onto the bench across from him and said, "You'll never win him over with that attitude."

"Who says I *want* to win him over?"

Before Maggie could reply, Annie showed up to take their orders, which was really excellent timing. "Annie, what would you say if I told you that Jackson doesn't want to make friends with Genghis Khat?"

"I'd say he might as well give up on making friends with *you,* in that case."

Maggie grinned. "You already know me so well. I'll have the burger and fries today."

"Good choice. Anything for Genghis Khat?"

"I think just water to drink."

Genghis Khat let out a tiny growl, startling Maggie and making Annie laugh.

"Sounds like he doesn't agree with that choice," Annie observed.

"Okay, fine. A *small* saucer of milk." Maggie had been reading up on cat care and it turned out dairy wasn't the healthiest of choices for cats, but then again, Genghis Khat probably hadn't had much milk—or really any treats at all—in his life up to now, so maybe she should just let him enjoy his newfound good fortune.

"Jackson?" Annie asked.

Maggie stared across the table at Jackson and raised an eyebrow.

He let out a huff and said, "Bring the demon cat a can of tuna. And I'll have the burger and fries as well."

"You got it." Annie winked at Maggie and headed back to the kitchen.

"Interesting," Maggie said.

"What's that?"

"You not only believe in multiple gods, but also that my cat is possessed by a demon."

Jackson grinned. "Not exactly what I meant, but it'll do. Anyway, there's something I wanted to talk to you about."

"Yes?"

"You see, this town's a little—"

He seemed to be searching for the proper words, but Maggie already knew a bunch of them. "Unusual? Unique? Strange?"

He laughed. "Well, sure, all of the above, but that wasn't really what I was going to—"

"Maggie!" Kate shoved her way into Maggie's side of the booth. "I'm so excited! You and the sheriff are—"

"Kate!" Jackson snapped.

"—dating!" Kate glared across at Jackson who glared right back at her.

They weren't dating, were they? Based on Jackson's scowl, the answer was definitely not. Maggie ignored the sinking feeling inside and said, "Oh, um, no, of course—"

"We are," Jackson said. He reached across the table and grabbed Maggie's hand.

Maggie's eyes widened. She glanced from Jackson to Kate and back again. "We are?"

"We definitely are." He nodded emphatically.

"Oh, okay." She turned to Kate. "Yes?" She didn't really mean to say it like that, like it was a question, but she was still too stunned to really process what any of it meant. "Yes," she said again, this time with a bit more confidence.

Kate grinned, threw her arms around Maggie and hugged her tight.

Jackson still had hold of one of Maggie's hands and her other hand was busy petting Genghis Khat, who was stretched out on the table as if the entire thing belonged to him. So with neither hand being free, Maggie couldn't exactly hug Kate back, but that was okay because Maggie had zero experience with hugs and wasn't quite sure of the etiquette involved.

Before she could even decide whether she liked being on the receiving end of a hug, Kate pulled back and exclaimed, "You're perfect for each other!"

Jackson scowled.

He couldn't prove it, but he was pretty sure the damn cougar had done that on purpose.

The shifters in the diner weren't exactly making it a secret that they were all listening intently to Jackson's attempts to woo his mate.

If they thought he hadn't noticed how their conversations pretty much died the minute he said he wanted to talk to Maggie about something, they were crazy.

Then for Kate to show up right when he was about to blurt out the truth—her timing was entirely too suspicious. She had to have done it on purpose, he knew she had.

Then she'd actually demanded to know whether they were dating, not that Jackson believed that was the word she'd been about to use. She'd almost given away they were mates.

He glared at Kate as she gushed about them dating and how perfect they were for each other.

Jackson happened to agree, of course, but Kate needed to butt out so that he could prove it to Maggie, who clearly wasn't as certain as he was that they were meant to be together.

Maggie never really said anything in reply to Kate's babbling, but Jackson had already noticed that silence tended to be Maggie's go-to response when most people attempted to engage her in conversation.

He wasn't even convinced that she heard them half the time, but if she did, she was an expert at ignoring them.

In Kate's case, however, Maggie actually appeared to be listening to her if the tiny smirk on her face was any indication.

Finally, Kate's rambling dwindled away and she gave Maggie one last hug and exited the booth.

Jackson glared at Kate's back as she walked away, but then realized Maggie was watching and tried to school his face into a more neutral expression.

"Did you really mean that?" Maggie asked.

"Mean what?"

"That we're dating now."

Jackson grinned. "How could you possibly doubt it after last night's kiss?"

Maggie blushed, then shrugged one shoulder. "I just wasn't sure, that's all."

"Yes, well, the thing is, Maggie, um, I wanted to talk to you about the town because, you see—"

"Oh, you don't have to explain the town," Maggie said. "I already know it's a little weird. I mean, look at Genghis Khat." She spread her hands to indicate the ridiculous feline currently sprawled across the table.

Jackson couldn't believe the cat had exposed its belly to a roomful of predators.

Zero respect.

That's what the feline was showing him.

Jackson scowled down at the cat. Maybe if he pricked it with one of his claws.

Just a little bit.

He wouldn't actually hurt the cat, of course, just teach it a lesson.

"Jackson!"

He jumped, then looked up to find Maggie glaring at him. Shit.

He surreptitiously curled his fingers a little. Thank goodness his claws were still retracted.

He cleared his throat. "Ah, sorry. What were you saying?"

"Just that it's a little weird for a restaurant to allow a cat inside, let alone a cat that sits on the tables. Aren't they worried about a visit from the health department?"

"Eh, not really. People in these parts—they're not that worried about a bit of fur in their food."

Someone snorted.

Jackson refused to look to see who it was.

Didn't matter anyway.

They were all bastards.

He should never have brought Maggie here. He should have suggested they go back to her house or that she come to his.

"Brother! Fancy meeting you here."

No. Freaking. Way.

Jackson glared as his twin brother, Jefferson, shoved his way into the booth, right next to Jackson's mate.

Jackson let out a small growl and fisted his hands.

He would *not* attack his brother in front of his mate.

He would *not.*

Later, however, all bets were off.

Jefferson grinned across the table at Jackson, as if he knew exactly what Jackson was thinking, then turned to Maggie and grabbed the hand that was busy petting the demon cat. "You must be Maggie. I'm Jefferson, the hand-some Hewitt."

Jackson rolled his eyes. Jefferson had been telling that ridiculous joke since they'd hit their teens and discovered girls.

Maggie giggled.

Jackson scowled.

That was the first time he'd heard her laugh and *Jefferson* was the one who made it happen.

Not cool.

It was now Jackson's mission in life to get Maggie to laugh. Often.

And why was Maggie staring at Jefferson so intently? Damn his brother. He might just have to—

At that moment, Maggie turned and stared at Jackson with the same amount of concentration.

That's when Jackson realized what she was doing. She was obviously searching for differences, but he knew she'd never be able to tell them apart, as they really were identical in every way.

Maggie switched her attention back to Jefferson, studied him for a couple more beats, then shook her head and said, "Sorry, Jefferson, but I'm afraid Jackson has you beat in the handsome department."

Jackson burst into laughter.

Jefferson grinned. "I expect you have to say that, since you're–hmmm–*dating*. So *this* is the infamous Genghis Khat." He held out a hand for the demon cat to sniff and Jackson grinned in anticipation.

He would *not* be warning his ass of a brother that he was risking life and limb. Literally.

Genghis Khat rolled over and stretched to a standing posi-tion. He then nudged Jefferson's hand with his nose.

Jefferson chuckled and began petting the demon cat.

"Excuse me?" Jackson growled. "How is that right?"

Maggie giggled again, which admittedly, brightened Jackson's day, but he did *not* appreciate the smug look the cat sent him over its shoulder.

Damn cat!

Nine

THE LATEST HUMAN, who introduced himself as Handsome Hewitt, smelled a lot like the sheriff, only a bit wilder.

Genghis Khat liked that wildness.

He also liked that Handsome Hewitt made Maggie laugh.

Maybe Bygul had gotten it wrong.

Maybe the sheriff wasn't Maggie's mate after all. Maybe it was Handsome Hewitt instead.

It'd be an easy mistake to make since they smelled a lot alike.

Genghis Khat liked the idea that Handsome Hewitt was Maggie's mate and not the sheriff, so he decided to explore the situation further.

He climbed to his feet and nudged Handsome Hewitt's hand, just to see what he would do.

As it turned out, Handsome Hewitt took the nudge as an invitation to pet Genghis Khat. A nudge did mean that in certain situations. Maggie belonged to him, so of course a nudge to her hand meant pet me now.

A nudge to a stranger's hand, however, was often just a test. To see what the stranger would do.

And to determine whether claws and teeth were required or not.

In this case, Genghis Khat decided they weren't required, mainly because the sheriff's scent had changed the minute Handsome Hewitt had joined them, going from a bit nervous and uncertain to irritated and impatient.

This led Genghis Khat to believe that the sheriff would be quite pleased if Genghis Khat clawed his rival.

Therefore, he restrained himself, and made friends with the rival instead.

At that moment, Genghis Khat's second favorite human (after Maggie, of course) arrived with her arms full of tasty morsels on plates.

"Can I get you anything, Jefferson?" Annie asked.

"He's just leaving," Jackson said, glaring at his brother.

"No, thanks, darling." Jefferson winked at Annie. "Gotta get back to work. Just stopped by to see my brother."

Right. Like anyone believed Jackson's brother was there to "see" him. *Torture* him was more like it.

"Well, let me know if you guys need anything else." Annie grinned and walked away, a slight spring in her step.

"I should be heading on." Jefferson climbed to his feet. "It was nice to meet you, Maggie, and you, Genghis Khat." Jefferson scratched the cat's head one last time, winked at Jackson's mate, then turned and sauntered out of the diner.

Jackson was only mildly appeased to notice that Maggie

didn't once look Jefferson's way as he spoke to her nor did she turn to watch his retreat.

Instead she was focused on cutting her burger into what appeared to be four perfectly equal portions.

Annie, Jackson noticed, had set the can of tuna on *his* side of the table.

Jackson scowled.

Was he actually supposed to feed the cat himself?

At least it had a pop top, but still.

He glared at the can of tuna, then looked at his burger.

Damn cat could wait.

He reached for the burger, then jerked his hand back when the cat snapped at him with its teeth.

No. Not at him.

At his burger!

With one lunge, the demon cat managed to extract an entire piece of bacon right from the middle of his burger, dislodging the top bun in the process.

"Hey! Why you little bacon thief!"

A spate of giggles from across the way drew Jackson's attention away from the cat and back to Maggie.

Her shoulders shook with laughter as she tried to get the bacon away from the demon cat. "Come on, now, Genghis Khat. Bacon isn't good for you. Too much salt."

The cat just growled low in his throat as he quickly gulped down the piece of bacon Maggie hadn't managed to pry from what Jackson was convinced were jaws of death, then turned his head to look speculatively at Jackson's burger.

"Oh, no, you don't." Jackson wrapped a protective arm around his plate and with the opposite hand, quickly set his burger back to rights and lifted it to his mouth where he took a giant bite.

Maggie giggled again.

Jackson had thought her beautiful from the first minute he saw her, but when she smiled, her eyes lit up and she was simply stunning.

"You should probably feed him some of that tuna," Maggie advised. "Then he won't be after your lunch."

Jackson scowled. "I notice he's not trying to steal *your* bacon."

"Of course not. Genghis Khat loves me, don't you, darling?" She kissed the cat on his forehead and crooned soft words to him as Jackson set about popping the top on the can of tuna.

"Here." He shoved the can across the table.

The demon cat gave it a dismissive look, then turned away.

"Seriously?"

Maggie snickered. "Oh, come on, Genghis Khat. It's perfectly good tuna."

In response, the cat actually put his nose up in the air.

"Fine," Jackson said. "I'll just enjoy the tuna myself then." He reached for the can.

In one swift move, the cat whirled and swat at him.

Jackson jerked back and let out a soft, rumbling growl.

Maggie jumped, startled, while the rest of the diner erupted in laughter.

Jackson scowled at the lot of them, then transferred his attention back to the cat.

The cat who had defended the tuna with a rather scary amount of viciousness, but who had not yet taken even the smallest of nibbles.

"Well, go on, then. You wanted it, eat it!"

Maggie shook her head. "You aren't doing it right. You have to feed him by hand."

"Excuse me?"

"It's why Annie brought the saucer. You have to scoop it out onto the saucer and then take a bit at a time and feed him."

"Are you seriously telling me that you hand–feed this monster cat like he's a baby?"

Maggie gasped. "He's not a monster, are you, Genghis Khat? And I only hand-feed him here at the diner."

Jackson groaned. "Great. Only here, where the entire town is witness."

Several snickers and chuckles rolled around the room, but he was too busy watching Maggie to pay them any mind.

She'd pulled the can toward her and was scooping the tuna onto the saucer. As he watched, she carefully divided the contents of the can into four equal parts, much like she'd done with her burger.

What followed was the strangest eating ritual Jackson had ever seen.

The cat, who had rejected the tuna from him, graciously accepted every tiny morsel Maggie offered. As she fed the cat, Maggie ate her burger. At first, Jackson thought it was his imagination, but no, as time passed, it became clear that Maggie was pacing her meal consumption right alongside the cat's. One-fourth of the burger and one-fourth of the tuna were consumed in approximately the same amount of time. She then went to work on the second-fourth of both.

Jackson couldn't decide if he was more disgusted or charmed. He really wanted to be disgusted, but he just couldn't find the process anything less than adorable.

Even though he still hated that damn cat.

He was so mesmerized by the process, he almost forgot to eat his own burger. For a while, the only sound at their table was Maggie murmuring soft words of encouragement and praise to the demon cat.

Jackson scowled. He wanted Maggie murmuring words of praise to him, damnit!

How ridiculous.

Jealous of a demon cat.

He wracked his brain for something to say to draw Maggie's attention back to him.

Wasn't there something he was supposed to be telling her?

Something important.

Oh. Right.

He cleared his throat. "So, Maggie, I wanted to talk to you a bit about *why* this town is so unusual."

Maggie glanced up from where she was feeding the cat another bite of tuna and said, "Oh. I didn't realize there was an actual reason for the strangeness." She looked disturbed for a moment. "You don't have to make up a reason for me. I'm perfectly fine with strangeness for its own sake."

Jackson didn't have the faintest clue how to respond to that. "Right. Well, there is a reason though and it's not one that I made up."

"Oh."

Damned if she didn't look *disappointed*.

"Well, I guess you'd better tell me then." She straightened in the booth, almost as if she was bracing herself.

"Okay, so it's like this. Everyone in this town is—"

"Maggie!" Livi slid into the booth beside Maggie and reached out a hand to pet Genghis Khat.

Unbelievable.

Jackson was beginning to think it was a conspiracy. He also couldn't help but notice that the cat didn't flinch or hiss or swat at *Livi*.

What *was* it with this cat?

He tolerated everyone but Jackson!

It was almost as if the cat *knew* Jackson had designs on Maggie, but that was preposterous. Right?

Jackson eyed the cat suspiciously.

Maybe it really *was* possessed by demons.

"You're coming to the party tomorrow, right?" Livi's question caught Jackson's attention.

Seriously? "Livi!"

"What?" She gave him an innocent look. "What on earth is taking you so long, Jackson Hewitt?"

Jackson glared at her and she only grinned unrepentantly back.

"Oh, I'm not much for parties," Maggie said.

"But you've never been to one of our parties," Livi said. "You'll love it!"

Maggie made a face. "Doubtful."

"I'm holding you responsible, Jackson," Livi said. "You get on with it right now and you bring her to the party tomorrow, you hear?" With that, she gave Maggie a quick peck on the cheek and was gone.

Jackson waited for Maggie to ask what Livi had been talking about, but realized after a few moments that she wasn't going to ask. At first, he thought she was just being patient and waiting for him to share, but the more he studied her body language, the more he realized she just didn't care.

Livi had left and as far as Jackson could tell, Maggie had put Livi and the entire conversation out of her mind.

Maggie sat there, no tension in her body at all as she continued to croon to her ridiculous cat and feed him tuna, all while taking bites of her burger in between. She didn't rush either one. She never took a bite of her burger without first feeding the cat a bit of tuna and not once did she glance at Jackson for his reaction.

Lord, she was such a breath of fresh air.

How in the hell was he going to break the news to her about the town and him and that he was her mate?

Although, now that he thought about it, he was probably blowing everything out of proportion.

If he was lucky, she already knew about the town. After all, her mother and aunt had both been shifters, so none of this should be too big of a shock.

Right?

Ten

EVEN THOUGH THE humans in this town smelled wilder than most humans, Genghis Khat had begun to doubt Bygul's claim that some of them could change into animals.

In all their trips into town, Genghis Khat hadn't seen a single human shift, not even once, which was rather disappointing. It was also, in Genghis Khat's mind, pretty compelling evidence that Bygul had been sniffing too much of the catnip.

Then the sheriff went and ruined that theory by claiming he could shift into a panther.

Genghis Khat had never met a panther before, but he was pretty sure it was just a fancy name for cat.

Of course, until Genghis Khat saw the panther with his own eyes, he wasn't going to be falling for these ridiculous tales.

Maggie must have agreed with him because the next thing he knew she'd snatched him up off the table and was storming through the diner and out the door.

Genghis Khat smirked at the sheriff over her shoulder.

The last thing he saw before the door closed behind them was the sheriff lunging from the booth and running after them.

At least the idiot realized Maggie was *worth* chasing after.

MAGGIE COULDN'T BELIEVE IT!

The one man she'd kissed, the one man she really liked, was making fun of her. Just because her best friend was a cat whom she loved to talk to didn't mean she was gullible enough to believe people could actually change into animals.

There was *zero* scientific data to show that such a thing would ever be possible.

Jackson must believe she was an idiot.

It was the only explanation.

"Maggie, wait!"

She jerked open her car door and set Genghis Khat inside, then whirled to face Jackson. "Don't even say it."

He skidded to a stop in front of her. "Say what?"

"Whatever you're going to say. I don't want to hear it. I can't believe you think I'm so gullible as to fall for such a ridiculous tale. People shifting into animals. Oooh!" She was so angry, she couldn't even think of words to express how upset she was.

"I know this is a lot to take in, Maggie, but I promise you I'm not lying. I made the mistake of thinking you already knew about shifters, I'm sorry about that."

"Why would I know about—you know what? Forget it. It doesn't matter. I'm going home." She turned to open the car door.

"Because your mother was a shifter," he said quickly.

Maggie froze with her hand on the car door handle.

"Your aunt was too. They were both cougars. This town is mostly home to cougars, bears and wolves. Jefferson and I are the only panthers in town, and we're a bit of a scandal in the family, to be honest. There's this family legend, you see, about one of our ancestors, a wolf, having an affair with a panther. Nobody believed it, of course. It seemed preposterous, but then Jefferson and I were born."

Maggie didn't even know what to say.

Her brain was busy screaming, *but science,* while her heart really wanted to believe him.

It was a fabulous story and she was now imagining two panther cubs running around with a bunch of wolf cubs. It was a rather adorable image.

Dragging in a deep breath, she turned and said, "Fine. Then prove it to me."

"What?"

She waved a hand in the air and said, "Shift and show me your panther."

"I'm not saying no. I just can't do it here."

Maggie rolled her eyes.

"No, really. It's illegal to shift downtown. It's for the town's protection and since I'm the sheriff, I really kind of have to set the right example."

Maggie sighed. "Fine. Then where *can* you shift?"

"Pretty much anywhere else."

"My house?"

He smiled. "I'll follow you there."

Maggie didn't respond, just climbed into her car and pulled out of the parking space.

Deja vu filled her at the sight of Jackson standing in the parking lot, hands on hips, watching her drive away.

She couldn't believe she was even entertaining this possibility.

It was ridiculous.

Why she was catering to this madness, she had no idea.

She should have asked the others in the diner before leaving.

She probably could have proved he was lying right then.

After all, no one else had mentioned being able to shift into an animal.

Annie, Kate and Livi didn't mention it once, even though Maggie had spent an entire afternoon and evening hanging out with them. In fact, no one in the salon or the movie theater had mentioned it either. Mr. Wilson and his assistant didn't mention it when she was in his office signing papers.

Yet Jackson acted as if the entire town was made up of shifters.

If that was true and everyone in town believed they could change into animals, maybe they were having a mass hallucination.

She wasn't sure there was any scientific evidence that mass hallucinations were real, but that seemed a more viable possibility than believing shifters were.

She was pulling up the long driveway when she realized she'd invited someone whose sanity she now doubted back to her house.

What would happen if he couldn't shift and prove it to her, something she figured had a high likelihood of occurring?

Would he completely lose it?

Was she going to have to pretend that he'd shifted into a panther, just to keep him calm?

Maggie shook her head.

No way.

She'd spent her entire life telling the truth, even when it hurt. She wasn't about to start lying now.

When she got to the house, she scooped Genghis Khat into her arms and retreated to the porch.

She stood there, behind the railing and watched as Jackson approached. "That's far enough," she said when he was about ten feet from the front stairs. "Go ahead and shift now."

He cleared his throat. "I have to take my clothes off in order to shift."

Okay, that was unexpected.

Perhaps she should have realized clothes would get in the way of a shift, but since she didn't really believe he *could* shift, she hadn't thought that far ahead.

"Fine. Just hurry up."

She wanted to look away, but she also didn't want to turn her back on the potentially crazy man standing in her front yard, so she just watched as he stripped.

Good night, the man was hot.

He peeled his tee-shirt over his head, the muscles in his chest flexing as he revealed a thin trail of dark hair that disappeared into his jeans.

Maggie wasn't used to lusting after anyone. Mostly, she just ignored people, but there was no ignoring this man or the way he made her feel.

Dear heavens, it would be a sincere tragedy if he turned out to be insane.

She set Genghis Khat down on the porch.

It didn't seem right to be lusting after the man while holding the cat in her arms.

She slowly straightened back up, her eyes trained on Jackson's form the entire time.

He kicked off his boots, dropped his belt and unbuttoned his jeans.

The sound of his zipper sent a shiver of lust down her back and she couldn't have looked away if she tried.

He peeled his jeans away and she caught her breath at the first glimpse of his cock rising thick and long.

She could barely breathe, he was so boldly beautiful.

It was because she couldn't look away that she caught every second of the shift she'd completely forgotten was the reason he was stripping in the first place.

His whole body shuddered as he dropped to his hands and knees and *morphed* into a completely different being.

Maggie didn't even realize she was moving until she was in the yard, standing in front of him, one hand outstretched, stunned at the beauty of the wild animal in front of her.

Then, Genghis Khat attacked.

Eleven

G ENGHIS KHAT GROWLED as the wild scent of the sheriff intensified, filling the air.

Then the sheriff became something else.

Genghis Khat had one moment to realize Bygul hadn't been sniffing too much catnip after all, then he panicked.

Not because the sheriff became a giant, predator cat.

Not even because the giant cat was on Genghis Khat's territory.

No. The reason he panicked was because Maggie left the porch and got entirely too close to the predator.

Genghis Khat let out a yowl, hurtled around Maggie and dived onto the intruder's back, claws fully extended.

ONE MINUTE, JACKSON WAS MESMERIZED BY THE sight of his mate, reaching out a hand as if to pet him, her eyes bright with a kind of joy he never expected.

The next minute, a demon had landed on his back.

Jackson howled as ten claws sank deep.

He tried to shake the cat from his back, but that just made it sink its claws in deeper.

Jackson crouched low to the ground, turned his head and aimed his loudest, most threatening growl at the demon on his back.

"Don't you growl at my cat," Maggie shouted, startling Jackson.

Why was she angry with *him*? He was the one getting clawed to death over here.

"You scared him!"

Seriously? Who was she kidding? The demon cat was growling louder than Jackson, for heaven's sake!

"You should have shifted differently so he wasn't so intimidated by you!"

That was just ridiculous. It's not like he had a thousand different ways to shift. Or that one way was more intimidating than another. If anyone should be intimidated, it was him! He had the demon cat's claws in his back.

"Just hold still," Maggie snapped, "and I'll get him loose. Poor Genghis Khat. It's okay, baby. The big, bad panther isn't going to hurt you, I promise."

Poor Genghis Khat, his ass!

Jackson held as still as possible, trying to ignore the continuous growls from the demon cat while Maggie attempted to coax the cat's claws from Jackson's back.

Unfortunately, Genghis Khat didn't seem inclined to go anywhere and sank his claws in deeper.

Jackson let out another howl of pain and tried to shake the cat off again.

"Oh, stop being such a big baby!" Maggie smacked his shoulder, which seemed unjust in the extreme.

Jackson was the one with claws embedded in his back, and yet, he was the one getting smacked by his mate!

"It's okay, sweet pea," Maggie crooned to the damned cat. "I've got you. One minute and we'll get you away from the mean, old panther."

Jackson could feel her peeling the claws of one paw out of his back and it didn't exactly feel awesome. He growled low in his throat and tried not to move.

He let out a huff of relief when the claws of that first paw were completely extracted.

On to the second.

He held his body tense as Maggie slowly extracted the claws from a second paw, then began working on the cat's hind claws.

Jackson was just starting to think freedom was imminent when Jefferson arrived.

"Yo, brother—" Jefferson broke off, let out a bark of laughter and that was all it took.

The demon cat yowled, scrabbled at Jackson's back with his hind legs, causing *Jackson* to yowl, launched forward and landed on Jackson's neck and upper back this time, claws sinking deep once more.

The real issue, though, was when the demon cat leaned forward and chomped Jackson's ear.

Hard.

MAGGIE WASN'T EVEN SURE WHAT HAPPENED.

One minute she had Genghis Khat in her arms and was coaxing him to unclench his hind claws from the panther's rump area and the next Genghis Khat was hissing and yowling.

One minute he was mostly in her arms, the next he was attached to Jackson's neck, teeth firmly clamped on his ear.

One minute, both of them were right beside her, the next Jackson let out a yowl to wake the dead and took off running.

"No, Jackson!" Maggie shouted. She stamped her foot. "Stop catnapping Genghis Khat!"

It was too late though. Jackson had disappeared around the corner of the house.

The sound of laughter penetrated Maggie's fury. She whirled around and glared at Jefferson, who was rolling on the ground, roaring with laughter. "Jefferson, do something!" She kicked the bottom of his foot.

Jefferson choked back his laughter and climbed to his feet. "Okay, okay, I'll do something." He pulled out his phone, tapped the screen a couple times, then held it up as Jackson came barreling around the house, Genghis Khat still attached to his neck and ear.

Jefferson turned his body so that he followed the two as they raced across the front lawn and back around the side of the house. He then turned the phone toward Maggie. "Maggie, sweet love, could you explain what's going on here?"

Maggie scowled. "Are you recording right now? Genghis Khat is traumatized and your brother's catnapped him. Again! Do something!" She waved an arm toward the side of the house where they had disappeared.

Jefferson obligingly swung the camera that way, then back to the other side of the house, just in time to capture Jackson barreling by a third time.

"Well, there you have it, residents of Greensboro. Our sheriff has been defeated by the Mighty Genghis Khat."

Maggie let out a growl of frustration.

"Aw, don't worry, sweet Maggie. Jackson'll get tired soon

enough and then he'll bring Genghis Khat home." As he was saying this, Jefferson was on his phone, undoubtedly doing something stupid like sharing the damn video with everyone in town.

"We might as well sit and relax." Jefferson gestured toward her front porch. "Trust me. When Jackson gets going, it can take a while before he gets worn out."

Maggie sighed. "I don't care about Jackson. He's a panther. I'm worried about Genghis Khat!" She stamped up the stairs onto the porch.

"Eh, he'll be fine. Watch when they come back around. You'll see."

So Maggie took a seat and this time, rather than panicking, tried to pay attention as they raced by.

It was hard to tell what with Jackson running so fast. "Was Genghis Khat still chewing on his ear?"

"Nope. Here." Jefferson held out his phone so she could watch their last circuit in slow motion. "See there?" He zoomed in so Maggie could see the look on Genghis Khat's face.

He *definitely* wasn't chewing Jackson's ear anymore.

In fact, it didn't look like his claws were embedded in the panther's skin either.

Instead, Genghis Khat was crouched low on Jackson's back, his front legs dangling down either side of the panther's neck. His fur was flying, ears flattened to his head, and if Maggie wasn't mistaken, he seemed to be *enjoying* himself.

She zoomed back out so she could Jackson's face.

He didn't look quite as happy as Genghis Khat.

Ha.

Served him right.

At that moment, cars started pulling up Maggie's drive.

"What in the—" She stood and stared as people started pouring from the cars.

Jackson raced by again, Genghis Khat clinging to his neck.

"Ten bucks on the cat," Bud shouted as he walked by carting a long, collapsible table.

"Which cat?" someone called back.

"The house cat, of course," Bud said to a round of laughter.

Maggie watched, flabbergasted as more and more people called out their bets, good-naturedly debating whether the cat or the panther would come out the winner.

Jackson and Genghis Khat flew around the corner again and the crowd shouted encouragement as they raced by.

"Get him, Genghis Khat!"

"Show him who's boss, Genghis Khat!"

"Aw, you can't let a house cat get the better of ya, sheriff!"

"Would someone please just stop them?" Maggie exclaimed.

"Stop them? Now would we want to do that, lass?" someone asked. "This is hilarious. Tell me someone's got pictures."

"Oh, I've gotten a video every time he runs by," Jefferson said, "and plenty of pictures to boot. Y'all missed what started it. The cat had hold of Jackson's ear something fierce!"

Everyone laughed.

Maggie wrung her hands. Why wasn't anyone listening to her? "I'm really worried about Genghis Khat. Someone needs to rescue him."

"Rescue the cat?" Bud asked with a roaring laugh. "Looks to me like Jackson's the one who needs rescuing."

Maggie scowled. "Jackson is ten times the size of Genghis Khat. He scared my baby and now he's refusing to shift back!"

"Aw, Maggie, don't worry," Jefferson said. "I told you. Jackson will get tired soon enough and he'll just stop running. Once he stops, the cat'll let go, you'll see."

At that moment, Jackson came around the corner again, only this time he was walking. He reached the base of the porch stairs and settled into a heap.

Maggie raced down them and fell to her knees beside Genghis Khat, who was still lying on Jackson's back, but seemed to be sound asleep. "Are you okay, baby? Genghis Khat?"

Genghis Khat opened his eyes and yawned.

Maggie scooped him into her arms. "Oh, I was so worried. Did the big, bad panther catnap you again?"

Genghis Khat nudged her on the chin.

She settled him against her chest and walked up the stairs and into the house.

GENGHIS KHAT WAS A LITTLE PUT OUT WHEN HE heard Maggie telling the sheriff *and* Handsome Hewitt that the sheriff had scared him.

He wasn't scared of that stupid sheriff.

He'd been trying to save Maggie from him.

Didn't she realize he was *brave*, not scared?

Of course, Maggie also called the sheriff a big baby, which Genghis Khat found to be both accurate *and* hilarious.

In fact, Genghis Khat's ride on the sheriff proved exactly who was the brave one and who was the baby. After all, Genghis Khat never fell off once, no matter how fast the sheriff ran, and now the sheriff was completely worn out, just like a baby in need of a nap.

Genghis Khat broke that panther in good.

Maggie must have recognized his bravery because when she carried Genghis Khat into the house after that exhilarating ride, she kept telling him that he was the bravest, strongest cat in the world.

Now *that* was more like it.

He had to be brave and strong if he was going to protect her from mutant human-panther sheriffs.

"Dude," Jefferson appeared at Jackson's side and stared down at him. "That was hilarious, but I'm not sure it helped your courtship of Maggie."

Jackson growled and climbed to his feet, slowly stretching upward into his human form. He stalked around Jefferson to his clothes that were still sitting in a pile in the middle of the front lawn and pulled them on, wincing as they settled against the multiple puncture marks along his back and shoulders.

What a nightmare that had been.

Stupid demon cat.

"I have no idea what I'm going to do now. Maggie's never going to forgive me for endangering her cat."

"Why *should* I forgive you?"

Jackson looked up.

Maggie stood on the porch, arms crossed. "You scared him and then you wouldn't shift back. If you'd just shifted back, he would have let you go."

Jackson sighed. "If I'd shifted back, I'm not sure what would have happened to his claws. They were buried in my panther form, Maggie. What if I shifted back and they got destroyed in the shift? He's not part of me, he doesn't shift with me. I couldn't take the chance."

"Oh." Maggie looked stunned. "I–I hadn't thought of that. I didn't know there was a risk like that. Thank you, I guess, but why run in the first place?"

"The first lap was just in response to the pain. It was instinct and that's all. The second lap was because I could sense the cat relaxing and thought if I kept running, he might be willing to jump down. The rest of the laps were because he was enjoying them."

Jefferson let out a hoot of laughter. "Told you! That cat is badass!" He whirled to face all the people in Maggie's lawn. "Let's get this party started!"

A bunch of cheers resounded in response.

"Wait. What's going on?" Maggie looked around, seeming to finally realize that her front and side yard was crowded with the entire town of Greensboro.

"The party's been moved to your place," Annie explained.

"What?" Maggie screeched.

"Oh, don't worry," Annie said. "We'll take care of everything for you. You don't have to do anything at all."

"But, but, I'm not a—I can't—parties aren't my thing," Maggie wailed.

Jackson chuckled and bounded up the porch steps to hug her. "Don't worry, babe." He wrapped his arms around her and swayed with her, back and forth. "The party will stay outside for the most part, so you can escape inside whenever you need to." He pulled away, settled his hands around the sides of her neck, and used his thumbs to tilt her chin up.

"Everything's going to be just fine." He leaned down and kissed her, then kissed her again, simply because he couldn't bear not to.

His mate was simply amazing, beautiful, everything he could possibly want in a mate and he had no words for how incredibly grateful he was for this unexpected gift in his life.

He was determined to earn that gift, to be deserving of it.

She may have calmed down and even forgiven him for the fiasco with the cat, but he knew he was on thin ice.

One misstep and he could lose it all.

With this in mind, he focused on wooing his mate, giving her everything he thought she needed as the hours of the party wore on. He took her inside when the socializing became too much, ran interference for her when it was obvious she was done with the talking, danced with her when he thought she needed to be held and fed her whenever she seemed hungry.

Unfortunately, the entire town seemed to be in a conspiracy to constantly interfere with his efforts though.

Jefferson kept stealing Maggie away whenever someone distracted Jackson.

Then Jackson would be informed by some other townsperson that he'd better step up his game or his brother would end up stealing his mate.

It was a constant cycle of Jackson reclaiming his mate, dancing with her, wooing her, kissing her, stoking their passion, only to have Maggie stolen away when someone distracted him again.

Then there was the constant teasing and the paying of bets as videos of his panther and Genghis Khat flickered on the white screen off and on all night.

At first, Jackson was annoyed.

The videos were just a reminder of how worried Maggie had been about Genghis Khat, but somewhere in the middle of the fourth cycle of those damn videos, she finally saw the humor in the entire experience and actually started to giggle at the ridiculous pictures of the demon cat clinging to his panther.

He wasn't exactly thrilled that his brother had recorded the entire situation for posterity's sake, but he did love hearing Maggie laugh.

They spent the final hours of the party, dancing in each other's arms on the driveway, waving goodbye as one after the other of their friends headed off into the night.

Twelve

GENGHIS KHAT AND Bygul were stretched out on the porch, watching the party wind down.

"Pretty good party, G.K."

Genghis Khat had to agree.

He'd especially loved the part where they played pictures and videos of him attacking Baby Sheriff.

He'd looked so fierce while locked onto the panther's ear!

Everyone had cheered and laughed and congratulated Genghis Khat.

He'd been the hero of the event.

"Good treats too," Bygul said.

Those were thanks to Annie.

"Hm. Maybe I'll have to find this Annie a cat companion too," Bygul said.

Genghis Khat let out a small growl at the idea.

Annie might decide to feed the companion cat instead of Genghis Khat and he wouldn't like that at all.

Bygul stood and stretched. "Well, I'll let you get back to your human and her mate. Looks like things are progressing quite well there. Overall, really nice job with the mate-matching, G.K."

Then Bygul was gone.

Genghis Khat hadn't exactly enjoyed the whole mate-matching gig.

And he definitely didn't like the mate in question, but he did love Maggie so he'd keep trying to help, even though he knew Baby Sheriff wasn't anywhere near good enough for her.

Though Maggie had always hated parties, to her surprise, she wasn't exactly hating this one. In fact, she found herself having fun as the night wore on.

Jackson was so attentive and sweet.

He always seemed to know when she needed a break and would sweep her into the house without ever seeming disappointed or annoyed. He was happy to just sit with her in whatever room she retreated to where she would listen to music and pet Genghis Khat, who *always* followed them inside.

Even if he'd been nowhere near them when they retreated, Genghis Khat always seemed to know when Maggie needed him and was always there within a few moments, nudging her hand and purring.

Those few moments when she retreated inside, cuddled Genghis Khat and just basked in the quiet seemed to rejuvenate her and gave her the energy to go back out and socialize a bit more.

Jackson followed her everywhere, catering to her every need.

Before she even realized she was thirsty, he was slipping a coke into her hand.

Hunger was just around the corner when he brought her a plate full of foods she loved.

When she was tired and needed to sit, he had a collapsible chair ready for her.

When she was feeling overwhelmed, he pulled her onto the driveway and into his arms and just swayed with her.

Those were her favorite moments.

Wrapped in Jackson's arms, feeling safe and cherished.

He took all the teasing good-naturedly, even when she stiffened at the memory of her worry when he'd first bolted with Genghis Khat clinging to his shoulders.

He even refrained from punching his brother, something he clearly wanted to do, given his glares every time Jefferson absconded with her.

She was fairly certain Jefferson was just messing with him, which was why she'd asked him, "Why are you torturing your brother?"

Jefferson had just laughed. "He's just too easy and it's fun. Besides, believe me, your ma—uh—your man will get his revenge. He always does." He'd then spun her out on the driveway and danced with her a couple minutes before Jackson managed to get away and steal her back.

They made her laugh and she didn't think she'd ever really laughed before she met the two of them.

In the end, the party was magical and Jackson utterly charming.

When the evening finally ended, she was in Jackson's arms, swaying and kissing him.

The last of the shifters had left—she *still* had to process the fact that shifters were real and her mother had been one of them—and now Maggie was alone with the one she cared about the most.

He helped her with the last bit of clean-up—as Annie had promised, there really wasn't much left to do—then he kissed her good night (multiples times), before leaving her at the door with a promise to see her in the morning.

He was supposed to pick her up at eleven for a surprise.

He ended up seeing her much earlier than expected, however, when he woke to discover Genghis Khat hanging out in his bedroom.

He returned the cat to Maggie and they got an earlier start to the day than expected.

He took her on a picnic breakfast to one of the lakes in the area and they spent the entire day getting to know each other better.

He told her about growing up as a panther among a family of wolves and about the mischief he and Jefferson got into around town. He told her about the tricks they used to play on their family, friends and neighbors and about one memorable double date when the twins switched places mid-way through.

"We thought we were so clever." Jackson laughed.

"Your dates didn't notice?" Maggie exclaimed incredulously.

Jackson shrugged. "Most people can't tell us apart, Maggie."

She rolled her eyes, then told him about growing up with parents who didn't understand their only child, about dropping out of school and getting her GED because school was a torture chamber from the first day in kindergarten and about the spiral notebook where she'd kept a list of all the jobs she'd worked through the years, sorting them into various categories like factory jobs, office jobs, service industry jobs and retail jobs.

Jackson scowled at the story of the employer who harassed

her, cheered when she related how she'd knocked him out with one punch and laughed uproariously when she described her fear of the dead rising as zombies and devouring her at the morgue.

It was probably the most talking Maggie had ever done in her lifetime in one day. The most amazing part, though, was that Jackson didn't seem to mind when the conversation lapsed into silence. He seemed perfectly content to wait for Maggie to start up the conversation again.

It was crazy.

She'd only known him a couple days and she was already falling deep under his spell.

The following week passed in a blur of moments all strung together like precious diamonds—the picnic by the lake, cuddling and kissing on her couch while a movie played in the background, hiking in the woods, going for a hayride, endless meals at the diner—and every day with Jackson began, inevitably, with the catnapping of Genghis Khat.

Jackson swore up and down that he was not the one letting Genghis Khat out or transporting him to a new location every day, even though that new location was *always* where Jackson happened to be in that moment.

More and more, it seemed like Jackson's illogical theory of god magic was the only one that made sense.

It was a full week after the party that Jackson said to Maggie words he'd said once before, words that had changed her entire world view.

"Maggie, I have something to tell you."

Not again.

"What is it this time? Vampires are real?"

He chuckled. "That I don't know. I'd say no, but we exist, so maybe?"

She could totally deal with that answer because as far as she was concerned, there was *zero* scientific proof that vampires existed, and therefore, she considered that answer to be a no. "So what then?"

"It's about shifters. And us."

"What about us?"

Jackson led her to the sofa, where he sat down beside her, turned and faced her and with her hands in his, said, "Maggie, I think you're my mate." He shook his head. "No, that's not right. I *know* you're my mate."

"What does that mean? Your mate?" She was afraid to hope. Afraid to believe.

"Shifters only mate once and they do it for life. They usually know their mate from the minute they meet, though there have been times when mates knew each other from childhood and didn't realize it until well into adulthood. In our case, though, I knew the moment we met. You're my mate, Maggie."

"But what does that *mean*?"

"It means you're mine and I'm yours and I'm falling in love with you."

Maggie shook her head. "That's not even possible. You don't even know me. We've only known each other a week."

"Eleven days, to be exact."

"You can't count those first two days. We only talked on the phone for a couple minutes at most. And you were annoying."

Jackson chuckled. "Say what you will, I'm still counting them. Besides, we shifters don't need that much time. I've learned everything I need to know about you."

Maggie shook her head. "You're insane if you believe that's true. And even if it is, I'm not a good bet, Jackson."

"Of course, you are, Maggie. You're the best bet in the world, at least for me."

"You don't understand. I'm too weird. You'll get tired of me and then you'll leave me, so it's best we don't get our hopes up. So far, everything's great, but it won't last."

"You're not weird. You're perfect."

"I'm not polite. I'm too honest. I say things without really thinking about them and people's feelings get hurt or they get mad and they don't like me anymore. It'll happen eventually, even with you, Jackson."

"I love that about you."

"No—"

"Yes. Listen. I *love* that about you. I love that I know exactly where I stand with you, that you'll never pretend to be happy when you're not, that you'll never say you're fine when you're really hurting, that you'll never say something you think I want to hear rather than what you're really thinking. I *love* that about you."

"I'll ignore people when they want to talk to me, they'll complain to you and you'll find that annoying."

"I absolutely won't. I'll always be happy to run interference if you need me to, to get you away from any situation if that's what you need, whatever is necessary for your happiness, Maggie."

"You won't feel that way when *you're* the one I'm ignoring."

Jackson chuckled. "Part of being mates is understanding each other and giving each other what we need. If you're ignoring me, I'll know it's because you've hit the wall and it's *not* a good time. I will always take care of you, Maggie, even if that means waiting until you're ready to talk. *This* is what being mates means. I'm here for *you. You're* my number one priority, no one else, not even me."

She stared at him, trying to decide if she could trust that he would stay the course, that he wouldn't one day decide she was just too much work.

"Maggie. I'm falling in love with *you.* Not the idea of you, but *you.* Crazy, wonderful, you. Maggie who talks to her cat like he's a person who might respond at any minute. Maggie who shouts at me when she's angry, who doesn't hesitate to smack me, even when I'm in my panther form when she needs me to pay attention. Maggie who always says what she means and does exactly what she says she will. You're the one for me, Maggie. Not anyone else. *You.*"

Maggie flung her arms around his neck and hugged him tight.

He pulled back, then kissed her.

She clutched his shirt and kissed him back.

Shivers raced up and down her spine as his tongue tangled with hers and a growl rumbled deep in his throat.

"Jackson," she whispered.

His hands clenched on her hips and he dragged her into his lap so she straddled him and held on.

They kissed and fumbled in the dark and kissed some more.

He put her from him when they were so breathless, she was gasping, and her whole body felt like it was going up in flames.

"You're mine, Maggie," he growled, "but we'll wait until you're feeling completely secure in this mating." He pulled her back into his arms for one last devastating kiss, then in a display of strength she found astonishing, surged to his feet and carried her to the door, kissing her the entire way there.

When he reached the door, he set her on her feet, kissed her one last time and murmured, "Lock the door behind me. I'll see you tomorrow, my love."

"Tomorrow," she whispered back, then watched as he stepped out onto the porch.

She closed and locked the door, then darted to the picture window in a ritual she'd been following since the first night he'd kissed her. She watched, as she had that night and every night since, as he sauntered down the walk, climbed into his car and drove away.

This time, when she picked up Genghis Khat, she wasn't shaking and she had no questions. Instead, she whispered in his ear a secret she'd been holding close to her heart. "Genghis Khat, you won't believe it, but I think I'm falling in love with that man."

Thirteen

GENGHIS KHAT DIDN'T exactly approve of Maggie falling in love with Baby Sheriff.

Nor did he approve of the romance that followed.

However, he did have to admit that Baby Sheriff was doing everything in his power to prove how important Maggie was to him.

He courted her and made it clear that she was the center of his world.

Genghis Khat still liked Handsome Hewitt more, especially since the man always brought him treats whenever he visited.

As a bonus, it made Baby Sheriff annoyed whenever he saw Genghis Khat scent-marking Handsome Hewitt.

Unfortunately, Bygul had insisted Handsome Hewitt wasn't in the running for Maggie's mate, so Maggie and Genghis Khat were stuck with the sheriff instead, leaving poor Handsome Hewitt all alone.

In Genghis Khat's opinion, it wasn't exactly fair that the more deserving of the twins had no mate of his own.

Therefore, even though Genghis Khat had been looking forward to retiring his mate-matching skills, he decided to make one more match.

He'd need to recruit Bygul's help, of course.

After all, Bygul was the reason Genghis Khat was stuck with Baby Sheriff, so as far as he was concerned, Bygul owed him big.

Unfortunately, Bygul refused to even consider it without bringing in another cat, so Genghis Khat grudgingly agreed Bygul could recruit a companion cat for Handsome Hewitt as well.

As long as the new companion understood, of course, that Genghis Khat was in charge.

THE FOLLOWING MONTH WAS THE MOST WONDROUS of Maggie's life.

She'd found a home that was populated with people who didn't mind her strange habits or her unwillingness to talk at times.

They didn't mind when she was silent or when she was what other people had called "rude and unfriendly." They just accepted her and were kind to her.

Then there was Jackson.

Her mate.

He wooed her with kisses and sweet words and made her realize how incredibly lucky she was to have such a wonderful mate.

And somewhere, in the process of gaining friends, a town, a home and a mate, she also gained a big brother.

She'd never had any siblings before and found Jefferson to be everything she could have ever wanted. Protective and funny, sweet and charming, and as a bonus, he *never* said what he didn't mean.

Neither did Jackson or any of her friends in Greensboro, for that matter.

She'd eventually come to realize it was because shifters could somehow scent deception.

Even a well-intentioned lie had no chance of success among the shifters.

As far as Maggie was concerned, this was a dream come true. She'd finally found the perfect place for her.

The only annoyance was the continued catnappings that Jackson *still* insisted he was not responsible for.

Maggie wasn't sure she believed him since Genghis Khat kept disappearing from her house and reappearing wherever Jackson was.

Every day, at some point during the day, Jackson would text Maggie to let her know where Genghis Khat had shown up that day.

The sheriff's office.

The diner.

The library.

The bookstore.

The courthouse.

The mayor's office.

The town square.

By the time a month had passed, Maggie had been inside every public building in Greensboro and some private ones as well.

It was rather awkward when she had to pick up Genghis Khat from Jefferson's house.

Awkward because Jackson had gotten a call out and forgot

to let Maggie know, so when she arrived to pick up Genghis Khat and found him in Jefferson's lap in the backyard, she'd come up behind Jefferson and had kissed him on the cheek before realizing he was the wrong twin.

She'd leapt away in horror while Jefferson had roared in laughter.

He'd then asked how she'd figured it out since most people couldn't tell the twins apart.

Maggie had just shrugged and said, "I don't know why people can't tell the difference. To me, it's obvious."

In truth, they were pretty damn identical. They even had the same haircuts, but somehow Maggie could always tell them apart.

She'd known the second her lips had brushed Jefferson's cheek.

There was just no spark.

She should have realized it sooner, but she'd been too focused on sneaking up on him.

Cat hearing made that almost impossible, but she kept trying.

At some point, weeks into her relationship with Jackson, she realized she no longer worried that he would change his mind or that he would find her annoying.

In a month of spending almost every free minute together, he'd been treated to *all* of Maggie's idiosyncrasies and not once had he seemed impatient or angry.

He accepted when she needed quiet time.

He was fine when she didn't want to go outside or socialize.

He didn't even get upset when she ignored him for almost forty-eight hours that one time. She'd just retreated into her head for a while. She wasn't sure why. It just happened sometimes.

When she'd finally surfaced, she'd asked why he hadn't gotten upset with her and he'd told her that he could sense she was okay and nothing was wrong, so that was enough for him.

He'd still spent time with her each evening, not pushing for anything from her, and when he'd left, he'd brushed a kiss on her cheek and had admonished her to lock the door as usual, but that had been it.

That was when Maggie finally began to trust that Jackson would never let her down, that this mating was truly solid and would last a lifetime.

She waited another week, just to be sure.

Then, one Friday night, when they were making out on the sofa, as they did every night, Maggie whispered in Jackson's ear, "I want our mating to be real. I'm ready."

He pulled away and stared into her eyes. His were lit with joy, but still he asked, "Are you sure, Maggie?"

She nodded. "I'm positive."

He swept her back into his arms and kissed her.

Maggie thought she knew everything about Jackson's kisses by then.

How incredibly tender and sweet they could be and how devastatingly hot and passionate.

In that moment, though, she realized how much he'd been holding back.

He devoured her mouth, tongue tangling with hers, as he lifted her in his arms and carried her to her bedroom.

He laid her on the bed and followed her down, still kissing her, still driving her mad with passion.

"Jackson," she whimpered, clutching at his shoulders,

trying to get closer, trying to find some relief from the unrelenting heat.

"Maggie," he murmured. He sat up, pulling her with him. He peeled his shirt off, then hers, then unhooked her bra and flung it away. He caught her breasts in his hands, tweaking both nipples and making her gasp.

She collapsed back onto the bed and he followed her down, capturing one nipple in his mouth while tweaking the other with his hand.

She writhed on the bed and gasped out his name. "Jackson, please." She grabbed the back of his head, clutching the hair there, holding him to her, but wanting, needing more. "Please, I need you."

He groaned, then jackknifed up and off the bed. "Should have stripped first," he muttered, struggling out of his jeans and boxers, only to get hung up at the boots.

He stumbled around the room, trying to kick them off, almost losing his balance in the process.

Maggie would have laughed, but she was frantically trying to get out of her own jeans without leaving the bed.

It didn't help that she couldn't pull her eyes away from Jackson.

Even hopping around the room with his jeans half-on and half-off, one boot on and one boot off, he was the sexiest man she'd ever seen.

She was so busy watching him that she forgot her own mission, so when he finally got free of his boots and jeans, he had zero patience for her own. He stripped them off her so fast she was once more in awe of his strength as he lifted her entire body with one hand while the other made short work of her jeans and panties.

He dropped her to the bed, settled his shoulders between

her legs, leaned forward and swiped his tongue through her folds.

Maggie gasped and fisted the sheets beneath her hands.

Jackson settled one arm across her belly, pinning her to the bed and with his other hand, opened her wide for another swipe of his tongue.

"Jackson!" she wailed. She couldn't escape his questing tongue, could only lie there and *feel*.

White sheeted across her vision as he caught her clit in his teeth and tugged gently.

For one long moment, she was frozen on a precipice and then she broke.

Everything clenched hard, then shattered.

The first sense that came back was her hearing.

The room still echoed with the sounds of her cries of ecstasy. Beneath that was her ragged breathing and a soft growling from Jackson.

She lifted her head and looked down her body to see that he was still between her legs, nuzzling her pussy, growling softly as he slowly licked it clean.

She whimpered at the sight. "Jackson."

He raised her head and looked at her. His eyes were wild, almost as feral as the panther's.

Her heart skipped a beat, then began pounding an impossible rhythm. "Jackson. I need you."

He let out another soft growl, then slowly prowled up her body until he reached her face. He settled one hand against her cheek and kissed her.

Slow. Gentle. Tender.

He settled over her, lodging his cock right at the entrance to her pussy, then waited.

She arched up slowly and begged, "Please, Jackson. Now. Please."

He reached down, grabbed one leg and pulled it up, then slowly began to penetrate.

Maggie's eyes fell shut at the sensation.

Jackson growled and her eyes flew open again, catching his.

Staring into his eyes, she could barely breathe as he slowly, so slowly, plowed forward, stretching her, claiming her, welding them together as one.

"Maggie," he growled. In that one word, she heard a wealth of passion and affection.

Finally, he was fully seated inside her. She could feel him everywhere, in every part of her being. He was hers and she was his.

"Jackson," she whispered.

He leaned down and growled, "Are you ready?"

"Yes. Yes, Jackson."

He pulled back and powered forward, the sensation so intense, Maggie whimpered and clutched at him tighter. "Please, Jackson. More."

As if that was all he needed to lose control, Jackson braced his arms on either side of her and let loose.

The friction, the incredible sensation of being filled with him, then empty, then filled again had Maggie crying out and begging for more.

She lost track of time and space. All she felt, all she knew was Jackson.

He was her everything.

When she broke this time, she didn't even know it was coming. It just came in a wave so powerful, it swept her under and it kept going and going and going.

"Jackson!" she shrieked.

He let out a growling roar and plunged deep.

Warmth bathed her pussy and another orgasm wrenched through her, causing everything inside to quake.

Jackson collapsed on top of her, then carefully rolled them both so that they were still connected, but she was on top.

For several long moments, they lay in each other's arms, gasping for breath and shuddering through the aftershocks of pleasure.

Into the silence, Jackson said, "God. *Damn.*"

Maggie giggled. "Is it always so…"

"Intense?"

"Yeah."

"Not in my experience, but I have a feeling you and I have just hit the tip of the iceberg when it comes to the intensity of our mating."

"We may not survive."

"Eh, maybe not, but what a way to go."

Maggie laughed, then lifted up to see his face. "Jackson?"

"Yeah, babe."

"I love you."

He rolled them so that she was on her back again and he was crouched over her. He settled his hands to either side of her neck, sliding his fingers into her hair so they cradled her head. "I love you too, my Maggie, my mate, my everything."

They got very little sleep that night as they spent it solidifying their mating, catching tiny catnaps between bouts of loving, only to rouse and love some more.

At some point in the wee hours of the morning, Maggie felt Genghis Khat jump onto the bed and smiled.

Her world was now complete.

Genghis Khat walked across Baby Sheriff's stomach, flexing his claws and making the panther hiss, then curled up on Maggie's pillow.

Even though the sheriff had intruded on their space, Maggie didn't hesitate to cuddle Genghis Khat close and to whisper to him, as she did every evening, that he was the sweetest, best cat ever.

Baby Sheriff made a scoffing sound in the background, but Maggie slapped her hand over his mouth and snapped, "Knock it off, Jackson."

She then turned back to Genghis Khat and finished their ritual with a kiss on his nose and a whispered, "I love you so much, Genghis Khat."

Best. Human. Ever.

The Real McCat

<h1 style="text-align:center">Description</h1>

A matchmaking cat may be Jefferson's only hope for a happily ever after.

Jefferson wasn't thrilled when his sister-in-law hired a new receptionist for his auto repair shop without first consulting him. He was even more annoyed when he realized the new hire was a bear, and not just any bear. She was Kate Worcester of the Worcester bears and even worse, the only sister of Mason Worcester, the scariest grizzly of them all. And to top it all off, Jefferson was pretty sure Kate Worcester was his mate.

Kate Worcester was sick of her brother's interference in her life. His latest antics included tossing a client out a window simply because he was standing too close to his baby sister. If the only way she could end this ridiculousness was to quit her job and go to work for a panther mechanic, then that's what she'd do. Even better if that mechanic turned out to be her mate.

Cleocatra has a mission: keep Jefferson to herself. He's her human companion and no one else's. That bear needs to go find herself someone else to snuggle up to because Jefferson belongs to this kitten and no one else!

One

BYGUL WAS THE top matchmaker at Pawsitively Purrfect Matches. Of all the matchmaking cats in the place, *he* was legendary.

Until recently, however, this hadn't been a good thing. In fact, the other cats had looked down on him for meddling in human affairs, which as far as he was concerned, made no sense at all.

After all, their entire mission at PPM was to match homeless cats to their purrfect human companions. If this wasn't already meddling in human affairs, he didn't know what was.

Meddling or not, though, Bygul took great pride in bringing his matches to the next level. Not satisfied to simply match his cats with a human companion, he also insisted on mate-matching those humans as well. After all, PPM *was* in the business of happily furever afters.

Besides, being the cat companion of a goddess gave Bygul insight and skills the other matchmaking cats lacked. Skills that honestly made him a matchmaking genius, one who brought endless joy to the world.

So Bygul did what he did best.

He matched cats to their human companions and he matched their companions to their true mates. It was the whole true love thing that most of the other cats (and to be entirely honest, the goddesses as well) objected to.

Bygul had his suspicions as to why the goddesses objected the way they did. He had no doubt it had something to do with power and control. True love, after all, should be the purview of the gods and goddesses (and the occasional demons and demonesses), but as Bygul continually pointed out, he was the cat companion of a goddess, and therefore, he acted on her behalf whenever he mate-matched a human.

He wasn't sure Freyja completely agreed with his logic, but she didn't try to stop him either, so as far as he was concerned, that was as good as giving him permission.

Then, he made the match of the ages.

A human, so completely withdrawn from the world, that matching her to a cat was a true challenge. Yet, Bygul managed to match her in such a way that she forged bonds, not just with the cat, though she did, and not just with her true mate, though she did that as well, but also with an entire community of shifters.

Suddenly, everyone at PPM was realizing what Bygul had always known: he truly was a matchmaking genius.

Now everyone wanted his advice and half the cats at PPM had it in their heads that they too could bring true love to the masses.

And that's when Bygul's genius backfired.

Ceridwen, that interfering goddess from hell, came up with the brilliant idea that Bygul should offer mate-matching classes for the cats interested in expanding their services.

Ridiculous.

Bygul had tried to protest, explaining that it was an innate ability, not something one might learn, but Bastet had smirked and agreed with Ceridwen that this was a fabulous idea.

Freyja, outnumbered by the other two, had sighed and agreed.

So now, five times a week, Bygul was responsible for teaching an hour-long class on mate-matching humans.

He blamed the human, Maggie.

If she hadn't been so stubborn and difficult to match, no one would have recognized his genius and he could have continued to mate-match under the radar and been perfectly content. Instead, he was standing in a giant classroom at the center of Pawsitively Purrfect Matches, trying to wrangle fifty matchmaking cats into a semblance of order.

"For goddess' sake, Tivali, would you settle down?" Bygul bellowed as Cleopatra's idiotic cat companion barreled around the room, chasing some unknown demon only she could see.

This was going to be a nightmare.

"For goodness sake, Maggie!" Jefferson bellowed. "Stop being so rude to the customers. You'll drive all my business away!"

Maggie glared at her brother-in-law. He had a lot of nerve, complaining about her customer service skills. "You do realize I'm only doing this as a favor because you're my mate's brother and he begged me to help you out. So really, I'm doing this as a favor to him, so he doesn't have to listen to you whine anymore."

"Yes, well, I had no idea this favor would involve you hanging up on my customers—"

"He was rude!"

"—insulting their vehicles—"

"It's ugly as sin!"

"—and refusing to answer the phone more than once an hour!"

"It rings entirely too often!"

"How is this any better than me not having a receptionist at all?"

"I don't recall promising it would be any better. In fact, I'm pretty sure I said I couldn't promise to be personable or friendly or even to do a good job."

"I thought you were joking!"

"Well, I wasn't. And frankly, if you don't want me to be rude to your customers, then you should recruit a better set of them. I have no idea why you can't just stick to customers from our own town."

Jefferson let out a furious growl, then spun around and stormed out of the office, probably back to the bay where he was working on some useless sports car. At the last moment, he yelled over his shoulder, "And stop painting your nails in my office. It reeks!"

Maggie grinned down at her nails. They were now a beautiful shade called Lucky Lavender and they were a perfect match to the flowers on her skirt. Who cared about scents when the result was this awesome?

She supposed she should feel bad about driving Jefferson crazy and about being rude to his customers and possibly losing him some money along the way, but really, she just didn't.

Because as far as she was concerned, none of this was her fault. In fact, she'd told both Jackson and Jefferson that they wouldn't like the results of her doing this favor for them, and they just hadn't listened.

Okay, so Jackson *had* warned her that Jefferson's shop was a ways out of town, at a crossroads between three different towns, and that one of those towns was full of humans, but that didn't mean Maggie had to like it.

She thought she'd left the whole customer service, dealing with strangers, human existence behind! Yet here she was, helping out her brother-in-law doing a job she didn't need and that she absolutely hated, just because her mate had asked.

This was what getting mated got you.

Fabulous sex, incredible friendships, romantic picnics, a big brother and *favors*.

A nudge on her arm ended Maggie's stewing. "Oh, Genghis Khat, you're so sweet." She leaned over and kissed the gray forehead of the best cat in the entire world. "Sorry for all the yelling, sweetie pie. And sorry we're stuck here in this ugly monstrosity of a building, instead of back at home in our awesome garden. Give it a few more days though. I may be his sister-in-law, but I guarantee Jefferson won't last much longer. He'll fire me before you know it."

"Um, excuse me?"

A woman stood in Maggie's office door, looking uncertain. She had short, black hair that kind of spiked outward in a really sassy way and was dressed in jeans and a tee-shirt.

"I saw the help wanted sign and—"

Maggie leapt to her feet. "Come in, come in. What's your name?"

"Kate Worcester."

"Nice to meet you, Kate. I'm Maggie. So, tell me what your qualifications are."

"Oh, well. I don't really have any. I mean, not as a mechanic anyway."

"Good because what we need is a receptionist."

"Oh, well, I don't exactly have receptionist experience either, but—"

"No problem." As far as Maggie was concerned, experience didn't really count for anything. After all, *she'd* worked as a receptionist plenty of times, but was absolutely *not* qualified for the job.

In fact, despite all her work experience, Maggie had *negative* qualifications, which meant that Kate, who probably had social skills, was higher than her on the qualifications ladder. "You're hired."

Kate's eyes widened. "Oh. Wow. Well, great. I mean—are you sure?"

"Absolutely! Okay, here's the deal. The phone rings and you answer it. Make appointments if they need one. Answer questions. If you don't know the answer, make something up."

Kate raised an eyebrow.

"Okay, no, probably don't do that. Just ask Jefferson. He's the boss."

"Um. Okay."

"I think that's it. Have a great rest of the day. The hours are eight to six, six days a week. You get Sundays off. If you need anything, well—just ask Jefferson." Maggie grabbed her bag, scooped Genghis Khat into her arms and headed for the door.

Kate swung around and followed her. "So what do I say when I answer the phones?"

"I usually just say whatever comes to mind. Usually hello. Sometimes car central or mechanics-r-us or whatever." Maggie wrestled the office door open and stepped through.

"Wait. Is that the name of the shop?"

Maggie threw a grin over her shoulder at Kate. "Nope. Never bothered to learn what it is. You could ask Jefferson that as well. He probably knows. Good luck!" With that, she let the office door swing shut behind her and bounced down the two steps leading into the garage.

Dropping a kiss onto Genghis Khat's head, Maggie giggled and whispered, "Let's go tell Jefferson the good news."

JEFFERSON FELT LIKE HE WAS LOSING HIS MIND AND might come unhinged at any moment. This was all Jackson's fault. He should have known not to trust his idiotic brother.

What a terrible idea, hiring Maggie as his temporary receptionist. What had he been thinking? He'd been desperate, true, but surely not *that* desperate? And now what was he going to do? Fire her?

Jackson would never forgive him.

Then again, if Jefferson was stuck with Maggie for the rest of his life, *he'd* never forgive Jackson.

"Jefferson, you're all set," Maggie called as she swept through the shop, Genghis Khat hanging over her shoulder.

Jefferson swung away from the car he was working on to glare at Maggie. "What's that supposed to mean? I'm all set for what?"

Was she leaving in the middle of the day? He didn't know whether to celebrate or mourn if that was the case. He had no one to cover the phones, but then Maggie barely covered them anyway, so it wouldn't be much of a loss.

"Your new hire's in your office, all ready to go."

"New hire? What new hire?"

"The receptionist I just hired for you." Maggie grinned at

him as she walked out the bay doors and headed for her car, calling back over her shoulder, "You're welcome!"

Jefferson shuddered. What now?

Who could she possibly have hired in the fifteen minutes since he'd last spoken with her?

He stormed across the garage and bounded up the two stairs leading into the office, muttering, "I bet she hired some bum off the streets," as he slammed through the door.

Just inside the office, he stumbled to a halt, stunned at the sight of the woman sitting at his receptionist's desk.

"I assure you I am not a bum," the woman informed him.

Speechless, Jefferson just nodded, then turned and stormed back out of the office into the shop.

She'd hired a bear! And not just any bear, a freaking grizzly! And not just any grizzly, but Kate Worcester, of the ritzy, real estate Worcester grizzlies.

High maintenance, snooty as hell, full of themselves Worcesters.

Jefferson had never actually met Kate Worcester before, or really any of the Worcesters, but that didn't mean he didn't know about them.

Rich. Spoiled. Completely detached from their own roots. He doubted a single Worcester had ever run through the woods in grizzly form, let alone shit in them.

And Kate Worcester was supposed to answer his phones?

What the freaking hell?

Well, that went well. Kate rolled her eyes.

If that was Jefferson, she was probably in trouble.

A search through the paperwork on the desk had turned up

a number of invoices with JH Automotive at the top, so she had at least one question answered.

There were so many others, though.

Like why she was working there in the first place.

Sure she'd walked in and asked for the job, but that was beside the point. She'd just been so angry and then she'd seen the sign. It had seemed like a message from the gods.

But now that she had a minute to think about it, she was realizing there was no way she could do this job *and* everything else. On the other hand—

At that moment, her cell phone began to ring.

Great.

She considered ignoring it, but no. He'd just do something really obnoxious, like invade her privacy and track her down.

With a sigh, she dragged out her phone and connected it, but didn't say anything.

"Well?" Mason bellowed after a few seconds.

Kate swallowed a giggle. "What? You called me."

"So you don't even bother saying hello anymore?"

"It seemed unnecessary."

"Unne—whatever. Where are you?"

"Oh, didn't you get my note?"

"You couldn't possibly be referring to this ridiculous post-it note that says 'I quit,' now could you? I know that can't be right because my sister would never walk out on the family business that way." Mason's voice rose as he spoke until he finished with a very bear-like roar.

Kate raised an eyebrow. "I don't see why not. I made it very clear, Mason, that one of these days you would go too far. Well, that day is today!"

"Oh, come on, Kate, it wasn't that bad."

"You threw the alpha of the McDonald clan out the window! Of a two-story building!"

"Eh, I'm sure he landed on his feet."

"That's not the point. And they're wolves not cats!"

"He was flirting with you."

"He was negotiating to buy the Wheeler property!"

"Oh."

"I was this close to offloading those acres, then you came along and ruined everything."

"Well, that'll teach him to keep his distance when negotiating."

"Oh, please."

"So when are you coming back?"

"What do you not understand about the words, 'I quit'?"

"You can't quit, Kate. You're not a quitter. Besides, we need you."

"Well, I'm sorry, but I've already got another job."

"You what?"

"I've given my word and have already started, and you're right. I'm not a quitter. There's no way I could leave them in the lurch, now is there? Not after they've gone to all the trouble of hiring and training me." Kate hit the mute button so he wouldn't hear her snickering.

"Training—you only left the building an hour ago!"

Kate cleared her throat to get rid of any telltale amusement and hit the mute button again. "Who said anything about the training happening today?"

Mason let out a growl. "You're making this up, aren't you? You couldn't possibly have found a job and been trained in the hour since I last saw you."

"I certainly am not making this up. I'm the new receptionist at JH Automotive."

"Receptionist? Now I know you're joking! There's no way you'd take a measly—hold on a minute. JH—are you talking about Jefferson Hewitt?"

"I believe that's my new boss's name, yes."

Dead silence, then, "You went to work for the panthers?" Mason roared.

Two

THERE WAS A reason Bygul had never been chosen to teach any of the matchmaking classes at Pawsitively Purrfect Matches. He wasn't exactly blessed with patience, nor did he have a single teaching bone in his body.

His idea of teaching was to throw the cats into the middle of a situation and see if they could manage to make a match. If they did, they passed and became matchmakers. If they didn't, they failed and went off to do something else with their tenth life.

Apparently, though, this was not considered to be good teaching.

Bygul didn't care though. After all, he'd never claimed to be a teacher and yet, he'd been roped into this nonsense anyway.

He was especially annoyed because he'd been unable to continue his matchmaking endeavors while arguing his case with the goddesses. Then, when he'd lost, he'd spent an entire day prepping for a class that ended up involving more cat-wrangling than teaching.

He had cats to match with their human companions and humans to match with their mates, and yet, instead, he was teaching witless cats nothing at all. Not because he had nothing to teach, but because they had no discipline whatsoever and apparently lacked the ability to sit still and to learn.

The only good news was that the torture only lasted sixty minutes, and was then followed by an entire twenty-four hours of freedom.

The minute the bell sounded, Bygul exclaimed, "That's it for today, class."

"That can't be right," Muezza exclaimed from the corner where he'd been giving himself a very thorough bath. "We haven't learned anything yet!"

Bygul didn't bother to answer. He simply transported himself to his rooms, where he'd stowed his purrfect match on the way to class. "Well, little one," he said to the tiny, black kitten, curled up in the middle of his bed. "Are you ready to meet your human?"

The kitten leapt to her feet and bounced a couple times there, clearly overwhelmed with joy at the prospect.

"That's what I thought. Well, come along now. Your human's name is Jefferson and I'm sure he's going to adore you."

Jefferson stormed back into the bays and paced back and forth furiously.

It wasn't that she was a grizzly. After all, he lived in a shifter town full of bears and wolves and all sorts of different shifters. It wasn't even that she was rich.

It was that she was beautiful.

Beautiful *and* rich. Beautiful and rich and impossible to ignore.

How in the hell was he going to get any kind of work done with Bombshell Grizzly in his office?

Beautiful and rich and entirely too—

"Mew."

Jefferson froze and looked down.

A tiny black kitten stood in front of him, staring up at him.

He glanced around the shop.

"Yo, Ryan, this your kitten?"

Ryan peered around the hood he was under to stare at Jefferson. "You kidding me, boss?"

Jefferson let out a snort of laughter. "Okay. Sorry. What about you two?"

Lyle rolled out from under the car he was working on, took one look at the kitten, who was now standing on its hind legs, front paws rubbing against Jefferson's jumpsuit, and let out a snort of derision before rolling back under the car.

Pete didn't even bother to respond, just shook his head and kept working on the motorcycle chain he was repairing.

Clearly, none of them would be claiming the kitten anytime soon.

With a grunt of exasperation, Jefferson leaned over and picked it up. "What are you doing in here with all these wolves, huh?"

The kitten started to purr and rubbed its head against his jaw.

"Well, aren't you a sweetheart?" Jefferson stared speculatively at the office door. It seemed unlikely and yet, the timing—

Jefferson strode back across the service bays, leapt up the two steps, swung open the office door and demanded, "Did you bring a kitten into the shop?"

The grizzly was still sitting at the desk, staring at the cell phone in her hand. She slowly raised her head and stared at him.

The look on her face was so incredulous, Jefferson let out a huff of exasperation, swung on his heel and stormed out again. He got halfway across the bay when he realized this was probably Maggie's doing.

Fishing his cell out of his pocket, he texted her. *What's up with the kitten?*

Within seconds his phone buzzed with her reply. *What are you talking about?*

Don't act so innocent. You're the only one I know who would have the audacity to sneak a kitten into my shop.

What kind of kitten?

Rolling his eyes, Jefferson held the kitten out in one hand and snapped a photo with the other and sent it.

His phone rang.

"You'd better be on your way back here to get what you left behind," he snapped into the phone.

"That kitten is adorable. Where did you get it?"

"Oh, stop acting so innocent. You're here with Genghis Khat and almost immediately after you leave, I have a kitten. You couldn't have been more obvious."

"Are you implying that Genghis Khat had kittens while in your shop?"

"Kittens!" Jefferson roared. "Are you telling me there are more of these around here somewhere?"

"Of course not! I mean, I assume not. I don't know where that kitten came from, but it wasn't from Genghis Khat. He's a boy, for heaven's sake!"

"I know that. Besides, the kitten isn't a newborn. Just come back here and pick him up."

"No way. Genghis Khat would not approve. So is it a girl or a boy?"

Jefferson held the kitten high to take a peek. "Girl, I think."

"Yay! Give Cleocatra a kiss for me."

"Cleo—hold on a minute. Did you just name my kitten?"

"Ha! I knew it. She *is* yours."

"Hey, that's not what I—hello?" Jefferson held the phone away from his ear and stared at it. "She hung up on me!"

Chuckles from the shop brought his head up. He glared at his men. "Who wants to adopt a kitten?"

The chuckling came to an abrupt end.

"Yeah, that's what I thought. Wolves. So damn useless." He stared down at the purring kitten in his arms. "Cleocatra, huh? It's not a bad name. But don't get any ideas." He stroked the kitten on her nose. "I'm the Big Cat around here."

Cleocatra lunged for his finger, catching it between her two paws and swiping it with her tongue.

Jefferson grinned. "Okay, fine. I guess you can stay." He settled her on his shoulder and headed back toward the sports car he'd been working on. "Let's get back to work, shall we?"

Used to spending her days in high-powered negotiations for major real estate deals, Kate was rather bored.

It had taken her about twenty minutes to figure out the computer system and how to make an appointment.

It had taken her another thirty to figure out the shop's filing system (practically non-existent) and an hour to get the stacks of paperwork scattered around the office into a semblance of order.

Once this was done, there really wasn't anything to do, except answer the phone when it rang, which wasn't very often. Mostly people wanted to set up appointments or to find out when their vehicles would be ready.

She kind of winged it on both and hoped she hadn't set up an appointment for when the shop was closed or told someone their vehicle would be ready sooner than it would (she pretty much told everyone not today, call back tomorrow).

Sure, she could have gone out into the shop and asked the surly cat, but she didn't really feel like it, so she stayed in the office, surfing the net on her phone and ignoring the many, *many* repeated phone calls and texts from her overbearing brother.

Constant glances at her phone told her that time was moving at an excruciatingly slow pace, every minute seeming to take years to tick by. This was something she was willing to endure, however, simply to teach her interfering, arrogant brother a lesson.

The desk phone rang.

With a sigh of boredom, Kate punched the speaker button. "JH Automotive. How may I help you?"

"So that's the name of the shop!" the woman on the other end exclaimed.

Kate rolled her eyes. "I found it on an invoice."

"That's great. This is Maggie, by the way. Listen, I'm not much for talking on the phone. Or really talking anytime, but I wanted to see how things are going. Not that I'll come back and help out if they're going terribly or anything, but I thought I should check anyway."

"Other than extreme boredom—"

"Yeah, I almost lost my mind sitting there for two whole days. Well, I guess it was really only one and a half since you saved me. Thanks for that, by the way."

"You bet," Kate said dryly.

"Anyway, if things are going well, I'll leave you to it. Oh, and I recommend painting your nails as one way to fight the boredom."

Kate wrinkled her nose. So that was the stench inside the office. She wanted to ask why Maggie didn't use the scent-free polishes developed by shifters, but then she realized she didn't really care. "Okay, well, thanks for checking in."

"You bet. Good luck and all that."

A dial tone filled the air before Kate could reply.

She pushed the speaker button to disconnect and sat there staring at the phone. Was this seriously her life now?

Sitting in an automotive shop, waiting for the phone to ring?

Maybe she could sneak in some work without Mason ever finding out.

Yes.

She liked this idea.

She grabbed the phone and called her assistant.

At the end of the day, Jefferson walked into the office in time to hear the grizzly say into her cell phone, "Excellent, Mr. Wong. You'll receive those contracts within the hour."

"Contracts?" Jefferson glared at Kate.

Kate just held up a hand and kept talking. "Absolutely. That sounds great. Thanks so much, Mr. Wong. You too. Bye now." She lowered the phone and looked at Jefferson. "What's up?"

Jefferson glared at her suspiciously. "What's going on?"

"Nothing at all. I've made four appointments for you this afternoon. All the details are in the system, but here's a list in case you need it." She handed him a piece of paper. "If you're looking for any papers that were scattered around the room, they're now filed appropriately in your mostly unused filing cabinets." She waved a hand toward the three cabinets he'd bought when he first opened the shop, but had given up on using within a month of opening their doors.

"Three people left messages, wanting you to call them back and I basically told everyone asking about the status of their vehicles to check back tomorrow."

Jefferson raised an eyebrow. "You can call Cecily Adams back. Her Ford's ready for pick up. Were you negotiating a deal for The Worcester Group when I came in?"

Kate didn't reply, just stared him down.

Damn.

Grizzly sows were freaking scary.

Still sexy, but damn scary.

At that moment, Cleocatra popped her head out of the pocket on his coveralls.

Kate's mouth dropped open. "I could have sworn I smelled wolves when I arrived."

"Yeah, the other three mechanics. Why?"

"I can't believe they haven't eaten that thing yet."

"Seriously? She's just a baby." He stroked a finger down the kitten's forehead. "Don't listen to the mean ole grizzly, Cleocatra. She's just grumpy."

"*I'm* grumpy? Wow." Kate shook her head, grabbed the phone and stabbed out a number. Ignoring him, she made the call to Cecily Adams, then, *still* ignoring him, she gathered her things and headed for the door.

"You're leaving?"

She shrugged. "There's really not much going on at this point."

"You just arranged for Ms. Adams to pick up her vehicle! I need you to get her invoice together and take payment when she gets here."

Kate let out a huff. "Seriously? Is this the way it's always going to be? Nothing to do most of the day, then a ton of work right at the end when you want nothing more than to leave this den of boredom?"

Jefferson couldn't help but grin. "Only here a day and you've already figured things out. Let me know when Ms. Adams arrives." He headed out the door, calling over his shoulder, "And do something about the stench in this room, would you?"

Truthfully, the office no longer smelled only of nail polish. Now it was some weird combination of both the polish *and* grizzly musk plus some other indiscernible scent he couldn't quite make out. If he was being honest, he didn't really mind the grizzly musk and he was definitely intrigued by the third scent.

As the door slammed behind him, he heard Kate let out a roar of frustration that rattled the windows and sent the three wolves in the bays diving for the floor.

Jefferson let out a chuckle and said to Cleocatra, "Well,

that's one perk of having a grizzly work here, don't you think? I can use her to terrorize the wolves."

Three

D AY ONE OF Bygul's matchmaking efforts had been a resounding success.

At first, Bygul had worried he was losing his touch as Jefferson had seemed determined to pass the kitten on to someone else.

The grizzly, the wolves, even Maggie—he'd tried them all. Luckily, none of them had agreed to take the kitten, and by the time the shop had closed that first day, it was clear Bygul had nailed it—Jefferson not only adored the kitten, he'd clearly fallen in love with her.

And so, phase one of Operation Match Jefferson was complete, with Jefferson taking the kitten home with him, thus proving Bygul's matchmaking skills were as flawless as ever.

Day two brought the bigger challenge, however: he now had to find the perfect mate for the panther.

When the grizzly had walked into the shop right after Bygul arrived with the kitten the day before, he'd actually thought she might be a good candidate, but she didn't seem too fond of cats so Bygul was reserving judgment there.

After all, she *was* a grizzly. One had to be patient when training the less evolved animals about the superiority of cats and Bygul imagined the same was true of shifters.

Unfortunately, Bygul had a very long list of cats needing matches, and even worse, the class from hell to teach, which meant he wouldn't be able to stick around the shop the way he had the day before, trying to monitor how the matchmaking was going. This was unfortunate because he needed time to figure out whether the grizzly and the panther were meant for each other.

And so, as he'd done when matching Maggie to Jefferson's brother, Jackson, Bygul recruited a helper.

Last time, it was Genghis Khat who was his partner in crime.

This time, it would be the kitten, Cleocatra.

A name that caused him endless hilarity and he couldn't *wait* to share it with all the matchmaking cats at PPM, but until then, he had to make sure Cleocatra was up for the job.

"You need to stick with Jefferson. Try to pay attention to any potential mates he encounters. I believe it will be a woman, but don't discount a man. It could really be either one. I'm currently leaning toward the grizzly, you understand, but— what? What's that supposed to mean?"

Cleocatra had a leg in the air and was washing herself thoroughly.

"Okay, so the grizzly wasn't exactly friendly. But—now don't exaggerate. She didn't threaten you. She just mentioned the terrible tendency of canines to attack our brethren. I'm sure she'd protect you from them if it became an issue."

Cleocatra stood and pounced.

"What are you doing now? There's nothing there. Nothing

at all. It's air. You're pouncing on air, Cleo. This isn't helping at all."

"Okay, Cleocatra. I'm heading in to the shop," Jefferson stepped into the living room where Bygul was lecturing Cleo, scooped her up and kissed her on the nose. "Be a good kitten while I'm away, okay?" He set her on top of a cat tree and headed out.

"Oh, now, this won't do at all. He's leaving you behind, Cleo. How can you possibly mate match him if you're not with him?"

Cleo didn't seem too concerned as she continued pouncing invisible beings from one level of the cat tree to the next.

Kittens.

With a huff, Bygul leapt up onto the cat tree, caught Cleo in his mouth by the scruff of her neck and transported them both to the office at Jefferson's auto shop.

They arrived into a bustle of activity.

The grizzly, Kate, was barking orders and people were moving furniture, setting up computers, installing what appeared to be phone lines and basically rearranging the entire office.

Bygul didn't know the panther that well, but he was pretty sure this was not going to go over well. He transported them back out of the hive of movement into the shop where everything was quiet.

Jefferson hadn't arrived yet and neither had any of the workers from the day before. Remembering they were wolves and that the grizzly had seemed to believe they might enjoy eating a kitten, Bygul wasn't certain leaving Cleocatra there without Jefferson to protect her was the best choice either.

Fine.

He'd recruit Genghis Khat as security for the kitten.

He believed this was a fabulous idea until he arrived at Maggie's house and faced G.K.'s wrath.

"I don't know why you're so upset. I said I'd help, didn't I? And I'm here, with the kitten, trying to match Jefferson to a mate, which is exactly what you wanted, right?"

G.K. gave Cleo a look of disdain.

Cleo didn't even notice. She was too busy attempting to catch the grouchy tom's tail.

Pounce. Pounce. Pounce.

The more she pounced, the more the tail swished back and forth, taunting her, yet never pausing long enough for her to catch it.

"If you really want a mate for Jefferson, you're going to have to go to the shop with Cleo here. The job is to check out the grizzly in the office."

G.K.'s one good ear flattened against his head. The other ear was pretty flat anyway, having been mostly chewed away in a cat fight at some point.

"Look, here's the thing. The grizzly needs to learn a lesson about how superior and fierce cats are. I figured you'd be the perfect candidate for that job and while you're at it, you can check her out. See if she's good enough for our panther."

G.K. straightened a little, his tail swishing even faster.

"Awesome. Let's go then." Without waiting for a reply, Bygul quickly transported all three of them to a corner of the shop, where he left them with a quick, "Be good. I'll check back in later. I have a class to teach."

A moment later, he faced a classroom full of chaos and cats.

"There's nothing there!" He bellowed at the cats who were rolling around and pouncing on nothing. "It's not a ghost, it's not a demon, it's just air!"

Day two on the job was much better than day one. This was because Kate came prepared.

Her assistant, Nick, met her at the shop early that morning and by the time the mechanics started arriving for their shifts, the office had been completely transformed from the office of JH Automotive to the offices of JH Automotive *and* The Worcester Group.

She had the ratty old, scarred desk hauled away and replaced with two exceptional work stations, one for herself and one for Nick.

She had the phone company in, installing three new lines for The Worcester Group, she upgraded their internet to the fastest available and she had both work stations set up with sophisticated computer systems.

She even set up a Bear Necessities Station with coffee and snacks in one corner of the office that kept the mechanics visiting all day long.

It was probably a good thing that Jefferson came in late on Wednesdays, and as a result, missed all the activity, as Kate anticipated extreme grouchiness in response to all the changes.

They had just finished setting up the new computer systems when Lyle showed up in the doorway with Genghis Khat sprawled across his shoulders and Cleocatra cuddled in his hands.

"What are they doing here?" Kate exclaimed.

"Not a clue," Lyle said. "We tried calling Maggie, but she's apparently on a hike with the sheriff, so Genghis Khat is stuck with us, and Jefferson won't be in until later. You'll have to keep them in here. It's just not safe out there, what with all the equipment and tools and everything."

"What I don't understand is why an auto shop would have shop cats in the first place," Kate said.

"Yeah, this is a new development," Lyle said, "and I can't say I approve much. We sent Pete for pet supplies. He should be back soon." He dumped Genghis Khat on Kate's work station and handed her Cleocatra. "Good luck."

"Great."

"What are we supposed to do with *those*?" Nick asked incredulously.

Kate shrugged. "Your guess is as good as mine. Just don't eat them."

Nick looked horrified, which made Kate laugh.

The hours passed quickly as Kate and Nick made progress on several negotiations, one of them major, the others relatively minor, and even had time to iron out the details on a new development aimed at shifters.

Of course, the cats got into everything, Cleocatra in particular. She loved batting at all the paper and specialized in knocking over Kate's container of pens.

After the third such occurrence, Kate just left the container and pens on the floor and tried not to be charmed by the kitten, who clearly believed each of those pens were enemies to be destroyed.

With cats weaving in and out of their legs, Kate and Nick also managed to answer every call for JH Automotive, print out several invoices for customers arriving to claim their vehicles, put together a number of estimates for additional customers and, when hunger struck, order lunch for themselves and the mechanics.

As an afterthought, Kate requested a can of tuna for the cats as well.

All of this meant that on day two of her new job, Kate was most definitely *not* bored.

Jefferson took Wednesday mornings off to volunteer at Greensboro High School, where he helped out in their shop classes and mentored a bunch of high school shifters, who were interested in auto mechanics.

It was really one of the highlights of his week and he always came into work in a pretty good mood.

Today was no exception.

Mostly because he headed straight for the bays and got to work on one of the vehicles waiting there. All afternoon, he kept his eyes firmly away from the office and pretended he had no idea there was a sexy-scary grizzly working inside it.

He was peripherally aware that the other mechanics were wandering in and out of the office fairly regularly, but he assumed they were asking Kate to call a customer or to order a part for them.

It was only when Lyle came to ask him a question about one of the jobs he was working on that Jefferson began to put things together.

"Where'd the coffee come from? And is that a donut?"

Lyle stuffed the last piece into his mouth and chewed quickly.

"Haven't you been listening to anything we've been saying, boss?" Pete asked. "We totally approve of your new hire."

"Definitely," Ryan called from the other side of the shop.

"She makes a mean pot of coffee and did you try those brownies?"

"Oh, man," Lyle groaned. "They were delicious!"

"Yeah, she said it's Wolf Down Wednesday," Pete explained. "That means we get to wolf down snacks all day long."

"She said if anyone deserved to wolf down on Wednesdays, it was a bunch of hardworking wolves," Ryan said, wandering over with a rag in hand. "I've been trying to decide if I'm going to have another brownie or one of those giant chocolate chip cookies."

"I recommend the bear claws," Lyle said.

"No one makes bear claws like grizzlies," Ryan agreed.

Jefferson was literally speechless. He had no idea what to say. Okay, yes, he did. "Are you guys serious right now? I mean, is this a party or is it a damn auto repair shop?"

Pete chuckled. "Apparently it's both on Wednesdays, boss."

Jefferson let out a grunt of exasperation. "All I have to say is we'd better not fall behind because you yahoos are eating instead of working!"

"Not a chance, boss," Lyle said.

"Yeah, the sugar rush has me super charged," Ryan said. "I finished the Johnson job in half the time I expected."

"Whatever." Jefferson turned back to the car he was working on. "Just get back to work."

"You should really try one of those bear claws, boss, before they all disappear," Lyle said.

The more Jefferson thought about it, the more annoyed he became.

What was up with Kate Worcester Fancy-Pants-Grizzly designating Wednesdays as some ridiculous calorie-ridden wolf-down day?

This was *his* shop, wasn't it?

He got to decide if people were going to eat inside the shop or not and he decided not.

Not!

What if crumbs got in the engines they were working on?

Or what if they got rats because they were munching down on cookies all damn day long?

After about five minutes of stewing and rapping his knuckles a number of times due to inattention, he finally gave up and headed for the office to give that grizzly a piece of his mind.

Except the minute he stepped into the office, he completely lost his train of thought.

He actually spun around to make sure he hadn't walked through a portal into a different realm, but no, that was his shop right outside the office door.

And yet, when he spun back around, the office bore zero resemblance to the office he'd locked up the night before.

"What the—who the hell are you?"

A man stood on the opposite side of the room, talking on a phone, pacing back and forth in front of a huge work station. He sent Jefferson an impatient glance, turned his back to him, and continued talking.

At that moment, Kate came out of a door at the back of the office.

For a moment, Jefferson couldn't even remember where that door led to, but then it came to him. It was a giant storeroom that he'd initially planned to use to store parts, but then he'd discovered it was more convenient for him to store the parts in the garage where they were easily accessible, and thus, the space had never been used.

"That should work. I'll have to order the part, but it should be in by then," Kate said as she walked toward a massive desk area and starting typing into the system. "Yes, that works. We'll see you then." She disconnected the phone, then swung in Jefferson's direction. "What?"

For the second time in as many days, Jefferson was utterly speechless.

"Coffee and Wolf Down Wednesday snacks are over there." Kate waved an arm toward the corner directly opposite the door he was standing in. "Otherwise, if you don't need anything, shoo. We're busy."

As if to prove her point, the phone rang and she answered it, "Kate Worcester. Oh, hello, Mrs. Simmons. Yes, yes, we received the offer. I've forwarded it to our attorney to go over it. I expect we'll have an answer or a counter-offer no later than noon tomorrow. Absolutely. All right then. I'll chat with you tomorrow. Bye now."

"What the hell—"

Kate held up a hand when the phone rang and answered it, "JH Automotive. How may I help you? I'm not sure. We're pretty backed up. Hold on a moment." She pushed a button, looked at Jefferson and said, "Can you fit in an oil change in about thirty minutes?"

Jefferson shook his head, not really in reply, just in reflex because he was pretty sure he must be hallucinating.

Apparently Kate took that as a response because she stabbed the button again and said, "I'm really sorry, we just don't have the room today. Would you be able to bring it in tomorrow? We have a couple slots available, one at ten in the morning and another at three. Three works? Wonderful. And your name? Excellent. And is this the number I can reach you at? Perfect. We'll see you tomorrow. Bye now."

The moment she ended the call, Jefferson exploded. "What the hell is going on around here? Where'd all this stuff come from? What do you think you're doing and who is he?"

"Oh, right. Here you go. My lawyer drew up this contract. I think you'll find it's quite generous."

Jefferson stared down at the paper in his hands. "Rental agreement?"

"Indeed. You do realize you don't need a full-time receptionist. You were paying an awful lot of money for someone to sit around for the majority of the day answering the occasional phone call and printing out invoices and estimates. If you'd trained your men, they could have taken shifts in the office and saved you a ton of money."

"You don't think I haven't tried that? It was always a nightmare. The men could barely handle the phone system, let alone the computers. And there's no way I want to be doing that work myself. There have to be some perks for being the boss."

"Hmm. You're telling me that those men are capable of making highly advanced automotive repairs, but can't figure out a computer software program."

Huh. That was a good point.

"I'm guessing they screwed everything up to force you to hire a receptionist you didn't need."

Jefferson scowled. They probably had. Damn wolves.

"So here's what I'm thinking. Nick and I—this is Nick, by the way—"

Nick, whose back was still turned to them, who was still muttering on the phone, waved a hand in acknowledgment and continued with his conversation.

"So Nick and I feel this is a perfect location for us. As a benefit, it's not in Worcester Falls. We can continue to do our work for The Worcester Group without my brother's interference—"

"Would that be Mason Worcester, the Grizzly CEO who recently threw a would-be suitor out a window?" He'd heard the story the night before when the gossip had finally reached the diner where he'd eaten dinner and he'd immediately known why one of the real estate Worcesters was slumming in his shop.

Kate let out a growl that had his panther hissing in response. "He wasn't a damn suitor. We were negotiating a deal and my idiot brother completely overreacted. As usual."

"So I shouldn't be expecting Mason Worcester to storm in here at any moment and tear me and my mechanics limb from limb?"

"Well." Kate hesitated just long enough for his knees to turn to water before she laughed and said, "Don't worry. He never causes permanent damage."

"Oh, that's comforting." Jefferson glared at Kate. How had he gotten into this mess and how was he going to get out of it without being mauled by either an angry grizzly boar or an angry grizzly sow, or worse, by both of them?

"Anyway, back to the contract. Nick and I would like to rent this space. We've made a very generous offer." She tapped her finger on the document Jefferson was holding and his eyes nearly bugged out when he saw the figure listed there.

"Monthly?"

"The space is worth it. And as a bonus, you'll get Nick, and me when I'm here, as your part-time receptionists. We'll answer the phones and take care of your filing and print your invoices and estimates when needed. In return, we get to use the space and we're taking over your storage space back there as well."

"For what?" Jefferson asked.

"You'll see."

At that point, Jefferson decided he just didn't want to know. "Whatever. I'll see you later."

"Don't you want your kitten?"

"What?" He swung back around.

"I rescued her from the wolves this morning. Well, they brought her to me, but I'm pretty sure if I hadn't provided all the snacks I did, this little kitten would have been the first victim of Wolf Down Wednesday."

That's when Jefferson noticed Cleocatra was stretched out on a keyboard in the middle of Kate's work area. "How in the world did you get *here*, sweet baby?" Jefferson scooped her up into his arms and cuddled her close, eyeing Kate and Nick suspiciously.

"Oh, please. Like we'd steal your silly little kitten. Though she is rather sweet. Surprisingly so for a cat, in fact." Kate raised an eyebrow at Jefferson. "I have some pretty solid evidence that most cats, no matter how big or small, are obnoxious, cranky *and* sneaky."

"Not true, Cleocatra," Jefferson murmured in her ear. "Cats are well-bred, refined, dignified and *always* sweet."

Kate let out a snort. "How do you explain Maggie's monstrosity then?"

"Are you referring to Genghis Khat?"

Kate laughed. "Yes, and a more appropriate name for a cat I've never known."

"He's always been incredibly sweet to me. You must have riled him up somehow. How'd you meet him anyway?"

"He was here with Cleocatra this morning. Maggie came to pick him up around lunchtime."

"So that's how you got here," Jefferson said to Cleocatra. "I should have known."

"Known what?"

"Genghis Khat is notorious for escaping and showing up all over town. Not that we're in town or anything." Jefferson frowned. This was much further than Genghis Khat had ever traveled before and it seemed a bit preposterous to think he'd managed to get all this way with a kitten at his side. "Maybe Jackson's right after all."

"Jackson?"

"My brother. He blames Genghis Khat's traveling on god magic."

"I hope you're joking," Kate said. "God magic is nothing to play around with."

Jefferson shrugged. "Eh, I'm not too worried." He had much bigger things to worry about, like the grizzly who was transforming his mechanic's office into a satellite office for The Worcester Group, and her terrifying brother who may or may not want to tear him limb from limb, and Wolf Down Wednesdays.

Shaking his head, Jefferson went to leave the office, but the temptation was entirely too much.

The entire office was flooded with the scent of coffee, which was a much more enjoyable scent than yesterday's nail polish. The grizzly musk was still there, along with that elusive scent he couldn't quite identify yet, and—he glared across the office at Nick.

Not cool.

Gritting his teeth, he stormed over to the snacks table and snorted at the ridiculous sign above it.

Bear Necessities Station.

He poured himself a cup of coffee, grabbed a bear claw—because Ryan was right, no one made bear claws like grizzlies—and stormed out of the office.

As he stalked back into the garage, he seethed.

Her assistant was yet another wolf. Like he wasn't already surrounded by wolves, he had to have another one in his office?

He took a bite of the bear claw and froze.

Dear goddess of all sweet things, it was utterly divine.

He swallowed and took another bite.

Incredible.

He hated to admit it, but that sign was probably right after all because this bear claw was now an absolute necessity in his life.

Four

CLEOCATRA MIGHT BE just a kitten, but she knew when someone was trying to steal her human.

Unfortunately, she'd completely misunderstood the situation the day before.

Bygul had kept talking about finding the perfect mate for Jefferson and she'd assumed he was referring to her.

Because *of course,* she was perfect for Jefferson in every way.

But then, this morning, Genghis Khat said they needed to get serious about evaluating the grizzly and that's when she realized they weren't talking about her at all.

They were actually planning to give her Jefferson to someone else. And the first candidate was that grizzly she'd been nice to the day before.

The Betrayer.

Kate.

Well, Cleocatra wouldn't stand for it!

So, when Bygul dropped them off at the shop for the third

day in a row, Cleocatra did everything in her power to make the grizzly realize Jefferson belonged to her.

When Kate was reading, Cleocatra attacked her papers.

When Kate was writing, Cleocatra chased her pen.

When Kate was typing on the computer, Cleocatra did her best to catch the words as they ran across the screen.

Cleocatra chased the phone cord when Kate was talking on the phone and chased her shoelaces whenever she was pacing the floor.

And whenever the woman turned her back, Cleocatra knocked something off her desk.

Papers.

Paperclips.

Pens.

Books.

More paper.

She even let Kate clean everything up and acted like she was no longer interested, but the minute Kate's back was turned, Cleocatra went into a whirlwind of movement, knocking everything over again.

It was really quite fun!

Genghis Khat didn't approve at all. He just sat on top of a filing cabinet and stared as Cleocatra tore around the office, causing chaos.

He did lecture her in the beginning, telling her she'd never make friends with the grizzly that way, which was entirely the point.

As if Cleocatra wanted to make friends with the woman trying to steal her Jefferson.

It would *never* happen because Cleocatra had already claimed Jefferson as her own and that was that.

JEFFERSON WASN'T EVEN SURPRISED TO FIND Genghis Khat and Cleocatra waiting for him in the shop when he opened it the next morning.

"Seriously?" he said to Genghis Khat. "You've got to stop this, you hear me?"

Pete walked in at that moment, so Jefferson delegated. "Call Maggie, will you? Tell her Genghis Khat's at the shop again."

"Oh, man, come on! You know she's going to yell at me."

"Better you than me."

Ryan walked in at that moment and Pete was quick to delegate. "Yo, Ryan, boss needs you to call Maggie and tell her Genghis Khat's with us."

Jefferson grinned at Ryan's groan. "Come on, Cleocatra." He headed toward the bay at the end where he had a Honda waiting.

Cleocatra trotted in his wake. He found it utterly adorable, the way she followed him everywhere. The last two nights, no matter where he was in the house, there was Cleocatra, following him from room to room, sitting on his lap or on his shoulder or right next to him on the couch whenever he sat down.

"Now stay out of mischief, you hear me?"

A few moments later, Ryan reported that he'd endured a very angry Maggie yelling that they'd better take "damn good care" of her baby until she managed to come get him.

"Wonderful. Something to look forward to. Now if only Lyle would show up, we'd be in business."

At that moment, the office door opened and Lyle came trooping down the stairs, bearing coffee and—treats again?

"It's Therapy Thursday," Lyle announced.

"Therapy Thursday?" Ryan and Pete chorused.

"Yep. Kate says food is the best therapy there is, so today there's hot apple cider and coffee *plus* the most amazing muffins and breads you'll ever taste. I've already had three muffins and a slice of zucchini bread."

Jefferson wanted to scoff, but based on the bear claws from the day before, he was afraid Lyle was probably right.

The only question then, was whether he was willing to subject himself to the craziness that had become his office, just so that he could try those delicious breads and muffins.

No, the real question was whether he had the self-discipline to resist the temptation.

He tried his very best, but only actually made it about forty minutes before he started sending his men into the office at regular intervals to grab another snack for themselves and while they were at it, to grab something for him too.

In this way, he managed to avoid the chaos of the office *and* being mauled by a grizzly because he was pretty certain, the more exposure he had to Kate, the likelier it was that he'd lose it one day and set her off in a crazed grizzly sow rage.

So he avoided the rage and still reaped the rewards of the best coffee he'd ever tasted and a truly magnificent supply of delicious breads and muffins to keep him going throughout the day.

"You know what the worst part is, Miss Cleocatra?" he said to the kitten after rescuing her for about the tenth time from a shelf full of tools. How she managed to make the leap with those tiny legs, he had no idea, but she kept doing it. "The worst part is I guarantee within a week, we'll all be sporting an extra hundred pounds."

"Speak for yourself," Ryan scoffed. "I'm going for extra runs tonight, just to work off these calories.

"I'll be working off my calories in a much more enjoyable fashion," Pete said with a leer.

"Burying the bone," Pete, Ryan and Lyle chorused at the same time.

Pete laughed. "What can I say? I'm a true ladies' wolf."

"Yes, well, do me a favor, Ladies' Wolf. Take Cleocatra into the office." Jefferson handed the kitten to Pete. "I just can't keep a close enough eye on her and she keeps getting into trouble. And while you're at it, take Genghis Khat too."

"I told you cats don't belong in the shop, man," Lyle said.

"Yes, well, if I could figure out how they're showing up here every morning, we wouldn't have this problem."

"You've clearly angered the gods," Ryan said.

Day three on the job was chaotic and not quite as organized as the day before.

Somehow, Cleo and Genghis Khat showed up in the shop for the second day in a row and within an hour of opening, Pete was bringing them into the office.

"Boss says it's not safe out there for them," he said as he dropped them off.

"Then why does he keep bringing them to work with him?" Kate exclaimed in exasperation.

Her only answer was the door closing behind him.

Great.

The rest of the morning was spent trying to work while

cleaning up disasters caused by Cleocatra, who seemed to have been possessed by a demon overnight.

"Weird how she's entirely focused on your desk," Nick said.

"Yeah, weird. I bet that damn panther put her up to it."

"Oh, come on, he's not that bad."

"Not that bad?" Kate stomped over to the windows that looked out over the shop. "He avoids us like the plague, but don't think I haven't noticed how he sends the others in here to get snacks and coffee for him. He enjoys all the treats we provide, but every time he looks this way, he scowls like he wants to tear us limb from limb."

"Well, you did imply your brother might do the same to him."

"Oh, please, I did nothing of the sort. In fact, I assured him that wouldn't happen."

"Yes, by telling him Mason wouldn't cause *permanent* damage. You and I both know a shifter can heal an awful lot of damage."

"But we can't regrow limbs. Therefore, I think it's perfectly obvious his limbs are safe!"

Nick let out a snort. "And I'm sure that brings him great comfort."

"So he said," Kate muttered.

"You did warn him about the contractors coming in this afternoon, right?"

"Now why would I do that?"

ONCE CLEOCATRA WAS IN THE OFFICE, THINGS GOT A little quieter in the shop, though if he were being perfectly truthful, Jefferson would have to admit he missed having Cleo-catra for company.

Still, he got a lot more done without having to catsit and did his best to avoid looking toward the office, even when he became aware there was a lot of activity happening, people and things being carted in and out followed by a lot of banging and cursing.

He just kept ignoring it.

Because he absolutely didn't want to know.

He'd probably lose it if he did, thus running the risk of becoming a victim of raging sow syndrome.

So he avoided it.

Even as the other men wandered away and wandered back and began talking about scary things like shelves being torn out and walls being knocked down and electricians and plumbers and he didn't even want to know what else, he continued to ignore it all.

"Hey, boss, you should see what they're doing back here," Lyle called.

"Not interested," Jefferson yelled back.

Actually he was very interested, but wasn't about to let the grizzly know it. He'd read the rental agreement last night and had signed it despite his many reservations. At the end of the day, though, he just couldn't turn down that amount of rental money.

He'd been a bit concerned about the whole section titled improvements, but then he'd figured whatever they did to the building couldn't possibly make it worse, and since they could only "improve" the sections they were renting, which was the office and the storage room, whatever they did probably wouldn't impact his business, so what did he care?

He was not only getting an astronomical amount of rent

every month, but was also getting free receptionist work, so of course, he signed it.

He'd slid it under the office door this morning, once again avoiding the grizzly, and hadn't even thought about it since.

Until all the banging and cursing started.

Until plumbers and electricians arrived and his men started talking about walls going down and now he was drowning in curiosity and anxiety.

Damn that grizzly.

How had he gotten into this situation anyway?

Oh, right.

Maggie.

As if his thoughts had produced her from thin air, Maggie's voice thundered through the shop. "Jefferson Hewitt!"

He jerked in surprise and banged his head on the undercarriage of the car he was working on. "Ow. Dammit." One hand to his forehead, he rolled out from under the car and stared up at Maggie, who stood, hands on hips, glaring down at him.

"I can't believe you, Jefferson! How could you?"

With a sigh, Jefferson climbed to his feet, wiped his hands on a rag and asked as patiently as he possibly could, "How could I what?"

"How could you catnap Genghis Khat? You know how upsetting it is when he just disappears on me and to take him all the way out here, not once, but twice! It's not right." She glared around the shop. "Where is he anyway?"

Shit.

Shit!

Jefferson bolted past Maggie, leapt up the stairs and flung open the office door.

Kate looked up from her desk. "What?"

"Where are the cats?"

Kate pointed to the corner where a giant pet crate was sitting.

"You locked up Genghis Khat?" Maggie shrieked, then pushed around him to rush to the pet crate.

Kate shrugged. "The kitten was out of control and this environment isn't exactly conducive to cats at the moment."

That's when Jefferson noticed the door to the storage room was missing as was a portion of the wall it had been on. "What the—" He closed his eyes and deep breathed for a moment.

He wanted to be annoyed that Kate was knocking out walls, but he'd signed the damn agreement.

He wanted to be annoyed that she'd locked up Cleocatra, but it was why he'd bolted in here in the first place—because all that banging and rumors of walls coming down had sounded terribly dangerous for a kitten.

This was why he'd avoided the offices today.

Because the grizzly made him crazy!

"You know what? I don't want to know."

"Probably a good idea," Kate agreed.

"Oh, my poor, poor Genghis Khat. Did they lock you up like a prisoner?" Maggie crooned through the cage door.

"Mrawr," Genghis Khat replied.

"Mew," Cleocatra said.

"You poor darlings. Don't worry, I'll have you out in a moment." She opened the door and Genghis Khat lunged forward into her arms.

She fell backward and hugged him tight. "I know, baby, I know."

"Mew, mew," Cleocatra said as she stuck her head out of the cage.

"Oh, you sweet thing," Maggie crooned, picking her up and cuddling her close as well.

Genghis Khat, Jefferson thought, didn't look as if he appreciated that development at all. In fact—

Jefferson leapt forward, intending to rescue Cleocatra, but Genghis Khat turned on him and lashed out with claws.

Jefferson leapt back, shocked. "It's me, Genghis Khat. I'm your friend. Jefferson, remember?" Sure, Jefferson had been terribly amused when Genghis Khat used to lash out at his brother, Jackson, but he didn't like the shoe being on the other foot.

"Don't touch him," Maggie said as she climbed to her feet, cradling both cats in her arms. "You don't *deserve* to be his friend."

"What's that supposed to mean?"

"Locking him up like that!"

"I'm not the one who locked him up! That was your new hire. Remember her? The grizzly?"

Maggie looked surprised, then swung around to face Kate. "Really? You're a grizzly shifter? I've never met a grizzly shifter before."

Jefferson groaned. "Can I have my kitten back please?"

"I don't know," Maggie snapped. "Are you going to lock her up again?"

"I didn't lock her up in the first place. Once again, that was the grizzly *you* hired."

"Whatever." Maggie looked down at Cleocatra. "What do you think, baby? Do you want to give Jefferson a second chance?"

Cleocatra responded with a tiny meow, which Maggie must have taken for agreement because she passed the kitten to Jefferson.

"Last warning, Jefferson Hewitt. No more catnapping. Got it?" Without waiting for an answer, Maggie stormed out of the office, leapt down the two stairs and stalked out of the garage.

Silence fell in her wake.

"All done in here, Ms. Worcester." A man stepped into the room from the storage area. "You're all set up for the builders and installers."

"Excellent. And the bathrooms?"

"We'll come back for them, probably the day of installation."

"Perfect. Thank you so much, Andy."

"You bet." With a nod to Jefferson, Andy slipped by and was out the door before Jefferson could get the power of speech back.

"Bathrooms?" He croaked out. They had one at the base of the stairs between the office and the bays. It was perfectly functional and as far as he was concerned, needed no improvements.

"You really don't expect Nick or me to use that disgusting bathroom, do you?"

"It's quite revolting," Nick said. "Understandable, of course. This place *is* very blue collar. Oil and sawdust and all the accoutrements of hardworking manual laborers are certainly to be expected, but still, don't you think your men deserve a bit of luxury when they go to the restroom?"

Jefferson was once again speechless.

Luxury.

For working class wolves and cats.

In an auto mechanics shop.

Hold on a minute.

"I'm pretty sure all improvements were to be limited to the areas you rented, which did not include the bathrooms."

Kate looked surprised. "Are you telling me that as part of

our rental agreement, we aren't being given access to the restroom?"

Dammit.

"Not explicitly. It's not written that way in the contract."

"Pretty sure it's implied, dude," Nick said.

Jefferson scowled.

Damn wolf was probably right.

Blast it.

Five

BYGUL WAS LOSING it.

It was a miracle these cats had ever learned how to make a pawsitively purrfect match between a cat and a human. There was no way they'd manage to arrange a true love match between humans.

Or humans and shifters.

Or shifters and shifters.

Or whatever.

As far as Bygul was concerned, they were *all* humans.

Flawed.

Difficult to match.

Picky.

Hindered by their lack of animal instincts.

Well, the shifters had *some* instincts, but nowhere near as many as Bygul.

And so, they needed all the help they could get.

Unfortunately, if these cats were the best they could hope for, the human race was probably doomed.

Bygul had argued with the trio goddesses something fierce the day before.

It was why he never made it back to the garage to check on Genghis Khat and Cleocatra.

He'd been too busy trying to make his case that fifty cats were just too many to wrangle at once.

"The other teachers manage it just fine," Ceridwen had snapped, which really got him going, since he had never claimed, nor ever would claim, to be a teacher.

"Then let *them* teach the cats how to match a human and its mate," he'd snapped back.

"Now, Bygul," Freyja had said. "You know, they're not the experts like you are."

As if he'd fall for that bit of flattery.

Freyja should know better.

He'd spent hours arguing with them and the best he'd managed was a promise that they'd come observe his class today.

Which was just great.

He was most definitely *not* looking forward to the humiliation of having three goddesses observe his lack of control over a full clowder of cats.

What ensued that morning was chaos, as it did every morning.

An entire hour of Bygul shouting at cats to stop chasing invisible demons and to stop wrestling each other and to pay attention!

He'd get five or six listening, but then a pair of wrestling cats would barrel by and off those five or six would go.

He'd wrangle another three or four and a cat toy would roll right into the middle of their group and the next thing you'd know, they'd all be chasing that toy all over the room.

When it was finally over, Bygul didn't even have the energy to look up when the goddesses appeared beside him.

"Poor Bygul," Freyja crooned and picked him in her arms to cuddle him.

He adored being cuddled by Freyja, but didn't want to show too much joy in front of the other two goddesses, so he tried to keep his purring to a very subtle rumble.

He was afraid he didn't succeed.

"You do realize the best teaching technique involves modeling," Bastet said as she paced in front of them.

Bygul didn't even know what that meant. Was he supposed to strike a pose for the cats?

Freyja let out a soft, tinkling laugh. "Not a pose, sweet Bygul. You have to show them how it's done. Talking about it is, well, boring. Showing them, though, they might actually enjoy that."

Bygul was appalled.

Was she seriously suggesting that he bring fifty cats with him into the earth realm to assist in mate-matching Jefferson?

Surely not.

"Exactly," Ceridwen said. "I think that's the perfect solution. Tomorrow, Bygul, you'll take the cats on a field trip."

"They'll learn so much better that way, I'm sure," Bastet said.

"You'll do an absolutely fabulous job, Bygul," Freyja said, all the while stroking his back and scratching his chin and making his entire body vibrate in joy from the attention. "I just know it, darling."

"You know, the panther *is* rather cute," Nick said the minute Kate walked into the office, arms full of pastry boxes.

She gave him an incredulous look. "He's cranky and unappreciative."

She stamped over to the Bear Necessities Station and began laying out pastries. "Case in point. All these goodies we've been providing will be gone by this afternoon and the panther will certainly have eaten his own share. But will he show any appreciation at all? Of course not! And why is that, you might ask? Because he's an unappreciative jerk, that's why."

"But a cute one."

Kate let out a huff of exasperation, grabbed a chocolate croissant and crossed to her desk, where she flopped down and glared at the computer screen.

Well, of course, the panther was cute.

She took a huge bite of the croissant and chewed angrily, thinking that cuteness should be outlawed.

She took another huge bite.

Sexiness too.

Not to mention being hot as hell.

Damn Nick for bringing it up.

She'd been doing everything possible to keep from noticing the panther's dreamy eyes whenever he stamped in here or his epic ass when he stamped out.

And now they were all she could think about.

She finished the croissant and snarled a little.

Nick grinned. "I know that snarl."

"Oh, stop it!"

He let out a hoot of laughter. "I have no idea how you've resisted temptation so far. I was tempted to flirt myself, but I'm pretty damn sure he doesn't swing my way."

Kate let out a huff. "He probably doesn't swing mine either."

"Um, I'm pretty sure that man is straight as they come."

"Yeah, but is he into bears?"

Nick snickered. "You know what they say."

Kate grinned.

"Once you go bear," they chorused together, "there's no other were."

"You should definitely give the panther a whirl," Nick said.

"Only if you make a play for Ryan."

Nick waved a hand. "Nah, that boy's way out of my league."

"You sure? Because he certainly checks you out every time he comes in here."

Nick swung around to stare at her. "Really?"

Kate grinned. "Yep."

"Huh."

Silence for a moment, then, "All right, I'll give it a shot with Ryan if you'll do the same with Jefferson."

"Seriously?"

"Absolutely."

"Okay, but don't hold your breath. I firmly expect him to bolt and run the minute I make my move."

"Doubtful. The chemistry between you two is off the charts."

"That's not chemistry. It's—"

"Yes?"

Kate sighed and propped her hand on her fist. "Lust. Good, old-fashioned lust. At least on my part. On his side, I'm pretty sure it's all irritation."

Nick snickered. "I'm pretty sure his irritation is just a cover. And here comes your chance to find out."

"Huh?"

The door to the office opened and Jefferson walked through, Cleocatra cradled in his large hands.

"Again?" Kate exclaimed.

Jefferson shrugged. "I have no explanation. Every morning, I leave her at the house and when I get here, she's waiting inside the shop."

"Maybe there are two of them," Nick said. "You know, like twins."

"I doubt it," Jefferson said, "especially considering I take her home every evening and there's no twin waiting at the house for us."

"So what you're telling us is that we're not only your part-time receptionists and renters," Kate said, "but we're also your cat sitters."

"Afraid so." Jefferson set Cleocatra on the floor and watched as she darted across the room and began wrestling with nothing he could see. He hesitated, then, "Do you mind if I—" He waved a hand toward the snack station.

"Help yourself," Kate said.

Jefferson nodded and headed for the coffee.

The minute his back was turned, Nick reached across their desks and tried to slap Kate upside the head.

She jerked back and scowled at him.

He grinned, nodded toward where Jefferson was doctoring up a cup of coffee and raised his eyebrows.

Kate shook her head.

He nodded emphatically and made a shooing gesture.

Kate rolled her eyes, let out a big sigh, then stood and headed for Jefferson. She couldn't believe she was about to try flirting with the cranky panther!

"So." She leaned against the table, set a hand on Jefferson's shoulder, leaned in and murmured into his ear, "What are you up to today?"

Jefferson froze, container of creamer in one hand, cup of coffee in the other and didn't reply.

Kate grinned. This could be fun. "I was just wondering about your tools and whether you needed any help," she paused for a heartbeat, then continued, "getting them ready for use."

Jefferson slowly set the cup of coffee and creamer back onto the table, but other than that, he stayed frozen in place, and still had nothing to say.

"What's the matter? Bear got your tongue?"

Later, Kate wasn't quite sure what happened first.

Whether Jefferson jerked away because he was totally freaked out by her flirting or if he jerked away because of Cleocatra.

All Kate knew was that she was so focused on Jefferson, she never even noticed the demon kitten stalking her.

One second, she was plastered to Jefferson's side, murmuring in his ear, the next she had a kitten on her back, front claws fully embedded in her left shoulder, back claws scrabbling at Kate's back, attempting to find purchase.

Kate let out a roar that rattled the windows and caused Nick to hit the deck and Jefferson to leap from where he stood to the opposite side of the office in one giant bound.

"Get her off me!" Kate shrieked as she tried and failed to get a good grasp on the swaying kitten.

Jefferson leapt back to her side. "Calm down. She's only a little kitten. She couldn't possibly hurt you."

His words were almost drowned out by Nick, who was rolling on the floor, laughing and crowing, "Kitten–1, Grizzy–0."

"Yo, boss," Ryan called out. "Everything okay?"

Jefferson didn't have a clue how to answer that question.

He had no idea what was going on. No idea!

"Mew," Cleocatra nuzzled his chin and gave it a swipe with her tongue.

Jefferson wanted to tell her that everything was fine and to give her plenty of praise and loving words.

The problem was his vocal cords were paralyzed.

In fact, he was pretty sure every part of him had completely shut down the moment the bear touched him. That elusive scent had coiled around him and suddenly, everything had become clear.

"Boss?" Lyle waved a hand in front of his face, Ryan and Pete on either side of him, all of them staring at him in concern.

"Jeez, Jefferson, what'd that bear do to ya?" Pete demanded.

"I think—" Jefferson broke off. She'd broken him, that's what she'd done! His voice sounded like a dying frog, not the mighty panther he normally was.

"You think what?" Ryan asked.

It couldn't be, could it?

Surely the gods wouldn't mess with him that way, would they?

"He's muttering about the gods again," Lyle reported.

"Yeah, this can't be good," Pete said.

"Maybe the bear's a goddess," Ryan suggested.

"A grizzly goddess?" Pete and Lyle chorused together.

All three of them turned and stared at the office.

"She doesn't dress like a goddess," Pete said.

"True," Lyle said. "But she doesn't dress like the rich either."

"Yeah, but if you'd asked me how a grizzly shifter would dress, I'd pretty much say jeans and a tee-shirt," Ryan said, "so maybe she dresses the way a rich grizzly goddess would."

Jefferson shook his head.

His men were idiots.

"She's not a goddess," he rumbled.

Cleocatra clearly agreed because she let out another meow and rubbed her face along his jaw.

"Well, then what's wrong with you?" Lyle demanded.

"I think the damn bear's my freaking mate."

"Well, that went well," Nick said. "I especially loved the part where you offered to handle his tools."

Kate snickered. "He really is quite adorable. He didn't know what to do. Or say. He was putty in my hands. Then that demon kitten ruined everything."

Nick snickered. "I had no idea bears could reach that high a decibel."

"What are you talking about?"

"You shrieked."

"I most certainly did not! Bears do not shriek."

"Not usually, no, but you hit the high pitch on that one." Nick laughed. "It's a miracle the windows didn't shatter."

"Whatever."

A loud burst of laughter came from outside in the garage and Kate stalked to the window to see what was going on.

"What on earth do you think they're doing?" Nick asked as he came to her side.

"Not a clue."

The wolves were rolling around on the garage floor, hooting with laughter, while Jefferson stood over them, glaring.

Cleocatra was perched on his shoulder and seemed to sense they were watching because she turned her head and looked right at them.

"Is she hissing at us?" Kate demanded. "I think she's hissing at us. How rude. She needs to be taught a lesson."

"No, no," Nick said. "No lessons today, especially if they involve roaring at a tiny, defenseless kitten."

"Defenseless? Did you see her attack me?"

"Yep. My guess? She knew you were putting the moves on her human and wanted to tell you 'Hands off, Sister.'"

"Oh, for heaven's sake. That's ridiculous."

"Do you have a better explanation?"

Kate let out a huff and stamped back to her desk. "You want to know the weirdest thing about the whole situation?"

"What's that?"

"My bear actually perked up when I got close to the panther."

"That doesn't sound weird at all. Sounds like business as usual. Your bear does like to size up its prey before jumping right into the maiming and mauling."

"Yeah," Kate drawled slowly. "Except that's not the reason she was checking him out."

"Wait a minute. Your bear *didn't* want to maim and maul him?"

"Nope."

"You're telling me you got close to the panther and your bear was what? *Interested* in him?"

Kate shrugged. "Or something. I honestly don't know. But it wasn't her normal reaction to most males."

"Well, this is unexpected." Nick grinned. "You know what I think?"

"What?"

"I think the panther could be your mate."

JEFFERSON HAD JUST MANAGED TO GET THE WOLVES calmed down when a loud explosion of laughter came from above.

They all turned and stared at the office.

From their angle, all they could see was Nick standing hands on hips, chin lowered, gaze aimed at the office floor.

He must have sensed their stares because he turned and looked out at them.

He flashed a grin and shrugged.

Jefferson sighed. "I'm freaking doomed."

Six

BYGUL DIDN'T THINK it bode well that the wolf mechanics were rolling around on the floor, laughing like loons, in response to the idea that the panther and bear might be mates.

Call him crazy, but that seemed a bit discouraging.

Especially since he was there to try and get a handle on the mating situation before all fifty matchmaking cats descended on the garage tomorrow.

That was a disaster just waiting to happen, so he was there to try and lay the groundwork so that things went as smoothly as they possibly could the next day.

But now, with the wolves laughing it up and the panther looking like he'd been hit over the head by an anvil and—was the bear laughing too?

Bygul popped into the office in time to hear the bear say in between giggles, "My mate? Don't be ridiculous. I think I'd know if the panther was my mate."

Nick was standing beside her, hands on hips, staring down

at her. "And how would you know if you haven't shifted around him yet?"

Kate's giggles tapered off, then she said, "I think my bear would have given me a clue if that were the case!"

"Correct me if I'm wrong, but didn't you just say your bear perked up when you got close to the panther. Don't you think that might have constituted a clue?"

Kate scowled. "You suck."

Yeah, this was a disaster already.

Bygul popped back into the garage. "G.K., Cleo, I thought you were supposed to be helping this mating along! What's the big idea? The panther looks sick at the thought of being mated to the bear and the bear's in total denial. How is this helping their romance along?"

Cleo, who happened to be hanging out on Jefferson's shoulder at that moment, turned her head and hissed at Bygul, startling Jefferson, who stroked her fur and murmured, "it's okay, sweetie."

She let out a plaintive meow and Bygul growled in frustration.

"What do you mean you don't like the bear?"

Cleo meowed a couple additional times and G.K. let out a sound that Bygul could only describe as the cat version of a snicker, then plopped on his side, lifted a leg and began cleaning himself quite vigorously.

Great.

Perhaps the bear wasn't the right mate for the panther after all.

Cleo seemed extremely put out, but then again, Bygul had a feeling she'd hate anyone he suggested given her extremely possessive stance on Jefferson's shoulder at the moment.

Her back legs were planted on his left shoulder, while her front legs were draped across the top of his head and every once in a while she leaned over to swipe his forehead with her tongue.

Jefferson didn't seem to mind.

In fact, every time she licked him, he let out a chuckle and tickled her on the forehead or chin or wherever he could reach at that moment.

Clearly, those two were a match made in heaven, or in this case, a match made by Bygul.

As for the match between bear and panther, however, apparently there was much work to be done there.

Either that or Bygul was in desperate need of new candidates.

"I thought you wanted a mate for Jefferson," he admonished G.K. "So what are you doing lying about, not helping this romance along?"

G.K. stretched, let out a yawn, then sauntered toward the office. When he reached the stairs, he looked back at Bygul as if to say, "Well, get me in there already."

Bygul sighed. These earth-bound cats were just so needy.

Kate was back at her desk, supposedly reviewing an offer for a piece of property they were looking to buy a couple towns over.

Unfortunately, she couldn't stop thinking about Nick's preposterous suggestion that the panther was her mate.

Preposterous for no other reason than that she'd always assumed she'd know right away.

Not to mention she'd also assumed her mate would be a bear.

Not that there was anything wrong with other shifters, per se, it's just that life would be so much easier with a bear.

Another bear would understand her need for fuel all day long and wouldn't be surprised to discover that she pretty much only stopped eating when asleep.

And if she'd been lucky enough to mate with another grizzly, well, a grizzly would understand her obsession with nuts, fruit, fish, and well, really, anything tasty at all. It would be a match made in foodie heaven.

Unfortunately, a quick search of the internet told her that panthers in the wild might only eat once a week.

Once a week!

How on earth would they survive such insanity?

She consoled herself with the knowledge that she'd seen Jefferson partaking of the snacks she'd provided on Wolf Down Wednesday and on Therapy Thursday, but now that she thought about it—she glanced toward the table—he'd left without his coffee and hadn't had a thing to eat during Feast on Friday.

In fact, none of the wolves had come inside for Feast on Friday either.

Perhaps they had no idea Fridays were for feasting.

That seemed terribly tragic.

She'd have to educate them immediately.

Kate stood and headed around the desk, almost tripping on Genghis Khat who was lying in the middle of the floor. "What are you doing in here? How did you get in here anyway? Did that panther just drop you off in here without a single word about it?" She leaned down and hefted him into her arms.

She crossed to the door, flung it open and shouted into the garage, "It's Feast on Friday, lads." Genghis Khat, who had been relaxed in her arms, stiffened like a board. "Oh don't worry. No cats are on the menu today!"

"Not even the panther here?" Ryan called out.

"As I said, not today, though no promises about tomorrow!" Kate whirled and headed back into the office, allowing the door to slam behind her.

"Way to impress your mate," Nick said.

Kate rolled her eyes. "Stop with the mate nonsense. Besides, if it's true, he's just going to have to get used to my bearish ways."

"Right."

"You heard her, Jefferson, no cats on the menu today," Ryan said.

"Yeah," Lyle said. "I think that was an invitation to go flirt with your mate."

"And while you're in there, grab us some snacks," Pete said.

Jefferson groaned. "I can't flirt with her. She's a predator."

The wolves all gave him a look, then cracked up laughing.

"Dude!" Pete exclaimed.

"What are you then?" Ryan asked.

"A fluffy bunny rabbit maybe," Lyle said.

"I had no idea panthers were such wusses," Ryan said.

"Not that kind of predator!" Jefferson exclaimed. "You should have seen her. She went from cold and haughty to stroking a hand across my back and whispering in my ear about helping me get my tools ready. She was freaking out my panther!"

"Seriously?" Ryan exclaimed.

"Dude, this is going to be the easiest mating on the books,"

Lyle said. "Just go in there and let her do her thing. You'll be mated before you know it!"

"Right," Pete said, "and no running away."

"Maybe try and flirt back this time," Ryan said.

"Fine," Jefferson said. "But don't—" He didn't finish his sentence on account of Cleocatra who instead of licking his forehead this time, leaned into his field of vision and bit him on the nose. "Yeow!" He scooped her away from his face and held one hand up to his nose, probing it.

No blood, thank goodness.

He glared at the wolves, who were back on the ground, rolling around and laughing hysterically.

"Kitten–1," Ryan chortled.

"Panther–0," Lyle and Pete chorused.

GENGHIS KHAT WAS SPRAWLED ACROSS KATE'S DESK, right next to her keyboard, occasionally stretching out one lazy paw and slapping it down right on the keys, causing a barrage of letters to stream across the document she was reading.

Each time, she gave him a scratch on the head, scooted his paw off the keyboard, erased his additions and kept reading.

They'd been playing this strange game for about ten minutes when the office door opened and Jefferson walked in, Cleocatra perched on his shoulder.

He looked nervous, Kate thought, and yet he'd returned to the office.

The question was whether he'd come back for the flirting or for the coffee.

Jefferson hesitated in the doorway for a split second, then made a beeline for the Bear Necessities Station.

Kate rolled her eyes.

Of course, it was the coffee.

She was debating approaching him to continue the flirting when Cleocatra turned completely around on his shoulder to stare at Kate while Jefferson poured a cup of coffee.

Cleo bared her fangs at Kate, who leaned forward and was about to release her own fangs when Nick slapped her upside the head.

She glared at him and he shook his head emphatically. "Make friends," he hissed.

Kate scowled, climbed to her feet, walked around her desk and headed over to join Jefferson at the Bear Necessities Station.

"So, Jefferson." She leaned up against the table and nudged shoulders with him—the opposite shoulder from where Cleocatra was perched, of course. "Where were we?"

Cleocatra leaned down from Jefferson's shoulder, setting her front paws on his chest, turned her head and hissed at Kate.

Kate let out a soft rumble of annoyance.

Stupid kitten.

Kate would never admit it out loud, but she was rather upset that Cleocatra, who had been perfectly adorable and sweet the first day they'd met, had since decided she didn't like Kate.

Kate had no idea what she'd done, but she was starting to think Nick might be right.

The kitten was emphatically staking her claim on Jefferson.

"It's okay, Cleocatra, baby. The crazy bear isn't going to hurt you." Jefferson scratched her under the chin, kissed her on the top of her head, then lifted her down to the floor.

The kitten immediately darted to Kate's side and attacked her ankle.

Since Kate was wearing jeans and ankle-high boots under them, she barely felt the kitten's claws as she scrabbled around in a circle, growling and attempting to make it through all the material to Kate's skin.

Jefferson stared down at Cleocatra, a strange look on his face.

Was that—

He glanced up at Kate, eyes twinkling and she knew it was.

He was amused!

Kate scowled.

He probably even thought the kitten's antics were adorable.

Kate peeked down at the kitten just in time to see her back legs disappear as she scrabbled around Kate's ankles. A second later, her head popped out from the opposite ankle as she began the journey again.

On her side the entire time, claws scrabbling at Kate's jeans, Cleocatra hurtled around the front of Kate's legs and disappeared once more.

Okay.

Maybe she was a little adorable.

Jefferson let out a snort of laughter as Cleocatra rounded Kate's ankles again.

Genghis Khat came out of nowhere and slapped one paw down on Cleocatra's whipping tail as she hurtled by.

Cleocatra let out a screech and leapt up. Her small body collided with the back of Kate's left knee, buckling it.

Kate slammed into Jefferson, who caught her in his arms, stumbled back a couple steps, but managed to keep them both upright.

Kate's face planted right against his neck and she got a

whiff of his delicious scent, a mix of oil and man that had her blood humming.

She couldn't resist a taste.

One tiny lick.

Jefferson inhaled sharply and she scraped her teeth along the pulse point that was *right there.*

Jefferson set a hand at the base of her neck, took a firm grip of her hair and pulled her back.

Kate had a split second of searing disappointment, then his mouth landed on hers.

Holy hell.

Who knew that panthers could kiss like that?

Shivers climbed up Kate's spine as she gripped Jefferson's shoulders and kissed him back.

Their tongues tangled and waves of heat washed over Kate as she shoved him, all the while kissing him, until his back hit the wall of windows and she had him right where she wanted him.

His mouth was devouring hers or maybe hers was devouring his.

Her head was spinning with lust and she just couldn't get close enough.

One of his hands clamped on her ass and lifted her closer.

She hitched her legs around his waist and pulled herself up so she was a little above him, forcing his head back and giving her a new angle.

She ran her fingers through his silky, black hair and pulled back a little to see his eyes.

Glazed, like she was sure hers were, and full of lust.

He pulled her back and kissed her again and she lost all train of thought, all rhythm, all coordination and everything narrowed down to Jefferson and this one incredible kiss.

"Don't see that every day," Ryan said.

"What's that?" Lyle asked from under the hood of an old Chevy.

"That." Ryan waved a hand toward the office.

Lyle peeked out from under the hood and let out a snort of laughter. "Yo, Pete!" He called across the bays. "Check it out!"

Pete looked up from where he was working on a motorcycle, glanced over at what had caught the other two's attention and let out a bark of laughter.

Jefferson's back was against the office windows, the bear plastered to him. Her hands were all over his hair, which was standing on end and the two were clearly kissing.

"I'm guessing he either flirted back or found out he didn't really need to," Lyle said with a laugh.

"The way she's all over him, I'd say he didn't need to," Ryan said.

"Uh-oh," Pete said. "Here comes Maggie."

"Where is he? Where's that catnapping bastard, Jefferson?" Maggie demanded.

"Uh, he's kind of busy at the moment, Maggie," Ryan said.

"He'd better be busy taking care of my cat," Maggie retorted.

"I think he's more interested in taking care of the bear," Lyle said, pointing to the office windows. "You should come over here to get the full effect."

Scowling, Maggie stalked across the first bay to where Lyle was standing, then followed his gaze to the office windows.

Maggie gasped. "Is that my new hire?"

"Yep," Ryan said.

"We heartily approve of her, by the way," Lyle said.

"She's kissing the boss!" Maggie exclaimed. "How is that worthy of approval?"

"Because today's Feast on Friday," Pete said.

"Feast on—what?"

"I think it's a bear thing," Pete said. "Every day of the week so far has had a theme."

"Seriously?"

"Yep. Yesterday was Therapy Thursday," Ryan said.

"I particularly enjoyed Wolf Down Wednesday," Lyle said. "The bear claws were to die for."

"You got bear claws?"

"Yep, you were here. You should have grabbed one," Lyle said.

"No one told me there were bear claws! What have you got up there today?"

"We don't know yet," Pete said. "We sent Jefferson to scope things out and bring us back some snacks."

"Well, I don't know about finding snacks for you guys, but he's clearly managed to find one for himself," Maggie said dryly.

Peripherally, Jefferson was aware that Cleocatra wasn't happy with him.

She was racing around them in half-circles, jumping at his legs, trying to get his attention, and meowing incessantly.

That was all background noise though because all of Jefferson's attention was on Kate.

Glorious Kate, of the absolutely sinful mouth, who had

sent all thoughts fleeing his head with a single lick of her tongue.

He'd felt that tiny swipe of her tongue, then the scrape of her teeth and he'd completely lost his mind.

But what a glorious way to go.

The woman was simply luscious and Jefferson couldn't get enough of her.

The taste of her, the scent of her arousal, the feel of her under his hands, the sexy aggression she showed as she shoved him against the windows, all of it combined to shred his thoughts and bring his blood to boiling.

A yowl sounded from a distance followed by a crash and Kate jerked away from him with a roar.

It took Jefferson a moment to catch his breath and from there a couple more moments to realize what had happened.

The Bear Necessities Station was still upright, but several platters of goodies had fallen to the floor and Cleocatra was firmly attached to Kate's head.

"What is up with your kitten?" Kate growled as she tried to remove Cleocatra's claws from her scalp.

Into this chaos, Maggie arrived. "Catnapper!" She shouted at Jefferson as she stormed over to the Bear Necessities Station where Genghis Khat was sniffing at all the treats that had landed on the floor.

Maggie swept him into her arms. "Don't worry, baby, we're going to the diner where we'll get you some treats that haven't been dumped on the floor."

Genghis Khat sprawled across her arms like a king in his throne and looked as content as Jefferson had ever seen him.

"Why are you wearing that kitten as a hat?" Maggie demanded, staring at Kate, who had apparently given up trying to extract the kitten's claws and was now petting her.

Jefferson wasn't sure Kate was aware that she was petting Cleocatra nor was he certain the kitten knew that her growls were starting to sound more like purrs. Still, he figured he should probably refrain from pointing out the waning of hostilities.

"I'm not wearing the kitten as a hat," Kate informed Maggie. "The kitten's wearing me as a person."

"But why?"

Kate shrugged. "Who knows? She's a kitten. She's probably got all kinds of kitteny thoughts we'll never understand."

Nick cleared his throat and Jefferson froze.

Dear shifter gods, he'd forgotten about the wolf.

Had he been there the entire time?

One glance at the grin on the wolf's face and Jefferson was sure the answer was yes. At least the wolf was standing in the doorway to the storage area, so maybe he'd been in there part of the time at least.

"I told you," Nick said. "The kitten's been warning you for days, 'Hands off my man.' You failed to listen and now you're paying the price."

"Must you always be right, Nick?" Kate demanded.

"What can I say? It's my specialty."

Seven

T HE NEXT DAY was everything Bygul feared it would be.

It began early in the morning when he stepped into the PPM classroom, ready to take fifty cats with him to the earth realm.

As usual, they weren't cooperative at all.

"Settle down," he shouted at the cats milling around.

They were entirely too excited about the expedition, bouncing around all over the place.

"Yesterday, the bear and the panther kissed for the first time, thanks to my unparalleled matchmaking skills," Bygul lectured them. "Today's goal is to further that romance along, to see if the bear and the panther will suit long-term. We are *not* going to earth to play or to make friends."

"Not even one?" A tabby from the back asked.

"Not even one! We're matchmakers, not kittens. Get it together."

"Well, this sucks," a calico snapped.

"Yeah," a tuxedo groaned. "I was really looking forward to interacting with the humans."

"Personally, I can't wait to meet Cleocatra," Tivali said with a giggle. "Cleopatra was not amused when I told her what you named the kitten, Bygul."

"I didn't name her," Bygul snarled. "Maggie did."

"It's still hilarious and I still can't wait to meet her," Tivali said.

"Fine, whatever, let's just get this over with," Bygul said. "First stop is to pick up Cleocatra."

"Yay!" Tivali exclaimed.

Bygul couldn't think of any activity less deserving of a yay than carting fifty cats around while trying to make a match, but whatever. "From there, we'll grab Genghis Khat and then head for the shop. Everyone follow me."

The only good news was that Bygul didn't have to transport any of them. They could all transport themselves so all they had to do was keep up with him.

Of course, they probably couldn't, so that was the second piece of good news. If he was lucky, he'd lose about forty of them along the way.

Not that they'd be lost permanently or anything. After all, they could all find their way home again, but if he was lucky, they wouldn't be able to track him down.

When they arrived at Jefferson's place, Bygul was disappointed to see that most of the cats had managed that first leg of the journey just fine.

With a harrumph, he went to grab Cleo, to transport them to Maggie's house, only Cleo bounced away at the last moment and he missed her entirely.

Whirling around, he scowled as she tore around the room,

weaving in and out and around other cats crowding the living room.

She bounced over a lazy tom who had collapsed in the middle of the floor, slid under the belly of a black cat, then bounced up and pounced on a Persian's tail.

"Mrawr!" The Persian cried out, but Cleo was already gone, bouncing over more cats, wrestling with one, chasing another's tail, pouncing on a third's back.

"Cleocatra!" Bygul cried out. "Stop playing around. Jefferson's already at the shop."

The minute he said Jefferson's name, the kitten slid to a stop, whirled and raced toward him, sliding to a stop right in front of him. She tilted her head back and stared up at him.

"Yes," he told her, "it's time to go to Jefferson now. But I'm warning you, Cleo, if you keep causing trouble instead of trying to help this matematching along, I'm leaving you behind tomorrow."

Cleo let out a pitiful meow and Bygul sighed. "Just keep it together today, okay? Everyone else, try and keep up."

He transported the two of them straight to Maggie's house, where Genghis Khat was impatiently waiting, pacing back and forth, tail swishing in agitation.

Bygul sighed. "Yes, you're right, Cleo. That's not Jefferson, but we're headed there next. And it's not my fault we're late, G.K."

At that moment, cats began popping into the room, one after the other.

G.K. let out a yowl of fury and started attacking at will.

Bygul groaned.

He should have known this would happen.

It really was too bad earthbound cats could see their heavenly counterparts. It would be so much simpler if they were blind like the humans.

Then again, if they were blind, Bygul couldn't have recruited their help for his matchmaking efforts, so he supposed it was just as well.

All over the room, cats were popping in and out, running into each other as they tried to escape a rampaging, snarling Genghis Khat.

"That's enough!" Bygul bellowed. "Genghis Khat, you did really well yesterday. Your efforts were critical in getting Jefferson to kiss the bear. If you want to help again today, you need to settle down and get over here now."

G.K. skidded to a halt, so that he was standing face-to-face with a Maine Coon who had refused to run when G.K. challenged him and who now stood, fur on end, growling incessantly.

G.K. growled back and for a moment, the room was filled with a crescendo of growls.

"Mew," Cleocatra said plaintively.

"I said knock it off, G.K. You're scaring Cleo," Bygul said.

"Oh, it's all right, sweetheart." Tivali sidled up to Cleo and began to groom her. "Don't worry. Those toms are just letting off steam."

With one last huff of annoyance, G.K. whirled around, his tail moving so fast, the Maine Coon wasn't quite able to avoid being smacked in the face with it.

G.K. sauntered up to Bygul, a smug look on his face.

Bygul sighed.

Some days it just wasn't worth getting out from under the covers.

SATURDAYS WERE BUSY DAYS AT THE SHOP, WITH SO many people coming in for last-minute oil changes and other car repairs they didn't have time to take care of during the week.

They were usually fully booked with appointments, but then had a ton of walk-ins begging to be squeezed in.

It was a crazy, fast-paced day with very little time for enjoying the Bear Necessities Kate and Nick provided for what they called Snarf It Saturday.

This meant that Kate ended up making coffees for each of the mechanics and delivering them along with a plate of goodies right at the start of their day. She and Nick then continued to keep them supplied all day long.

Adding to the chaos of their typical Saturday was Cleocatra, who had apparently gone insane in the thirty minutes she was away from Jefferson.

As usual, Jefferson had left her at home, but when he'd arrived at the shop, there she was, Genghis Khat at her side.

He had no idea what was going on with her that morning, but she was full of way more energy than usual and that was saying something, consider her usual was pretty energetic.

All morning long, she was constantly racing around the shop, pouncing on nothing and wrestling with no one.

"It's like she thinks there's someone there," Ryan observed.

"More like a lot of someones." Pete laughed.

Jefferson just shook his head as he rolled beneath a Ford Tempo. He was just getting started when Cleocatra shot beneath the car and snuggled up next to him.

"Well, hello there, darling. What's up?"

She couldn't have been with him more than five minutes before she shot out from under the car and started rolling across the garage again.

B ygul couldn't believe the chaos of the garage once they arrived.

Of course, he did bring fifty-two cats with him. Yes, somehow all fifty blasted cats managed to make the journey.

Not a single one got lost!

He was purely disgusted at the sheer bad luck of that.

In any case, Genghis Khat clearly didn't consider the garage his territory the way he did Maggie's place because he seemed uninterested in the other cats.

He simply plopped down in the middle of one of the bays and began to groom himself.

Meanwhile, the other fifty cats raced around the room, chasing each other, wrestling with each other and into that chaos came Cleocatra, who had clearly made it her mission to catch at least one of the cats.

Not that the cats were going to let that happen.

They went insubstantial anytime she got near so that poor Cleocatra skidded through, fell through and ran through a number of cats without ever physically connecting to a single one.

She got close and they popped away.

Over and over and over again.

"Stop torturing Cleocatra!" Bygul bellowed. "And stop playing around. We're on a mission here, matchmakers!"

At that moment Nick came out of the office, sauntered

down the two steps there and made his way across the bays toward Ryan.

"Is that the bear?" Tivali wanted to know.

"And is that the panther?" Muezza asked.

"No, no. Those are both wolves," Bygul said.

Tivali made a sound Bygul associated with furballs.

"Dogs?" A siamese named Soraya slid to a stop by Bygul and stared at the two wolves. "You're mate-matching dogs now?"

"Of course not! They're not the targets at all." Bygul scanned the garage. "Jefferson's under that car over there. You can just see his legs."

"Why is he under there?" Tivali asked.

Bygul sighed. "It's his job or something. Anyway, he's a panther. The bear's up in the office."

"I'm more interested in the wolves," Tivali said.

"Why?" Soraya asked.

"I think it would be funny. After all, they'd probably never make a go of it without a cat's influence."

"Good point," Soraya said. "I think I'll join you."

"What do you mean you'll join her?" Bygul exclaimed. "They're not the targets!"

"They're rather cute together," a ginger cat said. "Look at how they're leaning toward each other. Just a little push and they'd probably end up living happily ever after."

"Not if they're not mates," Bygul said. "Besides, *they're not the targets*!"

The ginger cat had already walked away though and with her went about fourteen other cats, all of them following Tivali and Soraya.

Bygul let out a huff. "Is no one going to observe the match

we came here to make? You know the one—the panther and the bear."

"I think we can do both," a black cat said as he sauntered by, two other cats on either side of him.

"Yes," agreed Muezza. "Let's do both."

KATE GRINNED AS SHE WATCHED NICK SAUNTER UP to Ryan and begin flirting.

Nick was an exceptional flirt.

He had body language and innuendo down to a science.

If Ryan leaned even partly that way and if he found Nick to be even minimally attractive, well, he didn't stand a chance.

Cleo rolled across the garage floor right then. It really looked like she was wrestling something, but nothing was there.

"Crazy kitten." Kate would have continued watching, but a customer arrived to pick up their vehicle and another arrived asking if they could squeeze in an oil change.

The day went by fairly quickly, with Nick and Kate taking turns wandering into the garage with refills from the Bear Necessities Station and to flirt with their chosen target.

The more time Kate spent around Jefferson, the more intrigued she became.

She adored how gentle and loving he was with the kitten and couldn't help but imagine those large hands stroking her from top to bottom the way he did Cleocatra, except with a lot more vigor and passion.

She loved his sense of humor and the sound of his laughter when joking with the other mechanics.

Her heart about melted when he spent fifteen minutes

flirting with Mrs. Williams, an elderly retired widow, making her face light up in joy. He'd been working on her car off and on all week and Kate had prepared the invoice, which she'd thought was a terrible use of funds for such an old vehicle that had long since gone past its prime.

When it came time to check Mrs. Williams out, though, Jefferson shook his head at Kate, walked Mrs. Williams to her car, helped her into it, spent five minutes chatting with her, then sent her off with a wave.

He came back into the office, grabbed a cookie from the Bear Necessities Station and told Kate as he passed Nick, who was on his way back in from another round of flirting and coffee delivery, "Zero out that invoice. I've got it covered."

The minute the door shut behind him, Nick exclaimed, wide eyed, "How big was that invoice?"

"She needed a new transmission, new brakes, new belts, I don't even know what all. He was mining parts from all over the country. I have a feeling there were more costs than I know about, but what I added up came to a little over eight thousand dollars."

"Damn."

That was when Kate knew she was in trouble.

A man who would care for an elderly woman like that, a *shifter* who would care to that extent for an elderly, *human* woman, was absolutely someone she could fall in love with.

"So how's it going with you and Ryan?" she asked, a little desperate to think about anything other than how she might be falling in love with a panther.

"Not so great," Nick said to her surprise.

"Why? What happened?"

"I'm not really sure, but one minute we were flirting and

the next he pitched headfirst into the engine he was working on."

"What were you thinking?" Bygul bellowed at Soraya.

"I'm sorry," she said. "But you told us what Genghis Khat did to get the panther to kiss the bear. It worked for him!"

"Yes, but Genghis Khat's an earthbound cat which means he probably has better instincts than we do. Besides, it worked for him because the bear and panther were facing each other. The wolf you targeted was facing the car he was working on."

"It really wasn't the best of timing," Tivali said.

"I know." Soraya sighed. "The minute he fell and the Nick wolf didn't catch him, I knew I'd messed everything up. And now the Nick wolf's in the office and the Ryan wolf's sulking and they're not talking to each other. I may have completely ruined that romance, Tivali."

"Oh, don't worry, we'll fix it somehow."

"No!" Bygul exclaimed. "You'll not be fixing anything. Those two aren't the targets anyway. We need to focus on the panther and the bear!"

Kate gasped. "Is he all right?"

"Mostly, yeah. He has a little burn mark on his forehead, but he seems okay. Just embarrassed. He wouldn't look at me at all after that. I had to walk away to let his ego recover. You know how we wolves are."

"Oh, yeah."

"So anyway, hopefully he'll get over it. If not, well, that may have been the shortest romance on record."

"Oh, I'm sorry, Nick."

"Eh, it's fine. It's not like we're mates or anything, but that doesn't mean we couldn't enjoy a bit of flirtation and sexy times, right?"

"Absolutely. And who knows? Maybe you *are* mates and you just don't know it yet."

"Wolves aren't like bears, Kate. We usually know our mates right away."

She sighed. "I know."

The rest of the afternoon passed in a flurry of customers.

At a certain point, Jefferson dumped both Cleocatra and Genghis Khat into the office. "She's out of control today," he said to Kate. "Sorry, but we're knee-deep in oil pans and we just don't have time to keep an eye on her, and where she goes, Genghis Khat goes."

And so, Cleocatra spent the rest of the day in the office with them, wrestling air, pouncing on air, swiping at air and racing around and around the office before starting it all over again.

The day finally ended, with all of them exhausted and worn out.

Nick and Kate were sprawled in their chairs, having just checked out the last two customers, when Jefferson walked in the door.

"I take it back," Kate said. "You did need a receptionist. On Saturdays only, though."

Jefferson chuckled. "Well, thank you. This day was actually a lot easier than usual with the two of you here."

"Definitely," Ryan agreed, pushing in behind Jefferson. He headed for the Bear Necessities Station. "Need some fuel and coffee and then I'm headed home." He slid a glance Nick's way. "What are you up to this evening?"

Nick straightened in his chair. "I have no plans. You want to get dinner?"

Ryan grinned. "Absolutely."

"Awesome." Nick leapt to his feet, grabbed his jacket and said to Kate, "I'll see you Monday, boss."

"See you. Don't do anything I wouldn't."

Nick chuckled, grabbed Ryan by the arm and dragged him toward the door. "Don't worry. That leaves us an awful lot of wiggle room."

The door closed on the sound of Ryan's laughter.

"So how about you?" Kate asked Jefferson. "What are your plans for the evening?"

"I usually go to the Greensboro Diner for dinner. You want to join me?"

"Sure. What about the cats?"

"They're used to cats at the diner. Genghis Khat's a regular and Cleocatra's becoming one as well." He glanced down at Genghis Khat. "It's odd that Maggie never picked him up today."

"Does she know he's here?"

Jefferson's eyes widened. "I didn't call her. Did you?"

Kate shook her head.

Jefferson swung around and opened the door to the garage. "Yo, any of you guys call Maggie to let her know Genghis Khat was here?"

A chorus of negative responses made his shoulders slump.

"Damn."

Eight

BYGUL COULDN'T BELIEVE how completely undisciplined these cats were.

He'd spent the entire day trying to wrangle the cats, reign them in, convince Cleo to stop chasing them and begging Genghis Khat to do something, *anything*, to help.

By the end of the day, he was exhausted, and not convinced that anything had been accomplished or that any of the cats had learned anything at all.

In fact, he was pretty sure the only cat that learned a damn thing was Soraya and that was not to attack wolves who were working on a car's engine.

How that would help in any matchmaking scheme, he had no idea.

So basically, the entire day was a complete waste.

Not that he'd expected it to be anything else, considering the number of cats he was dragging along with him all day.

Then again, Jefferson and Kate left the garage together and she followed him all the way to Greensboro, so perhaps it wasn't a total waste.

As long as they kissed at the end of the evening, Bygul would consider this to be their first date.

A date he'd somehow managed to make happen despite being hampered by fifty-two useless cats all day long.

WHEN JEFFERSON WALKED INTO THE DINER, WITH Cleocatra on his shoulder, Genghis Khat in his arms, and Kate at his side, a cheer went up from the patrons.

"Does Maggie know you catnapped Genghis Khat again, Jefferson?" George called from the back of the diner.

Jefferson rolled his eyes. "I texted her, no worries."

"And what was her reaction?" Annie asked as she approached them with a couple menus. Normally she didn't bother, which told Jefferson that this was probably the first time Kate had dined there.

"Haven't heard back from her yet."

"Who's the bear?" Bud called from the kitchen.

Kate grinned. "Knock it off, Bud. Like you don't know who I am."

Jefferson's jaw dropped. "You know Bud?"

"We went to school together. So this is why you left Worcester Falls." Kate crossed the diner to lean on the bar and chat with Bud through the window.

Jefferson followed, flabbergasted and a little annoyed the bear was stealing Kate's attention.

"Yep," Bud said. "Had a chance to open my own diner."

"I bet your parents were annoyed."

"Eh, they got over it. It wasn't like they were planning to retire anytime soon and I'm not one for taking orders."

"Yo, three triple cheeseburgers with the works," Annie called from across the room.

"On it!"

Kate grinned. "Yeah, I can see that. Well, it was good to see you."

"You too, Kate. Stop by before you leave."

She nodded, turned, grabbed Jefferson's hand and dragged him through the tables to an empty booth at the back of the diner.

The minute they reached the table, Genghis Khat lunged from Jefferson's arms, landed on the table and stretched out.

Kate rolled her eyes. "You weren't kidding when you said he was a regular here. Clearly, he's staked out his spot."

"Yep." Jefferson ushered Kate into the booth and settled across from her. "Pretty much everything here is to die for. You can't go wrong with anything on the menu."

"Oh, I'm sure of that, especially if Bud's doing the cooking. We bears are very particular about our food and he comes by his cooking talent naturally."

"I guess so. I never knew Bud grew up in Worcester Falls or that he had family there."

Before Kate could reply, Maggie arrived in the diner like a whirlwind. "You're a catnapping criminal, Jefferson Hewitt, and I'm done making excuses," she shouted from the doorway as stormed toward their table, dragging Jackson in her wake. When she reached them, she stopped, put her hands on her hips and demanded, "Jackson, arrest him!"

Jackson just shook his head and shoved his way into the booth, sitting beside Jefferson's date.

Jefferson scowled, but Jackson just grinned at him.

"So, who have we here?" He turned toward Kate, who was clearly flummoxed.

Jefferson had a moment of deja vu as he remembered how Maggie had studied the twins in just that same way, looking back and forth between them as if she were memorizing their features or searching for a difference.

She wouldn't find one, he knew, because they were truly identical. Most people wouldn't be able to tell them apart if it weren't for the fact that Jackson was usually in his sheriff's uniform and Jefferson typically had oil under his nails.

"I'm the Handsome Hewitt," Jefferson informed Kate, becoming a bit impatient with her scrutiny.

She chuckled. "Well, if you are, I hate to break it to you, but you probably share that title with this one here." She tilted her head toward Jackson, who grinned triumphantly.

"Nah. He's just the copy," Jefferson said. "*I'm* the Real McCat."

Jackson made a scoffing sound. "He's been saying that since we were kids, just because he was impatient and kicked his way out first. He thinks he's hilarious, but I'm not sure he understands the concept of identical twins."

Maggie and Kate both giggled.

"Move over, Jefferson." Maggie shoved his arm and he scooted over to make room for his sister-in-law. "Kate, you're sitting next to my mate, Jackson. Jackson, this is Kate Worcester."

"I'm completely intrigued right now," Jackson said. "You didn't tell me she was a bear, let alone a Worcester."

"I didn't know she was a bear when I hired her, and then, when I found out, I forgot to mention it. And what's a Worcester? You mean like the sauce?"

"That's Worcestershire sauce," Kate said.

"So, what's everyone eating?" Annie asked as she stepped up to the table.

"Oh, we're not staying," Maggie said.

"Hey, I'm hungry," Jackson exclaimed.

"We just came by to pick up Genghis Khat."

"And to give Jefferson a hard time. I owe him," Jackson said.

Maggie stood and scooped Genghis Khat up into her arms. "And you've given him that hard time and now we're leaving." She walked away without saying goodbye to any of them.

Jackson sighed. "I guess we're leaving. It was nice to meet you, Kate."

"You too."

Jefferson watched as Jackson caught up with Maggie and pulled her around.

He was relieved to see Maggie smiling at his brother, so she wasn't really annoyed. She'd just hit her limit for socializing, which Jefferson had learned could be pretty brief some days.

As the two walked out together, Maggie glanced over her shoulder and sent Jefferson a wink.

Holy hell.

She hadn't hit her limit at all. She'd clearly seen this meal for what it was and had done her part to protect it from her interfering, idiotic mate.

Jefferson grinned. "I owe Maggie big."

"What do you mean?" Kate asked.

"She just dragged Jackson out of here to give us time together."

Kate looked surprised. "Really?"

"Yep. So let's take advantage of it. Tell me everything."

As the hours passed, Kate found herself completely entranced by the panther.

He was funny and charming and full of humorous stories of what it was like growing up as part of a set.

He was interested in hearing about her own childhood and laughed at her stories of her overbearing, older brother who made dating practically impossible throughout her teens and twenties. She shared her underhanded methods for distracting him so that she could actually have a life, including on one memorable occasion, sprinkling itching powder all over his bed.

He'd been so miserable, he had no idea his little sister had sneaked out of the house for a school dance. That was the night she'd lost her virginity, she confided, and Mason hadn't a clue.

She got better at the subterfuge the older she got and things got way better once she moved out on her own, but Mason was still overbearing and controlling and she'd learned to mostly live with it, except for those rare occasions when it interfered with her job.

The hours slid by slowly as Kate and Jefferson laughed and talked. They were the last customers in the diner when they finally left as it was closing.

Cleocatra had made her presence known many times throughout the evening, demanding Jefferson's attention.

Somehow he'd managed to kiss her, pet her and adore her all while keeping his focus on Kate.

She found that to be incredibly sexy, that he could soothe Cleocatra and make her feel so important, all the while never taking his eyes off Kate and never making her feel as if he'd chosen the kitten over her.

He'd make an incredible father, she realized, for he also never made Cleocatra feel as if he'd chosen Kate over the kitten.

Jefferson walked her to where their cars were parked. He settled Cleocatra inside his car, then turned and backed Kate up against hers. He captured her lips in a searing kiss and long moments went by in a heartbeat.

Kate lost herself in the heat of the moment.

Shivers ran up and down her spine and if Bud hadn't driven by and honked his car in farewell at that very moment, she might have climbed Jefferson like a tree and taken him against the hood of one of their cars.

They broke apart and stood there panting, staring at each other, wanting.

Kate caught movement in the car behind him, but couldn't really see what was going on.

It was probably Cleocatra, blending in with the dark night, spying on them.

Yep. Definitely Cleocatra.

Kate could see just her eyes, glaring out at them from the side window.

She giggled.

Jefferson turned and let out a bark of laughter. "Guess that means it's time for us to go." He turned and swept Kate into his arms again, for one last kiss. When he set her back down, her knees were wobbly.

He helped her into her car, then watched as she pulled away.

The entire way home, she was tempted to turn right back around and go to his place. She knew his address because they'd made plans to meet there tomorrow. They were planning to spend the day together and she couldn't wait.

Nine

THE DATE THE night before had ended in kisses, which meant the romance was progressing nicely.

Except for one thing.

Cleocatra.

The kitten continued to be a problem.

Jefferson was pretty good at paying attention to her most of the time, but the minute he had to do something like work on a car, or was focused on kissing Kate, Cleocatra went nuts.

She definitely did *not* like sharing her human companion with anyone else.

Bygul had no idea how to convince her to accept Kate's presence in their lives.

Even worse, Jefferson wasn't his only client. Bygul had a long list of matches still to be made and several were reaching a critical stage where his presence was absolutely necessary to ensure success.

He had no choice but to focus his attentions on these other matches and hope things didn't fall apart in his absence.

This was probably a futile hope, considering Jefferson had invited Kate to his house.

His house, where Cleo lived, a dwelling he was certain she considered to be all her territory.

Jefferson had invited another woman into Cleo's territory and Bygul did not predict good things would come from this scenario.

He could only hope that Cleo didn't ruin everything.

"Bygul, Bygul." Tivali raced across the lawn of PPM, headed straight for him.

Great.

What on earth did she want now?

"Don't worry, brother. She has a fabulous idea to help you."

Bygul jumped. He hated it when his brother, Kalyn, sneaked up on him like that, and he absolutely had zero trust that Kalyn would recognize a good idea if it bit him on the tail.

"I'm so glad I caught you, Bygul." Tivali skidded to a stop in front of him, Soraya at her side.

Even worse.

Soraya was apparently involved.

"We know you have so many matches on your plate and you probably don't have time to monitor Jefferson and the bear today, so we thought we'd offer to take care of that for you."

"Take care of what?"

"Monitoring the panther and bear, of course. We know this match is at a very sensitive moment and delicacy is everything."

Delicacy. Right. Because they'd shown so much of that when trying to match the wolves the day before.

"We'll take care of everything, brother," Kalyn said. "You have no need to worry at all."

Bygul glared at his brother.

He had no doubt the other two had roped Kalyn into this idiotic plan because they assumed Bygul wouldn't say no to his own brother.

Well, they were wrong!

Of course, he'd—

"I'm really looking forward to this opportunity to help you with one of your matches since you were so helpful with one of mine last month," Kalyn said.

Bygul froze.

Dear goddess of all matches everywhere.

He'd completely forgotten that disaster!

Blocked it from his mind, more like.

In front of others, Kalyn pretended that Bygul had helped him out with that horror show, but the two brothers knew the truth.

In fact, Bygul had made a terrible situation that much worse.

Which meant he definitely owed Kalyn a tremendous favor.

Too bad Jefferson and the bear would have to be the ones to pay that price.

WHEN JEFFERSON HAD FIRST REALIZED THE BEAR WAS probably his mate, he'd panicked a little.

A panther with a bear just didn't seem a good idea.

And him with this particular bear seemed completely outrageous.

She scared his panther, made him whimper just a little.

It took a while for Jefferson to realize his panther actually enjoyed the sensation of being a tiny bit scared of their mate.

In fact, he seemed to get off on it.

Once Jefferson realized that, and once they'd kissed once or twice or a couple hundred times, he was all in.

The woman was sexy as hell and she lit every single one of his nerves on fire when she touched him.

He couldn't ask for more in a mate, not really.

So she intimidated him a little.

He imagined that would simply result in sexy times being that much sexier.

The only hitch in the entire situation was Cleocatra.

She didn't seem all that fond of Kate.

Not that Kate seemed to mind.

Oh, she'd roared when startled, and on one memorable occasion, had even shrieked, but mostly she just tolerated it with a tiny smirk on her face.

Like when Cleocatra was attached to her head the day before.

Kate had given up her attempts to remove the kitten's claws fairly quickly and instead had seemed amused by the entire situation.

He knew he was.

So maybe it wasn't that big a deal, after all.

Except he wanted Cleocatra happy, not stressed out.

With this in mind, he tried to prepare the kitten for the arrival of their guest.

He talked to her about the bear and how much Kate liked Cleocatra (a bit of an exaggeration, to be sure, but he was certain she was headed that way) and how lucky Cleocatra was to have two shifters who absolutely adored her.

Cleocatra had seemed to perk up when he mentioned

having two shifters, so he was mildly optimistic that today might not be a total disaster.

Kate arrived with three bear-sized picnic baskets.

She'd debated only bringing one, but there was no way just one basket would fill her bear and then she'd end up forcing the panther to feed her every morsel he had in the house, which to her seemed a bit rude.

Sure, showing up with three picnic baskets meant he'd clue in, if he hadn't already, to Kate's ravenous appetite.

It wasn't a fact she'd ever had to worry about when dating other bears.

She'd had to completely hide it from the one human she'd dated and she typically didn't reveal her full appetite to non-bear shifters until at least the fifth or sixth date.

However, if her suspicions were true and this panther really was her mate, he would need to know what he was getting into and she would need to know if he couldn't handle it, so they could both run away if need be.

Therefore, hiding her bearish nature just didn't seem like a good idea.

Besides, the truth was going to come out no later than tomorrow anyway, because that's when he'd discover the latest renovations at the garage.

She'd stopped by there on her way to his house and found everything progressing nicely. She had high hopes she'd be cooking in their office kitchen no later than tomorrow morning.

Hopefully Jefferson wouldn't be too terribly upset, especially since it would mean more scrumptious pastries all day long, but if he was, oh well.

He did sign the rental agreement, after all.

Of course, if she'd been his attorney, she would never have advised him to sign it.

He gave away entirely too much control of a good portion of his garage space in that agreement, not that he seemed to care.

Of course, if she'd been a good employee, she would have advised him to consult an attorney, but that wouldn't have been in her best interests, so she didn't.

And now they'd just have to deal with the consequences. He with a full-fledged kitchen in his garage and she with his temper if he wasn't pleased.

First, though, she was going to enjoy Snack Through Sunday by going on a hike and a picnic with the sexiest panther in existence and by eating through the contents of three bear-sized picnic baskets.

To Kate's surprise, Cleocatra seemed quite happy to see her when she first arrived.

The kitten bounced over to her and stretched up on her hind legs.

Kate leaned down to pick her up and wasn't quite fast enough to avoid the snap of Cleo's teeth.

"Seriously?" Kate slid a hand beneath the kitten's bottom and lifted. Her teeth were wrapped around one of Kate's fingers and she was letting out tiny, adorable growls as she tried to chew through Kate's admittedly tough hide.

Even in her human form, Kate's skin wasn't easily dented.

"What is she doing?" Jefferson chuckled.

"Apparently she thinks my finger is a chew toy."

"Now, Cleocatra, come here, darling." Jefferson worked to

detach Cleo from Kate's finger and for a moment, Kate thought he wouldn't be successful and she'd be stuck with a kitten hanging from her finger for the rest of her life, but then with one final adorable growl, Cleo let go.

Jefferson cuddled her to his chest, and with laughter clear in his voice, said, "Sorry about that," then leaned in close and caught Kate's lips with his own.

Kate forgot the kitten and everything else in the heat of his kiss. She stepped forward, needing to get closer, to feel his chest against hers, to—

"Ow!" Kate jerked away and slapped a hand to her left breast. "Ow, you little demon cat. I think she bit my nipple!"

"Sorry," Jefferson choked out. "I'll set her down now."

"Yeah, yeah." Kate pulled her tee-shirt out and stared at it. "See those tiny holes?" She smoothed her shirt back down and stared at her breast.

Yep. Those little puncture marks framed her nipple exactly. Little beast.

She glared down at Cleocatra, who was clearly feeling no remorse as she ran around the room in happy, darting sprints.

"Would you like me to examine your nipple?" Jefferson offered in a much-too-serious voice. "I'd be happy to blow on it, to soothe it with my tongue and to stroke it better, if you'd like."

Kate tried to maintain her composure, but really he was too much. "Oh, you would, would you?" She burst into laughter. "You're incorrigible."

He grinned. "That's me. Ready to go on a hike? Or would you rather stay here and have me provide a bit of nipple relief?"

Kate snickered. Though she thought she'd probably enjoy his brand of nipple relief, she decided it would be smarter to go on that hike. Besides, she was hungry. "I vote for hiking."

Jefferson shook his head in mock disappointment. "You have no idea what you're missing, but let's go then."

He led her across the field at the back of his house and into the woods that stretched from his town all the way to Worcester Falls.

She wondered how often they'd both been inside these woods at the same time, miles from each other, with no idea the other even existed.

They each carried one of the picnic baskets Kate had brought and stopped often for some Bear Necessities.

"You know," Jefferson said on their first stop. "I believe kisses should be included among these Bear Necessities we can't live without. What do you think?"

Kate grinned and crawled across the blanket they were sitting on to straddle his lap. "I think you may have a point. We should test this out and see."

And so the kissing began.

Every break, every pause even became punctuated with kisses that raised the heat level between them to almost unbearable degrees.

By the time they reached the waterfall Jefferson had chosen as the site for their picnic lunch, Kate was practically panting with desire.

They'd barely set the picnic baskets down before she was on Jefferson and the two of them were on the ground.

They rolled around and kissed and indulged in more heavy petting before breaking for lunch.

"We'll need the energy," Kate pointed out.

Jefferson just nodded in agreement and they set about pulling out the lunch Kate had prepared.

They spent hours at the waterfall, consuming everything left inside both picnic baskets. Well, Kate ate most of it, but

Jefferson ate his fair share and as the day wore on, he made eating a truly erotic experience as he fed her little morsels and followed it up with devastating kisses.

By the time they made it back to his house (because Jefferson insisted he wasn't going to take her for the first time on the hard ground—"I have at least that much self-control," he proclaimed loftily), Kate was a mass of hormones, just waiting to explode.

Then they walked in the front door.

Cleocatra was *not* happy her human had gone off with the bear, leaving her behind. She was even more annoyed when Bygul didn't show up to transport her to Jefferson.

He sent in three substitute cats instead and even put together, they weren't as smart as Bygul.

Cleocatra had met Tivali and Soraya already, but the one named Kalyn she'd never met before. He looked a lot like Bygul, except he didn't sound like him at all.

Not as bossy.

Or as smart.

The minute they arrived, Cleocatra demanded they take her to Jefferson, so they transported her to the garage, but Jefferson wasn't there.

Instead, there were all kinds of people wandering in and out, banging on things and tearing down walls and basically destroying the place.

Cleocatra couldn't believe it!

Jefferson would be so angry when he returned.

They also messed with her stuff. She had a litter box in the bathroom and another one in the back storage room and both of those rooms were being destroyed!

This was a disaster.

Cleocatra wanted to stay and protect the place from the destroyers, but she also missed Jefferson and hated that he was with the bear without her.

So she demanded once again that the cats take her to Jefferson.

The problem was they didn't seem to know where he was, so they ended up popping in and out of various places like the diner and a place called a barbershop and Maggie's place where they saw Genghis Khat and Maggie and even Jackson, but no Jefferson.

After spying on the three of them for a moment—Cleocatra was surprised Genghis Khat didn't seem upset when Jackson kissed Maggie, and in fact, when the kiss was over, had nudged Jackson's hand and got some pets in return—they all returned to Jefferson's house.

"I have no idea where they are," Tivali said. "And this is exhausting, popping in and out all over the place."

"Agreed," Soraya said.

Cleocatra flopped down and placed her head on her paws. Her human was out there somewhere without her and the bear could be eating him right now and she wasn't there to protect him.

What if he never came home?

What if she was left all alone again, without Jefferson by her side?

"Oh, sweetheart, don't be sad." Tivali dropped down beside her and began grooming her. "Everything's going to be just fine. They'll be home soon and he'll give you lots of attention."

"Absolutely," Soraya said.

Or he'd have so much fun with the bear that he'd completely forget about Cleo and not pay her any attention at all.

"I doubt that will happen," Kalyn said. "Bygul says he absolutely adores you."

"Exactly," Tivali said.

"I've got an idea," Soraya said. "Let's have some fun. We can play a few games. What do you guys say?"

"What a wonderful idea," Tivali said. "You'll be cheered up in no time, Cleocatra."

So that was how they ended up racing around the room, playing with anything that remotely resembled a cat toy and when Cleocatra recognized the scent of the giant basket sitting on the floor in the entryway, they had a ball shredding it with their claws.

Jefferson and Kate stumbled into the house late that afternoon, frantically kissing each other and were seconds from tearing each other's clothes off when a yowl from Cleocatra had them pulling away from each other, just in time for Jefferson to catch the kitten as she leapt straight up into his arms.

Cleocatra's fur was on end and she was clearly agitated. She hissed at Kate and swiped at her with both front paws, claws extended.

If Jefferson hadn't had a good hold on her, she would have completely overbalanced herself what with the reach of those swipes, especially when they came one right after the other, right paw, then left, then right again.

"It's okay, Cleocatra," Kate crooned, but Cleocatra was clearly not interested in being soothed.

Jefferson cuddled her close to his chest and murmured, "What's the matter, sweet love?"

She let out a distressed meow and buried her face in his neck.

"Holy hell," Kate muttered.

Jefferson glanced up, saw she was staring into the living room and turned to get a good look.

"Damn."

A side table had been knocked over and the lamp that had been on it had rolled across the floor.

At one time, his coffee table had sported a couple auto mechanic magazines, several remotes, a couple bills and some junk mail. None of those items were on the coffee table any longer. It was completely cleared off and scattered throughout the living room were the remnants of those bills and magazines and junk mail.

Jefferson could see what he thought might be the light bill sticking out from under the couch while shreds from the magazines were pretty much everywhere.

It also looked like Cleo had somehow managed to get onto the shelf where he kept the basket of cat toys because the entire basket was on the floor and toys were scattered everywhere.

In addition—"I think she found the third picnic basket. Doesn't look like she got inside it though."

Kate snickered. "It's pretty much bear-proof, so I'm not surprised. She shredded the outer layer pretty good, though. Is this the first time you've left her alone?"

"Pretty much, yeah. I mean, I leave her alone every morning, but you know how that goes, which means this is the first time she's been alone for any length of time, considering she didn't join us when we were hiking like she does when I'm at the garage."

"Which is probably a good thing. The woods aren't the safest spot for a kitten, but I'm thinking she didn't appreciate being left behind."

"Yeah." Jefferson sighed. "This is a disaster."

Cleo let out a soft meow and nuzzled the underside of his jaw.

"Oh, now you want to play nice, huh? Well, unfortunately, I'm going to have to clean things up, so there won't be any playing for a while." He went to set her on the ground, but she stiffened in his hands and let out a yowl.

Jefferson winced, pulled the kitten close again and glanced at Kate helplessly.

Kate grinned. "I'll clean. You soothe the beast."

"You don't have to do that."

"Of course, I don't, but it's the least I can do since you left her alone because of me."

Jefferson settled on the couch with Cleocatra and focused on petting her and soothing her temper away.

Cleocatra cuddled close, but no matter what he did, she wouldn't start purring, and in fact, kept her eyes open and trained on Kate the entire time, no matter where Kate was in the room.

Kate bustled around picking up cat toys, sweeping up remnants of paper and returning items to wherever they'd fallen from.

Once the basket of toys was mostly full, she carried it to the couch and settled it next to Jefferson.

Cleocatra glared at Kate balefully and let out a tiny hiss of warning.

Kate chuckled. "Yes, I know. He's your human, but do you

think I could maybe borrow him for just a moment?" Kate leaned forward as if to kiss Jefferson and Cleocatra let loose with a series of hissing snarls.

Kate laughed and pulled back. "All right, guess not. Well, Jefferson, I think maybe I should let you and Cleocatra have the evening to yourselves. You know, repair that bond of yours."

Jefferson groaned. "I'm so sorry." He should have said to hell with his self-control and taken her in the woods. Now he'd be taking cold showers all night instead.

Kate giggled. "It's okay. We'll work on it."

Jefferson stood and followed her to the door, cradling Cleocatra in his arm furthest from Kate.

Kate opened the door and stepped out onto the porch.

Jefferson stepped out after her, turned and set Cleocatra down in the entryway, then quickly closed the screen door, trapping the kitten inside the house.

He turned and pulled Kate into his arms. "One more kiss for the road," he murmured against her lips before pouring all of his passion into the kiss.

Ten

IT WAS MONDAY.

Bygul's least favorite day of the week.

In his experience, humans were less cooperative, more stubborn and far crankier on Mondays than any other day of the week.

After listening to Kalyn's report from the day before, Bygul was feeling quite cranky himself.

Apparently, they'd been unsuccessful in tracking down Jefferson and the bear the day before, which meant they were unable to monitor that romance.

However, according to Kalyn, things had been looking quite promising when the two stumbled into the house, clearly on the road toward a passionate mating.

Unfortunately, Cleo had her own mission.

And it apparently was to keep that mating from ever happening.

Per Kalyn, the bear had gone home alone and Jefferson had gone to bed with only Cleo for company.

Based on this information, Bygul decided it was time to

leave Cleo out of all plans because she was obviously trying to sabotage their mate matching efforts.

Therefore, he skipped right over Jefferson's house and went straight to Maggie's that morning where he picked up Genghis Khat, who informed him it was about time he left Cleo behind.

Bygul figured G.K. was simply tired of the kitten chasing his tail all the time.

He transported the two of them to the garage, then said to G.K., "Look, I have to get back to teach my class. Just do everything you can to get the bear and the panther together before Maggie comes storming in and takes you back home. Maybe without Cleo around, this romance will finally start moving forward."

SEEING AS CLEOCATRA ALWAYS ENDED UP AT THE garage anyway, that morning, Jefferson just took her with him.

He figured he might as well, especially since he didn't want to leave her for even the short amount of time it would take him to drive to the garage, given how upset she'd been the night before.

The minute he arrived at the garage, he knew something weird was going on.

Ryan and Pete had already arrived, but were standing just inside the garage door, staring.

"What's going on?" Jefferson nudged Ryan forward. "Why aren't we moving?"

"Uh," was Ryan's only response before he stepped to one side and Lyle to the other, so that Jefferson could move into the building.

Once he was inside, he knew exactly why the other mechanics were acting so weird.

At some point in the last thirty-six hours, the entrance had been transformed.

The garage had four bays with four garage doors that lifted. To the left of those garage doors was the single door they'd just entered. That door usually led into a largely unused garage space that was about two times the size of one of the bays.

The back half of the space was taken up by the office and storage room.

There were two stairs leading up to the office and to the left of those stairs had been a very small bathroom.

Jefferson had considered setting up a lobby area in the unused space that led up to the office, but had eventually decided he didn't want to encourage customers to hang around while they were working, and so he'd just left it as is.

About half that empty space was now gone. A wall had been built directly to the left of where they now stood, running from the door to the stairs and ending where the original bathroom had once stood.

The new wall had two doors labeled "Mechanics" and "Customers and Office Personnel."

The hiss of annoyance he let out startled Cleocatra whose claws came out and prickled his skin a little.

Jefferson dropped a kiss on her head. "Sorry, little one. Let's go check out the craziness." He walked over to the first door and flung it open.

His jaw dropped.

"Wow," Ryan said from behind him.

"Didn't expect that," Lyle said.

"What's going on?" Pete walked up behind them.

Jefferson didn't reply, just walked slowly into the new restroom that had clearly been built with them in mind.

The room was split in two. The area he walked into was a carpeted lounge, with two leather armchairs, a table with flowers and—Jefferson looked closer—yes, the exact magazines he'd had on his coffee table that Cleocatra had shredded the day before.

To the right was an open doorway that led into a tiled bathroom with a couple stalls and urinals.

"You should check this out!" Lyle exclaimed from inside the tiled room. "There's a pumice stone in here and nail brushes and lotions and wow—this is some high-end, expensive mechanics' soap."

"Damn," Pete said from the lounge area. "I'm spending my breaks in here from now on."

Jefferson just shook his head and walked out.

Cleocatra meowed at him.

"It's okay, baby." He dropped a kiss on her nose and scratched her under the chin.

She purred in response.

He wanted to be mad, but really how could he? He'd signed the agreement, after all, and Kate had warned him. It's just that when nothing happened, he'd assumed she'd changed her mind.

Obviously, she hadn't. There was no way he could complain, though, not when the bathroom had clearly been created with his comfort in mind.

Curious now, he wandered next door into the other restroom.

The setup was exactly the same, but in reverse with the lounging area on the right and the tiled bathroom to the left.

Just like next door, there were two leather armchairs and a

table sporting flowers and magazines (though these appeared to be focused on news and entertainment).

The bathroom looked similar as well, with three stalls and a variety of lotions and soaps and nail care utensils.

What impressed him the most was that neither bathroom was nicer than the other. Usually, men were thought to not need the special fancy additions that were so common in women's restrooms.

He also liked that the doors weren't labeled according to gender, but instead according to roles, which made sense considering the accessories in each.

Jefferson stepped out into the garage, just as Lyle exclaimed, "Hey, there's a third door back here!"

There was indeed. It was right at the base of the stairs, where the original bathroom had once stood.

Jefferson hadn't noticed it before because it didn't have a sign like the other two.

Except, now that Jefferson looked closer, he realized it did have one; it was just much lower to the ground.

He let out a bark of laughter.

The door was full-sized, but it sported a pet door at the bottom and above the pet door was a sign that featured a black cat.

Grinning, he opened the door and discovered inside a cat bathroom about half the size of the human ones, but with many of the same features. The area was split in two just like in the other rooms, with one half being carpeted and the other half tile.

In the carpeted area, there was a single armchair—not leather, but instead patterned in cats at play—a couple cat beds and a basket of toys that Jefferson noted included many of the same toys Cleocatra loved playing with at the house.

The tiled area to the right had two covered litter boxes (both decorated with cat images) on either side of a sink which had a tiny trash can in the shape of a cat sitting on its countertop.

There was also a cabinet with cat-shaped doorknobs standing against the wall across from the sink and litter boxes. A quick peek inside revealed bags of litter, a litter scoop and a box of trash bags.

Jefferson was literally speechless.

She'd created an entire bathroom just for Cleocatra.

The kitten who had made it clear she didn't like Kate.

Jefferson walked back out into the cat lounge area and murmured to Cleocatra, "Look at all the toys she bought for you." He set her down in front of the basket and watched as she sniffed it and the toys inside it, then sniffed around the chair, then investigated both cat beds, before heading back to the basket of toys.

She climbed into the basket and batted a ball out, then followed it onto the floor where she sent it skittering across the room, then chased after it.

Jefferson waited a few moments and when he was certain she was fully entertained and wouldn't even notice when he left, he sneaked out the door, letting it close behind him.

He glanced around and found only Pete waiting.

He raised an eyebrow.

"They went upstairs for coffee and snacks and to see if there were any other changes."

Jefferson sighed. "Well, we might as well endure all the shocks at once. Let's go, then."

They walked up the two stairs into the office.

The first thing Jefferson noticed was the door to the storage unit had been moved further down the wall from where it had originally stood, and was now a swinging door. The wall it was on had been completely rebuilt and looked quite natural, blending into the rest of the walls of the office, as if it had never been torn down.

He wasn't at all surprised to see Lyle at the Bear Necessities Station, clearly perusing the day's offerings, while Ryan was leaning against Nick's desk, flirting with him.

Ryan insisted they weren't mates, that they were just having a bit of fun, but Jefferson wouldn't be at all surprised if he was wrong about that.

"Where's Kate?" Jefferson asked as Pete made a beeline for the food.

Nick waved a hand behind him toward the swinging doors and said, "Kitchen," without taking his eyes off Ryan.

Jefferson was already walking toward the swinging doors when the word "kitchen" registered. He shook his head, convinced he couldn't have heard right, then shoved his way into the former storage room to discover that yes, he had indeed heard correctly.

The storage room had been completely transformed into what looked to be an industrial kitchen, with high-end appliances and a large island in the middle. The only thing that appeared to have remained the same from before was the wall to the right, which was still covered with the original shelves that had been part of the storage room, which were now clearly being used to house every ingredient known to man or shifter.

He really shouldn't be surprised.

The way Kate (and apparently all bears) ate, having a kitchen and full pantry available twenty-four seven was probably a matter of survival.

Just one more of those Bear Necessities.

And speaking of Kate, she stood with her back to Jefferson

and was in the process of transferring cookies to a cooling rack she'd set up on the island.

Jefferson waited until she'd finished and had set the hot tray aside before saying her name.

She whirled and smiled. "Jefferson!"

KATE DIDN'T WANT TO ADMIT IT, BUT SHE WAS nervous.

Super nervous.

After leaving Jefferson's place the night before, she'd stopped at the garage again, to check on the progress, and had been thrilled at the results.

The workers had just been finishing up and the foreman had given her a tour.

It was incredible.

Everything had worked out.

Even the furniture had been delivered on time.

She'd been especially thrilled with the cat room.

Not that the little demon deserved it or anything.

Still, she'd gone out the night before and made some extra purchases for a few final touches.

She'd picked up the magazines she'd seen on Jefferson's coffee table and some of Cleocatra's favorite cat toys.

Vases of flowers for the bathrooms, which was really quite ridiculous, and of course, a huge grocery run for everything she needed to be able to bake at a moment's notice.

She'd arrived home with a full SUV and a whole pile of nerves.

Shopping had helped to settle her raging hormones, but had done nothing for the nerves.

She'd slept very poorly the night before, thoughts on Jefferson the entire time, imagining how the night might have ended if it weren't for the demon cat and worrying about his reaction to the bathrooms and the kitchen.

She'd given up on sleeping around four in the morning and had decided to go ahead and come in and begin the day early.

She'd been baking since just after five and it had gone a long way toward calming her down. Well, that and being able to snack as she baked.

As long as she focused on the baking (and the eating) and kept her thoughts away from Jefferson, she thought she should be able to keep the nerves at bay.

Of course, that was easier said than done, but she did her best.

Then, in the midst of all that baking and eating, Jefferson arrived.

The minute she heard his voice, all her nerves just flew away.

She whirled with a grin, exclaimed his name and hurried across the kitchen to hurl herself into his arms.

Jefferson caught her close, settled one hand at the base of her neck and slid another down her back to cup her ass and lift her.

Kate wrapped her legs around his waist and kissed him.

Or maybe he kissed her.

Either way, their lips were melded together, tongues twining deep with tingles spreading all over her body as heat blanketed her in waves.

Jefferson carried her a few steps further into the kitchen and then she was on the kitchen island and he was between her legs and they were devouring each other with no end in sight.

Kate heard Nick yelling, "Yo, Kate, you've got a visitor!"

She could tell from the tone that he was trying to warn her about something. The words should mean something, but all she could do and feel was Jefferson.

His lips, his hard cock right against the part of her that ached for him, his hands on her back, on her neck, slipping beneath her pants to cup her ass, and then there was a horrendous roar that rattled every pot in the kitchen and Jefferson was gone.

Kate was left all alone, swaying in place on the kitchen island, so close to climax, it actually hurt for it to be yanked away.

She heard the sound of another roar—a roar she recognized —and then a huge crash.

Oh, shit!

She leapt down from the island, hurtled through the swinging doors and came to a screeching halt.

The first thing she noticed was Nick cowering under his desk.

She sent him a demanding look and he pointed to the windows overlooking the garage.

One was completely shattered with Mason standing in front of it, glaring down into the shop,

"Mason!" Kate shrieked. "What the hell is wrong with you?"

She raced out the door, leapt down the steps into the garage and hurried to Jefferson's side, falling to her knees beside him.

He'd landed flat on his back, but was struggling up onto his elbows when she reached him.

"What happened?" He seemed disoriented and had several cuts from the glass, but mostly looked okay.

"My idiot brother tossed you through the window."

Jefferson chuckled. "I'm pretty sure you assured me that wouldn't happen."

"No, I just said he rarely caused permanent damage." Not that that made it any better or anything. She was seriously going to kill her brother.

"Kate, stop fussing over that panther and get your ass in here," Mason bellowed through the shattered window.

"Excuse me?" Kate leapt to her feet and stormed back up the stairs into the office.

Mason disappeared from the window as he turned to face his angry sister.

"PSST. RYAN!"

Jefferson looked up and watched, a bit stunned, as Nick passed several things through the now broken window to Ryan.

"You okay, boss?" Lyle asked.

Jefferson nodded. "Survived a bear attack. I think I'm pretty good."

Nick hopped through the window, then grinned down at Jefferson. "Man, you're better than good if you can stand after an encounter with Mason Worcester. Let's see how you do." He reached out a hand, Jefferson grasped it and allowed the wolf to pull him to his feet.

Jefferson shook out his hands and arms and looked up toward the office, where Mason and Kate were still roaring at each other.

"Should I try to intervene?"

"Nah," Nick said. "Mason would never hurt Kate, but this'll probably go on for a while." He turned to the other wolves. "We might as well get comfortable and enjoy the show. It's Munch Away Monday so I brought popcorn and pastries."

So that's what he'd been passing through the window to Ryan.

At that moment, Cleocatra came bolting through the pet door and raced across the concrete toward Jefferson.

"What's the matter, baby?" Jefferson scooped her into his arms and cuddled her close. "Is the roaring too loud for you? They're just bears, sweetie. You can't expect them to be quiet."

A few moments later, once he was done soothing Cleocatra, he noticed the wolves had taken the opportunity to somehow locate his set of collapsible chairs and had arranged them in a row facing the office windows.

Inside, you could see Kate pacing back and forth, arms waving, while Mason stood back, arms crossed, glowering. Both bears were roaring at the top of their lungs, making it hard to understand anything they were saying.

The wolves were all eating popcorn while keeping up a running commentary.

"He's pretty intimidating," Lyle observed.

"Yeah, but so is she," Nick said.

"Who do you think's going to win this argument?" Ryan asked.

"I'm betting on Kate myself," Nick said.

"Fifty on the brother," Pete said.

"I'll take that bet," Nick said.

Jefferson shook his head and rolled his eyes. "You know, there is work to be done around here. Car repairs, oil changes, ring a bell?"

Ryan looked at Jefferson, then back at the shouting bears. "I hate to say it, but I'm pretty sure our boss is doomed."

"No shit," Pete said.

"There's no way he'll ever win an argument against that," Lyle said with a wave of the hand toward the raging Kate.

"Yeah, she is kind of scary when in a rage," Nick said.

"Glad it's not me," Pete said cheerfully.

They all looked at Jefferson, who just glared back at them.

"Dude, that grizzly kicked your ass," Pete said.

"Well, you can't blame the grizzly," Ryan said. "I mean, Jefferson *was* fooling around with his sister."

"Yeah, but Jefferson didn't even get one punch in," Pete protested.

"True, but it's not every day you get attacked by a giant grizzly," Lyle pointed out.

"He wasn't even in his bear form," Pete said. "You'd think Jefferson could have at least fought back a little, not just gone belly up."

"Hey, he ambushed me," Jefferson defended himself. "One minute I'm kissing Kate, the next I'm flying through the window."

"You mean to tell me you didn't smell that grizzly coming?" Pete exclaimed.

"All I could smell was Kate," Jefferson said morosely.

"You need to come back to work!" Mason roared at Kate.

"I *am* at work and I'm doing all the work I used to do, but in a new location and one where I don't have to deal with your controlling nature on a daily basis."

"Well, who can blame me when the second my back is turned, you're fraternizing with wolves and kissing panthers!"

"He's my mate!" Kate roared.

Dead silence.

"Say it isn't so, Kate," Mason shouted.

She shrugged. "Well, I haven't let my bear out yet, so I'm not positive, but considering my bear wants to get closer and to roll in his scent, rather than tear him limb from limb, I'm pretty damn sure we're mates."

"You've broken my heart, Kate."

"Why? Because he's not a bear?"

"No. Because he doesn't live in Worcester Falls."

"Oh for heaven's sake, he lives in Greensboro. It's a forty minute drive tops."

"Harumph. Whatever. Introduce me to this panther of yours."

Kate let out a huff. "Fine. Let's go." She stamped out the door and down the stairs into the garage, where for some reason, the wolves were all sitting in chairs she associated with outdoor events.

She grinned at the sight of Nick and Ryan, leaning toward each other, sharing a bucket of popcorn, clearly into each other in a massive way.

Jefferson was the only one not eating popcorn *or* sitting down. Instead, he was standing off to the side, cradling Cleocatra in his arms, and glaring at the wolves.

"Jefferson," Kate said, drawing his attention to her. "This is my idiot brother, Mason." She waved a hand behind her.

Mason glared at Jefferson, who just glared back.

"Mason's sorry for overreacting," Kate said, sending an elbow into her brother's gut.

He grunted, then held out his hand to Jefferson.

After a brief hesitation, Jefferson reached out and accepted the handshake.

From the wince on Jefferson's face, Kate was pretty sure

Mason was trying to grind his bones into dust. "Knock it off, Mason." She slammed her elbow into his side again, then slid under Jefferson's arm to stand at his side and glare at her brother.

Mason scowled, but relented.

Jefferson reclaimed his hand and discreetly flexed it.

"You're coming to dinner Wednesday night," Mason said to Kate, "and you're bringing the panther with you."

Kate sighed. "Fine. Whatever. Just go. We have a business to run here."

Mason gave her a look that clearly expressed his disdain for that business, then turned and walked out.

"Nice fellow," Lyle said.

"Sorry, guys. I would have introduced you, but then you'd have been subjected to The Mason Handshake of Doom like Jefferson here and I thought I'd spare you that. At least for now."

"And we appreciate it," Pete said.

"Most definitely," Ryan agreed. "I'll be needing my hands later." He waggled his brows suggestively at Nick, who snorted in amusement.

"So." Jefferson turned to Kate, a huge grin on his face. "I hear that I'm your mate."

Eleven

W HEN BYGUL POPPED back into the garage after his class was over, he was dismayed to find complete and utter chaos waiting for him.

What had he said about Mondays again?

Oh, right.

They were an absolute nightmare.

First of all, he saw immediately that Cleo was in Jefferson's arms and he had no idea how that had happened.

He'd deliberately left her behind today!

The next thing he noticed was that Genghis Khat was stretched out in the middle of the floor, apparently taking a nap.

What kind of matchmaking cat was he?

The third thing he noticed was that Jefferson was standing with all the wolves and Kate was nowhere to be seen.

So, apparently G.K. was not only napping on the job, but not even doing the bare minimum to ensure the panther and the bear spent time together.

The fourth thing he noticed were the very loud roars coming from the office.

Okay, maybe that was the first thing he noticed, but it certainly wasn't the most important.

Although it did prove his point about Mondays: humans were less cooperative, more stubborn and far *crankier* those days of the week.

It was at that moment, Kate's voice roared out louder than every other sound in the place, including that of the other bear, "He's my mate!"

Dead silence followed.

Bygul happened to be staring at Jefferson right at that very moment, so he saw the look of pure joy that crossed the panther's face before he quickly schooled his features back into a neutral expression.

Perhaps G.K. hadn't abandoned the mission after all. In fact, if the smirk on his face was any indication, the cat was definitely taking credit for this turn of events.

Cleo, on the other hand, looked quite worried.

Bygul made his way over to her. "Don't worry, Cleo," he started to say, but then realized Jefferson was already taking care of it.

"No worries, my sweet little Cleocatra," Jefferson murmured into her ear. "She may be my mate, but you'll always be my precious baby girl."

Even with all the bearish arguing coming from the office, Bygul could hear Cleocatra's purring in response.

Perhaps this romance wasn't doomed after all.

Having finally admitted out loud that Jefferson could be her mate, Kate was thrilled when he told her his panther agreed.

Over the next several weeks, they spent all their free time together.

Now that they knew they were mates, they slowed the pace of their romance, getting to know each other and limiting their physical encounters to kisses and heavy petting.

They spent every evening together, sometimes double dating with Nick and Ryan, who had discovered to their mutual surprise, though no one else's, that they were mates.

They also had dinner at the Worcester family home, something Mason insisted happen every Wednesday and Sunday like clockwork.

The first dinner was awkward, to say the least, but after enduring dire threats from Kate, both men had been on their best behavior and so the night had ended with no bloodshed.

Each subsequent dinner was easier and though Kate doubted either man would ever admit it, she thought they were probably growing on each other.

Maybe in another ten years, they'd actually be friends.

When Maggie found out they were having dinner with Mason twice a week, she became extremely insulted on Jackson's behalf and insisted they join her and Jackson two other nights of the week.

Jackson was clearly stunned at this turn of events, as was Jefferson, who explained that Maggie wasn't one for entertaining or enduring people very long.

This, Kate witnessed firsthand, when Maggie just up and left the table mid-way through dinner one night and never returned.

At this point, Kate decided perhaps four nights out of

every seven having dinner with family was a bit absurd, so she suggested they invite everyone to Jefferson's house for dinner together instead. By doing it this way, they could cut those days in half and Maggie and Jackson could leave whenever they wanted and not have guests still in their house when Maggie was done socializing.

Jefferson was appalled at the suggestion. "But that means we have to cook!"

Kate rolled her eyes. "Fine. How about this? I make Mason host one night a week and we host the other."

He sighed. "Fine."

So that's what they ended up doing. Every Wednesday, Mason, Jackson, Maggie *and* Genghis Khat came to dinner at Jefferson's place and every Sunday, they all went to Mason's for dinner, *including* Cleocatra.

Everyone else thought bringing the cats into bear territory was a terrible idea, but Kate insisted. She felt it was the least Mason deserved.

The look on Mason's face was quite hilarious when they first arrived, but even funnier was what happened at The Worcester Group the following Monday.

Someone posted in every break room a large photograph of six-foot-eight Mason cuddling Cleocatra.

Kate had no idea how that picture had managed to make the rounds so quickly. She'd texted it to Nick and the next thing she knew, Mason was calling to roar at her for ruining his reputation as a ruthless bear.

Of course, that didn't stop Kate from bringing the cats back the following Sunday.

In fact, she was now contemplating giving Mason a kitten for Christmas, especially since he clearly adored Cleocatra, scooping her from Jefferson's arms the minute they arrived at his place on Sundays and making a beeline for her at Jefferson's place on Wednesday nights.

The most annoying part was that Cleocatra clearly loved Mason as much as he loved her, yet was still prone to crankiness around Kate.

Kate tried wooing her with cat treats and toys and endless petting. Of course, Cleocatra didn't allow the last to happen very often as the kitten had very good Kate radar and would swipe at Kate whenever she got too close.

Still, Kate kept trying and every once in a while, she managed to pet Cleocatra into a purring ball of joy before she realized what was happening.

Cleocatra always gave a little hiss when she finally realized who was petting her, but the hiss was only halfhearted at best, which Kate counted as progress.

All the while she was attempting to woo Cleocatra, Jefferson was wooing Kate. He took her on dates every evening after work and hiking in the woods every Saturday.

Jefferson was clearly much better at the wooing than Kate was, for he took her to every quirky food establishment he could find in the three-city area, making their dates not only fun, but exceptionally delicious.

Kate most heartily approved.

By the time they'd been dating a month, Kate had fallen so deeply in love with her mate, she knew they were meant to be.

This was one mating that would endure for all time.

Which meant, it was past time to let her bear out.

She decided the waterfall where they always ate lunch on their hikes would be the perfect location for their animals to meet.

So, the following Saturday, when they arrived at the waterfall, she stripped naked, stunning Jefferson silent, and dove into the water.

She came up in her grizzly form.

Jefferson let out a whoop of joy, stripped and dove into the water, shifting into his panther form on the fly.

The minute he hit the water, Kate's bear bellowed in triumphant recognition of their mate.

They spent hours in the water, splashing each other and playing, then more hours racing through the woods, chasing each other, each of them taking turns as predator and prey.

Eventually, Jefferson took to the trees and disappeared on her.

She tried to hunt him down, but he clearly backtracked and the next thing she knew, she had a panther on her back.

Even though her grizzly was quite a bit larger than his panther, he clearly didn't mind wrestling her in their shifted forms.

They rolled across the ground, panther and bear, until she eventually allowed him to pin her, then while pinned, shifted back.

She stared up into his panther eyes and watched as they shrank away until he too was in his human form.

She quickly rolled them so she was on top, then kissed him long and deep.

He surged to his feet, lifting her with him.

She wrapped her legs around his waist and held on as he walked them a few feet until her back was up against a tree and then they were kissing again.

Long, endless moments of heat and passion drove them until when they broke apart, they were both gasping for breath.

Staring at each other, he said, "Bed?"

"If we can make it," she said.

Laughing, holding hands, they ran through the woods.

Every once in a while, one of them dragged the other to a stop so they could kiss, caress and fondle before breaking away to run some more.

They reached his house and ran stark naked across the front lawn.

"I sure hope none of your neighbors are looking outside at the moment," Kate gasped, laughing as they stumbled in the front door.

He slammed the door closed, whirled her around and pushed her up against the door, kissing her senseless the entire time.

She surged forward, pushing him up against the opposite wall, still desperately kissing him.

He whirled them past the living room, stopping to press her against the wall opposite the kitchen, then she maneuvered him into the hall where she pressed him against the linen closet and slid a hand down to grope and fondle what she craved so badly.

And so they continued, ever so slowly making their way down the hall, kissing and fondling until they fell into his bedroom and landed on the floor.

They rolled across the floor, nipping and stroking, devouring each other.

She settled on top of him, lifted up and slowly sank down on his cock, taking him one glorious inch at a time.

He groaned and holding her hips, surged upward, thrusting deep.

She cried out in ecstasy and began to ride him.

That first time, they never did make it to the bed, but Kate had no complaints, especially since they did eventually make it there, where they spent the night indulging their passion.

After hours of endless lovemaking, Kate was lying, arm wrapped around Jefferson's torso, head pillowed on his shoulder, cherishing his softly murmured, "Sweet dreams, my love," when Cleocatra landed on her ass, claws fully extended.

Kate let out a grunt, then murmured into Jefferson's chest, "I love you, Jefferson mine. You too, demon kitty."

CLEOCATRA MADE SURE SHE DUG HER CLAWS IN A couple times, kneading the trespasser's skin thoroughly.

She'd never admit it, but she was pretty impressed the bear only grunted a little and didn't try to escape her claws.

When she was sure she'd gotten her point across, Cleocatra hopped from the interloper's butt to Jefferson's stomach, where she padded around, claws retracted—she would never deliberately hurt her Jefferson—until she found the perfect spot on his chest to settle down.

As soon as she was settled, one of his hands came up to stroke her back and scratch her head and chin.

She'd trained him well and now he truly was the best human companion ever.

She was sure, with time, she'd manage to train the bear too.

Of course, the bear was quite stupid so it would probably take her a lot longer to learn exactly how to serve Cleocatra, but no worries.

Jefferson would be around to show her how it was done and Cleocatra was a very good trainer indeed.

Cleocatra fell asleep, purring as she imagined the glory of having two human companions serving her well.

Unbearably Cute

Description

**Mason's fallen in love
with a kitten named Cleocatra.**

Too bad his new brother-in-law isn't willing to share her. Determined to adopt his own kittens, Mason visits an animal shelter and is stunned when the woman in charge insists that no bears need apply.

Rude!

Who does this woman think she is? Especially since Mason is pretty sure she's a bear herself. Even if she does keep denying it. Either way, those kittens are his and no woman is standing in his way, no matter how sexy she is.

The only way these two will ever make it to their happily ever after is if a matchmaking cat and an entire shelter full of kittens get involved.

One

BYGUL WAS THE top matchmaking cat at Pawsitively Purrfect Matches. That might seem a tad arrogant for him to claim, but since everyone else agreed with him, he was just being truthful and that was all.

Bygul had a number of earthbound cats assigned to him at the moment, all of them needing human companions. These were the matches PPM was known for and Bygul, like all the other working cats of PPM, specialized in these types of matches.

What set Bygul apart from the rest of them, though, was his additional specialization in love matches.

The goddesses hadn't exactly approved in the beginning. They considered love matches to be *their* domain, but when Bygul pointed out that a love match made by the cat of a goddess was really the same as a love match made by the goddess herself, they began to see the possibilities.

Unfortunately, those possibilities included having Bygul train fifty other matchmaking cats to make their own love matches on behalf of the goddesses.

This was when Bygul's purrfectly wonderful job acquired a few additional, not-so-purrfect responsibilities.

Being asked to train others might seem like a compliment at first, but Bygul knew the truth.

It was punishment!

He was being punished for his excellence, which was entirely unfair.

At first, there seemed to be no escaping his fate.

However, after weeks of trying to train unruly cats in the art of romance (and failing miserably), the unexpected happened.

It was a miracle really.

Slowly, one by one, the cats began to lose interest in learning how to make love matches and stopped showing up for classes.

This was excellent news as far as Bygul was concerned. In a matter of weeks, he'd gone from fifty trainees to only three.

Unfortunately, those final three were the most stubborn of the lot and they showed no signs of giving up anytime soon.

That was when he began plotting against them. With the nicest of intentions, of course. He was only trying to save them from a lifetime of failure and disappointment, after all.

Hopefully, the goddesses would notice if the cats made a disastrous match, or if they failed to make one at all, and would release all of them (but most especially Bygul) from this training nightmare.

To get started, all he needed was a suitably impossible matchmaking mission.

Happily, he had the perfect candidate in mind.

Grumpy, unruly, rude, loud, obnoxious, alpha bear shifter *Mason Worcester*.

The bear's personality was bad enough, but add in his

penchant for throwing other shifters through windows and doors and off rooftops and over the side of mountains and the results were clear.

Mason Worcester was (and Bygul did not use this word lightly) *unmatchable*.

Which made him the purrfect target.

"YOU WANT TO WHAT?" JEFFERSON EXCLAIMED incredulously.

"Well, you don't have to say it like that." Kate had no idea why her mate was so astonished. It was a perfectly brilliant idea.

"You're mad," Jefferson said, "and I won't be a party to it. It's cruel."

"It's a kitten, not a torture device."

"Exactly. A poor, defenseless kitten you're planning to feed to your psycho brother."

Rude! Kate let a minuscule roar escape and smirked when Jefferson leapt backwards, clearing the span of the office in one leap.

At the same time, her assistant, Nick, jumped, sending his chair flying out from under him and dumping him on the floor. He glared over his shoulder at Kate, but she didn't know why he was so upset.

It's not like he wasn't used to it by now.

If he didn't like it, he shouldn't sit down in the first place. He had a standing desk for a reason, after all.

Besides, that roar had been halfhearted at best. Why, the windows had barely rattled—she glanced through them to the garage below—and the mechanics hadn't even hit the deck this time.

"I tried to stop her, Cleocatra," Jefferson said mournfully.

Kate whirled and glared at him.

He was cradling his black kitten in his arms, stroking her fur and crooning to her in that way he had, the one that made Cleocatra believe she was the center of his world, something that also made her a holy terror when she felt someone else (usually Kate) was attempting to usurp her role as queen of his universe.

Which, to be honest, Kate did quite often, especially since the way he stroked Cleocatra made Kate imagine all sorts of naughty things involving him stroking her.

"I can't be held responsible for the tragedy to come, Cleo-catra," Jefferson said as he slowly stroked his hand down the kitten's back. "I've done my best and now we must all suffer for my failures."

Oh, for heaven's sake. She was surrounded by drama queens. "What are you going on about now?"

Jefferson ignored the question and continued his one-sided conversation with the kitten. "Just remember when the poor kitten gets eaten, or worse, tossed through a window—" he sent a scorching look her way "—it's all Kate's fault."

"My brother would *never*—"

"As someone he's thrown through a window—not once, but twice, mind you—I have to respectfully disagree. *He would.*"

"You were a stranger he'd never met before and you were kissing *me,* his baby sister. What did you expect?"

"Uh, for him to kindly wait until I stopped kissing you and then to introduce himself politely?"

Kate stared at him incredulously. "You do know my brother is an alpha bear, right?"

"So?"

Kate rolled her eyes.

"And while we're on the subject, what about the second time? So maybe he didn't know who I was the first time he launched me through the air, but that second time was pure maliciousness."

Kate turned away so her mate wouldn't see the smirk on her face. "Oh, stop being such a baby. The point is, yes, my brother might toss you around a bit every once in a while—"

"A *bit*?"

"—but he would never hurt a sweet kitten. He adores Cleocatra, you know that."

"I know he's trying to steal her from me," Jefferson growled, "but for what reason I have no idea. What would a psycho–bear want with a tiny kitten anyway? Nothing good, that's for sure."

"Oh, for heaven's sake. Melodramatic much?"

"All I'm saying is maybe you should consider a python or an alligator or — what am I saying? Your psycho brother's the top of every food chain, so really it's better if you choose an entirely different gift for him. No pets for the apex predator!"

Kate snickered. "It's not like I'm suggesting we give him Cleocatra."

The kitten, who was now perched on Jefferson's shoulder, turned her entire body so that she was facing Kate and bared her fangs.

Little monster!

Every time Kate thought she'd finally won the kitten over, Cleocatra went out of her way to prove that she only tolerated Kate and could, in fact, shred her to ribbons at any moment.

Kate lifted her lip, planning to unleash just one of her fangs when she caught sight of the amused look on Jefferson's face and scowled instead.

He should be defending his mate's honor instead of finding amusement in the antics of a tiny little beast who was constantly riling up her bear.

"Anyway," Kate growled, glaring at the two of them, "I'm going to the rescue organization and I'm choosing a kitten for my brother. Are you coming along or not?"

"Not," Jefferson said decisively, as he turned and strode toward the office door. "Even if I didn't have a garage full of repairs, I still would have nothing to do with this plan to feed a defenseless kitten to that psychotic bear."

"My brother isn't—"

The door slammed, cutting off her protest.

"Dude," Nick said. "You're brother's *so* psychotic."

Kate snickered. "Stop it. He is not."

"Okay, fine. He's out of control, overbearing, outrageously rude... come on, help me out here."

"I mean, all of that is true, but that doesn't make him psychotic."

"No, but throwing people off a cliff kind of does."

"He only ever did that once and it was totally justifiable. Assuming it even happened. I maintain the possibility of his innocence."

Nick raised an eyebrow.

"Besides, Dorian forgave him."

"Eventually. After he woke from that coma. How long did it take him again? A year?"

"Oh, don't exaggerate. It was only ten months."

"What were they fighting about again? Raisinets? Junior Mints?"

"Milk Duds. The last box. I mean, who could blame him? He was a hungry bear. Everyone knows you don't get between a bear and his food."

"But the food was *Dorian's*. And let's not forget that Dorian's a bear too."

"Sure, but Dorian wasn't the *alpha* bear."

"Neither was Mason. At least, not then."

"Are you insinuating that it wasn't obvious my brother was an alpha bear from the moment he let out his first roar?"

Nick made a face. "Okay, fine. Doesn't make it any less psychotic."

"He was five!"

Nick snickered. "And Dorian, how old was he again?"

"Sixteen!"

"Yeah. You do realize none of this is proving him any less psychotic. What kind of five-year old attacks a sixteen year old and wins?"

Kate let out a huff of exasperation. "Isn't it obvious? An alpha bear, of course."

Nick let out a snort.

"Besides, Mason's gained a lot of—okay, *some* control—since then. After all, he hasn't tossed anyone off a mountain since. Not even when they make him really mad."

"No, he just tosses them through windows and on one memorable occasion, from The Worcester Group's rooftop."

"That employee was embezzling funds. He's lucky Mason didn't kill him."

Nick nodded. "Yeah, I guess that is pretty indicative that he's gained *some* control. You shouldn't tell Jefferson that though."

Kate grinned. "Of course not. It's entirely too much fun torturing him. Especially after that second launching."

"You can tell me all about it on our way to the animal shelter."

"What do you mean I can't just adopt a kitten?" A woman's irate voice rang through the quiet of the shelter, breaking Isana's train of thought and making her lose track of the numbers she was currently crunching as she attempted to balance the shelter's accounts, a task she'd put off until the very last minute, like she always did.

"You have way more kittens than you need around here. Surely you can spare a few."

Isana rolled her eyes.

Great.

Yet another human convinced the entire animal kingdom had been set on this earth for their convenience.

Isana couldn't hear the volunteer's response, but she imagined it was apologetic, yet firm.

Not that it seemed to matter.

"Look, I filled out the application like you asked. Now I'd like to choose a kitten and get on with my day."

Isana heaved a sigh.

Clearly she wouldn't be finishing the accounts until this woman had either been satisfied or sent away.

Closing her laptop, Isana stood and walked out of her office and down a short hall into their reception area, where her volunteer Sarah was looking a bit agitated as she faced off with—

Isana dragged in a deep breath.

Oh, great.

Not a human after all.

"Can I help you?" Isana moved behind the counter and

nodded to Sarah, who looked terribly relieved as she scurried away.

As anyone would be, facing off against a grizzly.

Isana scowled at the woman. "Was it really necessary to intimidate poor Sarah? She's not a bear, you know."

The woman looked surprised. "I'm not intimidating." She whirled to face the wolf at her side. "Right, Nick?"

The wolf let out an odd choking sound, whirled and raced toward the outer door. He flung it open and disappeared outside.

He wasn't quite fast enough though, for the door hadn't quite closed when they heard his burst of hysterical laughter.

The woman rolled her eyes. "Wolves. So dramatic, am I right?"

She *was* right, but Isana wasn't sure she really wanted to bond with a grizzly, so she didn't reply.

"Right. Sorry. I'm Kate and I'm here to adopt a kitten for my brother. I've filled out the application." She shoved it across the counter toward Isana.

Isana picked up the paper, but didn't look at it. "I'm surprised your brother wants a cat and not a dog. I can recommend some dog rescues if he'd prefer that."

Kate looked confused. "Why would he want a dog?"

"Well, I just figured since he's a wolf—"

"Oh, goodness no. We're bears!"

"Oh, I'm terribly sorry. I thought he was a wolf." Isana waved a hand toward the front door, feeling a bit ashamed that she'd stereotyped the shifter based purely on scent, something she was always judging others for doing.

"Nick?" Kate snickered. "He's not my brother. He's my assistant and just came along to help pick out the kitten." She threw a scowl over her shoulder. "Lot of help he is right now, running away like that." She glanced back at Isana. "How can he help choose the perfect kitten for Mason if he isn't even in here to meet them?"

Isana shook her head. "I'm sorry. I'm not sure I understand. Is your brother here?"

"Oh, no. It's a surprise. For Christmas, you know."

Isana couldn't even express the horror she felt at the thought. "Absolutely not."

"Excuse me?"

"Do you have any idea how many cats and dogs and rabbits and other animals get adopted for birthdays and holidays and *surprises—*" Isana waved her arms in agitation, "only to be surrendered months later back to the same shelters they were adopted from, or even worse, are simply thrown outside and abandoned to the wild?" She glared at Kate. "Do you?"

"Well, no, but I assure you, Mason will be thrilled. He's fallen in love with my mate's kitten, you see, and well, Jefferson's rather attached to Cleocatra and isn't willing to give her away, so we're stuck with her, but Mason's awfully lonely, now that I'm not around as much and so I thought a kitten would be a lovely surprise for him."

"Kittens are not surprises!" Isana had no idea why people couldn't seem to grasp this very simple concept. "They're living beings and they need cared for every day for the rest of their lives. That isn't a surprise. That's a responsibility! It's a lifelong commitment. It's not to be taken lightly."

"Obviously, and I assure you, Mason would take the responsibility very seriously."

"He's a *bear*, isn't he?"

"What?"

"A *bear*. Clumsy, plodding, often completely out of control, irrational *bears.*"

Kate looked confused. "I'm sorry, but aren't *you* a bear?"

Isana jerked back in offense. "I most certainly am *not*!"

Kate raised an eyebrow, leaned across the counter toward Isana and inhaled deeply. "Well, you sure smell like a bear."

"I'm not a bear!"

"If you say so. Anyway, to get back to the point, I'd like to choose a kitten now."

"No kittens!" Isana bellowed.

"Well, that's quite rude. The other gal said you had many kittens."

"We do! We have kittens we'll happily adopt to people who are not giving them as *gifts* or *surprises*. We also have kittens for people who are not *bears!*"

"That seems rather harsh. I mean, I suppose I understand your anti-gift, anti-surprise stance. But your anti-bear attitude seems a bit much."

"What happens if your brother shifts into his bear form and then accidentally steps on the kitten?"

"Unlikely."

"Let me put it this way. What if he goes into a boar rage at someone who irritates him and accidentally stamps on the kitten while raging about?"

Kate seemed to think about that for a moment, then said, "He only goes into rages at work—people tend to annoy him there—so I'll just make The Worcester Group off-limits for cats."

Isana inhaled so quickly and deeply she went a bit lightheaded.

At that moment, Nick came slamming back through the front door. "Are we ready to choose some kittens yet?"

"No!" Isana stormed around the counter, planted her palms on the grizzly's chest and shoved. "Absolutely no gifts!"

She shoved again and this time, Kate actually moved. "No surprises!" Shove. "No bears!" Shove. "And absolutely, under no circumstances, will we ever allow Mason Worcester of The Worcester Group to adopt one of our precious kittens!" She shoved one last time and Kate skidded back into the front door.

"Um." Nick sent a wide-eyed look between Isana and Kate.

"Get out!" Isana yelled.

Kate sighed, gave her a sad look, then turned and walked out.

Nick hesitated, then said, though it sounded more like a question, "I'm sorry?" and followed her out.

Two

"T*HAT'S* THE TARGET?" Tivali demanded. She was pacing back and forth on the conference table —at the far end from the bear, of course.

"He *can't* be the target," Soraya wailed from where she was cowering under the conference table. She'd darted under there the second the bear had lost his temper.

"Bygul, please tell us you're joking," Muezza said.

"What's the matter with you guys?" Bygul asked. "You've been begging for weeks that I give you your own target to match and now that I have, you're complaining? I've been making matches like these all by myself for years. Surely you three can manage one measly love match."

"There's nothing measly about him," Soraya exclaimed. "He's absolutely ginormous."

"Not to mention terrifying," Tivali said. "I can't imagine a single cat ever falling in love with him, let alone an actual human being."

"This isn't right," Muezza said. "Admit it. You've saddled us with an unmatchable."

Bygul growled low in his throat. He couldn't believe Muezza had already figured it out! No matter though. Bygul was an expert at misdirection. "There's no such thing as an unmatchable," he informed them in a lofty tone. "There may be difficult matches, but that doesn't mean impossible ones. Sure, some matches might take a bit longer to complete, but who cares? All that means is those targets will cherish their match all the more for how long they had to wait for it."

"I had no idea you were so optimistic, Bygul," Tivali said.

"Not to mention romantic," Muezza muttered with a suspicious scowl. He clearly wasn't convinced.

"Seriously?" Bygul infused as much astonishment as he could into that one word. "I've outmatched every matchmaker in the system. I couldn't possibly have matched that many cats with their human companions and that many humans with their love matches if I weren't both optimistic *and* romantic."

"He's got a point," Soraya said.

"Of course, I do. Now get to work. Because everyone deserves a faithful cat companion *and* a true love match."

Mason was about two seconds away from a full-on boar rage.

He was surrounded by idiots and if there was one thing Mason abhorred over all else, it was stupidity.

"Get out!" He roared, slamming his fists down on the conference table.

Despite himself, he was once again impressed at the workmanship that kept the table from buckling beneath the force of his rage.

Mason's sister, Kate, liked to point out that the table wasn't just bear-proof or even grizzly-proof, but that it was Mason-Worcester-proof.

He missed Kate.

He hadn't realized how much she did to keep him sane throughout the work day until she moved her office to an entirely different town.

He blamed that damn cat, Jefferson Hewitt.

Mason was sure he could have convinced her to come back eventually, but then she'd found her mate and that was that.

Damn cat.

He was glaring at the table, contemplating going on a hunt when his phone buzzed.

All of his executives had fled the room when he roared at them, but he could still hunt them down.

He'd drag the wolves to the ground floor and toss them through the windows there.

The bears, though, those he'd drag to the roof.

Okay, no, not the roof.

That was reserved for thieves and true incompetence.

This time, he'd drag them to the seventh floor.

Or maybe the eighth.

But then his phone buzzed and it was almost like old times.

His sister, Kate, saving both the wolves *and* the bears from his wrath with a single text.

I need you to meet me at this address.

Mason stabbed his phone and scowled at the map that popped up, showing exactly where that address was.

What the hell? *That's not in Worcester Falls.*

No answer.

It's not in Greensboro either.

Still no answer.

Kate. Why am I meeting you in freaking Pleasantville? Mason avoided that town like the plague. Full of humans and —well—humans, they just didn't understand a bear's temperament. Or appetite.

He waited a moment, but when it became evident she wasn't going to answer, he let out a loud huff of exasperation and shoved away from the table.

He stormed out the door of the conference room and strode through the office, growling at anyone who even looked like they might approach him.

Within seconds, every shifter on the floor was somewhere else.

He let out a grunt of satisfaction.

It was good to be alpha bear.

Fifteen minutes later, he was leaving Worcester Falls, something that had been occurring with increasing regularity lately.

Ever since Kate mated that damn panther, Mason had found himself spending an inordinate amount of time in Greensboro, the shifter town to the west.

Though he'd never admit it to the panther, Mason actually liked the town, though it was no Worcester Falls, which despite the sheer number of wolves living there, was mostly still considered bear territory.

Today, though, Mason was not headed toward Greensboro, where Kate and the panther lived. Instead, he was headed east, straight into Pleasantville.

The only good thing Mason could say about this development was that at least he didn't live there and could escape any time he wanted.

When he first pulled into the parking lot, he was sure he

had the wrong address, but a quick check showed he was in the right place.

Mason climbed out of his truck, slammed the door behind him and stared at the monstrosity in front of him.

The building looked as if it had been built in stages, with different sections added on over the years. Nothing really matched anything else.

The left side of the building was short and squat and had a flat roof. It was also painted purple.

The right side of the building towered over the left and center sections. It was completely circular in shape and had an actual dome for a roof. It would have reminded Mason of a castle tower except for one thing. The entire section, *including the dome,* was painted a brilliant orange.

Between those two sections stood a third section that by itself might have been considered normal. The front wall projected forward beyond the other two sections and was painted a soft cream color. It also boasted a large entrance with a number of windows that looked out onto the parking lot.

Mason imagined this section had been built to try to mesh together the other two, but instead served as a dividing line between bizarre and more bizarre.

"Humans," Mason muttered. You really just couldn't understand them at all.

"Finally!"

Mason grinned at Kate as she stormed across the parking lot toward him.

"It took you long enough."

Mason slung an arm around her and dragged her close for a quick hug.

The moment she started to pull away, he tightened his arms, transforming their casual hug into a full-on bear one.

Kate, of course, immediately began flailing her arms about and struggling to get loose.

Ignoring her struggles, Mason rocked her from side to side and hollered, "Aw, my wee baby sister, how I've missed you so. It's been ages since you last graced me with your presence."

"You idiot," Kate growled, even as she tried desperately, yet futilely, to escape his embrace. "We had dinner two nights ago. Let me loose, you neanderthal!"

Snickers caught Mason's attention and he glanced up to see Nick was standing just a few feet away, grinning like a loon.

"Ah, Nick, good to see you too!" Mason cried out jovially as he moved across the parking lot, dragging his sister with him, maneuvering her just enough so that her face was now smushed into his armpit. He held out his hand and Nick grasped it in his, shaking it with a grin.

"Mason!" Kate howled as she slammed a fist into his gut.

He let out a grunt of both pain and pride—after all, he was the one who'd taught her that move.

"All right, all right, sister mine." He let her loose and grinned as she staggered away, coughing and waving her arms about.

"Grizzly musk," she groaned. "I've been asphyxiated by my own brother's stench."

"Oh, please," Mason said. "If that were the case, you wouldn't be able to talk."

"That'd be the day," Nick said.

"You know, she's always been terribly melodramatic," Mason confided. "Ever since she was a wee little girl."

Nick snickered while Kate just rolled her eyes.

"Now, tell me what we're doing *here*, in front of this odd-looking building, Kate." Mason faced the front entrance and for the first time, noticed the sign. "A cat rescue?" He whirled toward Kate. "Do you need help dragging the panther inside?"

Nick let out a hoot of laughter.

Kate grinned. "Not those kinds of cats. Domesticated ones. Cats and Kittens. Like Cleocatra."

"Hold on a minute. Are you planning to adopt another kitten? Don't you think Cleo might get a bit—"

"Psycho if we bring another cat into the house?" Kate asked dryly. "Yeah, she barely tolerates me as it is. We're here to adopt a kitten for you."

"For me?" Mason was stunned. He'd been so focused on trying to convince Jefferson to let him borrow Cleocatra, it hadn't even occurred to him that he could just get his own kitten. One who would adore him and follow him everywhere and ignore that pesky panther whenever he came around. "This is a great idea!"

"Yeah, well, don't get too excited," Kate said. "We've run into a bit of an issue."

"What kind of issue? Are they all out of kittens?"

"Thankfully, no. However, I made the mistake of mentioning this was going to be your Christmas present to the woman in charge of approving applications and apparently she's a tiny bit anti-gifts."

"Not to mention anti-bear," Nick muttered.

"Who could possibly hate gifts? That doesn't even make sense," Mason said. "This woman must be—wait. Did you say anti-bear?"

Kate grimaced. "Yeah, she's not our biggest fan so now she's holding all the kittens hostage."

"That's just rude!"

"Tell me about it," Kate said. "So we're counting on you to change her mind."

"She is anyway," Nick said. "I'm just along for the ride. And the entertainment value."

"She really said no just because we're bears?"

"Yep," Kate said.

"Unbelievable." The absolute gall of the woman.

Who did she think she was, trying to keep him from adopting his very own sweet, baby kitten?

Why, he could buy this entire building right out from under her, and all the kittens with it, if he wanted.

Not that he had any desire to own such a monstrosity, but just the fact that he could do it should be enough to drag her in line. And if it wasn't, well—

"Let's go. I'm about to steal me some kittens."

ISANA HAD JUST GOTTEN BACK INTO HER PAPERWORK when she heard Sarah let out a high-pitched squeak followed by a man speaking in an extraordinarily loud, booming voice.

"I'm here to adopt some kittens. Where do you keep them? Here?"

"Oh, no, you can't—"

"No? How about down here?"

"Wait, you—"

"Still no? Oh, I've got it. Through here, is it? Perfect. Come along, Kate."

"Wait!"

Isana had already been heading to the reception area from the moment she heard his voice, but when she heard him say the name, Kate, she broke into a run.

She skidded into the reception area just in time to see the

back of a very large man disappear through the door that led to their veterinary clinic.

"I tried to stop him, Isana," Sarah cried. "But he was determined."

"It's all right, Sarah." Isana glared at Kate, who had opted not to follow the man Isana assumed was her brother, and was instead leaning against their reception counter, grinning. "I know exactly who's to blame." She transferred her glare to the wolf, who was chuckling at Kate's side.

He sobered under her glare. "Hey, don't look at me. I'm too smart to get between a grizzly and his objective, whatever that might be."

"Great." The only reason Isana wasn't chasing after the idiotic bear was because there were no cats in the clinic at the moment. "I suppose your brother's lumbering around the clinic, searching for invisible kittens."

"Oh." Kate looked disappointed. "We thought that was where your cat rooms were." She narrowed her eyes at Sarah. "Did you deliberately look toward that door, just to mislead us?"

A quick glance toward Sarah told Isana that yes, she'd done exactly that. "I'm very impressed, Sarah. Good job."

Sarah sent her a shy smile, one that disappeared when they heard the sound of footsteps approaching.

Loud footsteps. Almost like a stampede really.

Sarah edged away from the door leading into the clinic as the sound of barking reached their ears.

Tarnation! She'd forgotten about the dogs. They didn't usually have dogs at the cat rescue, but a rescue two towns over had desperately needed the space, so Isana had offered up the kennels at the back of the clinic.

The dog rescue sent people over to care for the dogs and

some of her volunteers had chipped in as well, but Isana herself hadn't really had any interactions with the dogs. Mostly because dogs didn't really like her.

At all.

So she'd forgotten all about them.

Until now.

When a man came bursting through the door from the clinic, a wild look on his face. "Lion!" He whirled around to face the door he'd just come out of. "Killer lion!" The last word ended in a shriek when a huge furry creature barreled into him and knocked him to the floor.

Isana wasn't certain which rescue was currently sitting on Mason Worcester's chest and attempting to lick him to death, but she did know it wasn't a lion.

"Get it off me! Get it off me!"

Isana rolled her eyes. From the amount of shrieking and flailing, you'd think it really was a lion on his chest.

Isana waited for the bear's sister or for the wolf to help him, but neither seemed inclined at all.

In fact, they were entirely too busy rolling on the floor, laughing hysterically to be bothered with Mason Worcester's panic.

Isana raised an eyebrow at Sarah, but she simply shook her head and stepped back.

Great. No help there.

"For goodness' sake!" Isana exclaimed. "Are you a bear or a bunny rabbit?"

Nick and Kate, who were finally showing signs of sobering up, lost it again. Hanging onto each other, they laughed and laughed.

Rolling her eyes, Isana stalked over to the bear and stood over him, hands on hips, glaring.

He'd stopped shrieking and was now simply lying there, submissive to the giant, shaggy *thing* lying on top of him.

Isana circled around to try and find the thing's head. Ah. There it was. Shaggy fur spilled into its eyes, but that didn't seem to stop it from being able to see as it happily licked every inch of the bear's skin that it could reach.

"I'm not sure if you're aware, Mason Worcester," Isana said. "But *that* is not a lion."

The bear lifted his arm a little to peek out at Isana. "Are you sure?"

"Most definitely. In fact, it's not a cat at all."

Fresh giggling came from where Kate and Nick stood.

"Well, what is it then?" The bear demanded.

Isana grinned. "It's a dog."

And that set the rest of them off again.

From there it took some time to sort things out, getting the dog off the bear, tracking down how the dog had gotten out in the first place (it was the bear's fault, he'd opened the dog's kennel, hoping to find some kittens) and getting the dog back where it belonged.

"I'm adopting that dog," Kate announced.

"Don't be ridiculous!" Mason snapped. "Cleocatra would have a fit. And that dog's a menace."

"Oh, I'm not adopting it for *me*. I'm giving it to Maggie for Christmas."

Isana whirled around and glared at Kate. "Have you learned nothing? What did I say about animals for gifts?"

"But Maggie would adore him and I know it sounds kind of crazy, but I think Genghis Khat and that dog are a match made in heaven."

Mason rolled his eyes. "Forget about the dog. Where are my kittens?"

"There are no kittens available for adoption by bears," Isana said firmly.

"Well, why not?" Mason demanded. "You're a bear!"

"*I am not a bear!*" Isana shrieked. "Now get out!"

"But what about the dog?" Kate asked. "I want to adopt the dog."

"Out!"

Three

"THAT DIDN'T GO well at all," Soraya said, staring at the door through which Kate, Mason and Nick had just been ejected. "Are you sure we can't just pick a kitten from one of our case loads?"

"I told you. I've done my research," Tivali said. "The bear never leaves Worcester Falls. He works, he eats, he goes home, he works some more. He may be the CEO of The Worcester Group, but he's the biggest homebody I've ever seen. If someone has to travel, Kate does it, or one of the other executives."

"What's your point?" Muezza asked.

"My point is the bear's never met his mate, which probably means she doesn't live *or* work in Worcester Falls."

"Oooh, and now he's at the cat rescue in Pleasantville," Soraya said excitedly.

"Exactly." Tivali gave her tail a tiny, yet triumphant swish. "If we had just given him one of our kittens, he'd be back in Worcester Falls right now and not interacting with the two mate candidates we found for him."

"What candidates?" Muezza and Soraya chorused.

"Weren't you paying attention? The two women, Isana and Sarah. They're both definite possibilities."

"Sarah was terrified of the bear and Isana hated him," Muezza pointed out.

"Minor details," Tivali said.

"THAT DIDN'T GO WELL AT ALL," KATE SAID AFTER Isana firmly ejected them from the cat rescue.

"What kind of animal do you think she is?" Mason asked.

"She's a dog, dude," Nick said. "I thought we already established that."

"That doesn't make any sense. She smells like a bear."

"Wait. Who are we talking about?" Kate asked.

"The woman." Mason had been speechless the first time he'd seen her standing above him. Her hair was the purest shade of white he'd ever seen and her bright, green eyes had mesmerized him. Then there was the mystery of her animal. So intriguing.

"What about her?" Kate asked.

"She smells like a bear, but says she isn't one. How can that be? What kind of animal smells like a bear, but isn't a bear?"

Kate shook her head. "I have no idea and I really don't care. We need a plan of action."

"What kind of plan?" Nick asked.

"A plan to adopt a dog."

"But I don't want a dog," Mason said. "I want a kitten."

"Okay, fine. We need a plan to adopt a dog *and* a kitten."

"I don't want just *any* kitten. I need to meet them to make sure they won't be scared of my bear."

Nick snickered. "Dude, you went belly up for a dog. I'm pretty sure no self-respecting kitten will ever fear you again."

Mason lunged for Nick, who let out a high-pitched squeal and backpedalled fiercely. "It was just a joke. Calm down!"

Mason bared his fangs at the wolf. "Yeah, that's what I thought."

"We need to get back to the garage, Nick. We've got some planning to do."

"Yeah, you guys go on ahead. I'm going to hang out a while longer, see if I can charm the bear-not-bear into letting me meet a kitten or two."

Kate rolled her eyes. "Right. Well, good luck with that." As she and Nick walked away, she muttered to him, "We're doomed."

"I heard that!" Mason shouted after them.

Kate just laughed, climbed into her car, waited for Nick to get settled, then drove out of the lot with a tap of the horn.

Finally.

Mason turned and studied the building.

He'd already checked out the rectangular section.

It didn't have much to see.

Offices and some medical rooms, plus some storage spaces and some kennels at the back that had been unexpectedly filled with dogs.

Which made no sense at all since the building was labeled "Cat Rescue."

Of course, he'd assumed the giant, golden beast was a lion. It had more fur than any creature he'd ever seen, except for maybe Bigfoot, and had lunged at him like a predator going after its next meal.

Of course, he'd run away. What rational human being wouldn't run when faced with a hungry predator?

Okay, sure, Mason was a predator too, but his bear had apparently been sleeping on the job when the lion-not-lion broke free, which now that he thought about it, was probably a big freaking clue that the lion was a fake.

Mason scowled. That lion-not-lion had completely freaked him out. *Him. A bear.* He was so ashamed.

Not ashamed enough to give up though.

He studied the building some more.

The clinic was on the left and that was definitely a cat-free zone. The reception area was in the middle and he hadn't seen any cats in there either. So that left the circular tower-like segment to the right.

Excellent.

This time he wasn't going to bother with doors.

Isana gave up on the paperwork when it became clear she wasn't going to be able to concentrate.

All she could think about was that damn bear.

That huge, growly, demanding, sexy bear.

His scent had wrapped around her when she'd leaned over to drag the dog away and it had taken all of her control to restrain her fox.

Now the vixen was sulking because Isana had kicked out a potential mate, to which Isana reacted with nothing short of horror.

The gods couldn't possibly be so harsh and cruel as to send yet another bear into Isana's life, now could they?

Based on the vixen's state of mind, Isana was afraid they most definitely could.

With a soft growl of annoyance, she shut down her laptop and packed up.

Sarah had left about thirty minutes before, having completed one final round to make sure all the animals were safe and happy for the night.

Though Isana knew she could trust Sarah's report that all was well, she also never locked up without saying goodbye to each of their rescues one final time.

Though not the dogs, of course.

Visiting them would only rile them up.

She'd just set her bag down on the counter in the reception area when a crash from the cat side of the rescue made her jump.

She lunged across the reception area and flung open the door that led to the cats' quarters.

She loved this area of the rescue center the most.

Because of the cats, of course, but also because it was a truly unique bit of architectural genius.

The lower level of the tower was a giant playroom for cats, with an actual real tree growing at its center.

Around the perimeter of the room was a circular walkway that twined around and around leading higher and higher to the dome at the top. All along the walkway were cat kennels. Each individual kennel could be closed off if that cat needed to be quarantined, but could also be opened so that the cat had free range of several kennels, of an entire floor of kennels or even of the entire complex.

It was truly genius.

But what caught Isana's attention this time wasn't the brilliance of the architecture or even the kennel system that had been built to resemble a fox's intricate den of tunnels.

Instead, it was the giant bear sitting in the middle of the floor, legs forming a triangle that three of her favorite kittens were leaping in and out of.

"Seriously?"

Mason sent her a huge grin. "They're adorable. I think I'm in love."

The tiny colorpoint climbed onto his ankle and started attacking one of his shoelaces.

The two ginger kittens jumped into the bowl his legs had formed and rolled around, wrestling each other.

"How did you get in?"

He shrugged and kept his attention on the kittens, lifting one of the gingers up to his face so he could nuzzle its nose before setting him down and picking up his brother. "I've decided I'm going to adopt all three of them."

Isana's heart clutched. This was the hope for every bonded set of kittens and cats she accepted into the rescue, that they might be adopted together, so that their bond was never broken.

But to a bear? And not just any bear, but a grizzly. And not just any grizzly, but a *Worcester* grizzly. And for that matter, not just any Worcester grizzly, but the *alpha* himself.

It was enough to make her lightheaded.

"There's a process for adoption. You can't just come and decide you're taking three of our kittens and walk out the door with them."

"I don't see why not."

"Because we have to make sure you're the right fit, that the kittens will bond with you, that you have the right setup at your house, that they'll be safe and loved and happy there."

Mason slowly raised his head and stared at her. "I have

more money than I could spend in thirteen lifetimes. If there's something missing at my house that they need, I'll get it. As for bonding—" He looked back down.

The colorpoint had given up on the laces and was now sleeping on his ankle, her four legs wrapped around him securely. The two gingers had stopped wrestling and were now curled up in the curve of one of his knees, also sleeping. The sound of their purring filled the space between Isana and Mason.

Isana rolled her eyes. "There's more to being a pet owner than a few moments of play time."

Mason scowled. "Like what?"

"Like cleaning their litter boxes, feeding them, taking them to the vet for their shots and when they're sick—"

"That's what I have employees for."

"And what if The Worcester Group goes bankrupt tomorrow?"

Mason let out a scoffing sound. "*My* Worcester Group?"

"The point is life is unpredictable and if you're not fully prepared for everything taking care of these kittens entails, you're not getting them."

Mason let out a loud sigh of exasperation. "Fine. What do I need to do to prove I'm worthy of these kittens?"

Isana thought that question right there went a long way toward proving it, not that she'd ever admit it, and she was charmed in spite of herself. Still, she wasn't one to turn down a brilliant opportunity like this one.

MASON HAD NO IDEA HOW HE'D MANAGED TO GET himself into this situation. All he'd wanted was to adopt one tiny kitten—okay, three tiny kittens—but it shouldn't be that difficult.

Fill out some adoption paperwork, pay the damn fee, leave with the kittens.

But that is not what happened.

He was beginning to think this Isana woman was the devil herself.

Surely only the Dark One could convince him, Mason Worcester, alpha bear of the grizzly Worcesters and CEO of The Worcester Group, to *volunteer* for a cat rescue.

Even worse than volunteering were the tasks involved.

If it was just playing with kittens and cats, he'd have no problem at all with volunteering. He might even make it a permanent gig.

But no. That was *not* all that was involved.

There were the sick kitties who needed medicine, which was a bit like attempting to control the wind.

There was one cat in particular, a huge monster named Reaper (a more appropriate name Mason couldn't imagine) who wielded his claws much like Mason imagined the Grim Reaper did his scythe.

Unfortunately, Reaper was not a cooperative cat when it came time to give him his medicine, which came in liquid form.

"It's the easiest method of getting medicine down his throat," Isana informed Mason.

He firmly believed she was feeding him a line with that one because there was nothing easy about this shit.

He had Reaper wrapped in a towel, syringe ready to pour the medicine down his throat, and then everything went to hell.

His first attempt ended with a giant scratch across his nose and cheek and don't ask him how the demon cat managed to get his paws free while wrapped in a towel. Clearly, Reaper had ninja powers.

After chasing the cat around the damn room and finally getting him wrapped in the towel again, his second attempt ended with a bunch of medicine coating Reaper's fur instead of in his mouth. Damn cat moved his head at the last minute and all that medicine went to waste.

By the time Mason had caught the cat again and successfully delivered the medicine, he was exhausted.

The cat, on the other hand, was full of energetic fury.

Reaper stalked away and proceeded to ignore Mason for the next hour.

This shouldn't bother Mason as he had many other things to do in that hour, like clean out disgusting litter boxes (how had he gotten into this situation again?) but somehow in the battle between cat and bear, Mason had decided he actually liked Reaper.

Maybe he'd adopt him too. The cat could be a big brother to the kittens, help Mason watch out for them.

When he mentioned this to Isana, she looked horrified. "I'm sorry, now you want to adopt Reaper too? You do know Reaper's a crotchety old man who will probably make you miserable for the rest of his natural life."

Mason shrugged. "That's kind of why I like him."

"Hmmm."

By the time Mason was done cleaning kennels and litter boxes and had fed all the cats (forty-three in all!) he was completely done in.

This job was more exhausting than heading a multi-billion dollar real estate corporation, which was saying an awful lot.

Mason trudged out of the cat wing into the reception area, where Sarah was shutting things down for the evening.

"All finished?" She asked cheerfully.

Mason let out a grunt. "Where's Isana?"

"I'm right here," Isana walked into the room from a hallway at the back of the building. "Sarah, everything good on the dog side?"

"Yes, the volunteers from the dog rescue just left. They also gave us a stack of their applications, said they trusted us to process them if anyone wanted a dog. They've got their hands full what with taking in all those dogs from the fighting rings and that hoarder's house."

Isana groaned. "Fine. No one's going to come here for a dog though. I mean, it clearly says Cat Rescue on the door."

"You never know. I pass out dog rescue information all the time. This way we can actually show them some available dogs."

"I suppose." Isana sighed. "But we've got forty-three cats we need to find homes for. Forty-three! I'll never understand why people don't just get their animals fixed."

"Well, good news," Mason said heartily. "You'll only have thirty-nine once I'm out of here." He rubbed his hands together. "Now, what do you need me to fill out so that I can take my wee cats home?"

"He really thought that was going to work," Soraya observed.

"For supposedly running an entire corporation, the man isn't that smart," Tivali said.

"Yeah," Muezza agreed. "Even I knew one afternoon of volunteering wasn't going to convince Isana of anything."

Tivali winced as Mason stormed out of the rescue center, waving his arms and shouting about devil women. "He's never going to win a mate with that kind of attitude."

Mason paced in the parking lot a few moments, then turned and stormed back toward the building.

He flung open the door and shouted inside, "I'll be back tomorrow after work. I'm not giving up! Those cats are mine." He stormed away.

"Oh, that'll convince her," Muezza said.

"That man is hopeless," Soraya said.

"I'm telling you, Bygul saddled us with an unmatchable," Muezza said.

"Loosening Reaper's towel should have worked," Soraya said. "I can't understand why it didn't."

"Probably because it required someone with more empathy than Isana Meier," Tivali said.

"Or someone who hasn't been scratched as often as she has," Muezza said.

"True," Soraya said. "I guess when you're used to being scratched on a regular basis, you probably don't have much sympathy for someone who gets scratched just the once."

"Especially when that someone is a man-baby who's wailing and whining," Tivali said.

"It was pretty funny though," Soraya said.

"Personally, I enjoyed watching the bear chase Reaper all around the room," Muezza said. "It's always fun to see earthbound cats showing humans who the boss really is."

"Yeah, that was hilarious," Soraya said.

"Funny or not, I have no idea how we're going to match

that man with anyone," Tivali said. "He can't even convince a woman who works in cat rescue, who's overrun with cats needing homes, to let him adopt some kittens. The man has more money than most of the gods and she won't even let him have a cranky, old cat. This mission is doomed."

Four

"I'VE COME UP with a plan," Kate announced when Nick walked into their offices the next morning.

"Oh, great. This should be good."

"Isana already knows you, but she hasn't met Ryan, Pete or Lyle. So we'll have one of them go in and try to adopt the dog. Then we'll give it to Maggie for Christmas."

"Dude, maybe you should rethink this whole idea. What if Maggie doesn't want a dog? What if she's allergic? What if the cat decides to fight the dog?"

"Oh, I'm sure Genghis Khat will fight the dog. It'll be all kinds of entertaining, just like when he took Jackson for a ride."

Nick snickered. "That *was* hilarious."

"I think we should send Ryan first."

"If Ryan comes back with a cat, I'll never forgive you."

"Why would he come back with a cat? We're sending him after the dog!"

RYAN WASN'T SURE HOW HE'D BEEN ROPED INTO THIS situation. All he'd done was show up for work as usual and the next thing he knew, his boss's mate was sending him on a very important mission.

At least he'd managed to convince her to let him finish the car he'd been working on. Otherwise, they would have gotten even more backed up than usual.

As it was, Jefferson had been annoyed with Kate for pulling Ryan from the shop early to go on this ridiculous quest.

She'd given him a highly specific description of a dog and orders not to leave the rescue center without him.

The only good news about this mission was that the cat rescue was located in the middle of Pleasantville, a human town, thus reducing the likelihood that anyone from his pack would see him entering the place.

Dragging in a deep breath for courage, he made his way inside.

Two women stood behind the counter, talking with a woman. There was a young boy at the woman's side who turned and stared at Ryan when he walked in.

Ryan stared back.

Long minutes later, it occurred to him that he was in a stare down match with a kid who couldn't be more than ten years old.

Still, the wolf inside wasn't going to let him look away first. This kid was going down.

Just when Ryan was convinced he might end up spending the entire day there, the kid bared his teeth and made a fierce face.

It would have been more impressive if the kid had fangs.

Sadly, it appeared he was hampered by his humanity.

Ryan lifted his top lip and bared a single fang.

The boy's eye got huge and he jerked back. He slid to the other side of his mother, then peeked out at Ryan again.

Ryan grinned at him.

The boy sent him a tiny smile, then looked away.

A few moments later, the woman walked out of the center her boy trailing behind, throwing glances over his shoulder at Ryan all the way.

"You do realize they were human, right?" At first glance, Ryan had assumed the speaker was older than she was based on her white hair, but now he realized she was probably in her mid-thirties at most.

Interesting.

"I'm here about a dog," Ryan said, ignoring her question about the humans.

Both women looked surprised.

"But we're a *cat* rescue."

"Sarah." The other woman put a hand on her shoulder. "Did Underdog Rescue send you? Just because we agreed to house a few of their dogs doesn't mean we have the time to handle their adoptions for them."

"Isana, I said it was no problem."

"Fine. Fine. But they'd better start sending some cat people our way."

"Come along. I'll show you where the dogs are."

Ryan followed Sarah through a door into another reception area, this one empty. The silence was broken by the faint sound of dogs barking.

"This used to be a veterinary clinic that also offered boarding for dogs before we bought it." Sarah explained as she led him past a number of examination rooms, the sound of barking growing louder with every step. "We have a couple volunteers who come in and use the clinic to administer vaccinations and to spay and neuter our cats, but the kennels at the back of the clinic go unused." She pushed through a swinging door that led to a giant room with kennels lining the walls. "I was kind of glad Underdog Rescue asked us for help. The kennels have doggy doors that lead outside into a run. It's good to see all of this space being used again."

All of the kennels appeared to be empty, though the sound of barking continued.

'The dogs must all be outside." Sarah walked across the room and pushed open a steel door. She used her foot to shove a rock against the door to hold it open. "Come on. You can meet the dogs."

Ryan's attention had already been caught though.

One of the kennels wasn't empty after all.

Inside a large dog was lying, head on his paws, eyes on Ryan. He was pitch black and had the saddest of eyes.

"Well, hello, there, buddy, what's up with you?"

Sarah came back inside. "That's Cujo. I don't know why anyone would name him that because he's the sweetest dog of the lot. He's just sad because his owner died and no one in the family could take him."

Mason decided there had to be some benefits to being in charge. He had his assistant cancel his final meetings of the day and escaped the office in favor of the cat rescue center.

He wasn't sure why he couldn't stop thinking about the bear-not-bear, but when he wasn't thinking about the kittens, he was picturing all that white hair and remembering the bear-not-bear's scent.

The mystery of it was driving him mad!

He'd hinted repeatedly throughout his afternoon of volunteering, trying to figure out what animal smelled like a bear, but wasn't, but she'd refused to share. In fact, for the most part, she'd ignored him.

Including when Reaper had tried to scrape off his face.

He couldn't believe how mean she was!

He kind of liked it.

When he arrived at the center and found Isana standing at the reception counter, he was thrilled.

Sarah was nowhere in sight.

Even better.

"Did you miss me?"

She jumped and glared at him. "Like an itchy rash. What are you doing here?"

"I told you I'd be back. I'm here to adopt my kittens. I also brought some Bear Necessities, just in case. This countertop should do nicely." With that, he began unpacking the box he'd brought with him.

Box of donuts.

Platter of cookies.

Homemade breads.

Giant platter of fish lasagna.

Crockpot full of—

"What on earth is all of this?" Isana exclaimed.

Before he could explain, the door to the clinic opened and Ryan, of all people, came through it, leading a dog on a leash.

"What are you doing here?" Mason demanded.

"Are those Bear Necessities?" Ryan made a beeline for the countertop and grabbed a handful of cookies. "You and Kate are the best people I know." His words were mangled a bit due to his mouthful of crumbs, but Mason still understood him.

"Ryan's adopting Cujo," Sarah told Isana. "Here's his application paperwork and his credit card."

Isana stared at Ryan who was busy scooping lasagna onto a plate, then at Mason who was trying to decide whether he wanted to start off with some bread or with some cookies—maybe he should just go with both—then back to Ryan, who was now gagging and spitting out Mason's delicious fish lasagna—*wolves*. They had no taste whatsoever.

"You two *know* each other?" Isana demanded.

"Well, yeah, he works for my brother-in-law," Mason said.

"As in the mate of your sister, Kate?" Isana demanded. "This is unacceptable. You tell that Kate Worcester that she doesn't get to send her stooges in here to adopt pets on her behalf."

"Hey, I resent that. I'm not a stooge and I happen to be adopting Cujo on my own behalf." Ryan dumped his plate of rejected lasagna into a trash bin and grabbed a new plate that he started piling high with cookies and breads.

Damn wolf.

If Mason had known he'd be there, he would have packed more necessities.

"Right. And I suppose you didn't come here planning to adopt a different dog?"

"No idea what you're talking about."

The wolf was a terrible liar. Mason had a feeling even Isana could tell he was full of shit.

"Fine," Isana said, "but we're not a dog charity. We're a cat rescue. Therefore, if you want to adopt *that* dog, you have to take a cat with him."

"What?" Mason and Ryan roared at the same time.

"I don't need a cat. I don't want a cat," Ryan whined.

"*I* want a cat," Mason snapped. "In fact, I want four. How come you're letting *him* adopt a cat and not me?"

"Sarah, take Cujo back to his kennel."

"No!" Ryan exclaimed. "He wants to come with me."

"Then I guess you'd better go choose a cat," Isana said.

Ryan glared at her.

"Look I've got forty-two cats needing a home. The least you could do is check them out."

"Did you lose one?" Mason exclaimed. "You had forty-three yesterday."

"A mother and her son adopted one a little over an hour ago," Sarah said.

"She'd better not have stolen one of my kittens," Mason said. "Or Reaper. She didn't take Reaper, did she?"

Sarah and Isana stared at him incredulously.

"Only a bear would want that cat," Sarah muttered.

"The kittens and Reaper are still here," Isana said, "along with thirty-eight other cats, so let's get on with it, shall we?"

"Fine," Ryan grumbled. "Introduce us to the cats, but first —" He grabbed another handful of cookies that he added to the pile on his plate.

Isana rolled her eyes. "What's with all the food anyway?"

"It's Wolf Down Wednesday," Mason and Ryan chorused together.

"I almost starved yesterday," Mason said. "By the time I got home last night, my stomach was busy eating itself. Today I came prepared."

"Whatever."

"Come on, Ryan," Sarah said. "I'll introduce you to some of the cats." She headed for the cat tower and the rest of them followed.

The minute the door closed behind them, Mason made a beeline up the ramp to the left until he reached the section of kennels where he'd found the kittens the day before.

Only today the kennels were empty.

Before he could start roaring his rage, Isana called up to him, "They're in the playroom."

Now why couldn't she have told him that before he came bolting up here?

Since he was already halfway there, he figured he might as well check on Reaper before heading back down.

"Oh, man, you do not look happy," Mason informed Reaper when he finally arrived at his set of kennels.

Apparently Reaper was so territorial, he'd been given five kennels on his level, plus the five above his level and the five below it, which meant he had quite a bit of territory to lounge in. And still he growled the minute he saw Mason. "Hey, don't blame me. I'm not the one who locked you inside this luxurious kennel-palace. Nor am I the one who insisted you needed medicine. I was just drafted to do the dirty deed."

Reaper let out a yowl of annoyance.

"Fine. You can come with me if you behave." Mason waited, but the cat didn't reply. "Does that non-reply mean you *will* behave or that you're just waiting for me to open this cage door and then you'll be turning into a grimmer version of yourself, which is kind of hard to imagine, but still. You gonna behave?"

No reply.

Hmm. "I guess we'll see." Mason unhooked the cage door and slowly swung it open.

Reaper just glared at him balefully.

"Well, come on. We're going to go play with some kittens. Doesn't that sound like fun?"

Reaper stood and stretched, then sauntered nonchalantly toward the cage door.

Mason reached in and scratched him on the head.

Reaper let out a tiny grumble and nudged his hand for more pets.

Mason took that as permission to move forward with his plan and he carefully lifted Reaper out of his cage.

Mason held the cat up so that they could stare into each other's eyes. He pressed his forehead to Reaper's and let out a soft rumble. Reaper replied with a scratchy meow.

Mason settled the cat against his shoulder, latched the cage door closed again, then turned and stumbled to a halt.

Isana was standing against the opposite wall, watching them. "Well, come on then." She pushed away from the wall and led him down the ramp to the main level where the cat playroom was.

"Did Ryan choose a cat?" Mason asked.

"Not yet. I left them in the playroom. Sarah's been bringing cats in to meet them."

"Wait. They're in the playroom with *my* kittens? You're not going to let Ryan choose one of them, are you?"

"Relax. Ryan was adamant that it had to be a full-grown cat, probably a good idea given the size of Cujo."

"Maybe I should just take Reaper back to his kennel. I don't want Ryan choosing him either."

Isana snickered. "Trust me. That's not going to happen."

Mason saw she was right when they reached the ground floor again.

Ryan was relaxing under the tree at the center of the play-room and wasn't paying attention to any of the cats Sarah kept bringing by.

Instead, he was typing away on his phone, pretty much ignoring all the cats.

By comparison, he was constantly petting Cujo, who was lying on his side, nudging Ryan's hand for more pats and stretching out a paw to pat Ryan's cheek.

"They bonded so fast," Sarah said to Isana. "It's truly beautiful."

"Yeah, great, but I need him to bond with a cat," Isana said.

"I know," Sarah sighed. "Do you have any suggestions?"

Isana looked at Mason, who immediately scowled at her. "Not Reaper."

"Fine. What about Midnight?"

Sarah's eyes widened. "Good idea. I'll be right back." She bolted from the room.

"Who's Midnight?" Mason asked.

"A cat who's been living in a cage for three years. He's sweet as can be, but pitch black, which makes him harder to adopt out."

"Why?"

Isana shrugged. "It's the black cat syndrome. They're just much harder to place."

Mason frowned. "None of my cats are black."

Isana grinned. "That's okay. They need homes too."

At that moment, Reaper let out a low-pitched yowl.

"Sorry, Reaper. Let's go find the kittens, shall we?"

ISANA REALLY DIDN'T WANT TO LIKE THE BEAR, mostly because he was a bear, but also because she was very much afraid he might be her mate.

It was difficult not to like him when he sat and played with kittens though or spent time chatting with a cranky tomcat, trying to convince him to submit to being petted.

At this point, she was pretty convinced Mason would make an excellent cat dad, but that didn't mean she was willing to admit it just yet.

The bear would just get a swelled head if she gave in too soon.

Still, it was hard to resist the man, especially when he kept tugging on her heart strings like he was at that very moment.

Mason was now surrounded by cats and kittens—the three he'd chosen plus a number more. He was playing with all of them, petting them, tossing balls for them to chase, waving cat wands of fabric in front of them, leading them this way and that, almost like a pied piper calling his charges.

The only one not mesmerized was Reaper.

Instead of playing, he was perched at the top of a cat tree, not far from where Mason was playing with the kittens, and was observing the entire room, almost like a guard kitty standing sentry over his charges.

At that moment, Cujo came loping through the area with Midnight on his back.

It was only because Isana had been looking at Reaper at that very moment that she saw what happened next.

Reaper let out a yowl and leapt from the cat tree.

For one single moment, he was airborne, then he slammed into Midnight and the two of them tumbled to the floor.

Reaper landed on top of Midnight and swatted him in the face, then leapt up and onto Cujo's back. There he settled and stared down at Midnight with a superior look on his face, as if to say this was now his dog.

Midnight shook his head, climbed to his feet and yowled.

Ryan hurried over, picked Midnight up and murmured soft words of comfort as he glared at Reaper.

Mason let out a short whistle, Reaper whirled and jumped down to the floor. He sauntered unhurriedly over to Mason's side where he began grooming one of the ginger kittens.

"Wow," Ryan drawled out the word.

Isana chuckled. "Now you know why Sarah said only the bear would want Reaper. So I take it you're going to adopt Midnight?"

Ryan looked surprised, then glanced down at the cat in his arms, then over at Cujo, who hurried to his side and leaned against his leg.

Midnight stretched out a paw and patted the dog on the head.

Ryan grinned. "Yeah, I guess I am."

"Awesome," Sarah exclaimed. "Let's get the paperwork done, shall we?"

They hurried out while Isana tried to avoid Mason's glare.

"You're not going to make him volunteer to earn the right to adopt one of your precious cats?"

Isana shrugged. "We don't need a volunteer anymore. We have you." She turned her back so that Mason wouldn't see her struggle to keep from laughing.

"Oh, that's nice."

"You'd better get started. Those litter boxes won't clean themselves, you know." She hurried toward the door. "I'll be back as soon as I'm done processing Ryan's adoption paperwork."

ISANA WAS DRIVING HIM CRAZY.

Mason couldn't decide if he was more annoyed that she still hadn't agreed to him adopting his cats or that she seemed completely unaffected by him, whereas he could barely concentrate on anything else whenever she was around.

He hurried through the tower, scrubbing out kennels, refreshing food and water and scooping litter boxes. While he worked, he munched on Bear Necessities and occasionally shared tiny morsels of fish with the occasional cat.

Isana caught him, though, and that was the end of that.

"Sorry, Larry," he said to a gray, striped cat. "No fish for you."

The best part of the job was spending time with the cats and getting to know each one of them. There were so many and they all had different personalities from fun and energetic to sweet and skittish to hissing and cranky.

No matter what, though, he made sure to talk to each one and to pet as many as he could.

By the time Isana returned to the tower, all the stresses of his day at the office had disappeared under a barrage of kitten meows and purrs. "I think I might be in the wrong profession."

"What makes you say that?"

"I'm in love with your cats. They're so soothing."

Isana grinned. "Yeah, it's a pretty good gig. Doesn't pay anywhere near as well as CEO of a corporation though."

"Eh, money's overrated."

"Uh-huh. So says the filthy rich."

Mason chuckled. "I suppose that's true. And speaking as one of the filthy rich, are you ready to take my adoption fees yet? Or a donation? Or maybe both?"

"You know, I really thought we might be making some progress," Tivali said, "until the idiot bear went and ruined everything."

"What are you talking about?" Soraya exclaimed. "Mason barely spoke with Sarah today. She was too busy helping Ryan."

"What does Sarah have to do with it?" Muezza asked.

"She's his mate. I'm sure of it," Soraya said. "We just have to get them to spend more time together."

"Uh, that's insane," Tivali said. "There's no way Mason's mate is Sarah."

"I don't see why not. Sarah's nice. I think she deserves a mate."

"Isana's nice too," Tivali snarled.

"Yeah, but she hates Mason. Did you hear how she tore into him when he offered her that bribe?"

"What a moron," Tivali said.

"I'm telling you, he's unmatchable," Muezza said.

"Bygul wouldn't do that to us," Soraya said. "I'm sure he would only have us working on a match that's a sure thing and Mason and Sarah are *perfect* for each other."

Muezza let out a scoffing sound. "Mason would be bored out of his mind if we set him up with her."

"Bored!" Soraya exclaimed. "That's so rude. He wouldn't be bored. He'd be *adored*! She's a sweetheart."

"True," Muezza said, "but Mason doesn't need a sweetheart in his life. He'd walk all over a sweet girl like Sarah. He needs someone who will stand up to him and drive him crazy."

"He's right, Soraya," Tivali said.

Soraya sighed. "Damnit. I really wanted to matematch Sarah."

"Oh well. Maybe next time," Muezza said.

KATE COULDN'T BELIEVE IT.

She'd spent all afternoon waiting for Ryan to come back to the garage with the perfect Christmas gift for Maggie and instead he walked into the garage with a cat and some other dog.

"That's not the right dog," Kate exclaimed furiously, glaring at Ryan.

"And *that's* a cat," Nick exclaimed, coming to stand at Kate's side, also glaring at Ryan.

"This is Midnight." Ryan lifted his arms as he said the cat's name. "And this—" he dropped a hand to the top of the dog's ginormous head—"is Cujo."

"You adopted a dog named Cujo?" Pete exclaimed, then burst into laughter.

"Never mind about his name," Kate said furiously. "Who cares about Cujo? He's the *wrong* dog!"

"Well, it's a good thing it's not the right dog," Ryan said, "because if this was the dog you wanted for Maggie, you'd be out of luck. She's mine."

"Well, this sucks," Kate said.

"Yeah, how come they let *you* have a dog?" Nick demanded. "*We* went there first. Now *I* want a dog."

"You can have Midnight," Ryan said.

"I don't want a *cat.*"

"*I* want a cat," Mason bellowed as he stormed into the garage.

"Well, you can't have him," Ryan said. "Isana will take back the dog if she finds out I gave you the cat, so just get over it."

"I totally blame you for this, Kate," Nick muttered.

"Get over it? That bear-not-bear *still* won't let me adopt my cats. Plus, she won't tell me what kind of animal she is! She smells like a bear, but isn't a bear and it's driving me crazy!"

"I'll just have to recruit someone else," Kate decided. "Lyle, first thing tomorrow, you're up!"

Five

L YLE HAD NO idea how he'd been roped into this, especially after seeing Ryan return with both a dog *and* a cat.

His mistake had been telling his girlfriend, Heather, all about it when they met for lunch the day before.

He'd told her the story of Kate and the lion-dog she wanted to adopt for Maggie and how she'd recruited Ryan to go to the cat center later that day.

So when Lyle had gotten home the night before, Heather had demanded an update. Had Ryan succeeded in adopting the dog for Kate and Maggie?

Lyle thought the story was hilarious, how Ryan had returned with not only the wrong dog, but with a cat too, so he hadn't hesitated to share this with Heather.

Of course, when he told her that Kate wanted him to try next, Heather was thrilled. She actually had the next day off, so she immediately began making plans to go with him.

So this was how Lyle ended up walking into a cat rescue in the middle of a human town with his wolf girlfriend at his side.

"Now, remember, Heather, we're only here to adopt the dog Kate wants for Maggie. No other dogs and definitely no cats," he admonished as he opened the door.

"No problem. I can't wait to see this dog. He sounds so cute!"

"Well, isn't this interesting." A woman with white hair approached. "I'm Isana Meier, the director here, and I find it very interesting that so many wolves have been visiting lately. Interested in adopting a cat, are you? Well, come along, follow me." She turned and headed toward a set of doors to the right of the lobby.

"Oh, no, sorry." Lyle hurried after her, Heather at his side. "We're actually interested in—"

Isana whirled and snarled, "Cats first." She flung open the doors and ushered them into a giant tower room.

"Wow." Lyle and Heather stared, mouths agape, at the giant tree in the center of the room.

It was a real tree. Right there, growing through the floor and stretching up toward the dome.

Lyle looked up and realized there were skylights in the dome, letting natural sunlight trickle in.

There were two ramps, one to the left and one to the right, that appeared to travel around the room, all the way up toward the top of that dome.

"So, tell me the type of personality you'd like in a cat," Isana said.

"Oh, well, um—"

"I want a lap kitty," Heather said, shocking Lyle silent. "Actually, what I really want is a bonded pair. It wouldn't be fair to adopt a kitty and then go off to work, leaving them all alone all day long, so I'd like two kitties. Playful and affectionate."

"I have the perfect cats for you," Isana said. "You're going to love them. Right this way." She led them up a ramp around and around.

As they walked, cats came flying up to the cage doors to get pets as they passed them by.

"They're so cute," Heather said. "I'm so sad I can't adopt them all."

Lyle rolled his eyes. Great. Apparently he'd have to watch his girlfriend for cat hoarding tendencies. Who knew?

The worst part was that they were wolves.

What kind of self-respecting wolf wanted to adopt cats?

"We had barn cats growing up," Heather said. "Every spring, there would be a whole new crop of kittens and I had so much fun playing with them. One spring, I must have been about seven or eight, I sneaked a pair of kittens into my bedroom and I kept them in there for about a month before my parents discovered them. I was quite resourceful. I made litter pans from cardboard boxes that I filled with dirt and I fed them table scraps."

"Did you get to keep them?" Isana asked.

"I did. When my parents saw how attached I was to the kittens, they took them to the vet and got them all their shots. I named them Spooky and Spike. They even went away to college with me. We were inseparable until they passed away at ages fourteen and sixteen."

Lyle hadn't known any of this.

"That's the worst part of pet ownership," Isana said. "They never live as long as we'd like. Well, here we are. This one is Madison and that one there is Max. They're from the same litter and have been here at the center for over a year now."

"Why so long?" Lyle asked.

"They're black cats, honey," Heather said. "Black cats never adopt as fast as other cats, do they?"

"Exactly," Isana said. "Do you want to pet them?"

"Oh, yes, please!"

Lyle didn't even have to see what happened next. It was totally predictable.

Of course, Heather fell in love with the two cats, who were almost indistinguishable from each other. The only differences came in the form of a single white toe on Madison's left front paw and a tiny white dot on Max's nose.

"They're so precious," Heather crooned as she cradled Madison in her arms. "She's so soft."

So was Max, not that Lyle was about to admit it or anything.

Instead, he stoically waited for Heather to finish fawning over the cats, so that he could go find Kate's dog, then fill out the adoption paperwork for three animals instead of one, pay the adoption fees and get on with his life. A life that now included deciding where they would stash the litter boxes and how they would combat the cat fur.

It took a while, but they finally made it to the dog side of the center, where Lyle repeated to himself as they walked through the deserted animal clinic, the details of Kate's description. There was no way he was falling for any other dog. He was there on a mission.

Golden fur, looks like a lion, ginormous paws.

Golden fur, looks like a lion, ginormous paws.

Golden fur—

Ruf! Ruf! Ruf! Ruf! Ruf!

"Oh my gosh, he's so cute," Heather squealed as she fell to her knees.

"What is it?"

Isana chuckled. "Some sort of terrier mix, we're not sure. He won't ever get much bigger than that."

The dog leapt onto Heather's lap, then bounded out of it to race around her and Lyle, then jumped back onto her lap, then raced around again. This time, the dog stopped in front of Lyle, stood on its hind legs and scrabbled at Lyle's pants.

Lyle chuckled and settled down on the floor beside Heather. He scooped the dog up, which was met with ferocious excitement as the dog lunged forward and began licking Lyle's cheeks, nose, forehead, chin and pretty much anything else he could reach.

Lyle laughed and passed him to Heather then watched as she crooned and pet and loved all over that silly dog.

Without too much regret, he got to work adjusting his mental plans once more, this time making room for a dog bed and a dog crate.

MASON LEFT WORK EARLY. HE'D BEEN THINKING about Isana and the cats all day *again*.

The worst part was knowing he'd offended Isana with the offer of a donation, something he just didn't get.

He had money, so why shouldn't he share it with people and causes he cared about?

Still, he had to figure out how to make it up to her. Otherwise, he'd never convince her to let him adopt his cats.

If only he knew what her animal was. If he could figure that out, he'd probably know how to woo her.

For example, if she really was a bear, he'd try honey, but since she was a bear-not-bear, he was at a loss.

He walked into the center and screeched to a halt.

Lyle, the traitor, was standing in the reception area with his girlfriend, Heather. They were each holding a cat carrier and Lyle had the leash of a dog in his other hand.

Seriously?

Mason stormed forward, leaned over and peeked into each of the carriers.

"You're letting *them* adopt Madison and Max?" he demanded.

"Hey, Mason," Heather said. "What are you doing here?"

"I volunteer here," Mason said. "I also have a vested interest in four cats at this center, but *that woman—*" he glared at Isana "—hasn't seen fit to allow me to adopt them yet."

"Oh, we still have to have a home visit once the cats are settled, just to make sure things are going well, but then the cats are ours," Heather assured Mason. "Don't worry, I'm sure you'll get your cats in time. Isana just has to make sure every cat goes to a good home."

"Exactly," Isana said. "Thank you, Heather."

"Well, we're headed out," Lyle said. "Gotta get our new family members settled in."

"Good luck, Mason," Heather called as they walked out the door.

Mason didn't answer. He was too busy glaring at Isana, who was busy shuffling papers and ignoring him.

Well, two could play that game.

He stormed over to where he'd set his boxes of Bear Necessities and started unpacking them.

Cinnamon rolls.

Brownies.

Bear claws.

Popcorn balls.

"Oh, hey, Mason." Sarah came in from the clinic side of the

building. "How's it going? Oooh, bear claws. Yum." She grabbed a pastry and took a bite, then froze and stared at Mason. "Wow. Isana, you *have* to try a bear claw. I've never tasted anything so delicious in my life."

"It's a family recipe," Mason said. "One only shared with other *bears*." He sent a pointed look Isana's way. "It's really too bad your boss doesn't admit to being a bear. If she did, I could share the recipe with her, but since she insists she's *not* a bear—"

"*I am not a bear!*"

"—as I was saying, since she continues to insist she's not a bear, well, I'm afraid you guys are out of luck. When they're gone, they're gone."

Sarah let out a huge sigh. "Maybe, Isana, you could—"

"*I am not a bear!*"

"Okay, okay, sheesh. I just came in here to let you know I spoke with Brad over at Underdog Rescue."

"Uh-huh. What'd he want now?"

"So, the thing is they're actually quite thrilled we've managed to adopt out two of their dogs. So now they're wondering if we'd be willing to rent them the kennels on a permanent basis. They'll pay more rent if we agree to continue handling adoptions for them."

Isana scowled. "I'll think about it. We'd need to hire at least one more person though because this is getting a bit much for just the two of us."

"Agreed. Thank goodness we've had Mason the past two days. We'd be swamped otherwise. Thanks again for helping out, Mason."

"No problem. Is that what this is about? You're keeping my cats hostage so I'll keep volunteering?"

Isana rolled her eyes. "Don't be ridiculous. It's because you're a bear. I told you that."

Mason scowled. "That makes no sense! I know you say that you're not a bear, but you smell like a bear which means you're probably a bear. Which also means that you've been taking care of cats for years so obviously bears can be trusted around cats."

"How many times do I have to tell you?" Isana exclaimed. *"I am not a bear!"*

Mason threw up his hands in the air. "Fine. Fine. You're not a bear. Can I *please* adopt my cats now?"

BYGUL HADN'T CHECKED IN WITH TIVALI AND THE others since he'd presented them with their Mason mission. He'd been busy helping cats left homeless after a hurricane reunite with their families or find new ones if necessary.

It was heartbreaking work and he was exhausted.

However, he knew he really needed to check in with his trainees, if only to make sure they weren't destroying already existing matches.

You never knew with those three.

He could arrive and discover they'd managed to break up Jefferson and Kate or even worse, Jackson and Maggie.

It took longer than he expected to track down his trainees. He'd expected them to be at The Worcester Group, but everyone there was talking about how Mason Worcester kept leaving early to go visit some cat rescue in a human town called Pleasantville.

That was an interesting development for a bear known for never leaving his own town.

Bygul was now officially intrigued, especially once he

arrived at the cat rescue center and had a frontline view of all the drama happening there.

"Bygul," Tivali exclaimed. "What a surprise."

"Yes, well, I'm just checking in. I don't have a lot of time, but I thought I'd stop by and see how's it going."

"We're failures," Soraya wailed. "Epic failures!"

"What? Surely not."

"We are! I wanted to match Mason with Sarah, but Tivali and Muezza said he'd walk all over her, so then we thought maybe Isana, but there's no way that romance is ever getting off the ground. Isana hates him! We're terrible at this, Bygul."

"Oh, I'm sure it's not that bad." Bygul crossed the room and peeked into a side office where Mason and a woman—this Isana, perhaps—were squared off against each other, arms crossed.

Huh. That was some decidedly hostile body language.

Oh, well.

At least it wasn't any of his former matches going at each other. With these three, you never could tell whether they were going to help a match along or completely annihilate it.

"Don't worry so much," he said to Soraya, even though from what he could tell, there was plenty to worry about. "There are always sticky moments in any romance. You just have to get to the other side. If they're meant for each other, it'll all fall into place. Trust me."

"Are you sure?" Soraya asked.

"Positive."

Muezza made a scoffing sound and Tivali just stared at him suspiciously, but Soraya looked relieved.

Bygul should probably feel guilty since the truth was the situation didn't look good at all, but he really couldn't find it in himself to care, not if it meant he'd never have to train another group of cats to matchmake again.

Even though Mason seemed a really nice guy and probably deserved both a cat companion *and* a love match, Bygul simply didn't have the time to continue training and mentoring incompetent cats.

He'd taught them all he could and now it was up to them. Either the cats would fail and he could get on with his life or they wouldn't fail, in which case, he might be expected to train another group of cats.

Dear goddess, he hoped they failed.

Six

KATE WAS FURIOUS. She couldn't believe Lyle hadn't come to work at all the day before.

He'd even ignored her phone calls and texts.

When she'd asked Jefferson what was going on, he'd just grinned and said, "Lyle's spending the day with his girlfriend," which was *not* the agreement.

Lyle was *supposed* to be adopting Kate's dog and bringing him to her, not hanging out with his girlfriend.

This was why Kate demanded, "Where's my dog?" the minute Lyle walked into the garage the next morning.

Lyle ignored her question and made a beeline for the Bear Necessities table where he started piling pastries onto a plate. He shoved a cake donut in his mouth and set about making himself a cup of coffee.

"Lyle!" Kate exclaimed.

"What?" His voice was muffled due to the donut.

"Where's my dog?"

"What dog?"

Kate gasped. "What dog? The dog I sent you to Pleasantville to adopt. The dog for Maggie!"

"Oh, that dog. I didn't see him there, sorry."

"What do you mean you didn't see him? Did you even look?"

Lyle let out a huge sigh, set down his coffee cup and turned to face Kate.

She took a step back at the look on his face. "What's wrong, Lyle?"

"What's wrong?" He stalked across the office toward her.

At that moment, the office door opened and Pete and Ryan trooped across the office toward the Bear Necessities table, but Kate was too focused on Lyle to respond to their greetings.

Lyle seemed awfully upset, which was pretty unusual for the laidback wolf.

"Do you know what I spent my entire day yesterday doing?" he demanded.

"Um, no."

"I spent hours at a cat rescue center in the middle of a human town, then I spent hours inside a human pet store buying cat food and litter boxes and cat toys and dog beds and dog food. Do you know why I was buying those things, Kate?"

"Because you adopted my dog for Maggie?" She asked hopefully.

"Not even close," he said. "But I did adopt a toy dog. Do you know why they call them toy dogs?"

Kate shook her head.

"Because they're so small they look like little stuffed animal toys. Do you know what else I adopted yesterday?"

Kate shook her head.

"Two black cats."

"Do you know what I didn't adopt yesterday?"

Kate shook her head again.

"The mythical dog that looks like a lion that you sent me there to adopt! You know why I didn't adopt him?" He continued before she could shake her head again, "Because I ended up with two cats and Heather fell in love with the toy dog within two seconds of us entering the dog room. I couldn't risk exploring further in case she found another dog or two or *ten* that she wanted to adopt. So thanks, Kate. Brilliant idea. I now have two cats and a dog while you still have no gift for Maggie." He turned, stalked over to the Bear Necessities table, grabbed his coffee and plate of pastries and stormed out.

The minute the door slammed shut behind him, Ryan and Pete, who had been off to the side, eyes wide, clearly barely containing themselves, finally burst into laughter.

Kate walked over to stand in front of Pete.

His hilarity died instantly. "Oh, no. I've seen the writing on the wall. Everyone who does this little errand for you ends up coming back with a dog and a cat. Lyle just came back with two cats. Well, I am one wolf who has no problem saying no. So here it is: No. No. No. *No.* I will *not* be going to the cat rescue center anytime this century."

AN HOUR LATER, PETE WAS STANDING IN FRONT OF the cat rescue center, wondering how he'd gotten roped into this shit.

He drew in a deep breath for courage and went inside.

He recognized Isana from the description everyone had given him. He'd been hoping to find the other woman they'd described—Sarah—there instead.

Both Lyle and Pete had agreed if it weren't for Isana, they might have managed to escape the cat rescue center with only a dog, but Isana was quite determined and somehow they'd ended up with cats too.

Unfortunately, Pete was doomed to follow in his co-workers footsteps because Sarah was nowhere in sight.

"Another wolf. What a surprise," Isana exclaimed. "Come along. The cats are all in the Cat Tower." She flung open a pair of doors and led the way inside.

It was exactly as Pete and Ryan had described it.

He'd been sure they were exaggerating or just pulling his leg, but there really was a tree in the middle of the tower.

"You go right ahead and wander around. Sarah's in here somewhere. She can answer any questions you have about any of the cats. Just come find me once you've decided which ones you'd like to adopt."

He blanched. Had she just said "ones" as in plural? He didn't want to adopt a single cat, let alone multiples.

What was he supposed to do now?

Rather than head up one of the ramps, he decided to wander the playroom first. Maybe if he hid in there for a while, Isana would forget all about him and he could charm this Sarah woman into letting him adopt just the one dog and no cats.

He walked around the tree at the center of the room and discovered on the other side a wall of windows looking into separate rooms. These must be the individual playrooms Pete was talking about. There were three of them, all in a row, and a cat was sitting at the window of the third room.

He walked down to stand in front of the cat and that was when he saw the woman.

When the others had described Sarah, saying she had reddish blonde hair and green eyes, Pete hadn't thought much about it. Now he realized they hadn't done her justice because he couldn't take his eyes off her.

She didn't realize he was there, so he had the chance to observe her without her knowing. She had a cat toy in her hand, a wand with a long piece of fabric that she was using to entice the cats to play. There were two cats happily chasing her wand, but the third, he still stood at the window, watching Pete watch Sarah.

After long moments of feeling utterly bewitched by her beauty and the gracefulness of her movements as she waved the wand, sending the fabric swirling this way and that, Pete opened the door and stepped inside.

He drew in a deep breath and immediately knew.

Sarah looked up, eyes wide.

He walked toward her, settled on the floor across from her and told her his name.

And so the hours swept by without either of them noticing.

They played with the cats and talked.

They barely noticed when Isana stopped by to check on them, then left as quietly as she'd come.

Eventually Sarah remembered she had a job to do, so Pete accompanied her all through the cat tower, helping as she fed and gave attention to cat after cat.

She introduced him to all the cats she loved, which was basically all of them, and to the ones she'd completely fallen in love with, which was two. There were more she adored, but two she'd take home with her in an instant if only her apartment complex allowed pets.

When they were finished in the cat tower, they spent time in the reception area, answering the phone and talking about everything and nothing.

They ended the day outside, playing with the dogs, and it was out there, while surrounded by happy, barking, playful dogs, that they had their first kiss.

"Oh my goodness. Look at that! I'm a genius," Soraya exclaimed. "We just made our second love match. Or is it our third?"

"But we weren't even *trying* to match Pete *or* Sarah," Tivali exclaimed.

"Speak for yourself," Soraya said. "I've been all about matching Sarah this entire time and I think this is a wonderful development. I'm definitely taking credit for this match."

"Well, if you're taking credit, *we're* taking credit," Muezza said.

"Exactly," Tivali said.

"That's fine," Soraya said. "I have no problem sharing credit. My only question is whether this is our second match or our third."

"Why would it be our third?" Tivali asked.

"Kate and Jefferson, of course! We were definitely there for that match."

"Yeah, but I think technically that match belongs to Bygul," Muezza said.

"Okay, fine, but we do get to take credit for Nick and Ryan, right?"

"Absolutely," Tivali said. "Bygul was completely against that match. We made that happen without him."

"Sweet," Soraya said. "We're on a roll. Two matches down, one to go."

"Yeah, but that one is completely unmatchable," Muezza said.

"He's right," Tivali said. "We'll probably end up having to take credit for *failing* to match the bear."

Soraya scowled. "Well, that sucks. Maybe we should enlist some help from the natives."

"Good idea," Tivali said. "Bygul did say earthbound cats are one of his most valuable tools in making these matches."

"I vote for the kittens," Soraya said.

Muezza let out a growling snort. "Remember Cleocatra? I vote for some of the older, wiser cats."

"How about Reaper?" Tivali asked.

"There's no way that cranky cat is going to help us make a love match," Soraya said.

"Well, the kittens certainly won't be of much help," Tivali said.

"How about we just invite them all?" Muezza suggested.

"All of them?" Tivali and Soraya chorused.

"All of them."

MASON HAD A FULL DAY OF MEETINGS AND COULDN'T get away early like he had in days past. This made him especially grouchy when he finally arrived at the rescue center and passed Pete and Sarah leaving as he went in.

"Pete didn't have any carriers and no dogs on leashes," Mason said to Isana. "Are you losing your touch?"

Isana grinned. "Not at all. Pete took me aside and asked to adopt Sarah's favorite cats, Shadow and Bandit."

"That doesn't make any sense. Why would Pete adopt Sarah's cats? She's going to be so mad."

Isana chuckled. "Actually, since they're mates, I think she'll be fine with it."

"Seriously?" Mason whirled and raced to the door. He flung it open and stared. Ha, perfect timing!

"What are you doing?" Isana came up beside him.

"Just wanted to see if Pete would manage to convince Sarah to ride his motorcycle."

"Motorcycle? It's barely above freezing outside!"

Mason chuckled. "Like shifters care about a bit of cold."

Isana gasped as the rumble of a motorcycle reached their ears.

A moment later, Pete drove out of the lot, Sarah plastered to his back.

Mason chuckled. "Guess he convinced her. Good for him." He stepped back inside and closed the door behind them. "So what's the plan tonight, sweet Isana?"

Isana blushed. "Same as every night." She turned and headed for her office. "Paperwork, cleaning, cat cuddles."

"How about dinner after?"

She froze, turned and stared at him. "Why?"

"Because I find you intriguing."

"I'm not sure that's a compliment."

Mason grinned. "Trust me. It's a compliment. So what do you say. Dinner?"

"Sure. Why not? But first—chores."

"On it, ma'am."

Isana couldn't believe she'd agreed to go out with the bear.

A *bear*, for heaven's sake!

And especially for dinner. If a date with a bear was anything like family dinners with bears, she'd be at dinner for literally hours.

It could quite possibly take half the night, but even if it didn't, it would certainly last long enough for her entire meal to wear off, leaving her hungry again, all while the bear ate continuously without ever getting full.

She had no idea what she'd been thinking when she accepted his invitation. The bear just sent every rational thought fleeing from her head, especially when he grinned like that. Damn sexy bear.

Isana spent the afternoon putting together a list of excuses for canceling on him.

She planned to use those excuses as they walked around the tower saying goodnight to all the cats, but things got really strange before she could even pull out one excuse.

It all started with Pepper, a white cat covered in tiny black dots.

She was purring in Isana's arms when Mason got near and Pepper lunged for him.

Isana lurched forward to keep the cat from falling and somehow ended up in Mason's arms.

The first time it happened, she didn't think much of it, but then when two other cats did the same thing and she landed in his arms for the third time, she started to wonder if the cats were all possessed, then she wasn't thinking at all.

Three times was clearly one too many for the bear because the second she collided with him, he swept her into his arms and kissed her.

Heat swept through her and all thoughts were obliterated under the scorching fire of his kiss.

Long moments trickled by as heat spiraled between them.

Dear goddess, the bear could kiss!

It was only the plaintive meow of the cat they'd forgotten that brought her back to herself and gave her the strength to pull away.

And so the evening went, with cats conspiring to send Isana into Mason's arms where he'd kiss her breathless and then they'd go back to work only to repeat that scenario again and again.

By the time they finished their rounds, any excuses Isana had planned to provide for not going to dinner with Mason were completely lost in the brain fog caused by his kisses.

It was only after Mason had swept her up into his truck and had driven them out of Pleasantville that Isana's thought processes started to come back online.

She was now remembering the myriad of excuses she'd had and was thinking this would probably be a good time to bring one up.

The only problem was she no longer *wanted* to cancel.

Could it be that she was actually falling for the bear?

Could it be that she was beginning to hope he really *was* her mate?

She hadn't decided the answer to these questions before he pulled up into the parking lot of a restaurant.

Oh, dear goddesses in heaven.

She hadn't been paying attention.

Nor had she given proper consideration to the consequences of accepting his invitation.

She should have known that he'd take her back to his home turf, to Worcester Falls.

She should have considered the possibility that he'd take her to the most well-known bear restaurant in the shifter community.

She hadn't considered any of that, though, and now she was well and truly panicked. "Maybe we shouldn't go in, not here anyway."

"What? No. This is absolutely *the* best restaurant in all of Worcester Falls. They specialize in all types of bear gourmet foods."

"But then, *I'm not a bear*, remember?"

He looked crestfallen. "I keep forgetting. It's because you smell like a bear and if you smell like a bear, you have to *be* a bear. That's just the way it is."

Isana rolled her eyes.

"Truly, though, it doesn't matter. Even if you're not a bear, all the shifters in town agree. The Ice Box is one of the best Shenanigans restaurants around. If you prefer, though, we can drive to a different Shenanigans."

That really wouldn't help because the minute Isana stepped foot into any Shenanigans in the state, every bear she was related to would know she was dating a grizzly.

She really was an idiot for agreeing to this, but fine. She might as well get it over with.

"I'm sure this will be just fine."

"Are you sure?" Mason beamed at her.

"Absolutely."

As it turned out, it wasn't fine at all.

In the beginning, everything was wonderful, full of romance and laughter with Isana falling deeper under Mason Worcester's spell.

It was a truly lovely evening.

Until suddenly it wasn't.

"You know we're getting pretty good at this," Soraya exclaimed.

"Are you crazy?" Tivali exclaimed. "Those polar bears just threw Mason Worcester through a window!"

"Yeah, but think about all the progress we made up until then!"

"She has a point," Muezza said. "The cats *were* more effective than expected."

"And let's not forget *why* the polar bears tossed him out the window."

All things considered, even though it wasn't exactly the first date he imagined, Mason felt the night was overall a success.

After all, it wasn't often a woman stood between you and five pissed off polar bears.

It all began innocently enough.

Mason couldn't help but notice that all the wait staff in The Ice Box seemed to recognize Isana the minute they walked in the front door.

He also didn't miss the slight shake of the head Isana sent the hostess when she started to greet them.

From there, everyone acted like they didn't know who Isana was, but that was clearly just them pretending because *everyone* was inordinately interested in the two of them.

As they ate, the wait staff came to their table much more frequently than they visited any other table, to the point that Isana eventually snapped, "We're fine. Don't come by again unless you're delivering more food for the bear."

And this was why Mason had decided Isana Meier was the perfect woman for him.

She understood his appetite and though she rolled her eyes every time he unpacked his boxes of Bear Necessities, she never complained that he'd taken over her countertop for them.

She also didn't give him a hard time when he constantly visited that same countertop to get more necessities nor did she protest when he ate his way through the job from the minute he arrived until they minute he left.

She understood what it meant to be a bear.

Which had him even more convinced that she was a bear herself.

The evidence was piling high.

Exhibit A: she smelled like a bear.

Exhibit B: she understood bears.

Exhibit C: she was clearly well-known at the most famous bear establishment in Worcester Falls.

Little did Mason know, there would soon be an Exhibit D involving a bunch of psychotic polar bears.

The employees at The Ice Box were a mix of polar bears and arctic foxes, something Mason had always found to be very interesting. As a grizzly bear, he wasn't too fond of seals, but he did love how those polars prepped their fish, especially the salmon and the trout.

In fact, Mason loved their food so much, he had two accounts there. One was a personal account and the other was a business account under The Worcester Group. As a result, he was used to being catered to at The Ice Box and honestly, treated like a king.

He definitely wasn't used to the wait staff attempting to spy on his dinner dates nor had he ever been surrounded by polar bears halfway through his meal there.

He looked up, surprised to see five huge polar bears scowling down at him and Isana.

Mason bristled at the possessive look on the polars' faces.

"Isana, it's time for you to go home," one of them said.

Mason narrowed his eyes. Was this polar actually trying to lay claim to Mason's date? She was *his* and no one else's.

"Back off, Bryce," Isana snapped.

It was really too bad that Bryce didn't listen and instead grabbed her and dragged her out of the booth.

It was also too bad that when Mason saw the polar's hand on Isana's arm—*his* Isana—the grizzly woke with a vengeance.

This was why Isana had moved away from Worcester Falls.

In fact, *this* was why she lived in a human town away from shifters entirely.

Okay, so she'd had the thought that Mason should know what he was getting into by dating her, so she hadn't protested too much when she'd realized where they would be eating.

Now, though, she realized that was a severe miscalculation.

After all, she had never, as in *never*, brought a date to a family-owned establishment.

And this right here was why.

Her brothers.

And her cousins.

Were all *bears*.

In every meaning of the word.

Still, she didn't expect Bryce to manhandle her and she *definitely* didn't expect Mason to go into a rage as a result.

And if she were being entirely truthful, she would never predict that Mason would hold his own against the lot of them.

Sure, he might if he were only up against her two brothers *or* her three cousins, but put them all together and the grizzly didn't stand a chance.

But then Bryce touched her and Mason lost his ever-loving mind.

One minute, Bryce had his hand wrapped around her arm and was dragging her away from their booth, the next he was flying through the air and landing on a table clear across the restaurant.

Isana had no idea how Mason had done it without knocking her to the ground in the process, but somehow he managed to dislodge that hand, set her aside incredibly gently and throw her brother like he was nothing but a stuffed toy.

The rage in the air was palpable in that split second Bryce was airborne, a rage that came not just from Mason, but also from her idiot family when he roared, *"MINE!"*

Isana was pretty sure that up until that moment, her family had just been messing with her, and by extension, with Mason, but the minute the grizzly tried to lay claim to her, playtime was over and the rest of them attacked en masse.

At first, it looked like Mason might go down under the sheer weight of five polars, but then in an incredible burst of strength, he managed to fling the lot of them off so they went in every which direction, collapsing tables willy-nilly.

Isana was so stunned, mouth agape, she didn't resist even a little when Mason dragged her into his arms and caught her mouth with his.

His tongue stole inside and heat washed through her in a massive wave.

She clutched his shoulders and kissed him back, losing

track of where they were, who was watching, basically everything.

Then Mason was the one who was airborne.

And so, Isana's first date with the man who just might be her mate ended in chaos, with five polars and a grizzly roaring their displeasure at each other, arctic foxes taking pictures and videos of the insanity, and Isana pacing in front of her family's restaurant, screaming through the window at her idiot brothers and cousins, threatening them with dismemberment if they even thought to step out onto the sidewalk.

Basically, it was just another day in the life of a family of freaking bears.

Oh, well.

Like she said.

It was better if the grizzly knew *exactly* what he was getting into by dating *her*.

Seven

KATE COULDN'T UNDERSTAND what was wrong with these wolves.

She sent each one on a very simple task—adopt a dog, *one specific dog*—and they kept screwing it up!

Not to mention ignoring her.

According to Jefferson, Pete met his mate the day before.

This was awesome news and she was very happy for him.

However, that was *no excuse* not to call in and report the status of his mission.

How hard was it to send a simple text saying, "I got the dog and by the way, I'm mated now?"

But *no*.

Not a single update from Pete the entire day before and now she was stuck pacing back and forth waiting for him to come in so she could figure out whether she still needed a Christmas dog for Maggie.

If he'd failed in his mission, she had no idea who she'd recruit next.

She was out of mechanics!

"Stop pacing, Kate," Jefferson said. "I'm sure he'll be here soon."

"Yes, but will he come in with my dog?"

At that moment, the garage door swung open and Pete walked in, a sappy grin on his face.

Kate's eyes narrowed. "Where's my dog?"

Pete stumbled to a stop, a confused look on his face. "What dog?"

"The dog you were supposed to adopt yesterday!"

"Oh, yeah, that dog." Pete winced. "Sorry, Kate. I kind of forgot to ask about him."

"You what? You—how could you forget the entire reason you went to the rescue center in the first place?"

"Didn't Jefferson tell you I met my mate?"

"Well, yeah, but what does *that* have to do with my dog?"

"I met her at the rescue center. Not the dog. My mate. Her name's Sarah."

"Hold on a minute. Sarah, the one who sent Mason into the clinic where the lion-dog was?"

"Yep, that Sarah."

"Huh. I kind of liked her. She was quiet, but sneaky."

Pete scowled. "She's not sneaky."

"Please. Anyone who manages to send my brother in the wrong direction without tipping him off is definitely sneaky. In a good way, of course."

"Whatever."

"Anyway, I'm happy you found your mate, but that didn't help me get my Christmas shopping done, now did it?"

"You know, just a thought," Jefferson said, "but you could get Maggie something else for Christmas."

"Are you crazy? The lion-dog is absolutely perfect for her

and it's like a gift for Genghis Khat too, which will earn me brownie points with Maggie."

"What do you need brownie points for, especially ones from Maggie?"

Kate shrugged. "You never know when you're going to need a favor from a friend. Anyway, none of that matters because it isn't helping me *adopt a dog!*"

Jefferson sighed. "If you're absolutely determined to get this dog, you *might* consider asking Jackson. After all, he lives with Maggie now, so maybe you should get his opinion on this particular gift."

This idea actually had possibilities.

As long as Jackson didn't try to steal the dog for his own gift-giving. She'd probably have to go with him, just to be sure.

"Actually, now that I think about it, you might suggest Jackson bring Genghis Khat with him. You know, just in case the cat goes psycho when he meets the lion-dog."

JACKSON HAD NO IDEA HOW HE'D BEEN ROPED INTO this shit.

He was pretty sure Jefferson was to blame.

They were panthers, for heaven's sake, so why on earth he was driving out to some human town in the hopes of adopting a dog, he had no idea.

"Now remember," his sister-in-law, Kate yelled, trying to be heard over the sound of Genghis Khat yowling from inside his carrier in the backseat. "This is *my* gift for Maggie. You can't steal him from me."

"No problem," Jackson hollered back, "but if Genghis Khat doesn't like him, you're out of luck."

"Okay, sheesh, fine."

Jackson actually thought getting Maggie another pet for Christmas was a brilliant idea. The problem, of course, was Genghis Khat. Jackson would bet money on the cat attempting to destroy any animal thinking to live in his domain.

Basically, Jackson expected this entire trip to be a giant waste of time.

As soon as they arrived at the center, Kate turned to Genghis Khat and said, "Pipe down, would you? We're here and I need to talk to Jackson for a minute."

Jackson wasn't at all surprised when Genghis Khat fell silent. The cat was seriously smart.

"So, listen," Kate said, "the woman in there will probably try to get you to adopt a cat. If you explain that you already have an incredibly territorial one, she might back down."

"Why are you telling me this?"

"Just so you're prepared, you know, for all the possibilities. Anyway, the dog you're looking for looks like a lion."

"Again, why are you telling me this? You'll be right beside me. I assume you'll recognize the dog."

"Oh, no, I can't actually go inside the center."

He had to be hallucinating. "If you're not going in, then why did you insist on coming with me?"

"Because the last three times I sent a wolf to adopt this dog, they adopted the wrong animals. This time, I'm going to be right here to make sure that you exit that building with the right dog."

"If you come inside with me, you can make sure of that in person."

Kate shook her head. "Trust me. Isana, the woman in charge, will refuse to allow the adoption the second she seems me."

"And why is that exactly?"

"Because I made the mistake of telling her this was a gift for Maggie and apparently the woman is anti-gift."

"That doesn't even make sense."

"I know! What kind of person hates gifts?"

"There has to be more to this story. Wait here." Jackson slammed out of the truck and headed into the center.

KATE SET ABOUT GETTING COMFORTABLE.

She figured it'd be a while since Jackson would have to convince Isana to let him see the dogs, then he'd have to find the right dog and then he'd have to fill out the adoption application and pay the fee and then—

The door she was leaning against flew open and she squealed as she lost her balance and almost fell out of the truck.

"You're an idiot." Jackson said as he steadied her.

"What's that supposed to mean?"

"I just spoke with Isana Meier, the director of the center. I explained that I'm Maggie's mate and that I have Maggie's cat with me and that we'd like to see if there's a dog the cat might get along with as a special Christmas surprise. Do you know what Isana said?"

"Get you begone, you evil gift-giver, you?"

Jackson grinned. "Not even close. She said she thought that was a lovely idea and to bring the cat inside."

"You are *shitting* me."

"Nope."

"Are you sure you were speaking with Isana and not Sarah?"

"White-blonde hair, smells like a bear?"

Kate let out a huff. "Maybe it's her less-evil identical twin."

Jackson grinned. He opened the back door and picked up the carrier Genghis Khat was in.

"This makes no sense. She threw me out, yelling that pets aren't gifts!" Kate climbed out of the truck and stormed toward the building. "I hate this woman with a passion right now." She flung open the door and stormed inside.

Isana was leaning against the reception counter, clearly waiting for them.

"You told me pets weren't gifts!"

"That's true I did, but that was before you sent three other wolves to try and con me out of a dog. It was also before you sent in the mate of the woman you want to gift the dog to."

"Why does all that make a difference?" Kate demanded.

"Sending the wolves showed a certain amount of persistence. It was really quite impressive. However, I still wouldn't have allowed any of them to adopt the dog on behalf of someone else. I *will*, however, allow Jackson to adopt the dog on behalf of his cat *if* things go well between the cat and the dog."

"I don't get it," Kate said. "We can't adopt a dog to give to a person, but we *can* adopt it to give to the cat?"

"You, no. Jackson, as a representative of the household where the dog will live, yes."

Kate let out a low growl. "Are you telling me all I had to do was get Jackson and Genghis Khat to come up here and you would have allowed the adoption from minute one?"

"Pretty much."

Kate was speechless.

Jackson chuckled. "Let's go meet this dog, shall we?"

THE MOMENT JACKSON LET GENGHIS KHAT OUT OF his carrier, the cat went about exploring his environment.

Isana had taken them to an enclosed room that had tile floor, baskets full of cat toys and several cat trees.

Genghis Khat wasn't interested in the cat tree or in the toys.

Instead, he was busy sniffing out every corner of the room, making tracks from one end to the other and back again, nose to the floor, sniffing, sniffing, sniffing.

Jackson chuckled and settled down on the floor in the center of the room and just watched.

Kate was pacing back and forth, impatiently waiting for Isana to return with *her dog*.

Jackson thought it was hilarious that she kept referring to the dog as hers when she clearly planned to give it to Maggie.

At that moment, Genghis Khat raced up to Jackson and butted his head against Jackson's knee.

Jackson chuckled and scratched the top of the cat's head.

Genghis Khat let out a soft rumbling meow, then took off sniffing across the room again.

At that moment, the door opened and Isana walked in, a giant dog at her side.

"Holy hell," Jackson muttered. No wonder Mason thought the damn thing was a lion. It had so much golden fur around its face, it resembled a mane, and it was *huge*. It might even be bigger than Jackson's panther. If not, it was certainly close.

"The paperwork says they think he might be a Tibetan Mastiff," Isana said, "but they're not sure because he was abandoned and in pretty bad shape when they found him. We've been calling him Leo."

"Awww, poor guy," Kate said.

At that moment, Genghis Khat let out a yowl and charged Leo, who immediately flopped down on his belly.

Genghis Khat leapt over Leo's head and landed on his back.

The dog didn't move.

Genghis Khat rolled back and forth on the dog's back, then slowly slithered down to the floor, where he slunk toward Leo's tail and pounced.

Leo still didn't move.

Genghis Khat rolled over, dragging the dog's tail with him, then rolled back, dragging the tail with him again.

Still no movement from Leo.

Genghis Khat leapt to his feet and ran around the dog three times, pausing at his tail to pounce each time, then racing off again.

"Wow. I haven't seen Genghis Khat this animated in, well, ever," Jackson said.

After pouncing on Leo's tail, playing leap frog over his head and his back and climbing onto Leo's head and gently chewing his ear, Genghis Khat finally curled up on the dog's back and went to sleep.

"Right. We're adopting the dog," Jackson said.

"Yes!" Kate crowed.

Isana rolled her eyes. "I'll get you the paperwork."

Fifteen minutes later, Jackson handed back the completed adoption paperwork and Kate handed over her credit card.

"You do realize Christmas is still two days away," Jackson said. "Where are you going to keep the dog until then?"

Kate grinned. "Mason's house."

Isana's eyes narrowed. "Does Mason know this?"

"He will by tonight."

Isana had just finished emailing the adoption paperwork to Underdog Rescue when Mason walked in. She would never admit it out loud, but she was super relieved to see him.

After the way their date had ended the night before, she wasn't sure she'd ever see the bear again.

She certainly wouldn't blame him after her asshole brothers pitched him through the front window of their restaurant, but even if he'd been okay with that, she hadn't exactly shown her best side, what with all the pacing and screaming like a wild woman.

"I could have sworn I just saw that lion-not-lion in my sister's car as I was pulling into the parking lot and she was pulling out." Mason glared at Isana. "Do you have anything to tell me?"

"Nope, I'll leave that to your sister."

"Uh-huh. So what's on the agenda for today?"

"Same as yesterday."

"Excellent. Though I hope you're referring to the kissing and not the smashing through windows."

Isana could feel blood rushing to her face. "I'm so sorry about that. My brothers are such assholes!"

"Eh, it's fine." Mason laughed. "I really can't complain considering I did the same thing to Jefferson when I first caught him kissing Kate."

"Seriously?"

Mason nodded. "Must be a bear thing."

"Or something," Isana muttered.

"And speaking of bears, I knew you were conning me, claiming not to be a bear. I suppose some might say polars are a breed of their own, but still, at the end of the day, you really *are* a bear."

Isana shook her head. "I'm not a bear."

Mason scowled. "Your polar bear brothers and cousins tossed me quite literally out of their restaurant. I think it's pretty clear. You're a freaking bear."

Isana giggled. "If you say so."

He glared at her. "Come on. Tell me the truth. You're a polar bear, right?"

"You'd better get to work if you want to have time for dinner tonight."

Mason's eyes widened. "You mean I don't have to convince you with kisses this time?"

Isana grinned. "Well, I wouldn't say that."

"I TOLD YOU WE WERE GETTING GOOD AT THIS! WE might actually match our first unmatchable."

"Doubtful," Tivali said.

"Probable," Soraya insisted. "After all, they've been kissing all night and now he's taking her to his house for dinner."

"Yes, but she still hasn't agreed to let him adopt those kittens. Until she does that, this relationship is doomed," Muezza said.

"Exactly," Tivali said.

"That gives me a brilliant idea," Soraya said.

]

"This is actually perfect," Mason told Isana as he opened his front door. "You wanted to make a home visit anyway, to make sure it's a good environment for the cats. This way, we'll kill two birds with one—" His words ended in a shriek when a giant, golden creature slammed into him.

The force made him stagger back.

He tripped and landed flat on his back under the same lion-not-lion creature he'd seen in Kate's vehicle earlier that day.

At least this time he knew it wasn't a lion.

He tried to shove the dog off him, but the dog was too determined to lick every segment of Mason's face that it could reach.

The sound of laughter reached Mason's ears and Isana came into his field of vision.

"I feel like we've been here before," she said to him.

"Yeah, yeah, yeah." Mason shoved the dog back, bounded to his feet and held out his hand to Isana. "Let's go inside so I can call my sister and chew her out."

Isana giggled and accepted his hand in hers.

He led them into the house and got her settled in the living room. "Give me five minutes." He pulled out his cell and stabbed his sister's name.

Of course, Kate didn't answer the phone, so he left her a voice mail.

"I don't know exactly what's going on. All I know is there's a giant lion-not-lion in my house and he took me down like I was a bunny rabbit. You'd better not be giving this dog to me, Kate Worcester, or you and I will be having words. I'll be bringing this dog to Maggie's tomorrow for our Christmas Eve celebration and you'd better be passing him off to her because my cats will not be happy to come home and discover a dog has moved in, you hear me? All right. That's all. See you tomorrow. Love you. Bye."

ISANA WAS SO CHARMED IN THAT MOMENT, SHE FELL the rest of the way into love with Mason Worcester, a bear shifter who adored his sister so much, he couldn't stay angry with her for the length of even one voice mail message. That final "love you" melted her heart.

Then she noticed the kittens.

All three of them, bouncing past the entryway to the living room like they'd lived there their entire lives.

Except Isana recognized these kittens.

"You stole the kittens?" she shouted, leaping up from the couch.

Mason jerked in surprise and exclaimed, "What are you talking about?"

Isana stormed across the living room into the hallway and there they were, rolling across the floor, wrestling with each other.

"The kittens!" She waved her hands at them. "I can't believe you stole them." She leaned over and scooped up the colorpoint.

"I didn't steal them," Mason exclaimed. "You know I wouldn't do that. Kate must have done it when she took the dog."

"Kate didn't steal the dog. She came by with Jackson and they adopted it for Jackson's mate. They didn't even go near the kittens when they were at the center today so she couldn't have stolen them."

"Yeah, well, I didn't steal them either. They were still there when we left tonight, remember?"

"Oh, like one of the richest men in the world can't afford to hire someone to steal some kittens and sneak them into his house."

Mason looked confused. "Why would I do that? Especially when I knew you would be coming over."

Isana had no idea, but what other explanation was there?

"*THAT* WAS YOUR BRILLIANT IDEA?" TIVALI demanded.

"Well, yeah. I figured if Isana saw the kittens in his home, happy and safe, she'd approve the adoption for him. Never mind. I'll put them back."

"No!" Tivali and Muezza shouted, but it was too late.

A split second later, shouts of horror and surprise filled the air in response to the kittens disappearing.

"Are you crazy, Soraya?" Tivali demanded. "Way to freak out the humans."

"Hey, I didn't know what to do. At least this way, Isana knows Mason wasn't to blame."

"YOU KNOW," MASON MUSED OUT LOUD, "I NEVER really believed Jefferson when he talked about how he'd leave Cleocatra at home in the mornings, only to get to work and discover her waiting for him there."

"Seriously?"

"Yep. I always figured the panther was making shit up, especially since he kept claiming it had to be god magic, but now I'm not so sure."

"Do you think the kittens are back at the center? Or maybe they never left the center at all. Maybe we just had a shared hallucination."

Mason shrugged. "Well, whether it was a hallucination or it actually happened, we should probably go back to the center to make sure the kittens are safe and sound."

In the end, it wasn't quite the second date Mason had planned.

They ended up getting food from a taco truck on their way back to Pleasantville and then spent the evening at the center, eating tacos, playing with cats and kissing.

It may not have been dinner at his house, but in the end, it was still a perfect second date.

Eight

I T WAS CHRISTMAS Eve and Bygul thought it would be a good idea to check on his trainees again.

This time he found them all inside the kitchen of Jefferson and Kate's house. "What on earth are you three doing here? These aren't your targets. They've already been matched."

"We know," Tivali said. "But our targets are expected to arrive at any moment."

"Yes, and we're expecting a mate announcement at any time as well," Soraya exclaimed.

Bygul let out a surprised meow. "Hold on a minute. I thought you said this romance was doomed, that you were epically failing at the matchmaking."

"We were," Soraya said, "but then we recruited the kittens and things got a lot better. There was kissing and everything."

"Well, that's a great start," Bygul said. "My experience has been that once the kissing begins, the match either dies a natural death or it heats up and goes supernova. So which is it?"

"Supernova," the three chorused.

Huh. This was unexpected.

And not exactly good news.

Since it probably meant he'd be training matchmakers in the art of making love matches until the final day of his final life.

On the other hand, he'd have colleagues with whom he could talk about his love matches and compare notes and strategies.

He supposed it wasn't all bad, especially if he could convince the goddesses that one of these three would be better at the teaching gig.

"Oooh, look!" Soraya squealed. "Mason just arrived."

THEY'RE HERE, KATE TEXTED HER BROTHER.

Jackson, Maggie and Genghis Khat had just arrived and Kate knew from experience you could never predict how long Maggie's patience would last. When Maggie was done socializing, she would leave and they wouldn't see her again for days.

Therefore, Kate needed Mason to bring the dog immediately.

She didn't understand why he wasn't already there. He was supposed to be watching for her text so that he could show up within minutes of Maggie's arrival.

Where are you?

On your front porch, Impatient One.

Tamping down on the urge to squeal, Kate hurried to the front door. She stepped out onto the porch and grinned at Mason.

She pulled the door closed behind her, reached under the

rocking chair to the right of the door and pulled out the box with the giant bow inside that she'd stashed there earlier.

She hung the bow around Leo's neck and arranged the card so that it clearly showed Maggie's name. "Ready?"

"I'm right behind you."

Kate accepted the leash Mason handed her, turned and walked into the house with Mason on her heels.

She stepped into the living room and grinned at Jackson and Jefferson who were standing on opposite ends of the fireplace, their eyes on Maggie who was entertaining herself by playing with Genghis Khat.

Kate was about to say Maggie's name when Genghis Khat whirled away from her and lunged across the floor, racing toward Leo.

At the last moment, he launched himself into the air and landed on the dog's back.

Maggie gasped and leapt to her feet.

Genghis Khat stepped in a circle, then settled on the dog's back, facing Maggie.

For a split second, the room was dead silent, then Maggie let out a squeal of excitement and lunged forward.

She fell to her knees in front of the dog and flung her arms around him. "You're so beautiful." She pulled back and grinned at the cat, "And you look so regal riding him like that, Genghis Khat. I love you both so much!" She grabbed the card that had her name on it and turned it over.

Kate had thought long and hard about what to say on the card.

The first thing she'd written was "Merry Christmas, Maggie, from Kate." However, that hadn't seemed quite enough because it didn't really encapsulate the full measure of human effort that had gone into this gift.

So then, in smaller letters, she had added, "with completely incompetent help from Lyle, Ryan and Pete (but it's the thought that counts) and somewhat competent help from Mason and Jefferson, but mostly with truly exceptional help from Jackson and Genghis Khat."

Then, because Kate definitely wanted credit for the gift, she'd added one final thought, "But mostly, as in entirely, this gift is from Kate. Merry Christmas!"

Maggie sniffled a little, then stood and threw her arms around Kate, shocking everyone with the affectionate gesture. "Thank you so much, Kate. I love him." She pulled away and settled back on the floor to stare into Leo's eyes. "What's his name?"

"They were calling him Leo."

Maggie made a face. "I don't see it."

"Uh, he looks just like a lion," Mason muttered.

Kate shoved an elbow into his side and said, "That's what I thought. I figured you could come up with a better name than that."

"Let's see," Maggie said. "He's definitely a boy?"

"That's what all the paperwork said."

"So I guess Queen Elizabark is out of the question."

Genghis Khat growled softly and the dog let out a huffing sound.

Maggie giggled. "*King* Elizabark?"

Genghis Khat growled even louder.

"Okay, okay, that was just a joke. Let's see. It has to be a name worthy of such a majestic looking animal. How about... Spawtacus?"

Kate chuckled. "I like it."

"Genghis Khat and Spawtacus, a match made in heaven," Maggie exclaimed.

Kate grinned.

Success!

Of course, there was one problem with finding the perfect gift and that was realizing she'd never be able to top it.

Oh well.

Totally worth it.

They were all gathered in the living room, talking and laughing, when Kate's phone buzzed again.

As soon as Mason's attention was fully on Cleocatra, who was stalking Spawtacus, acting like she was going to pounce, Kate slipped out onto the front porch again.

This time, Isana was waiting.

Kate ushered her inside, opened the carrier Isana held and scooped the three kittens into her arms. She grinned at Isana and whispered, "Right, let's go."

She led the way back into the living room and headed toward her brother, who was sitting on the floor playing with Cleocatra. "Merry Christmas, Mason." She leaned over and set the three kittens in his lap.

Mason looked overjoyed for a split second, then that joy melted into horror. "You didn't steal them, did you? Isana will never forgive me if you stole them!"

Kate giggled and Isana said dryly, "Don't be ridiculous. Our security is exceptional."

Mason snickered, lifted each kitten for a kiss on the nose, then set them each, one by one, on the floor where Cleocatra hunkered down and glared at them.

Mason stood and pulled Isana into his arms for a kiss. "Thank you, sweet love."

"Hey!" Kate exclaimed. "She's not the one who gave you those kittens. Maybe I'll just take them back and Reaper too."

"Reaper?" Mason pulled away to ask.

"Kate's already filled out all the adoption paperwork and paid the fees on all four cats," Isana said. "You can pick up Reaper after the holiday."

"Aw, you've made my year, sweet Isana mine." Mason kissed her again.

"Hey!" Kate exclaimed. "I say again, Isana's not the one giving you the cats. *I am!*"

Mason laughed, flung an arm around Kate's shoulders and dragged her close, shoving her face into his armpit as he hugged her tight. "Thank you, sister mine."

"Argh! *Mason!*"

BYGUL WAS POSITIVELY STUNNED. HE'D WRITTEN Mason Worcester off as an unmatchable. And now his three trainees had somehow proven him wrong. They'd accomplished a match even he had deemed impossible.

"I have to say, I'm really impressed," he told them. "One of the things about being a good matchmaker is never giving up on your targets. Sometimes it seems impossible. Sometimes you just can't find that perfect match and you have to move on. That doesn't mean you might not find their match years later, when you least expect it though. This match may not have taken years, but it was definitely a difficult one and you three never gave up."

As Bygul spoke, he paced in front of them and watched as his words washed over them and their postures straightened, their ears pricked up and their chins lifted in pride.

"I have a status meeting with the goddesses tomorrow and I'm going to recommend that you three be given full match-maker status for love matches."

He waited as the three of them lost their composures for a moment and indulged in a bit of cheering. And some wrestling. And a whole lot of grooming.

When they finally came back together, he looked them over with pride.

Perhaps he'd be stuck training new cats for the rest of each of his remaining lives, but for now, he would bask in the glory of having trained three more cats to spread love matches far and wide.

"Congratulations, you three."

"I can't believe I'm finally meeting your kittens," Maggie exclaimed.

Mason grinned. She'd been nagging him ever since he texted her those pictures.

"I've been wanting to meet them ever since I named them."

"Wait, what?" Isana asked.

"Mason texted me for their names when he first met them."

"Why would you have their names?"

"Maggie's really good at naming pets," Jackson said.

"It's true," Maggie said. "I have a gift."

"So the names you made me put on their cages weren't names that *you* created for them?" Isana demanded.

"Of course they weren't," Mason said. He couldn't understand why she would think otherwise. "What do I know about naming kittens? I asked Maggie because she's the expert."

"Now I'm completely curious," Kate said. "What are their names?"

Isana picked up the fluffy orange kitten and showed him to the room. "This is Furcules."

"And this is Purrseidon." Maggie picked up the second orange kitten and showed him off. "This white mark here looks just like a trident."

Isana leaned over to look, then exclaimed, "It does! I never even noticed that."

"And this is Catphrodite." Mason showed off the white kitten.

"Because look at her!" Maggie exclaimed. "She's totally a goddess of beauty who knows how to accessorize."

"Accessorize?" Jackson asked.

"The face, the paws, the tail, the ears! The brown is just perfection against all that white."

"Well, all I have to say is those names are awesome," Kate said with a laugh. "Too bad you can't get a job naming cats, Maggie. You'd make a fortune if you—"

A loud thudding knock came at the front door, making everyone jump.

Isana would know that knock anywhere.

Kate sent her a sympathetic grimace. Obviously she knew the pain Isana lived with on a daily basis.

The only difference between the two of them was that Kate only had *one* brother bear to deal with whereas Isana was lucky enough to have five. The fact that three were cousins and not brothers didn't really signify.

They were still, *all of them*, brother bears.

Brother bears who didn't hesitate to invade as soon as Jefferson made the mistake of opening his front door.

The five of them sort of pushed their way inside and Jefferson just backed up all the way into the living room.

"Well, this is an interesting gathering," Steven said.

"What are you guys doing here?" Isana demanded.

"You abandoned us for Christmas Eve in Greensboro. Of *course*, we had to come see what was up. But don't worry, it's not just us." He grinned. "The rest of the family's setting up outside."

That was when Isana knew her family was going to give the bear a chance to prove himself worthy of her.

She knew this because the arctic fox side of the family had just arrived.

"I'M SO CONFUSED," MASON CONFIDED TO ISANA, HIS statement a bit garbled from the platter of fish kebabs he was working his way through.

The two of them were standing outside in the snow, watching as Isana's family of polar bears, plus a whole bunch of arctic foxes, mingled with panthers and grizzlies and the many other residents of Greensboro who kept stopping by.

At first, it had just been a few shifters who happened to be in the area and smelled the food.

Then it was a veritable stream of people as word spread that the cooks from The Ice Box were at Jefferson's place cooking enough food to feed an army of bears.

It seemed to Mason as if every employee of the restaurant, both polar bears *and* arctic foxes, were standing in Jefferson and Kate's front yard.

They all moved like a well-oiled machine. Some were cooking, others were serving and the rest were chatting and laughing with the people consuming their food. Then everyone would shift and those who'd been mingling would be serving or cooking and those who'd been working would now be mingling.

"Confused about what?" Isana asked.

"Yesterday your family wanted to kill me. Today they're at my sister's house, cooking for the entire community. This does not compute."

Isana chuckled. "They're bears. What do you expect?"

"Yes, let's talk about your family of bears again and why you seem to *still* think you're not one of them."

"Oh, I'm definitely one of them. I'm just not a bear."

Mason let out a growl of pure frustration.

Isana giggled. "Come on. I think it's time you met my parents."

"Wait. What? Your parents are here? *Now?*"

"Yes and yes. Come on." She caught his hand in hers and dragged him to the biggest grill in the front yard where an absolutely massive polar bear shifter was flipping giant slabs of meat. At his side was a tiny woman who looked so much like Isana, Mason immediately knew she was Isana's mother.

"Mom, Dad, this is Mason Worcester," Isana said. "Mason, this is my mother, Lisa Meier, and my father, Zachariah Meier."

"Pleased to meet you both," Mason lied, trying to sound as if he meant it when in reality, he was quite horrified.

Not that he didn't want to be accepted by Isana's family, just that he was quite terrified it would never happen and would have put off this meeting, as a result, for as long as he could.

Zachariah let out an aggressive-sounding grunt, but Lisa

beamed and stepped around her mate to hold out her hands to Mason.

He stepped forward and she clasped his hands in hers. "I'm so happy to meet you, Mason." She stretched upward as if she were going to kiss his cheek, but that never happened because her mate grabbed her around the waist and set her on his opposite side again.

"Zachariah!" she exclaimed.

He just glared at Mason and grunted, "Mine."

Since Mason completely understood the sentiment and thoroughly respected it, he nodded his head in agreement. "Yours."

The truly impressive part of that encounter was that Mason managed to restrain his grizzly who wanted nothing more than to do the same and lay claim to his own mate by roaring, "Mine!" in his mate's father's face.

It was only as they walked away from her parents, hand-in-hand, that Mason came to his senses and realized what he'd just learned.

He stumbled to a stop and pulled Isana around so she was facing him.

He then leaned forward, placed his nose in the hollow of her neck and inhaled deeply.

Bear was still the overriding scent, polar bear to be exact, but underneath that scent, almost completely buried was the tiniest strain of—

"Arctic fox," he breathed.

Isana giggled. "Exactly so."

He pulled back and stared into her eyes. "Your dad's a polar and your mom's a fox."

"Yep." She glanced around the yard. "I'm related to pretty

much all the foxes and polar bears here plus everyone who works at The Ice Box is a relative of one kind or another."

"Wow."

"Yeah. I'm an anomaly. Most of my family, what you smell is what you get, but not me. I'm an arctic fox who smells distinctly like a bear."

Mason grinned. "I find that incredibly sexy. Just one question."

"Yes?"

"Is your arctic fox the size of a fox or the size of a bear?"

Isana rolled her eyes. "Don't be an idiot."

Nine

B YGUL WAS ACTUALLY a bit nervous, which was somewhat shocking, but then he *was* about to meet with the goddesses to explain that most of his trainees had abandoned ship.

The most annoying thing about this meeting was that Freyja wasn't there yet.

Ceridwen and Bastet were, though, and they were demanding answers.

"So?" Bastet exclaimed impatiently. "Did my cats make it or not?"

"And what about mine?" Ceridwen demanded.

"Aw, well, the thing is, Bastet and Ceridwen, most of the cats just weren't interested in making love matches. They had other things consuming their attention."

"So they just stopped attending?" Ceridwen demanded.

"Pretty much."

"So how many completed your course then?" Bastet asked.

"Three."

Silence.

"I'm sorry," Ceridwen said. "Did you say three?"

"Exactly so. Three."

"Out of fifty?" Bastet exclaimed. "That seems awfully low, doesn't it?"

"Well, which three? And were any of them mine?" Ceridwen asked.

"Or mine?" Bastet asked.

"I'm terribly sorry, but none of your cats, Bastet, and none of your cats, Ceridwen, made it to the end."

"Not even one of them?" Bastet demanded.

"I'm afraid not."

"Were they all Freyja's cats?" Ceridwen asked.

"Uh, no."

"No? Well, who are we talking about then?" Bastet asked.

"Are you sure Fannar didn't make it?" Ceridwen asked.

"I'm afraid he abandoned class pretty early on."

"What about Firwen?"

"He made it to our first trip to the earth realm, but then he seemed to lose interest. Honestly, I don't think he cared much for the task of making love matches."

Ceridwen rolled her eyes. "Fair. He's not much for romance, but surely Gwyneira was interested?"

"She was, at least until the first snowfall. After that, we never saw her again. I assume because she was playing in the snow."

Ceridwen let out a huge sigh. "Well, this is thoroughly disappointing."

"We could spend all day asking names," Bastet said, "when it would be much simpler if you would just tell us who made it, rather than us having to guess."

"Right. They're waiting outside," Bygul said. "If you're willing, I could just invite them in."

"Fine, fine." Ceridwen waved her hand.

Five minutes later, Soraya, Tivali and Muezza stood in front of the two goddesses.

"Are you being serious right now?" Bastet demanded.

"Quite serious," Bygul said.

"Not one of these cats are the cats of a goddess," Ceridwen complained. "Sure, Muezza happens to be companion to a prophet, but that prophet's a *man.*"

"And what is up with the cats of the queens of Egypt?" Bastet exclaimed. "Why are Nefertiti and Cleopatra so special? They're just queens, not goddesses, no matter how much Cleopatra likes to pretend otherwise."

At that moment, Freyja walked in. "So sorry I'm late. I hear we have three graduates from your class, Bygul. How wonderful." She turned to the cats waiting at his side. "Soraya, Tivali, Muezza, congratulations. I know that Nefertiti must be so proud of you, Soraya, and Cleopatra of you, Tivali." She turned to Muezza. "Muhammad will undoubtedly not believe me when I tell him you completed the course. He will be most impressed, I'm sure."

"Yes, yes, but Muhammad has no need to be making love matches," Ceridwen said. "I wonder if he'd be willing to let me borrow Muezza so he can make some on *my* behalf from time to time."

Muezza didn't appear to have any sort of reaction to that suggestion. A pretty laidback cat was Muezza overall.

"I'd ask Nefertiti to borrow you, Soraya," Bastet said, "but you and I both know she'll want something in return."

Soraya let out a tiny rumble of agreement.

"I guess Soraya and Tivali can just go on making love matches on behalf of the Queens of Egypt, though honestly, Cleopatra probably won't even notice," Freyja said.

Too busy traveling incognito and interacting with the masses, Bygul assumed.

"Forget that," Bastet exclaimed. "If they're going to be making love matches on behalf of Egypt, they'll be doing so in *my* name. I'll negotiate with Queen Nefertiti for Soraya's time, but Queen Cleopatra can just suck it up."

Overall, Bygul thought the meeting went quite nicely. He was particularly impressed with how Freyja managed to manipulate Bastet into accepting both Soraya and Tivali as her representatives.

Bastet probably believed that was all *her* idea.

The biggest relief of all though was that Freyja didn't ask for any of the three to work on her behalf, leaving Bygul's position as her top matchmaker and *only* maker of love matches completely intact.

Even better news than that, though, was that none of the goddesses suggested he train any more cats.

Hallelujah to that.

The following month was the best of Mason's life.

Before he met Isana, he was well-known for arriving at the office just as it was getting light outside and not leaving until darkness had blanketed the land.

Work had always been his life.

Now his life was Isana.

He learned to delegate more just so that he could spend time with her. He continued volunteering at the center and spent his evenings courting his mate.

They went to dinner at The Ice Box once or twice a week

just to keep her brothers and cousins from interfering too badly in their relationship, and the rest of the week, they indulged in picnics in the snow and dinners at his place.

The first time she stayed the night, he felt as if he'd won the lottery. He truly was the luckiest man alive.

Isana couldn't understand how she'd gotten so lucky.

Mason was absolutely extraordinary. Even after the holidays, he continued volunteering at the center, despite no longer needing to convince her to let him adopt Reaper and the kittens.

He still showed up every afternoon with boxes full of The Bear Necessities, but now they regularly included some of her favorite foods and fresh flowers, plus quite often, he brought a blanket and candles for picnics in the cat tower.

It was no wonder that one Saturday afternoon after an entire week filled with picnics and cats and kisses from Mason that she decided to close the center early and follow him home.

The anticipation as she drove behind his truck built until she felt as if she was on fire by the time she pulled into the long driveway leading up to his house.

The moment Mason stepped down from his truck and turned to look at her, lust burning in his eyes, she knew this first time was going to be fast.

Thank goodness.

They burst in the front door and fell upon each other, kissing and struggling with their clothes, trying to get rid of them without losing contact with each other.

Finally, they were skin to skin.

Mason lifted Isana and pulled her legs around his hips, nudging her into position. He stepped forward, braced her against the wall and slammed deep.

She arched her back and cried out in ecstasy.

Right there, in the entryway of his home, he took her fast and hard.

She writhed against the wall, clutching his shoulders and whimpering as he worked his way in and out, dragging forward and back, hitting the right spot again and again and again until the world exploded into shards of searing heat and light.

Long moments later, they stood there, her hands clutching his hair, his hands clamped on her ass, both of them breathing heavily, gasping for air.

"Sweet mate," he rumbled in her ear.

"Yes," she breathed.

"Again."

Her heart, which had finally started to settle into a regular rhythm, missed a beat and heat rushed through her.

Her pussy, already soaked, softened further and he sank even deeper with a growling rumble.

The second time was as fast as the first and it wasn't until the third time that they made it out of the entryway.

It was then they discovered that though she was stark naked, he still had on his boots and his jeans were around his ankles.

They had to take a brief pause so that he could extract himself enough to be able to walk, but the minute he was free, he hitched her up in his arms, hooked her legs around his hips and sank deep again.

The third time happened along the way between the entryway and the top of the stairs.

Every step up had her whimpering in pleasure and by the time they reached the top, they were desperate.

He laid her down right there at the top of the stairs and proceeded to obliterate the world once again.

They did finally make it to his bed, but it was the wee hours of the morning by then and they ended up only sleeping once they got there.

When they woke a couple hours later, though, that was another story.

And so it was just one month after their first meeting that Isana ended up mated to a bear, something she'd always sworn never to do.

And it wasn't just any bear, but a grizzly and a Worcester at that, and it wasn't just any Worcester, but the alpha Worcester himself.

She was pretty amazed at how things had turned out, especially since it was probably inevitable that she would eventually move in with Mason, which meant she would be back in Worcester Falls, living among bears again.

Not to mention the fact that he was now responsible for her falling off the wagon of cat adoption. Sure, technically, Mason was the one who adopted Reaper and the kittens, but when her last cat had died three years before, Isana had promised herself not to start down that slippery slope again.

Because in her world, one cat always led to two, which often led to three, which could, for those who loved cats as much as Isana did, lead to a houseful of them.

And so she'd kept rigid control of her cat adopting ways and had succeeded in convincing herself that the cats she served at the shelter were cats enough for her.

The key was discipline.

Or at least it was until she met a bear, who quite possibly loved cats more than her, and she mated him.

Now she was on that slippery slope again, this time with him, and it didn't begin with just one cat. It began with four.

Fate truly was a bitch sometimes.

All in all, though, she really couldn't complain.

After all, she'd ended up with a bear who happily volunteered at the center, even going so far as to clean an untold number of litter boxes for her. What said true love more than that?

And he didn't just show true love for *her*.

He also showed it for all the cats, bringing them new cat toys and climbing trees and eventually, adding cat treats to his Bear Necessities boxes, thus earning him the undying love of all the cats at the center.

Even the grumpy ones.

In the end, Isana decided that perhaps fate wasn't so much a bitch as a very clever fox.

And speaking of foxes, there was still one final hurdle they had to overcome and that was for Mason to meet hers.

THE BEDROOM WAS INCREDIBLY COLD WHEN MASON woke one morning a couple weeks after Isana had started spending the night.

A quick glance outside told him they'd received an epic snowfall overnight.

There was white blanketing the land as far as he could see. His truck was buried to the top of its tires and there were snow drifts even taller than it.

He was disappointed to realize Isana had already left the bed, possibly to go in search of coffee.

He waited to see if she'd return, hoping to convince her to climb back into bed, but she never appeared, so he got up, pulled on a pair of jeans and went in search of her.

His house wasn't exactly small so there were any number of rooms where she could be hiding. However, her scent had dissipated just enough to make him think she was no longer inside.

He grabbed a cup of coffee from the kitchen, then wandered out onto the front porch.

He loved this type of weather.

Unlike full-blooded grizzlies, who preferred to hibernate in the winter, Mason and his grizzly loved to play in the snow.

Unfortunately, he wasn't seeing Isana anywhere.

He was pretty sure she was out there, though, and he was willing to bet she was in her arctic fox form.

He set his coffee cup on the railing, peeled off his jeans and lunged down the stairs, landing in the snow in his grizzly form.

He shook his head and took off running, following the scent of his mate.

Something huge and white lunged up from the snow in front of him and he let out a startled roar.

He toppled backward and stared at the vision hovering above him.

His mate was *not* the size of an arctic fox.

ISANA WAS SO EXCITED WHEN HER MATE CAME OUT onto the front porch.

She was crouched low in the snow, just waiting for him to come find her.

She inched forward, belly crawling from the woods where she'd been shaking snow from the trees, toward the porch where her mate stood.

She froze when he suddenly stripped nude and lunged down the front steps.

He landed in his grizzly form and raced straight for her.

Did he see her?

Her backside wiggled in anticipation.

Almost.

Almost.

Almost.

Now!

She exploded upward, snow flying everywhere, and let out a yip of excitement. *I'm here, I'm here, I'm here.* She leapt all around her mate, who looked a little stunned from where he'd fallen into a snow drift.

I'm here! She leapt on top of him and they rolled around in the snow, wrestling and breaking apart only to lunge back together and wrestle some more.

Finally, she broke free and ran across the lawn and around the house, her mate thundering after her.

It was a truly perfect morning and the start of a beautiful life together.

REAPER WANDERED THROUGH THE HOUSE, CHECKING all the entrances, peering through every window and growling a warning into the night.

All intruders beware! This house belongs to The Reaper, Guard Kitty Extraordinaire.

Once Reaper was certain his territory was secure, he stalked into the room where his humans slept.

First, he checked on the kittens.

All three were sound asleep in their cat bed.

Furcules and Purrseidon were wrapped around each other while Catphrodite was stretched out on top of them both.

He sniffed each of them, gave them each a nuzzle and a swipe of the tongue, then sauntered over to the bed where the humans were sleeping.

He leapt up and circled them both, searching for the perfect spot.

Eventually, he wiggled his way in front of the female, stretching out against her belly so the man's arm that had been around her waist was now around Reaper too.

Lying there, Reaper listened to the sounds of kitten purrs from across the room and the soft breathing of his human companions, and fell asleep to the realization that his own lost purr had been found again.

Read on for an excerpt from *A Catmas to Remember* in the next Pawsitively Purrfect Trilogy, Holly Jolly Pawliday.

Excerpt

Bygul wasn't happy about his latest assignment.

He might be the best matchmaker on the Pawsitively Purrfect team, but this case required a miracle worker.

"This particular cat is quite the troublemaker," Freyja informed him.

"He's been returned *seventeen* times," Bastet said.

"And by humans who adore cats, no less," Ceridwen agreed.

"Seventeen—how is that even possible?" Bygul demanded. He couldn't imagine that the director of the center, Isana Meier, had screwed up that many matches. After all, the woman was outrageously protective of her rescues.

"The cat's an asshole," Freyja said.

"Entirely," Ceridwen and Bastet agreed.

"But that's simply the nature of cats," Bygul protested.

Freyja raised an eyebrow. "Yes, but this cat takes it to unprecedented levels."

"He's smart," Bastet said.

"And devious," Ceridwen said.

"And he knows exactly how to make life miserable for his humans," Freyja said. "He's in a league of his own."

Now Bygul was intrigued.

Not that he would admit it, of course. "He can't possibly be that bad. Any true cat lover would put up with all manner of assholery from a cat."

"Not this one," the goddesses chorused.

Interesting.

Bygul did enjoy a challenge, but there were limits. "And how exactly am I supposed to get this cat away from the rescue?" Normally he just took the cats, but those were cats living on the streets, fending for themselves, with no humans to worry about them when they disappeared.

"You're just going to have to work with the humans to find the perfect placement for this cat," Freyja said.

"Have you *met* Isana Meier? Talk about uptight! *She's* the asshole in this scenario. She'll never let that cat be adopted by just anyone."

"Of course not," Ceridwen said.

"And why should she?" Bastet asked. "Every cat deserves the purrfect human."

"Exactly," Freyja said. "So your job is to find that human and somehow get them into the rescue to meet the cat."

"It's not enough that they meet the cat. Isana Meier has to approve their application and believe you, me, that's never an easy—"

"Bears!" Soraya exclaimed.

Bygul jumped a little. He'd completely forgotten the recent graduates he'd trained were in the room.

Great.

Now they'd want to assist in this match.

"Oooh, yes, bears," Tivali said.

"What are you two going on about?" Bygul glared at them.

"Who better to adopt an asshole cat than shifters who are assholes all the time?" Tivali asked.

"I vote for the polars," Soraya said.

"That's a crazy idea," Muezza said.

Bygul completely agreed.

"It's not crazy!" Soraya exclaimed. "It's purrfect!"

"Those polars are always fighting," Bygul said. "Besides, don't you remember how adamant Isana Meier was about bears *not* being an appropriate cat companion?"

"Yes, but that was before she mated one," Tivali said.

"Besides the polars are family," Soraya said. "She'd never deny family."

These cats were delusional.

Isana Meier would deny the goddesses themselves if she deemed them unworthy.

"Well, we'll leave the four of you to figure out the details," Freyja said. "Bygul, you're in charge. If you can't find a match for this cat, I fear for his future."

Great. Way to pile on the pressure. "What's the cat's name anyway?"

"Shredder," the goddesses chorused.

Wonderful.

"No," Mason said.

"He needs a home."

"That may be so, but his home's not going to be anywhere near *my* precious babies."

Isana rolled her eyes. "They're not even kittens anymore.

They're fully grown and thus, are capable of defending themselves."

"Against Shredder the Destroyer?" Mason demanded.

"Stop calling him that!"

"Look, you know I love cats, but *that* is not a cat."

"Really, Mason?" Isana glared at her mate. Some days, she doubted her own sanity. She'd had one rule and one rule only her entire life: *no dating bears.*

And now look at her!

Mated to one.

For life.

A stubborn, clumsy, rampaging, irrational *bear.*

"If he's not a cat, then pray tell, what is he?" she demanded.

"Best guess? A demon from hell."

Isana groaned. "Can't we just discuss this? I've exhausted every cat lover I know in three counties. *Everyone's* heard about Shredder. No one's willing to take him in."

Mason just stared at her.

"What? What's that look supposed to mean?"

He didn't answer.

"What?"

He just kept staring.

She *hated* it when he did that. "Just say it already!"

"I've already said it a thousand times."

"Oh, no. Forget it. I already told you, no. We're not foisting Shredder off on the shifters."

"I don't see why not. You've adopted out to shifters before."

"Those were exceptions, not the rules. You know I prefer adopting out to humans, Mason."

"Which makes absolutely no sense whatsoever."

"It makes perfect sense."

"Not to anyone who isn't you."

Isana let out a tiny growl of frustration. "Fine. Who would you suggest then?"

Mason grinned. This was going to be fun.

BRYCE HAD WORKED A DOUBLE AT THE RESTAURANT the day before and was sound asleep when the pounding on his front door began.

He let out a roar of rage that rattled the windows and shook the floor, but didn't bother to get out of bed.

His roar was usually enough to send even the most determined packing.

Unless they were family.

Or insane.

Or both.

The pounding began again, which told him it was probably family.

Either that or the nutcase next door.

Either way, he was ignoring them both.

He pulled a pillow over his head and tried to ignore the relentless pounding.

It finally stopped.

He smirked a little as he sank back into sleep.

Bam! Bam! Bam! Bam bam bam!

Bryce jumped so hard, he almost fell out of bed, then leapt to his feet with a roar.

Family!

It had to be family.

The woman next door might be crazy enough to risk his wrath, but he doubted she had the strength to make the windows rattle the way they did with that last knock.

It was probably Isana.

Only his sister would have the audacity to continue knocking despite it becoming clear he had no intention of answering the door.

"Bryce, we know you're in there!"

Yep. That was his sister all right.

There was a reason he'd taken away her damn key.

Apparently, that wasn't enough though.

He should have moved.

Out of the country.

Bryce stamped across the room and flung open the window. "What the hell is wrong with you?" He couldn't see his sister because the roof of the porch obstructed his view, but he knew she was there.

The roof shook a little as Isana stamped down the stairs, turned and glared up at him. "Get your ass down here, Bryce Meier. Right now."

"I worked a double yesterday. Now go away." He pulled his head back inside the house, slammed the window and turned away, fully intending to climb back into bed and continue ignoring his sister.

Bam! Bam! Bam! Bam! Bam! Bam!

Hands on hips, Bryce glared at his bed.

Surely she'd give up.

Any minute now.

Bam! Bam! Bam! Bam! Bam! Bam!

Bam! Bam! Bam! Bam! Bam! Bam!

Bam! Bam! Bam! Bam! Bam! Bam!

Damn her.

A more bearish arctic fox he'd never known.

Grabbing a pair of sweats, he dragged them on, then

stormed out of his bedroom, down the stairs to the front door.

He flung it open and glared at his sister and—great—her grizzly mate.

"It's about time." Isana shoved her way past him and as she moved by, he caught a strange scent of something foreign.

He whirled to follow and found himself shoved aside as Mason Worcester pushed by him with his arms full of bags.

Damn grizzly!

Scowling, Bryce turned to slam the door shut, but Mason shoulder checked him aside and stepped back out onto the front porch.

Bryce let out a low growl, went to slam the door shut *again*, only to have it flung back toward him by a massive grizzly paw in human form.

Bryce barely stopped the door from connecting with his face as Mason shoved by for the third time, this time carrying a strange box by the handle. "Now see here," Bryce snarled, turning to follow the grizzly down the hall. "What the hell is—"

He stumbled to a halt when he reached the door to his guest bedroom and finally realized what he'd been smelling. "Oh, hell, no!"

Don't miss the matchmaking cats of the goddesses' holiday adventures as they target a family of polar bear shifters!

Grab HOLLY JOLLY PAWLIDAY, featuring *A Catmas to Remember*, *This Cat's for You* and *Santa Kitty,* today.

Other Books by Pepper

THE MURRYSVILLE COALITION

The Crazy Cheetah Lady
One Sad Kitty

A PAWSITIVELY PURRFECT MATCH

Catnapped
The Real McCat
Unbearably Cute
A Catmas to Remember
This Cat's for You
Santa Kitty
Hocus Purrcus
Tridents & Tails
Abra-Cat-Abra
Satan's Kitty
Valen-Cats
Vampurr Lovin'
A Beautiful Cat-ship
Grave Cattitude

THE SHENANIGANS SERIES

Shifter Shenanigans

Witchy Shenanigans

Full Moon Shenanigans

Hotel Shenanigans

Dragon Shenanigans

Undercover Shenanigans

Spooky Shenanigans

Holiday Shenanigans

Valentine Shenanigans

Lucky Shenanigans

STORIES OF THE VEIL

Guardians of the Veil

Astra

Glory

Luna

Zara

Lotus

WICKED

No Rest for the Wicked

Wicked Is As Wicked Does

Anthologies & Collections

PAWSITIVELY PURRFECT TRILOGIES

THE CAT'S MEOW

Catnapped | The Real McCat | Unbearably Cute

HOLLY JOLLY PAWLIDAY

A Catmas to Remember | This Cat's for You | Santa Kitty

SHENANIGANS ANTHOLOGIES

CRAZED

Books 1-3

AMAZED

Books 4-6

HOLIDAZED

Books 7-10

SHENANIGANS

The Complete Collection

STORIES OF THE VEIL

THE UNVEILED

Astra | Glory

THE VEILED

Luna | Zara

WICKED DUET

WICKED

No Rest for the Wicked | Wicked Is As Wicked Does

About the Author

WWW.PEPPERMCGRAW.COM

PEPPER MCGRAW is a USA Today Bestselling Author of paranormal romance. Her life to date has sadly been paranormal-free, but she knows it's simply a matter of time before her fated mate finally appears. Until that glorious day arrives, she keeps herself busy writing (and reading) paranormal romances.

Pepper loves animals, especially cats, and spends her free time volunteering at local shelters and for Trap-Neuter-Release programs. She's had the supreme honor of winning occasional head butts and meows from the local ferals in her neighborhood and has even convinced a few to come inside and adopt her as their own.

BB bookbub.com/authors/pepper-mcgraw

f facebook.com/ShenanigansSeries

g goodreads.com/peppermcgraw

instagram.com/peppermcgraw_author

tiktok.com/@peppermcgraw

twitter.com/peppermcgraw